THE VALKYRIE ENCOUNTER

By the same author:

TOO MANY CHIEFS

THE VALKYRIE ENCOUNTER

Stephen Marlowe

NEW ENGLISH LIBRARY/TIMES MIRROR

First published in Great Britain in 1978
by New English Library

First NEL Paperback Edition July 1979
Reprinted October 1979

NEL Books are published by
New English Library Limited from
Barnard's Inn, Holborn,
London EC1N 2JR.
Made and printed in Great Britain by
Hunt Barnard Printing Ltd.,
Aylesbury, Bucks.

45004250 2

CONTENTS

'Men who make the mistake of contributing toward totalitarianism can never turn back. The totalitarians hang them as traitors; the other side condemn them as accomplices.'

Hans Bernd Gisevius

'If only life would at last stop demanding solutions from us.'

Gerhart Hauptmann

To my brother Frank,
who fought for them.

Foreword

On Thursday, 20 July 1944, six weeks after D-Day, a time-bomb of British manufacture exploded at 12.42 p.m. in the Conference Barracks at Wolf's Lair, Adolf Hitler's East Prussian military headquarters.

By sheer luck the Nazi Führer was only slightly injured. Had he been killed, the war in Europe might well have ended ten months before it did, at a saving of millions of lives.

The attempt to assassinate Hitler was the culmination of a carefully planned conspiracy of anti-Nazi Wehrmacht officers who had managed through secret contacts in Switzerland, Sweden, and elsewhere to keep the Anglo-American allies and the Russians informed of their plans.

Whatever responses these efforts drew from Washington, London, and Moscow remain to this day shrouded in secrecy. The relevant archives remain sealed.

The narrative that follows, although a work of fiction, attempts to reconstruct these events.

S. M.

Characters in order of appearance

ANTONIO DA COSTA, manager, Ritz Hotel, Lisbon

MONIKA JAEGER, secretary at Gestapo headquarters, Berlin

EUGEN, her lover

CAPTAIN RICHARD HALLER, O.S.S. agent

AXEL LINDSTROM, Swedish businessman, O.S.S. contact in Berlin

GILLIAN BENNETT, wife of

WING COMMANDER HARRY BENNETT, assistant chief, German Section, Special Operations Executive

MAJOR MILT GREEN, O.S.S. liaison officer to Special Operations Executive

PATTY, W.A.A.F. Section Officer, Special Operations Executive

ELISABETH LAUTERBACHER, niece of

GENERALOBERST LUDWIG BECK, former Chief-of-Staff, German Army

PROFESSOR LORENZ LIEBERMANN, a fugitive Jew in Berlin

FRAU LIEBERMANN, his wife

MAJOR ERNST OTTO JAEGER, Monika's husband, on leave in Berlin from the Eastern Front

WALTER ULBRICHT (alias COMRADE CELL), German Communist leader in exile in Moscow

COMMISSAR IVAN TERENCHEVICH PERESYPKIN, chief, Central Intelligence Directorate, Moscow

BINNICKER, hall porter

OBERLEUTNANT HARALD FREIHERR VON HEYDEBRAND, adjutant to Stauffenberg

RAMBOW, Gestapo and Red Underground double agent

OBERST KLAUS SCHENK, GRAF VON STAUFFENBERG, Chief-of-Staff, Home Army

SEPP, his chauffeur

GENERAL FRIEDRICH OLBRICHT, Deputy Commander, Home Army

ADOLF HITLER

GENERALFELDMARSCHALL WILHELM KEITEL, Chief-of-Staff, Armed Forces High Command

JULIUS ESSER, former Social Democrat delegate to Reichstag

RAFFAELLO MATTI, Swiss surgeon

WOLF HEINRICH GRAF VON HELLDORF, Berlin police chief

CARL GOERDELER, former Lord Mayor of Leipzig

GOTTFRIED RITTER, chief, Bureau of Student and Youth Affairs, Gestapo

HEINRICH MUELLER, chief, Bureau IV (Gestapo), Reich Central Security Office

FRANZ JACOB,
ANTON SAEFTKOW, } German Red Underground leaders

DRUNKENPOLZ, brewmaster

KRASKE,
DIECKHOFF,
LUTZE, } Gestapo agents

SISTER EUNICE, nurse at University College Hospital, London

MR MUSGROVE,
PETERS, } patients

REINHARD, café waiter

STEFAN HELD, student, University of Munich

KURT HUBER, professor of philosophy, University of Munich

HANS SCHOLL, } students
SOPHIE SCHOLL, }

PAUL GEISLER, Gauleiter of Bavaria

LUKAS MÖLLINGER, Gestapo agent

ROLAND FREISLER, chief judge, People's Court

WILLI GRAF, } students
ALEXANDER SCHMORELL, }
ZECHLIN, }

FRITZI, headwaiter at Hasenheide Restaurant, Berlin

STANDARTENFÜHRER DREHER, S.S. officer

ERNST KALTENBRUNNER, Director, Reich Central Security Office

OTTO OHLENDORF, chief, Bureau III (S.D. Interior), Reich Central Security Office

WALTER SCHELLENBERG, chief, Bureau VI (S.D. Exterior and Counter-espionage), Reich Central Security Office

ARTUR NEBE, chief, Bureau V (Criminal Police), Reich Central Security Office

BARBARA HELLMUTH, secretary to Gestapo Chief Mueller

MEISTER ADOLF RALL, Berlin police riot squad

ALLEN WELSH DULLES, head of O.S.S. in Europe

HANS BERND GISEVIUS, German diplomat stationed in Switzerland

NINA, GRÄFIN VON STAUFFENBERG, wife of Klaus Stauffenberg

GENERALMAJOR HELMUT STIEFF, Chief of Organisation Branch, Army High Command

STURMBANNFÜHRER OTTO GUENSCH, S.S. adjutant to Hitler

LEUTNANT BLEINER, Communications Officer, Grossdeutschland Guard Battalion

GENERALOBERST FRIEDRICH FROMM, Commander, Home Army

JOSEPH GOEBBELS, Gauleiter of Berlin, Minister of Propaganda and Public Enlightenment

SIEGLINDE MEIER, daughter of

MORITZ MEIER, portrait painter

FRÄULEIN BRAUN, secretary to Police Chief Helldorf

FRAU GALLENKAMP, landlady

ANDREAS PFLAUM, first sergeant, Two Company, Grossdeutschland Guard Battalion

OBERLEUTNANT SCHLEE, Commanding Officer, Two Company, Grossdeutschland Guard Battalion

LINGE, valet to Hitler

GENERAL WILHELM BURGDORF, Army adjutant to Hitler

OBERSTLEUTNANT STREVE, staff officer, Armed Forces High Command

GENERALLEUTNANT ADOLF HEUSINGER, Deputy Chief, Army High Command

OBERST HEINZ BRANDT, deputy to Heusinger

DELIA ZIEGLER, secretary to Olbricht and Stauffenberg

HERR GRUENBERG,
FRAU GRUENBERG,
MAXIMILLIAN GRUENBERG,
HANNAH GRUENBERG,
} fugitive Jews in Berlin

KURT FRANZ, who hid them

ALBERT SPEER, Minister of Armaments and War Production

PRINCE FRIEDRICH OF SCHAUMBURG-LIPPE, adjutant to Goebbels

OBERSTLEUTNANT GLAESEMER, Panzer officer

HEINRICH HIMMLER, Reichsführer-S.S., Chief of German Police, Minister of the Interior

Prologue

FIRST ENCOUNTER

Any number of uniformed flunkies at the Ritz Hotel might have gone from table to table in the bar to make the discreet announcements in those hushed tones reserved for the departure of an international aircraft from Lisbon. Even in wartime the Ritz was over-supplied with staff. Portugal, after all, was neutral. Still, having received not one but two phone calls in less than five minutes, an unusual occurrence, the manager Antonio da Costa decided to do it himself. With a final minute adjustment of his silk tie, he entered the large high-ceilinged ornate room which its waiting British occupants would have called Edwardian and its waiting Germans Wilhelmine.

Da Costa took considerable pleasure in announcing the flights for London and Berlin. There were few places in the world in July 1944 where Britons and Germans could sit down, more or less together, and drink the drinks of their native lands, more or less civilised, while waiting to go home. Da Costa's air was elaborately theatrical. His voice, soft and conspiratorial, suited the mood in the Ritz bar. International aircraft kept to no fixed schedule and notices of departure reached the Ritz with just enough time to get the passengers on their respective buses.

Antonio da Costa, with a broad smile and fair English: 'Madame, it pleases me to inform you that the flying-boat will shortly depart for England. The bus leaves for the harbour at once.' And Madame's pretty eyes fill with tears as she smiles at two children and in one of those high British voices tells them they are going home.

Antonio, with a lugubrious mortician's look and fair German: 'Meine Herren, Lufthansa has informed me that the flight for Berlin via Madrid, Barcelona, and Lyon will shortly depart. The bus leaves for the airport at once.'

Madame, it pleases me . . .

Meine Herren, Lufthansa has informed me . . .

Antonio da Costa, bald and paunchy but dignified, drifts from table to table, group to group, leaving in his wake joy or dismay.

The room shifts and stirs. Waiters hurriedly add their bills, present them, make change. Liveried porters troop in for the luggage. The Ritz bar cannot help resembling a waiting room these days.

Madame, it pleases me . . .

Mein Herr, Lufthansa informs me . . .

That Herr there is important; da Costa has an instinct for such things. A dark civilian suit, a Party badge in the left lapel, an air of admirably arrogant confidence somewhat spoiled by Teutonic impatience. With him is a Lorelei, poised in beige linen travelling suit, beautiful with what for da Costa is exotic German beauty at its exotic German best: almost as tall as the important Herr, younger by fifteen years; long dark-blonde hair bleached by the sun to a streaky wheat colour, eyes incredibly blue-white against the bronzed face. A holiday at Estoril or on the Algarve, while Berlin burns? The Lorelei looks bored and sulky. The Herr seems to have run out of conversation. Da Costa's instinct tells him that the Herr, important or not, will shortly lose her. The instinct, honed by thirty years at the Ritz, ten of them as manager, five of them in wartime, is rarely wrong.

Last to leave is the patient stolid Swiss courier. Tall, younger than the usual run of them but wearing the usual grey pinstripe so ill-suited to this place and this time of year. Da Costa is certain he has seen him before; his memory is the sort that can match faces to circumstances. Suddenly he has it. A cold January day a year and a half ago, the rain delaying the departure of the Sunderland flying-boat from the harbour. Even the imperturbable British were impatient, but not the Swiss courier. That one, tall and younger than usual, leaving now. Da Costa ponders for a moment: to the harbour bus that January, to the airport bus now. Then he shrugs. In this monster of a war, with Germans and Englishmen destroying each other's cities from the air, they still have interests to be looked after in the places they are bombing. The Swiss perform this function, maintaining diplomatic niceties in a world gone mad.

Antonio da Costa looks out past the palm court at the two buses, one for the harbour and England, one for the airport and Berlin.

Monika unfastened her seat belt and looked down at the toy city on its hills – a jumble of pastel-coloured children's blocks with red tile roofs, the miniature ships in the harbour, the white bird of the flying-boat that would shortly take those others to England. Then the Junkers tri-motor banked and Eugen deftly refastened Monika's seat belt, his hand lingering to caress her thigh. Soon they flew over bare tawny hills due east towards Spain, and a young officer in Lufthansa blue came back from the flight deck to inform them they could unfasten their seat belts.

'You're always in a hurry,' Eugen told her in his deep voice, more patronising than proprietary. 'Those things serve a purpose, you know.'

Monika accepted a cigarette, from a pack of American Camels Eugen had just opened. Eugen's hands were manicured, his face pink-tinged and unlined, undeniably handsome, his dark hair silvering at the temples. They said in Berlin he was up for the Golden Party Badge. He worked out of I.G. Farben headquarters on Pariserplatz, director in charge of the vast cartel's procurement office. He had long ago sent his wife and children to the country, to a villa he owned in a Black Forest village twenty miles from Freiburg and untouched by war. The self-conscious urbanity of his private self had so contradicted his aggressive public image that for a while he had fascinated Monika. The fascination had not lasted through a fortnight in the Iberian peninsula, where Monika, waiting on beaches in San Sebastian, Sagaró, and the Algarve, had little opportunity to see the aggressive public image that had first attracted her. He carried the self-conscious urbanity into bed, his dispassionate and unvarying efforts to give rather than take pleasure the mark of the extreme egoist.

Monika had felt safe for the first time in years, two whole weeks away from the endless night terror raids – safe but bored out of her mind waiting in the sun on the hot beaches while Eugen made the I.G. Farben rounds in Barcelona, Madrid, and Lisbon procuring wolfram – she thought it was wolfram – for the Armaments Ministry. Part of it, Monika admitted to herself, was the danger. She missed the danger, the living on precarious heights, the frantic terror leading to frantic joy so that one would be a fool not to try everything while one still could. She had had a brief affair with an impecunious Spanish count in San Sebastian. The one high point. She had left her fascination for Eugen in bed, a little more each time he made love to her with cool practised skill, unsweaty even in the heat of the Iberian summer. She would break off with him in Berlin, or allow him the sop of believing he was breaking with her.

And then? Gottfried might be a satisfactory replacement, she decided. He'd been after her for months in the office in his subtle, low-key, tentative way, but if she snapped her fingers he'd come running. Gottfried, with his easy charm and scholarly turn of mind, seemingly so unsuited to his position with the Gestapo – and yet she sensed passion there. She was rarely mistaken.

'What?' she said. 'I'm sorry.'

'I was saying, my dear, I know a little place on Hermann Goeringstrasse that's going for a song. Three delightful rooms and a little garden in back. Almost undamaged.'

'You're very sweet, Eugen.'

'It's French Empire inside, done in impeccable taste. Exactly the right setting for you.'

'We'll talk about it in Berlin.'

'It would not be necessary for me to . . . monopolise your time,' Eugen said. 'Hardly fair, my dear, since I travel so much. Besides, I'm no jealous schoolboy.'

The offer, so tendered, infuriated her. She wanted to rake his complacent I.G. Farben face with her fingernails.

They were seated in the rear of the Junkers tri-motor cabin. Eight seats two-by-two on their side of the aisle, four seats on the other, all occupied. She was the only woman, Eugen one of two male passengers in civilian clothing. The other sat in the single row across the aisle, close to the four large strapped-down canvas sacks that made up, along with three crates, the cargo they were carrying. For the rest, three uniforms of Luftwaffe blue, four of Wehrmacht field-grey, and directly in front of them a pair of S.S. officers in black with leather strappings that creaked whenever they moved. Across from them sat a major whose tunic was trimmed with the carmine piping of the general staff. He held the oaktag-bound report he was reading at arm's length, scowling fiercely at it through the monocle screwed into his right eye. The Black Corps officers in front of them, both smoking foul Portuguese cigars, punctuating the drone of the engines with loud phlegmy laughter, were depressingly low types. Monika dismissed them and returned her attention to the civilian seated near the cargo.

All she could see now were the broad shoulders and the back of his head, but he intrigued her. Boarding the bus in the dazzling sunstruck street outside the Ritz, Eugen had engaged him in an after-you-Alphonse routine. The man, tall, dark-blond and so ruggedly virile-looking that he might have stepped off one of those heroic nameless S.S.-man posters you saw on every advertising pillar in Berlin, had finally bowed with elaborate irony and a sweeping gesture of his right arm that Eugen had to accept or look like a damn fool. The S.S.-poster type had smiled at Eugen's stiff back as he climbed aboard.

'He's Swiss,' Eugen said now.

'I beg your pardon?'

'That man up front you've been staring at. I said he's Swiss,' Eugen told her dryly. 'Damned good looking.'

Complacent idiot! Monika thought. 'How do you know he's Swiss?'

'Those canvas sacks contain mail for British P.O.W.s. A Swiss courier meets them in Lisbon and escorts them to Berlin.'

Monika laughed.

'What amuses you, my dear?'

'He may be a foreigner, but he looks more Aryan than anyone on this plane.'

'Many Swiss are Germanic, after all,' said Eugen pedantically, and proceeded to lecture her on the demographic make-up of the Confederation Helvetique. Soon she was sorry she had made the observation.

They stopped over for two hours at Barajas airport outside Madrid, allowed the dubious privilege of a waiting-room sweltering in the late afternoon under its corrugated tin roof while the three-man Lufthansa ground crew did whatever they were supposed to do to an over-age Junkers tri-motor transport. Eugen sat her at one of the small round tables, ordered in rapid Spanish what turned out to be sherry and orange juice for both of them, and excused himself to make one of his inevitable phone calls. More wolfram for Armaments Minister Speer, she supposed.

She rummaged through her purse, placed one of Eugen's Camels between her lips and contrived to be out of matches for the benefit of the Swiss courier, who was seated nearby. He didn't respond. She raised one bleached eyebrow and smiled, white teeth gleaming against her sun-bronzed face. He acknowledged the smile with a stolid Swiss nod and lowered his head to the Spanish newspaper he was reading. Monika impatiently tapped a high-heeled straw sandal acquired in Lisbon, got up and went to his table.

'Would you have a light?'

He produced a box of matches, struck one, made flame. She ducked her head, her sun-streaked blonde hair falling in wings on either side of his hand, which she cupped in both of hers as if he were lighting her cigarette in a high wind on a Swiss mountain-top.

'Thank you.' She blew smoke at him.

He said please and resumed reading Spanish.

'I understand,' she said, beginning to feel annoyed because he showed no indication of rising to the bait, 'you're bringing mail to the Reich for British P.O.W.s.'

'Yes, that's right,' he said.

'It must be a good feeling, to have a job like that.'

'It's a job,' he said, not looking up from the newspaper.

Monika leaned down and crushed the cigarette out in the ashtray on his table. 'You don't like Germans, do you?'

He looked up for the second time. 'Do you know any reason why anybody should?'

She went back to her own table. Insolent boor!

She was trembling.

He said: 'Fräulein?' and tossed her the little box of matches. Eugen came back. The call had been a success, he told her. A little over an hour later, they were airborne again. There was another stopover at Barcelona. Eugen had no calls to make. From Barcelona to Lyon they were escorted across a corner of the Mediterranean and up the Rhone valley by an Me 109e, purely as a precaution, the co-pilot told them. They spent the night in Lyon, where she contrived to keep Eugen at arm's length until he woke her shortly before dawn. While he was making love to her in the darkness of their suite in the Hotel Royal she saw the face of the German-hating courier. She arched upward strongly to meet Eugen's thrusting weight and for the only time with him her cry of pleasure was real.

The tri-motor left from Lyon-Bron airport shortly before noon on Friday 7 July and reached Tempelhof in Berlin in late afternoon. The passenger facilities had been bombed out; Eugen's chauffeur was waiting outside the Mitropa dining car that had replaced them. A pall of smoke hung over the city, scratching her throat raw, stinging her eyes. The smoke glowed red north of the airport. The British had hit Berlin-East last night, Eugen's chauffeur reported as they drove towards the centre of the city. Ruins which she had taken for granted two weeks ago looked bleak and terrible now, like an archaeological excavation of a civilisation that had succumbed to barbarian hordes at the dawn of history. They had to wait while an Organization Todt salvage convoy crossed their route on Wilhelmstrasse. After Portugal and Spain, the Berliners looked apathetic, shuffling along the smashed pavements like sleep-walkers.

The convoy passed. A traffic cop in a soot-stained white tunic and white gloves waved them forward. Piles of rubble made Wilhelmplatz an obstacle course. Only the Ministry of Propaganda was undamaged.

Berlin made her want to scream.

For the first time in months, Monika Jaeger thought of her husband, fighting somewhere on the Eastern Front.

Part One

SECOND ENCOUNTER

One

A woman at the reception desk of the almost deserted Swiss Legation signed for the four sacks of P.O.W. mail, clocking them in at 19.56 hours.

'I don't know you, do I?' she asked Haller.

'No, it's my first run.'

'How are things at home?' She was plump and middle-aged and had a pleasant smile. Behind thick glasses her eyes looked wistful.

'Everybody hates the blackout,' Haller said.

'Are you from Zürich, perhaps?' she asked hopefully. She wanted to talk; Haller didn't.

'No,' he said.

'I volunteered to stay here. Volunteered. I must be crazy. Most of the Embassy staff is at a castle outside of town. But we get extra pay. For hazardous duty. Do you know the Veltliner Keller in Zürich? I dream of it. Some bundnerfleisch and then a schnitzel that overflows the plate. After that a glass of kirsch. And real coffee.' Her voice trailed off regretfully. 'Will you be staying long?'

'No,' Haller said. 'I have to get back.'

'Portugal?'

Haller nodded.

'It must be nice in Portugal. No blackout.'

'Once a week, for practice.'

Where *are* you from? I can't place the accent.'

'Bern,' Haller said.

'Ah, Bern. I started in the Foreign Office there, before the war.' She sighed. 'Was there ever a time before the war?'

Haller nodded his sympathy with this philosophic question. He picked up his worn leather suitcase.

'A pleasant journey,' the woman told him.

Haller thanked her and went outside. From the steps he could see across a weed-grown lot the skeleton of the Reichstag. The distance to the address on Mittelstrasse near the Prussian State Library wasn't far. He decided to walk.

Haller said: 'I'm told you repair watches.'

The door had been opened as far as the chain would permit. Haller could see a long nose, shiny round cheeks, rimless glasses.

'Not much these days, I'm afraid. I can't get the spare parts.' The voice was high-pitched, the accent Swedish.

'I don't require any spare parts,' Haller said.

He heard the chain grating. The door opened quickly and he stepped into the apartment. There was no hallway. Haller found himself in a small living-room jammed with red plush overstuffed furniture. The walls were lined with bookshelves. Books overflowed on to a long table against the right-hand wall and were stacked on the floor so that it was difficult to find anywhere to stand. A long-haired dachshund emerged from somewhere and yiped ecstatically at Haller's trousers, tail going like a frantic metronome. The man, whose name was Axel Lindstrom, was short and round.

'You're late. I was worried,' he said. 'I don't like to keep that sort of stuff around.'

'I don't blame you,' Haller said. 'I got here as soon as I could.'

The Swede chained the door again, first looking both ways along the dim hallway. Then he suddenly grinned at Haller. 'It's called "the German look". Everyone does it. A drink?' he asked. 'I have Steinhäger.'

Haller said he could use a drink, and the Swede finally motioned him to sit. Haller had to push aside a stack of books to find room on the overstuffed sofa. The Swede poured clear liquid from a stone bottle into shot glasses. He said: 'Skål,' and they drank. The Steinhäger tasted like a pre-bottled Martini cocktail. The Swede poured again. Then he left the room. When he returned with a large brown-paper package fastened with twine, the dachshund had finished bathing Haller's right hand and had started on the left.

'The clothing is all you'll need? They didn't say anything about papers.'

'I have papers,' Haller told him. 'I'd like to leave some things here with you.'

'They said nothing about that.'

'I have nowhere else.'

'What things?' the Swede asked unhappily.

'What I'm wearing, one set of papers.'

'You came through the streets with more than one set?' the Swede marvelled.

'Swiss. Diplomatic. It was all right.'

'How long will I have to hold your things?' the Swede asked. Then he brightened. 'Could I perhaps give the papers to someone else?'

Haller shook his head. 'I'll need them when I'm through here.'

'How long will that be?'

'I don't know,' Haller said.

'I don't like it. How could I explain Swiss papers?'

Haller said: 'How could you explain a short-wave radio transmitter?'

While he spoke, Haller was undressing. All his clothing, down to his undershorts and gartered knee-high socks, were of Swiss manufacture. He wondered about the watch. That was Swiss too. He decided it would be all right.

The Swede looked at the scar that ran from his shoulder to his left nipple. It was fully healed, but not an old scar.

'Combat?' he asked.

'More or less,' Haller said. He was cutting the twine on the package with a Swiss clasp knife. He decided he could keep that along with the watch.

The Swede was impressed. 'They thought of everything. Extra linen, a spare shirt, even a wound badge. Not to mention the Knight's Cross for valour.'

Haller packed the spare underwear and grey shirt in his leather suitcase, then put on German underwear, clean but not new. One of the grey socks had been darned at the heel. The iron-grey breeches were a good fit, the black jackboots polished to an anthracite finish. Haller fastened the five matt-grey buttons of the field-grey tunic – actually more green than grey and with darker green badge cloth at cuffs and collar. It was snug across the shoulders but good enough. Braids and stripes were of the 67th Infantry Regiment, formerly the First Regiment of Grenadiers in the Prussian Guards. They matched the papers Haller had brought with him. The forage cap fitted perfectly. It bore eagle and swastika embroidered in silver thread, as did the tunic above the right breast pocket. Shoulder straps and collar tabs showed Haller to be a Hauptmann of Grenadiers, an infantry captain.

'My God!' said the Swede, studying him. 'I'd never look twice. Are your documents as good?'

'They'd better be.'

Haller was folding his pinstripe suit. He gave it and the slim leather case containing his Swiss diplomatic passport to Axel Lindstrom.

'You can't give me any idea how long?'

'It had better be less than two weeks. That's how long my Wehrmacht leave warrant is good for.'

'May I ask why you are here?'

'You know better than that.'

The Swede nodded. Haller thought he was embarrassed.

Haller asked: 'If I had an emergency, could I use your transmitter?'

For the first time the Swede's face looked hard. 'You know better than *that*,' he said.

Now Haller nodded. It had been foolish to ask.

The hard look left Lindstrom's face. 'This was the only time I used it this year. You have to understand.'

The Swede looked him over. 'Is the suitcase all right?'

Haller said it was of German manufacture.

'I'd wear the Knight's Cross,' the Swede suggested. 'It could help.'

Haller took the heavy iron cross from one gusseted pocket of his tunic. He tucked the black ribbon under his badge cloth collar, so that the cross hung just below his throat. Perhaps the Swede was right; perhaps it would come in handy.

Haller knew that everything he did from now on would put his life on the line. One wrong move would finish him. It was not comforting to know that none of Berlin's four million inhabitants would give a damn.

The two men shook hands. The dachshund circled Haller's legs inquisitively, sniffing at the jackboots. Haller was another person.

Hauptmann Richard Haller, on leave from the 67th Infantry Regiment on the Western Front, went downstairs and outside into the streets of Berlin.

*

An old man came through the swaying U-bahn car punching tickets. The subway car was not crowded; just four other passengers. All of them looked exhausted except for the well-dressed man who gazed approvingly through his pince-nez at Haller and his Knight's Cross.

Haller got his ticket punched. It was good for one ride on the U-bahn and a transfer to the S-bahn or any Berlin bus line. Any bus line still operating, Haller thought,

The clatter of the metal wheels was thrown back in an instant echo by the close walls of the tunnel. Some of the train's shattered windows had been boarded over. Slogan cards had been tacked to the boards, telling Haller that hard work will beat every opponent in the end, that half measures were no measures, and that what couldn't kill him would strengthen him. One card exclaimed: 'Stick it out!' and someone had scrawled under that: 'Until we're all dead?' No one had seen fit to remove the graffito.

The train left the tunnel and hurtled along an elevated line. It was dusk, and Haller could see little in the blackout in the southern suburbs of Berlin. The ticket puncher came back through the car as the train slowed. 'Eberswalde,' he announced. 'End of the line. Everybody out.'

Haller asked him: 'Doesn't this line go as far as Lichterfelde?'

The old man smirked at the country-bumpkin question. 'The R.A.F. decided it should stop here,' he said, and then he saw the Knight's Cross. He stiffened. 'You can probably hitch a ride to Lichterfelde down below, Herr Hauptmann.'

Haller went with the other passengers along the platform. Dull blue lights, wide-spaced, lit their way feebly to the stairs that descended to the street. Or what was left of the street. Two large Organization Todt trucks were parked there. Men wearing protective masks and wielding acetylene torches were burning away sections of twisted steel girder that blocked the roadway. A large bomb crater had filled with water from a burst main. Beyond it in the dusk Haller could make out the silhouettes of destroyed buildings, like the stumps of decayed teeth. An Organization Todt foreman wearing the O.T. armband above the broader swastika brassard on his left sleeve came by, a fidgety little man in a soiled brown uniform.

'How can I get to Lichterfelde?' Haller asked him.

'It's worse than Eberswalde, down there,' the O.T. foreman said indifferently, and then his eyes went to the Knight's Cross.

Haller knew the Swede had been right. 'You're going to the Cadet Barracks?'

'Of course,' Haller lied. 'Where else?' He could almost see the large-scale map of Berlin he had studied so long. Six transparent overlays on which had been drawn anything that might conceivably matter. *Sorry, old boy,* someone had joked, *we didn't have room for public urinals.*

Goethestrasse was less than half a mile from the Lichterfelde Cadet Barracks.

'I'm heading down that way myself,' the O.T. foreman said. 'Come on.'

Together they crunched across broken glass to a Volkswagen with the O.T. symbol on its door.

Soon the rattle of the short-stroke engine pushed them slowly along the rubble-filled streets. The blackout headlights were of little help, but the O.T. man seemed to know the way. It took them half an hour to negotiate the four miles between Eberswalde and the Cadet Barracks in Lichterfelde.

'Been reassigned as an instructor?' the O.T. man asked.

'Something like that.'

'Your bad luck, friend. You know the joke that's going around. What's the definition of a coward?'

'You tell me,' Haller said.

'A Berliner who volunteers for front-line duty. Well, here we are.'

Haller stood in shadow outside the Cadet Barracks guardhouse. When the rattling Volkswagen disappeared into the darkness, he started walking.

The suburb of Lichterfelde had taken capricious punishment. On some streets no single house remained. Rows of small villas with steeply-pitched roofs stood undamaged elsewhere. The moon hung low in the east, its light diffused to an anaemic glow by the shroud of smoke smothering the city. Electricity lines had not been knocked out, or had been repaired; pinpricks of blue light aimed directly downwards revealed the location of street-lamps and those street signs that still stood. Haller found Goethestrasse that way. It was one of the less fortunate streets in Lichterfelde. On one corner a fireplace and chimney stood solitary sentry duty over a block of wasteland. Fifty yards beyond, Haller made out a grand piano standing canted on two legs on the pavement. He wondered if the house he had come to find would be bombed out, a pile of bricks or an empty lot. What then? Drop back five and punt, he thought.

Or if not bombed out, then under surveillance. But when he saw it, standing amidst shattered piles of brick and masonry, he knew it would not be under surveillance. Fifty-seven Goethestrasse stood alone. Even the picket fence enclosing the little garden was intact, street-number painted on the gate. Hardly as much as a wall remained in one piece anywhere near it. There would be nowhere for the Gestapo to set up shop.

Not even the faintest light escaped the blacked-out windows. Haller opened the gate and went up the brick path to the door. He knocked. After a few moments a woman's voice called: 'Yes? Who is it?'

She sounded young, and frightened. The fear didn't surprise Haller. The reports reaching London all agreed that General Beck had fallen under suspicion.

'Gröfaz,' Haller said. The irony of the password amused him. Gröfaz: Grösster Feldherr aller Zeiten – the greatest commander-in-chief of all time. It was the contemptuous epithet used by disillusioned Germans for their Führer.

Haller heard a quick intake of breath followed by a sigh. Then the countersign: 'From Kaiserslautern?'

'No. Kassel,' Haller said, completing identification.

He heard a bolt sliding back. The door opened on total darkness and he went in.

Two

At that same hour in London, a faint green twilight still lingered in the west. From the window of the flat, Gillian could see the uneven cobblestones of the mews, the carriage house in deep shadow across the narrow lane, and, were she to lean out and crane her neck to the right she might just see Sloane Street in the last light. Gillian resisted the impulse: she was stark naked. The husky, not quite lewd laughter – her own – surprised her. That was about the only impulse she'd resisted tonight.

She leaned on the sill and breathed the air of London. Home.

'If you think you're going to make your escape that way, my girl, you're very much mistaken.' Harry gave a parody of a lascivious chuckle. 'Come back to bed,' he commanded.

Gillian sighed dramatically. 'Not again.'

'I'm afraid so,' said Harry.

'Twice already and it isn't even midnight,' Gillian complained as she approached the bed. 'The man will wear himself out.'

In the faint light from the window she could just make out the tickets on the night-table. Eighth row centre at the Duchess. *Blithe Spirit* was in its third year, and it had seemed a good idea when she had picked up the tickets that afternoon. She doubted that Noël Coward had even begun writing it when she'd left with the children for America during the Blitz.

What had seemed a good idea in the afternoon had rather slipped away from them as evening approached. Philip and Mavis were with their grandmother in Bampton, only for a few days unless she and Harry decided that the buzz bombs necessitated an extended stay in the Devon countryside.

The children, especially six-year-old Philip, were still confused by it all – the long journey from New York to Lisbon, the flight aboard the Sunderland yesterday, the strange ruddy-faced man with the fierce guardsman's moustache who was their father. Last night had been a strain. They'd seen Philip and his younger sister off this morning. Then of course Harry had put in his day at Baker Street, not getting home until after six. So of course Noël Coward had been a mistake. Four years. She had anticipated a strangeness with Harry, a slow awkward searching out of one another. It hadn't been that way at all. Harry had taken her in his strong arms and obliterated those four years. Which he seemed about to do again.

Gillian pushed him firmly back on the bed. 'Just you lie still. My turn, Wing Commander Bennett. I'd far rather you *didn't* wear yourself out.'

Much later she awoke and rolled over languidly, reaching out for him. He wasn't there. She saw him silhouetted against the moonlight at the window, smoking.

'Darling? A penny?'

'Couldn't sleep. Nothing to it. Restless.'

She remembered that brusque, faintly querulous tone of voice, even after four years. Trouble.

'What is it, darling?'

'I knew a chap once who called it a white night. Dark outside, but white in here.' Harry tapped his temple. 'Touch of insomnia, that's all. Go back to sleep, love.'

There was a faint explosion, far away. The windowpanes rattled a few seconds later.

'Bloody bastards,' growled Harry.

Gillian knew the explosion had been a buzz bomb, its engine cutting out suddenly, somewhere over London, the small pilotless jet plane diving to earth with its ton of high explosive, bringing random destruction, random death.

'You'd think they'd know when to pack it in. You'd think they'd know they're only making it worse for themselves. Bloody bastards,' Harry said again.

'Worried about the children? Mother would love to have them stay. Philip could go to school in Bampton.'

Gillian slipped into her robe and went over to him.

'Grow up to be a pair of hayseeds,' said Harry, trying out a smile. His speech was laced with Americanisms, as was hers. Not surprising, Gillian thought; his work brought him into frequent contact with the Yanks.

But it wasn't the children, Gillian could sense that. It was almost as if the four-year separation had made their rapport more complete.

Gillian tried their old shorthand: 'I'm a good listener.' Harry had always been self-contained, and she *was* a good listener. The only one he allowed himself.

He drew the blackout curtains, switched on the bedside lamp and lit another cigarette. It was just after three in the morning. He chewed at a corner of his moustache, a remembered sign. His scowl was so fierce he looked like a little boy masquerading as Wing Commander Harry Bennett. He said:

'Something you told me just after you landed yesterday, love.'

'Did I say anything? I thought all I did was kiss you. Five hundred and forty-seven times.'

'Actually,' said Harry, 'you were babbling.'

Gillian truly didn't remember. 'Better remind me.'

'Waiting at the Ritz in Lisbon. The coincidence?'

'Oh, that. The two buses. It *was* rather grotesquely amusing. The Nazis boarding one for the plane to Germany at the same time we were boarding the other to take us to the Sunderland in the harbour. Almost as if there was no war on.'

'There's a war on,' Harry said flatly. He went into the sitting-room and returned with his large battered briefcase. He extracted a manila envelope, undid the clasp, withdrew a folder. From that he took an eight-by-ten glossy photograph and showed it to her.

It was a head and shoulders shot of an American officer. The two bars on the collar told her he was a captain. The American part was easy: the big eagle over the visor of the garrison cap.

'Know this chap?'

'Should I?'

'I'm asking the questions, love,' said Harry.

She studied the photograph. 'He's very good looking. He . . . he does look familiar. Do I know him from the States or what?'

Harry cocked a bristly eyebrow that complemented the guardsman's moustache. 'No guessing games,' he said, more than an edge of anxiety in his voice. Gillian knew this was terribly important to him.

'Sure!' she blurted, sounding totally American herself then. 'The bus in Lisbon. I'm sure of it.' Suddenly she was perplexed. 'But if he's an American, what was he doing boarding the bus for the German plane?'

'You saw him?' Harry said. 'You're certain of it? He got on the airport bus?'

Gillian looked at the photograph again. 'The cap put me off at first. Blond hair? Tall, athletic build?'

Harry said nothing for a while. Then he said, mostly to himself: 'We got our man in.' He didn't sound happy. He asked: 'What time is it?'

Gillian pushed his jaw so that he was staring at the luminous dial of the clock on the night-table. It was 3.15.

Then she turned his jaw back and kissed him on the lips. Harry was stiff and unresponsive.

'The hell with it,' he said. 'If I can't sleep, there's no reason why he should.'

'Who? the man in the photograph?'

Harry went into the sitting-room again and Gillian heard him speak a number down the telephone.

Three

This is where I come into the story, sort of a walk-on part. But if Harry Bennett went to anyone, it had to be me, of course. I was the one who suggested Dick Haller for the mission in the first place.

It had been a tangled kind of night and the girl wound up

sleeping on my usual side of the bed, where the phone was. She mumbled something that could have been hell-a-time-anyone-call as I reached across her. She was a W.A.A.F. Section Officer named Patty whom I'd met through Harry. She worked in his office, as she put it, sticking pins into maps and things. She was very Irish. I wound up leaning across her breasts, and she had come awake enough to start nibbling at my ear when I managed an angry hello at the phone.

'Milt? Milt Green? Harry Bennett here.'

'This number is out of service until seven o'clock,' Patty said. 'If not later.'

'Hullo? Milt? I've got to see you.'

'So, see me. In the morning. You know where to find me.'

'I've got to talk to you.'

Patty, now that she was awake, decided it was a good idea to wriggle out from under and unfasten the buttons of my pyjama jacket. I was propped up on one elbow.

'It's about Breakers,' Harry said.

I'd already guessed it would be. Harry had been the minority's leading advocate at 82 Baker Street. I could have gone either way, but once I'd suggested Dick Haller and the S.O.E./O.S.S. brass went for him, I got caught up in things.

With forthright dexterity Patty was working on the drawstring of my pyjama bottoms. There were strong indications that I seemed to like the idea.

'We've got to call our man off,' Harry said.

'The hell you say. And even if we had to, we couldn't. Go back to sleep, Harry.'

'There's a way we could.'

'How?' I asked.

Harry said: 'Through Bern, that's how.'

I was going to tell Harry I didn't agree with either his premise or the method of implementation, but then Patty's red head swooped down towards my belly.

I managed: 'Your office, first thing in the morning,' and dropped the phone.

Patty stopped what she was doing long enough to remark that the middle-of-the-night phone call had been a good idea after all.

I forgot about Harry for a while.

Start with what Napoleon once said. Not the bit about an army marching on its stomach; we've got that one pretty well sorted out. What Napoleon said was that he loved treason – I guess he meant in the enemy camp – but he hated traitors.

We tossed it back and forth on Saturday morning in Harry's office in the red brick building on Baker Street that the Marks & Spencer department store people had loaned to the Ministry of Economic Warfare for the duration. The brass plaque out front says 'Inter-Services Research Bureau' in the kind of discreet lettering you'd find outside a gentlemen's club. The front entrance is used mostly when someone wants to duck across the street to the French section. Otherwise, the grab-bag of civilian and military types who make up Special Operations Executive prefer the back entrance off a lane of abandoned carriage houses and a couple of functioning garages. They are forbidden by the Official Secrets Act to refer to S.O.E. by name outside the shop, and even among themselves call it The Old Firm or The Racket. Harry Bennett, Wing Commander Harry Bennett, was assistant chief of the German Section, until recently the poor relation of S.O.E. That's easy enough to understand. You can buy yourself some agents in neutral countries like Switzerland and Portugal, and you can drop agents by parachute or send them in the tiny Lysanders flown by Moon Squadron to organise underground operations in occupied countries like France or Holland. Pretty heroic stuff, and effective. Dick Haller was doing the same sort of work in France for O.S.S., but I'll get to that.

Buying agents or organising the opposition in Nazi Germany itself is something else again. It can't be done, of course. So what Harry's office did, most of the time, was listen. I worked as their O.S.S. liaison.

Where did we leave Napoleon? Not marching on his stomach, but loving treason and hating traitors.

Harry's office did its listening to traitors, or at least potential traitors, or at the very least friends of traitors or potential traitors. Not that they exactly grew on trees in Hitler's Thousand Year Reich. But every so often one or two of them came crawling out of the woodwork. That's how Harry's boss put it, and the brass at S.O.E. and our own O.S.S. tended to agree. The first question asked, inside the shop, went something like this: if they claim they want to overthrow Adolf and his whole sick gutter crew, what's in it for them?

Everybody hates a traitor.

Nobody on Baker Street – Harry excepted – could conceive of a patriotic Kraut going ape to get rid of his Führer.

Still, Harry's people and the O.S.S. set up listening posts.

There were the Wallenberg brothers in Stockholm, Swedish bankers who occasionally passed along sausage stuffing about the anti-Nazi Underground. There was the Countess Rocamora, the genuine article, whose husband was the Spanish military attaché in Berlin. The countess served as lady-in-waiting to the deposed Spanish Infanta, who was languishing in a fifty-room villa in Lausanne, and divided her time between Berlin and Switzerland, where she sometimes met with our man in Bern.

Maybe I'm prejudiced, but I think the best listening post of all was on Herrengasse in Bern. That's where Allen Dulles set up shop back in late '42, the last American to enter Switzerland legally because, right after he went in, the Krauts occupied Vichy France and sealed the Swiss border. Dulles's chief contact was a German named Gisevius, Ribbentrop's consular attaché in the Swiss capital. A potential traitor? Dulles thought so, anyway.

That was the situation until D-Day last month. After that the pinball machine really lit up.

Figure there *was* a conspiracy inside Germany to overthrow the Nazis. D-Day meant they had to hurry.

Back to the question: what's in it for them?

And the answer: a Fatherland more or less intact, a new German government that could negotiate peace terms short of the unconditional surrender called for by Roosevelt and Churchill. But time was running out. We were in France and moving, the Russians were at the gates of Warsaw and moving, and if the anti-Nazis didn't get the lead out of their pants, they'd wind up sharing Hitler's Götterdämmerung with seventy million Krauts.

The lights on the pinball machine said: assassination.

The lights on the pinball machine also said: military putsch in Berlin.

X-Day: mid-July. Say, a week or ten days from now.

Harry's office got that from Sweden and we got it from Dulles in Bern, and it even came through a P.O.W. cage in Normandy, courtesy of our C.I.C. interrogators. Dulles's code-word for the anti-Nazi operation was Breakers, and his coded W/T signals said Breakers was for real. Among themselves the anti-Nazis called it Operation Valkyrie. That was a nice touch, the Valkyries being those mythological Amazonian types who flew on horseback above Teutonic battlefields and decided who would die.

They had decided Hitler would die.

Napoleon one last time: Everybody hates a traitor.

Amended by Major Milt Green, Psych Warfare and O.S.S.: nobody trust a traitor.

That's what Harry and I were mulling over in his office. We were still going round and round in his club on Albemarle Street over a lousy wartime lunch.

Partly I was humouring Harry. Before the war he was an Oxford don – field of study, German culture. Harry hated the Nazis but he didn't hate Germany. The distinction, from where I sat in July 1944, was kind of minimal. But something else was bothering me: I'd given them Dick Haller.

Questions: what if Breakers or Operation Valkyrie or whatever you wanted to call it really could pull the job off? What if they could kill Adolf and overthrow the Nazi regime? Never mind what was in it for them.

What was in it for *us*?

That was when the pinball machine went tilt.

Answer, arrived at by S.O.E./O.S.S., Harry and few others dissenting: not bloody much.

Hitler, at this late juncture in the war, would serve the Anglo-American cause better alive than dead.

Make that stronger. If any Germans were capable of assassinating their Führer, we had to stop them. Fast.

The final reasoning went something like this:

1. The German motive: if a bunch of Kraut aristocrats and general-staff types – and that's who they were – knocked off Hitler, the benefits to us would be nil. It was debatable whether they were Adolf's tool or he was theirs. But say they did it, and say they formed a provisional government. They'd expect a *quid pro quo* from us, of course. Such as: never mind Unconditional Surrender, let's negotiate. How's about if we let them keep Austria, the Sudetenland, the Polish Corridor, and Upper Silesia. For starters.

2. The stab-in-the-back theory: the word for this in German is *Dolchstoss.* If they got rid of Hitler and were allowed to surrender to us before we kick their arses but good, we'd go right back to square one, where we found ourselves after the First World War. Meaning a Germany that saw itself 'undefeated in the field', busily nurturing the deadly notion that it had been defeated by traitors on the home front. Such a post-war Germany would cry out for revenge, first against the traitors, then against us. Let them knock off Adolf, end the war on terms short of Unconditional Surrender, and World War Three would be coming right up.

3. The pox-on-all-of-them viewpoint: Germans like Carl Goerdeler and General Beck, the civilian and military leaders of the conspiracy, we could do without. They were ready to follow a Hitler before there *was* a Hitler. Why had they decided to move against him now? One reason only. Because he was losing the war. That didn't make them any better than their Führer. They deserved him, and he deserved them.

4. Which led to this objective assessment: the real enemy was not Hitler. The real enemy was and always had been German militarism and German expansionism. We had to destroy the first and roll back the second.

5. Now look at it the other way round: say we give the plotters our blessing, make promises we would either keep or not keep. What if they fail? (This was my boss at Psych Warfare talking.) If they fail, why then, a little later on when the Nazis themselves are finally ready to call it quits, they might just turn to Russia, not us, for separate peace terms. Colouring the post-war map of Europe an interesting shade of red.

6. And if they succeed? It could result in civic breakdown in Germany, even a civil war between the Valkyrie provisional government and the S.S. This at a time when the Russians are a hell of a lot closer to Berlin than we are. Result: Uncle Joe stops the carnage, not Uncle Sam – and the map of Europe turns the same interesting shade of red.

7. To cap everything, there was the American-election angle, as seen by Harry's boss: what if Valkyrie succeeded, and we started dickering? Maybe Britain would hold out for Unconditional Surrender, but what about us? No Nazi bombs had fallen on American cities, a lot of folks in Ohio and Wisconsin and California thought our real enemy was in the Pacific, and since 6 June American boys were dying on European soil – more than 4,000 of them in the first month of combat. 'Bring the boys home' would make a pretty irresistible campaign promise in election year 1944. With Hitler dead, Unconditional Surrender might become a political hot potato even F.D.R. couldn't handle.

There was more, three days of rancour and reason, of scrambled transatlantic phone calls and ciphers, or hurriedly drawn position papers and woefully unprepared arguments. But you get the idea. If the Valkyrie people had to hurry, so did we.

Decision: Hitler had to survive to ignite Germany's funeral

pyre. Total war is total war. So let's get on with it, O.K.? They asked for it.

Implementation: we send someone in for a good long look at Valkyrie. If it showed out as cloud-cuckoo-land, we would simply wish them joy. If it turned out to be the real thing, we would stop them.

Enter Dick Haller, and my feelings of guilt.

Once the brass had a look at Dick's credentials – and a look at the man himself – there were no other candidates. You couldn't have invented a man better suited for the mission than my friend Dick Haller.

To begin with, he looked the part. I don't suppose you've seen the chart painted by Alfred Eydt for the Reich Ministry of Education, but every German has. Psych Warfare's got a copy. It's a straight propaganda job, showing how all the racially impeccable Aryan types are supposed to look – Westphalian, Rhinelander, Dinaric, and so forth. Anyway, Eydt's ideal Nordic type, full-face and profile, could have been a portrait of Dick Haller.

Then there's his background. Dick's father was a petroleum engineer who gypsied all over the Middle East and South America. So did Dick for a while. Then Dick's mother apparently decided it wasn't the perfect life. There was a divorce, and Dick got his education in boarding schools in Switzerland and at the University of Geneva in the thirties. He wound up speaking fluent French and fluent German and he had an amazing linguistic aptitude. He could cut over from Rhenish dialect to Bavarian or Berliner, not to mention Schwyzerdutsch.

He enlisted the day after Pearl Harbor, got assigned to Counter-Intelligence and through it to O.S.S. He spent a year and a half setting up Resistance circuits in France, including the most successful one of all, the Donkeyman circuit in Paris that was, and is, driving the Gestapo and S.D. nuts. He made a dozen drops in France, including the contact with Roger Peugeot that resulted in the destruction of the big plant at Souchet that made armoured cars and tank components for the Wehrmacht. To get those early circuits going he had to be an astute judge of character and, when necessary, one hell of a hard-nosed bastard. Equipment was allocated and dropped to the Underground on the basis of his evaluations. And he had another job. Local enforcers tend to lose their effectiveness: more than once Dick parachuted in to liquidate a traitor.

So from an intelligence viewpoint, Dick looked like the perfect agent. Ice-water in his veins. Nerves of steel. Superman on detached service to O.S.S.

Of course, there's more to Dick than that. He's human. In fact, he's the sort of guy who if you were a girl you'd be glad to bring home to papa. But that part of him is under wraps for the duration.

One final point. If the brass had had any lingering doubts, there was his name. When you go in under a cover identity, that's one of the little things that can keep your neck out of a noose. I mean how you answer to your name. In Dick's case, no phoney name was necessary. Haller's a good old German name. Austrian and Swiss too, for that matter.

Dick Haller was their man.

And he's in there now. Harry didn't have to tell me that. He got it from Gillian last night. I got it the day before by W/T from the O.S.S. field man in Lisbon.

Which is when I started feeling guilty. I got Dick into this.

Not that I'm worried about him succeeding. The first part, vetting the Valkyrie people, will be easy. They'll welcome him with open arms. They know through Dulles and Gisevius that he's going in, and they *think* they know what he wants – to discuss peace terms. Not exactly accurate, perhaps, but plausible.

If they haven't got a prayer, Dick comes out the way he went in, as a Swiss, and gives us the good word. If it looks like they can pull it off, if it looks even remotely possible, Dick blows the whistle on them.

I don't know the details there. I'd guess he'll contact a double agent, some good wholesome type we've bought information from once or twice, but probably as dedicated a Nazi as Heinrich Himmler.

After which Dick Haller has to live with himself.

Harry had changed his tack. Not having persuaded me on the level of global politics, he was now appealing to me as a Jew, an American, a soldier, and a humanitarian.

He said: if they succeed, the first thing they'll do is open the concentration camps.

He asked: if they fail, if we *make* them fail, how many G.I.s and Tommies will die?

He pleaded: if we betray them, we'll be betraying the only people in Germany with the guts to take a stand. Some of them might survive *their* failure, but not *our* betrayal. They're the sort of people we'll need after the war.

This was over lunch at his club. The white wine was too warm and too acid. It and the conversation gave me a sour stomach. I said no to the State Express cigarettes Harry offered and yes to the Rennies antacid tablets.

'Well?' he said.

'Well?' I repeated.

'Damn it all, fuck the brass.'

Harry was agitated, his voice louder than he'd thought, and it was that kind of club. Heads swung towards us. Harry reddened, lowered his voice:

'We can signal Dulles to tell that chap at the German consulate in Bern – what's his name? – to warn his people.'

'His name's Gisevius,' I said. 'Aren't you forgetting something?'

'That it might mean a court-martial for both of us? If it did come to that, I wouldn't mind blowing this thing sky high.'

'That's not what I meant,' I said patiently. 'What about Special Project Bennett?'

Harry gave me a furious look. 'Bloody-minded bastards. Are they still calling it that?'

Special Project Bennett had been his Baker Street colleagues' sop to Harry. He was so outraged over the planned operation they had to give him something.

The Wallenberg brothers in Sweden had learned about a list the Bureau of Student and Youth Affairs in the Reich Central Security Office had compiled, over two hundred dissident students slated for extermination. That list, according to the Swedish bankers' source, had not yet been delivered to Gestapo Chief Heinrich Mueller. Harry thought he knew why. He had met the Director of the Bureau of Student and Youth Affairs once or twice before the war, an historian named Ritter who had held down the contemporary history chair at the University of Munich.

Ritter, neither a fool nor a fanatic Nazi, according to Harry, was an ambitious man. Obviously, he was playing it cagey.

If he could deliver the list intact after the war, thus demonstrating that he had saved the dissident students from Nazi justice, his other activities at the Reich Central Security Office would conveniently be forgotten by the victorious allies.

Question: who would get the list?

The Wallenberg brothers weren't sure. Harry was.

Ritter saw the wave of the future rolling across Europe from the steppes of Central Asia. He would deliver his list not to us but to the Russians.

Those dissident students, Harry believed, were the hope for a new Germany. They would supply its leaders, good leaders from our point of view.

Not from the Russian point of view. Students capable of dissidence against the entrenched Nazi regime would cause even more trouble in a Russian-controlled regime. And it had seemed obvious, at least until D-Day, that the Russians would reach Berlin before we did.

Special Project Bennett, so-called, was a discretionary adjunct to Dick Haller's mission. If the opportunity presented itself, he would try to get his hands on the Ritter list.

As I said, that was a sop to Harry. No one took it very seriously.

Now he said: 'Come off it, Milt. You know Captain Haller better than I do, but I know him well enough. Bloody-minded like the rest of them. The Ritter list doesn't mean a goddamn thing to him.'

Harry was right, of course. Dick was pragmatic and, for the duration, as bloody-minded as Harry claimed. The Ritter list was eyewash for Wing Commander Bennett.

Outside, the air raid sirens began to wail. The chief club steward came around and said something about the cellar. Harry just shook his head. Hardly anyone left their tables. Buzz bombs were pilotless and haphazard, as impersonal as the Black Plague. One ignored them, as Harry put it. Otherwise one gave in to the terror.

It hit me then. 'Aren't you forgetting something else?' I asked.

'Now what?' Harry said, exasperated.

He had made a convincing case for signalling Dulles. I wasn't at all sure I didn't agree with him.

'If we do it,' I said, 'what happens to Dick Haller?'

We couldn't find a taxi outside Harry's club. We started walking, Dover Street and then Hay Hill over towards Berkeley Square. The little park was lovely, despite the sandbags and the squat ugly concrete A.R.P. box. London almost looked at peace. Nobody seemed perturbed by the air raid warning. Buzz bombs would hit where they would hit. Stiff-upper-lip fatalism, and to hell with you, Adolf. Few of the pilotless jet planes had struck the West End.

Harry kept talking. He was all British understatement until something riled him. And he was riled now. He talked my ear off along Mount Row and Carlos Place. By then we were approaching Grosvenor Square and the American Embassy. We could have taken another route. Harry chose this one. I think he had in mind to steer me into the Embassy. There was a cryp I knew there if I wanted to get through to Dulles in Bern.

We hit the south-east corner of the square, where Carlos Place enters it. Fifteen minutes more would see us back in Baker Street unless we showed our I.D.s to the marine guards outside the Embassy.

Maybe we would have. I honestly don't know.

Grosvenor Square was crowded with Londoners pointedly ignoring the air raid warning, taking the July sunshine. I could see the Stars and Stripes flying in front of the Embassy and the Officers' Club. By then I was only listening with half an ear. I hadn't got riled up the way Harry had, and I'm not as quick as Dick Haller. I was mulling it over.

Harry said: '... murdering the only good Germans there are, damn it all,' and I heard a buzzing, rasping sound.

You don't get much of a chance to see them. Sometimes a fiery tail of flame. Last month, when the Krauts first started sending them over from the Pas de Calais, those streaks of flame fooled people. They would fill the streets with cheering. They thought it was Kraut aircraft going down in flames.

The buzzing, rasping sound cut out. It just stopped.

Everybody looked up uneasily. Everybody kept walking.

'Harry,' I said. I grasped his arm.

'That cryp you know in the Embassy,' he said, unperturbed, and maybe I saw something. A few people had begun to run, looking for cover. I tried to pull Harry along with me. He broke my hold on his arm and kept walking.

I dived into a recessed doorway. Staff entrance to the Officers' Club.

The world went bright and loud, and the ground shook my feet out from under me. I got up fast the way a boxer sometimes does to prove he isn't hurt. A car lay upside down and burning on the pavement right in front of me. Across the square a wall floated lazily outwards, a slow-motion shot of an air raid in a movie, and came apart like the pieces of a jigsaw puzzle. Black smoke swirled and mushroomed over the park. Nobody was walking, nobody trying to run. People were down all over the place, like mangled and twisted ragdolls.

I wandered around looking for Harry. My left arm wasn't working. I couldn't hear. I tried to shout Harry's name, spat a mouthful of blood instead.

Through the smoke an A.R.P. warden in a steel helmet came towards me. He had a moustache like Harry's and blood all over his face. He looked horrified. I started to sway.

It's possible he caught me.

Four

Haller awoke on Saturday morning, 8 July, and slid effortlessly from sleep into his cover identity. He was Hauptmann Richard Haller on leave from the 67th Infantry Regiment on the Western Front, all the bits and pieces of the non-existent Wehrmacht officer in place in his head. Then he realised that wasn't necessary here in the tiny attic bedroom in General Beck's house in Lichterfelde. He went to the dormer window and looked out at early morning sunshine and the rubble that had been piled like snowbanks along what remained of Goethe-strasse.

He got into the iron-grey breeches, the jackboots. He was buttoning the grey shirt when he heard footsteps on the stairs and then a light knock at the door.

'Come in,' he said, and the door opened and he saw Elisabeth Lauterbacher. She was small and lithely curved, say a hundred and five pounds in a white skirt and what looked like a middy blouse. Twenty-two or -three years old, he thought. She hardly seemed German. She had an almost Mediterranean prettiness – the dark hair that hung straight to her shoulders with wispy bangs that half-covered her forehead, the dark-brown eyes flecked with gold when she faced the sunlight at the window, the delicate aquiline nose, the slight pout to her full lips that made her look wistful instead of sulky.

They had no dossier on her in London. He had tried last night to evaluate her, but it hadn't been easy. Elisabeth Lauterbacher was an elusive subject. For every question he asked, she had three of her own – soft eager questions about London, about the war, about himself.

He knew this: she came from Bad Reichenhall in Bavaria.

She had told him that. The Bavarian part he could confirm: the softness of her speech was south German.

He knew this: she had studied medicine at the University of Munich, but hadn't taken her degree. She had told him that too.

And he knew this: she was part of Valkyrie even if they had no dossier on her in London. It was obvious the general kept no secrets from her.

'You're up early,' he said.

'I couldn't sleep. I wanted to talk to you.'

There was no chair in the small room. He waved her to the bed, where she sat primly on the edge, looking suddenly like a little girl in a grown-up's room gathering her courage to confess some childish peccadillo.

Haller leaned against the windowsill and asked her: 'How is he?' There was no warmth in his voice. The danger of course would be to allow himself to feel anything for them – sympathy, pity, understanding, anything.

'He's not always agitated like last night. But your visit meant so much, Herr Haller. Can you imagine how it is for him – for all of them? They don't have contact with the outside world every day.' She looked at him defiantly. 'You were disappointed, weren't you?'

He evaded the question. 'I just got here. I'll have to meet the others.'

'General Beck is still convalescing,' she told him. 'You have to realise that too. He was only operated on in March. He almost died under the knife. Cancer of the stomach. They think they got all of it.'

He nodded impatiently. Ludwig Beck was an old man, aged even beyond his sixty-five years. Once his features might have been sensitive, those of an artist or a scholar, not of the former Chief-of-Staff of the Wehrmacht. The disease had blurred them, leaving the brooding eyes trapped in the ravaged face. Beck was an invalid. He would be good for a few hours a day, no more. That in itself wasn't damning. Valkyrie, like any political movement, revolutionary or otherwise, could use the wisdom of an elder statesman.

But this feeble old man was its leader, its driving force. If Valkyrie succeeded, General Beck would become Chief of State in the provisional government. Half a dozen years too late, Haller told himself. Beck had organised a coup in 1938 but thanks to Chamberlain's Munich appeasement the army had not moved against Hitler. That year he gave them military triumph without war.

Beck had learned nothing since the coup that had foundered on Chamberlain's compliance with the dismemberment of Czechoslovakia. He had resigned as Chief-of-Staff after vainly and incorrectly protesting that the occupation of Czechoslovakia would lead to a general war which would crush the unprepared German army.

Now in 1944 Operation Valkyrie was Beck's final attempt to protect the Wehrmacht, or what was left of the Wehrmacht, from the excesses of Adolf Hitler. To end the war with the German armed forces reasonably intact seemed the limit of his old soldier's vision. His eyes had glowed in the ashen face when he spoke of it. They had gone dull and listless when he mouthed the moral considerations he thought Haller wanted to hear. Ludwig Beck was a general-staff anachronism who made the death of Adolf Hitler seem somehow irrelevant.

The girl waited for Haller to speak. He said nothing. She licked her lips and told him, as if reading his thoughts: 'You have to understand he was a military man almost forty years. The army is his life.'

'It wasn't hard to see that.'

'That's not fair. He speaks in military terms because they are what he knows.'

'And the others?'

'The others? Oh, I see. Yes, most of them are army officers. What else can you expect? Only the Wehrmacht can overthrow the Nazis. Surely you understand that. You didn't come here expecting a popular uprising in the streets, did you?'

Haller started to speak, then checked himself. Beck's moral position did not matter. What mattered was whether or not Beck and his fellow-conspirators could pull it off. If Colonel-General Beck was typical, the Nazis would grind them to hamburger.

But wasn't that judgement premature? All of them wouldn't be in their sixties. All wouldn't be convalescing from major surgery.

The girl stood. She looked defiant. 'You're wrong about him. I can prove it to you.'

She led Haller downstairs and into the darkness of the living-room. The windows had been covered with boards. When she lit a lamp Haller could see travel posters tacked to the boards – Venice, the Norwegian fjords, the Eiffel tower – windows on saner places, saner times. She paused long enough to select three books from the shelves, then led Haller wordlessly through the kitchen to a flight of stairs going down.

The cellar wasn't quite dark. A single lamp had been lit there too. Haller saw two cots, a washstand, a battered wood table and two chairs.

'It's all right,' Elisabeth called softly. 'You can come out.'

Then, emerging from the shadows of the darkest corner of the cellar room, Haller saw a man and a woman, both gaunt in threadbare clothing. They were staring not at the girl but at him. When he got closer he saw that they were terrified.

'It's all right,' she said again. 'He's a friend.'

The woman kept staring at Haller's field-grey uniform.

The man patted her arm awkwardly. 'Fräulein Lauterbacher says it is all right,' he told her. He asked Elisabeth: 'Must we . . . leave today?'

'No. Here, I brought you more books.'

The man took the offered books, squinting at their spines. 'Rilke,' he said. 'André Gide.' He managed a tremulous smile. '*Mein Gott*, Thomas Mann. Ten years since I read Thomas Mann.'

'You can stay a few more days anyway,' Elisabeth told them.

'A few more days,' the woman said, her voice caressing the words as if each of those days was a year.

'Until Uncle Emil finds somewhere else,' Elisabeth said. 'I'll bring you something to eat later.'

'Potatoes?' the man said philosophically.

'Potatoes,' Elisabeth admitted.

The man smiled. 'If they are the difference between starving and not starving, potatoes are my favourite food.' He held the largest book out for the woman's inspection. 'See? It's *Buddenbrooks*.'

With difficulty the woman tore her gaze away from Haller.

'Is there anything else I can get you, Herr Professor Liebermann?' Elisabeth asked.

The man shook his head, as if the very thought of accepting more was outrageous. Then, in a marvelling voice he said: 'Herr Professor. I don't remember when I was last called that.' Again he shook his head. 'Herr Professor,' he repeated.

'Until later,' Elisabeth told them.

The man sketched a courtly bow. The woman impulsively came forward to kiss Elisabeth's cheek. 'You are very kind, Fräulein. How is the general?'

'A little stronger every day, Frau Liebermann.'

'He'll get well. A saint like him. God sees to such things.'

'These days I would rather depend on medicine,' Herr Professor Liebermann said dryly.

'But God too,' the woman said, 'or there is nothing.'

They stood at the foot of the stairs as Haller and the girl left. Haller fought down an impulse to look back.

In the kitchen Elisabeth got some potatoes from a sack and began scrubbing them.

'Are you any good at lighting stoves?' she asked Haller. 'There's wood in the pantry.'

It was an old-fashioned cast-iron stove. Haller found a pile of twigs and slats in the almost bare pantry. There was a slab of bacon, a small bag of sugar, part of a loaf of dark bread, another sack of potatoes. He returned to the kitchen with an armload of wood. He started the fire with two crumpled sheets of *The National Observer*. He fed twigs to it while Elisabeth put a pot of water on to boil.

'Who's Uncle Emil?'

'It's an organisation that hides Jews. They have to keep moving. One place more than a few days could be fatal. This house is one of the hiding places.' Elisabeth turned from the stove to face him. 'The penalty for hiding them is death.'

Haller said nothing. He nodded.

'Himmler declared Berlin Jew-free last spring. We think there are perhaps five thousand left. Most of them have no papers, no ration cards. They're called U-boats because they surface only when they must. Herr Professor Liebermann taught philosophy at the University – Plato and Aristotle, the German fascination with the Golden Age of Greece, all things in moderation. Now he's a U-boat.' Elisabeth was trying not to cry.

'It's a very brave thing, what you're doing.'

She looked at him bitterly. 'I didn't show you them to have you tell me that. It isn't brave. It's necessary, if you are to go on living with yourself. I know that. So does the general. Your general-staff officer with the Prussian mentality.'

'Was what I thought that obvious?' Haller asked her.

'Wait a few days, Herr Haller. I beg you to do that much. See the others. Give them a chance. And the general – don't you realise the risk he's taking, at a time like this? Hiding U-boats, a few days before Operation Valkyrie? That's the kind of man he is.'

Haller said nothing. She had it backwards, of course. The dangerous heroic gesture was the worst possible thing Colonel-

General Beck could do now. The old man had no judgement at all. If his Uncle Emil way-station was discovered, it could blow the conspiracy wide open.

Still, it was tempting to see it as Elisabeth did. The lives of two ageing Jews balanced against Operation Valkyrie – as if to prove what they would attempt to do was still worthwhile in Germany, still not too late. Or as if to prove they had earned the moral right to do it.

Five

Later that same afternoon, Major Ernst Otto Jaeger walked along Bellevuestrasse past what was left of the Esplanade Hotel. He set his heavy suitcase down on the pavement and stared up at the overly ornate Wilhelmine entrance to the apartment building. It had suffered only slight damage. Jaeger did not go in at once. He was still absorbing the idea that he was here, home in Berlin.

Two weeks ago he was sure he would spend the rest of the war as a prisoner slaving in an armaments factory east of Moscow. With luck he would have survived. The Communists, unlike the Nazis, knew that extermination and exploitation were incompatible. They did not work their slave labourers to death.

On 22 June 1944, the third anniversary of Barbarossa, the German invasion of Russia, four Red Army Groups of 179 infantry and armoured divisions under the command of Marshals Zhukov and Vasilevski had launched an attack against Army Group Centre in the direction Minsk–Vilna–Grodno. Objective: the East Prussian border.

With 32 under-strength infantry divisions, almost no panzer units, and even less tactical air support, neither General Busch nor Field Marshal Model could contain the assault.

Hitler sent the expected order from his command post at Wolf's Lair deep in the pine forests of East Prussia: no retreat.

Retreat would be regarded as treason.

This order suited the Russian plan of battle so well that it might have issued instead from Marshal Zhukov's headquarters. By 1 July 350,000 Wehrmacht soldiers were sealed off in pockets in the areas of Minsk and Bobruisk. A few score thousand were killed, the rest taken prisoner.

It was a worse defeat than Stalingrad, but by then both the Germans and Russians were used to such Wehrmacht debacles. Dr Goebbels, Reich Minister of Public Enlightenment and Propaganda, proclaimed no period of national mourning in Germany, as he had after the surrender of von Paulus's Sixth Army a year and a half earlier. Nor did the Russians bother to march their prisoners, more than a quarter of a million strong, through the streets of Moscow, as they had done after Stalingrad. The captives were delivered to transient camps near Mogilev and Bykhov in White Russia. From there they would be shipped as slave labour to the new underground armaments factories in western Siberia.

All but one of them. All but Ernst Jaeger.

The Red Army ambulance rumbled through the twilit streets of Moscow. An awkward, swaying, top-heavy vehicle built on a GAZ triple-A chassis, it had set out at dawn from the transient camp at Mogilev four hundred miles to the west. It could accommodate nine stretchers; it had none.

A solitary prisoner sat on the bench that ran the length of one side of the ambulance. Two non-coms in rumpled green uniforms with rectangular red and blue N.K.V.D. collar tabs lounged on the bench opposite him, both smoking and both with P.P.D. sub-machine guns across their knees. The sub-machine guns were unnecessary; the N.K.V.D. non-coms were too far down the chain of command to know that Major Ernst Otto Jaeger, former National Socialist Guidance Officer attached to General Busch's headquarters staff, was coming out of cold storage.

The ambulance stopped only long enough to discharge its three passengers outside the soot-darkened brick building on Kropotkin Square. For the same reason that the driver quickly put his vehicle in gear and sped away, no passers-by lingered to watch the two N.K.V.D. non-coms show their papers at the guardhouse and escort their package into the cobblestoned courtyard. The brick building housed Division III of the Commissariat of War, mistakenly referred to in the West and in Nazi Germany by the initials G.R.U. The Russians themselves used the acronym Razvedupr for the dread Glavnoe

Razvedyvatelnoe Upravlenie, the Central Intelligence Directorate.

Even the N.K.V.D. non-coms were in a hurry to leave. They delivered Jaeger to an office on the second floor, received a receipt, and hurried downstairs and outside.

Vodka was indicated. They found it in a tavern around the corner, where their red and blue N.K.V.D. collar tabs had the same effect on the patrons, most of them military, that the brick building had had on them.

'Whenever I go near that place I break out in a sweat,' one of the non-coms said.

The other managed a hard grin. 'Funny – the package walked in like he didn't have a worry in the world.'

'What does a Nazi know about Razvedupr?'

They drank another round of vodka. The second non-com said: 'I never thought I'd feel sorry for a fucking Wehrmacht officer.'

Even after fifteen years Jaeger recognised the man who had been called Comrade Cell by his Communist associates in pre-Hitler Germany. A stocky man of average height, balding, with bulbous forehead, pince-nez, a bold nose, salt-and-pepper moustache and spade-shaped beard, he had received his nickname for his organisational abilities on behalf of Josef Stalin and the Comintern. He had other abilities, which had saved his life in Germany when comrades like Rosa Luxembourg and Karl Liebknecht had been murdered. By coldly playing his rivals off against one another at home and by backing Stalin against the Trotskyites during the Great Purge in Russia, Comrade Cell had achieved the first requirement of historical necessity. He had survived.

So, too, had Ernst Otto Jaeger, who now allowed himself a brief smile in response to Comrade Cell's two words of greeting: 'Welcome back.'

They shook hands perfunctorily; Comrade Cell detested pointless gestures as much as he hated wasting words.

The room was furnished in green, its chairs covered with worn dark-green velour, its walls a pale green, the large desktop a slab of green stone streaked like marble. The expected photograph of Stalin in his undecorated marshal's uniform dominated the wall behind the desk. Comrade Cell did not sit, nor did he indicate that Jaeger should. He stood watching a door on the far side of the room, obviously expecting someone.

He had not long to wait. The door opened and a bulky man in an ill-fitting dark grey suit with wrinkled lapels and trousers that bagged over his shoe-tops came in. He didn't look like much to Jaeger, but Comrade Cell came to attention and, not quite clicking his heels, said: 'Comrade Director.'

'Sit, both of you,' said the Comrade Director in a mild, melodious voice.

He was Colonel-General Ivan Terenchevich Peresypkin, Deputy People's Commissar for Defence, Director of Razvedupr. No introduction was made for the benefit of Jaeger, and none needed. No one else would be called Comrade Director here. Nor, short of Josef Stalin himself or perhaps Lavrenti Beria, would Comrade Cell appear so deferential in the presence of another human being.

Comrade Cell recited quickly: 'Jaeger, Ernst Otto. Born 1905, Berlin-Moabit. C.P. member from 1924. M-school graduate 1927. Infiltrated into Reichswehr 1929. Lichterfelde Cadet School graduate 1935. Membership N.S.D.A.P. from 1936. Married 1940, no children. Wife, politically illiterate. Company commander, Afrika Korps 90th Light Armoured Division until late 1942. Awarded Knight's Cross with oak leaves. Promoted major same year. National Socialist Guidance Officer since last October, attached to headquarters of General Busch's 16th Army and later Army Group Centre, same commander. Relevant C.P. documents removed from Karl Liebknecht House, Berlin, prior to Nazi takeover. All cell associates and troika contacts eliminated. Deep freeze total.'

Only on completion of the recited dossier did Comrade Cell seat himself behind the desk. Commissar Peresypkin was already seated, sloppily, the base of his spine and the back of his head coming into contact with the green velour of the sofa to the left of the desk. Jaeger remained standing until Commissar Peresypkin said: 'Sit, comrade, sit. You make me nervous.'

Peresypkin, like Comrade Cell, was speaking Russian, which Jaeger had learned at the M-school here in Kropotkin Square in 1926–7.

He sat on the sofa to the right of the desk so that he might study the Commissar's face without seeming to do so.

There was an oriental cast to Peresypkin's features – the flatness of the cheekbones, the folds of flesh at the outer corners of the dark eyes, even the odd sallow-glossy complexion, almost like wet clay. He looked soft. That, Jaeger knew, was misleading. Peresypkin had survived the Great Purge in which his predecessor Uritsky was murdered.

'You became an N.S.D.A.P. Guidance Officer in October of last year,' he said in his melodious voice. He had reverted to almost accentless German. 'Can you tell me precisely why, comrade?'

It seemed a foolish question, but Jaeger responded carefully. 'I was cold-storaged the day I left here and returned to Berlin, with orders to infiltrate the Army. The effectiveness of such infiltration would increase proportionately with the importance of the position attained. One can learn much as a Guidance Officer in the Wehrmacht – precisely what one can learn as a Political Commissar in the Red Army.'

'And what did you learn?'

'That the Wehrmacht needs Guidance Officers for the same, or almost the same, reason that the Red Army needs Political Commissars.'

'Explain, please.'

'Nazism is the inevitable offspring of the decadent capitalist system, and like all populist movements it must promise more than it can deliver. The army quickly becomes disenchanted.' Jaeger paused. 'Communism is the inevitable goal of social revolution, and like all Utopian movements it must be ruthless as to means. The army quickly becomes disenchanted.'

Commissar Peresypkin laughed. Comrade Cell adjusted the pince-nez on the bridge of his nose.

'You will continue with your guidance activities,' Peresypkin told Jaeger. 'You will broadcast to Wehrmacht troops for the Free Germany Committee.'

Jaeger had heard such broadcasts, the opportunistic mouthings of turncoat prisoners of war, made in exchange for material comfort. He glanced quickly at Comrade Cell, who had allowed himself the indulgence of a faint scowl. Jaeger knew that this interview would be as important to Comrade Cell as it was to him. He wasn't the only cold-storage officer available, and Comrade Cell had chosen him. At a high enough level in the Communist Party, mistakes could not be tolerated. Marxism dictated with implacable logic that history would move in a certain direction. If a high-level decision impeded that movement it was no mere error, it was the treason of failure.

Jaeger took an enormous risk. He said: 'I can't believe that's why you brought me here, Comrade Director.'

Comrade Cell made an audible breathing sound. Peresypkin said: 'I had thought you'd be grateful.'

'Grateful?' Jaeger demanded angrily. 'To stay in cold storage from the age of twenty-two almost until my fortieth birthday, and then be told I'm to perform like a third-rate traitor?'

Again Peresypkin laughed. He nodded at Comrade Cell. 'Good,' he said. 'Very good.'

He told Jaeger: 'The Free Germany Committee is comprised of filthy little men who defecate on their own doorstep. There is no place among them for you and no place in history for them.'

Jaeger relaxed. He realised he'd been holding his breath.

'Consider this hypothetical situation,' said Peresypkin. 'A small determined clique of general-staff officers and Prussian nobility is planning the assassination of Adolf Hitler. How do you react?'

Jaeger waited three seconds. Then he said: 'That depends, Comrade Director. Am I still in cold storage?'

'If you were?'

'There is an odd sort of fraternity in the Wehrmacht. I've known anti-Nazi officers. They talk. Even to supposed pro-Nazi officers like myself. We do not betray them – even though we disapprove.'

'And if you were not in cold storage, if you were freed to act? How would you approach such a plot to assassinate Adolf Hitler then?'

'I would support the plot,' Jaeger said.

Comrade Cell removed his pince-nez and polished them with a small white handkerchief.

'Explain,' said Peresypkin. His hooded eyes were almost shut.

'This hypothetical plot of yours,' Jaeger told him, 'would reveal the enemy.'

'Whose enemy?' Peresypkin asked.

'Hitler's enemy now – ours after the war. They are the same people, Comrade Director. Officers, Junkers, former Social Democrat politicians, former trade unionists, dissident intellectuals and university students. A plot to assassinate the Führer would flush them into the open. For the Gestapo to deal with now. And for us to finish the job after we have destroyed the Nazis.' Jaeger leaned forward. His grey eyes narrowed. He spoke with absolute conviction. 'The closer to success the plot comes, the more value it would have for us – provided that, in the end, it failed.'

'Of what value would its failure be?'

'The Wehrmacht is weakening, Comrade Director, and already facing the inevitability of defeat. There is talk at high levels of relaxing resistance in the West and shifting troops to the Eastern Front, in the expectation that the Anglo-American victors would grant softer peace terms. If Hitler died prematurely, it could happen that way.'

Peresypkin's soft, rather feminine face wore a look of almost sensual satisfaction.

'To best serve the course of history,' Jaeger summarised, 'your hypothetical plot should come within an inch of success. And then be crushed.'

Peresypkin turned to Comrade Cell and said: 'I commend you on your choice, Comrade Ulbricht. To know history after the event is nothing. To know it before the event, everything.'

Walter Ulbricht's lips twitched. Jaeger knew that was his way of smiling.

'Had you answered in any other way,' Peresypkin told Jaeger, 'you would have been taken from here and shot. The plot to assassinate Hitler is of course not hypothetical. The attempt is to be made before the end of the month. You are going to Berlin.'

Jaeger's forty-eight-hour briefing began that night. He attacked it with a cold elation.

During seventeen years of cold storage, his faith had never wavered.

On the first day they told him he would be returned to Mogilev where arrangements would be made for his heroic escape back to the German lines. After that he would be sent to Berlin for a two-week leave and reassignment. He did not ask how that could be done. He was not the only infiltrator in the Wehrmacht.

On the second day they told him about his wife. And about that part of his mission which, when history rendered its irrevocable verdict, would be more important than whether Adolf Hitler lived or died.

A one-legged porter wearing a shabby suit and a swastika armband hobbled towards him with the help of a single crutch as Jaeger entered the apartment building on Bellevuestrasse near what was left of the Esplanade Hotel. The lobby was a pretentious clutter of leather furniture and glossy tropical plants in majolica jars, the overall effect that of the winter garden on a prewar Strength-through-Joy cruise ship.

Between his army pay and Monika's salary as a secretary at the Reich Central Security Office they had never really been able to afford the apartment. The three-storey sandstone building designed by Schinkel at the height of the Neo-classical period had been the Berlin townhouse of a baron from Upper Silesia. Such things mattered to Monika with her bourgeois background.

Jaeger himself had been born in the working-class district of Moabit and had spent his childhood in a cold-water flat on Lindenstrasse near the main fire station, where the family had moved so that his father could be close to his job as a typesetter at the government printing office. His father had lost a leg in the Great War and blamed it on the November Criminals – Jews and Social Democrats – who had stabbed the Army in the back in 1918. Once, in the early days of the Weimar Republic, his father had walked with Jaeger the short distance to Oranienstrasse where the printing office stood. Leaning heavily on his crutches, he told the fifteen-year-old boy: 'You will notice it is close to the fire station. There is a joke about that. All the paper, rolls and rolls of paper, tons of paper for official publications. German efficiency. It is why the fire station is nearby.' His father spat on the sidewalk. 'Totally unnecessary,' he said. 'Shit doesn't burn.'

He wore his Iron Cross Second Class always, and the Storm Troop brown shirt that stank of sweat. He never won Jaeger over to his viewpoint, even though the boy was far from enamoured of the Republic himself. Had the elder Jaeger not been a cripple, they might have found themselves on opposite sides in the nightly street fighting in Berlin in the 1920s. Jaeger joined the Red Front Fighters' League when he was sixteen. Walter Ulbricht discovered him at a Spartakus rally one year later, and his education began.

His father was murdered in the Roehm purge in 1934 when, except as a ceremonial organisation, the S.A. was destroyed by Himmler's élite S.S. guard on orders of Chancellor Hitler. This was Hitler's way of placating the officer corps, who feared that the S.A. rabble would supplant them. The elder Jaeger never had understood political reality. It was said that he died shouting a defiant 'Heil Hitler!' to the S.S. man who pumped four slugs from an Erma-38 sub-machine gun into his body at point-blank range.

By then Jaeger had been in cold storage seven years and the death of his father was an historical irrelevancy. He was mildly surprised that the old man had been considered important enough for execution.

Now the one-legged porter said 'Heil Hitler' in a bored voice and looked Jaeger over. The garrison cap with its stiffening removed and the silver-braid shoulder straps of a major did not impress him. Then he saw the Knight's Cross hanging on a ribbon at Jaeger's throat.

'Where'd you get that?'

'Africa,' Jaeger said.

The porter banged the stump of his left leg with his fist. 'The Argonnerwald,' he said, accepting Jaeger. 'We've come to a pretty pass,' he told him. 'A one-legged block leader. Next thing you know, they'll use women. Are you looking for someone?'

'Frau Jaeger.'

It was after seven. Monika should have returned by now from the Prinz Albrechtstrasse. Unless things had changed, she only worked until four on Saturdays. Jaeger's mouth was dry. He could almost feel her in his arms.

The block leader studied him more carefully. Then he gave a conspiratorial wink. 'Fifteen tenants,' he laughed. 'Half my time for fourteen of them, the other half for her. Well, she has the looks for it, not to mention the connections. Does she expect you?'

'No, it's a surprise,' Jaeger said. 'Is she home?'

'Got in fifteen minutes ago. Alone,' said the block leader, as if that were an unusual occurrence.

Picking up his canvas suitcase, Jaeger followed the one-legged man to his lodge in one corner of the lobby. Jaeger grasped his shoulder before he could press the buzzer next to the tenant directory.

'I said it was a surprise.'

'Strict orders, Herr Major,' the block leader said apologetically. 'That one would cut off my acorns and serve them to me for lunch if I let anyone surprise her.'

'I'm her husband,' Jaeger said.

The block leader turned slowly and lowered himself to the padded bench on one side of the directory. Jaeger admired his ability to smile at that moment, even though it wasn't much of a smile.

'Old women and hall porters,' said the block leader. 'They talk too much.'

Jaeger stuffed a ten-mark note into the breast pocket of his threadbare jacket. 'Forget it,' he said.

The block leader, like a good Berliner and particularly a good Berlin hall porter, recovered sufficient composure to have the last word. 'Still, you should have told me sooner,' he said reproachfully. 'Instead of pumping me for information, Herr Major.'

He let himself in with his own key, almost surprised that it still worked the lock, and heard a rushing sound which at first he could not identify. Then he grinned. Water filling the bath-tub, *dummkopf*, he told himself. He had been away a long time, all right.

When he put the canvas suitcase down at the entrance to the living-room, he realised he had never seen the Persian rug before. The same was true of the furniture in the room. It looked expensive and antique, all dark wood polished to a rich dull glow and tapestried upholstery that matched the tapestried walls. In a sideboard opposite the fireplace Rosenthal china was on glittering display. The cocktail table was a marble chessboard; the large, intricately carved chessmen looked like real ivory.

The rushing sound stopped.

Jaeger opened the hall door and shut it again, not gently. He heard Monika's voice: 'Gottfried? Did I forget to lock the door again? How'd you get past old Binnicker anyway? You're terribly early, darling. I'm still having my bath.'

By the time she said that, Jaeger had crossed the living-room and entered the hall that led to the bathroom. He heard a splashing sound.

'Why don't you be a dear and soap my back?' Monika asked.

He opened the door without breaking stride. 'Things are pretty tough on the home front,' he said, 'just like they warned us in Russia.'

The bathroom was steamy, the bubblebath in the tub thick as the head on a stein of good Berliner beer, Monika's bathing cap gold and white, her deeply suntanned face certainly no product of early summer in Berlin.

All things considered, her poise was amazing. She tried to say his name once, and failed. She rose from a reclining to a sitting position in the tub, exposing throat, shoulders, and high brown-tipped breasts as tanned as her face, and by then she was totally in command of herself.

She tossed a large sponge at Jaeger. 'Ernst, dearest,' she said, 'he wouldn't have done it with quite the same flair anyway.'

He did not know what he would do until he knelt at the edge

of the tub. Then he plunged his arms into the bubbles and pulled her fragrant body against him.

She made a sound that could have been a whimper or a laugh.

They lay side by side, their touching flanks shiny with sweat. A small lamp glowed on the night-table at Monika's side of the bed. She turned towards it, got a pack of cigarettes, lit two, put one between his lips. Real tobacco. Naturally.

Earlier, wrapped in a terrycloth robe, here in the bedroom, in Jaeger's presence, she had calmly telephoned someone named Gottfried to cancel a dinner date. Her end of the conversation indicated Gottfried had not asked for excuses; she offered none.

Hanging up, she had looked over her shoulder at Jaeger. 'Well, what did you expect? An old maid waiting for the war to end? Berlin's no convent.'

She was still seated at the telephone table alongside the big lacquered Chinese armoire. On impulse he pulled the doors open.

Twenty gowns? Thirty? Two dozen pairs of shoes?

'You're right,' he said dryly. 'Berlin's no convent.'

Only then, and only for a moment, her voice wavered. 'I deny nothing,' she said. 'Why should I? I could die in a terror raid tomorrow. So could you.'

He asked: 'Who's Gottfried?' and instantly regretted the question. Jealousy was a bourgeois weakness, like charity or forgiveness.

'How long are you on leave?'

'Two weeks.'

'Then for two weeks,' she said with total candour, 'you don't have to ask such questions. About Gottfried or anyone.'

'I'm being reassigned to Berlin.'

'Well now, that does complicate things, doesn't it?' she said.

Jaeger bunched the terrycloth robe at her shoulder and pulled her to her feet. He had forgotten how tall she was, almost his own height. If she had said a single word more at that moment, he would have beaten her.

She stared defiantly into his eyes and said nothing.

With both hands he caught the robe at her throat and yanked it down the length of her body. Still she did not speak. He examined her with calculated insolence, as if she were merchandise, trying to hurt her that way. She had always been a very private person, girlishly shy of her body. Too private, too shy. Undress in the bathroom. Make love in the dark.

That had changed too. 'Satisfactory?' she asked. 'Everything in order, Herr Major?'

He laughed. She wasn't Monika.

Four years of marriage, and how much time had they spent together? Two months, three?

She was a stranger. It had been ridiculous to think otherwise.

'Now you,' she said.

'What?'

'I said, now you. After all, it's my birthday. You didn't remember, did you? That's what I was going out to celebrate. I want a present.'

'Thirty-two, isn't it?' he said, feeling ridiculous again. 'Happy birthday.'

'Bastard. I'm thirty-one. Now get undressed.'

He did so, and she stood watching with a cool clinical appraisal that matched his calculated insolence.

'Not bad,' she said. 'In fact, better than most. Better than I remembered.'

He hit her once, a back-handed blow to the face that glazed her eyes and spun her half around and down to one knee.

'Satisfied?' she asked. 'Punishment properly inflicted, Herr Major?'

He flung himself on her, intending to have her quickly and brutally on the floor, more punishment, more subtle. But she met his thrust with a soft passive rhythm that absorbed it and changed it, bringing him high immediately, almost over the edge, then dropping him, bringing him higher still, dropping him less far, and soon he shared the rhythm with her, a rhythm he understood at once because it was like a sexual dialectic.

Somewhere along the line she said, 'If you ever mark my face again, I'll kill you.'

Six

Less than half a mile north of the Jaeger apartment, a twenty-five-year-old Wehrmacht Oberleutnant named Harald Freiherr von Heydebrand scowled his monocle into place and surveyed the drawing-room of his far more elegant apartment on Pariserplatz in the heart of Berlin.

The young Baron von Heydebrand wondered what was wrong with the scene he had set. Somewhere there was a jarring note. It could not be the room itself – with its gilded mouldings, cloud-frescoed ceiling, red damask drapes, and french doors looking out on a walled garden, it had a strange wistful Belle Epoque feeling, as if it had been transplanted against its will from turn-of-the-century Paris to wartime Berlin. The french doors faced south, and through them in the twilight Baron von Heydebrand could see, beyond the garden wall and looming over the Foreign Ministry, the badly damaged roof of the Reich Chancellory, long since abandoned by Adolf Hitler, as Berlin itself had been abandoned by him.

Which, of course, would make the task of killing him that much more difficult.

The view through the french doors was what disturbed Heydebrand, and he drew the red damask drapes, then lit candles on the sideboard and the small, perfect Louis XV table that had been set for two. The crystal reflected the candlelight and, now that the windows were shut and the drapes drawn, the scent of roses filled the room. Six dozen of them including the centrepiece on the table. Elisabeth's favourite flower. Whatever changes the R.A.F. wrought on Berlin, Heydebrand told himself, two things would remain – the Friedrichstrasse flower vendors with their inexhaustible supply of roses and, naturally, the flow of good beer from Berlin's breweries, sixteen of which were still in business on this Saturday evening, 8 July.

Heydebrand looked at his watch. 8.30. Elisabeth was late, as usual. Her prerogative, especially on the night he had finally decided to propose to her. It was the last day but one of Heydebrand's leave, and for the occasion he wore his old-fashioned full dress uniform with its stiffly starched, pocketless *waffenrock* tunic, its eight silver buttons gleaming against field-grey. Heydebrand's face just missed looking brutal in repose and just missed being handsome when he smiled. Under the kinky mat of blond hair, the bone structure was prominent – heavy ridge of brow, large high-bridged nose, slab of jaw. The necessity of flesh and the pale-blue eyes seemed an afterthought, the two-inch slash of sabre scar in his right cheek did not.

When the door-knocker thudded, the unexpectedly gentle smile won its battle with Heydebrand's foreboding features. He had seen little of Elisabeth during his five-day leave – one visit to General Beck's villa in Lichterfelde, one lunch with her here in town. The old general was on the mend, though, and Heydebrand had talked Elisabeth into staying the night. The proprieties would be observed if that was what Elisabeth wanted; another three dozen red roses waited in the guest room. On the other hand, there were more candles and roses in Heydebrand's own bedroom. A general-staff officer trained at the Lichterfelde Cadet School, the young lieutenant was prepared for any contingency.

Still smiling, he opened the front door with a flourishing bow – and saw that Elisabeth was not alone. He managed to keep smile and monocle in place as she said:

'Heydi, this is Hauptmann Haller. Richard Haller, Freiherr von Heydebrand.'

The thick-set Heydebrand saw a man taller than himself, perhaps six or eight years older, with the sort of rugged blond good looks that Heinrich Himmler liked to put on display in black S.S. uniform.

Elisabeth came briefly into Heydebrand's arms and offered her cheek for a chaste kiss before stepping back.

'Hauptmann Haller needs a place to stay in Berlin, Heydi,' she said.

Heydebrand's poise deserted him for a moment. 'You mean tonight?'

'For several days starting tonight.'

In the time it took him to shut the door and usher them into the drawing-room, Heydebrand had recovered. 'There's always room here for a friend of Elisabeth's, Herr Hauptmann,' he said. 'How long will I have the pleasure of your company?'

'I'm not sure yet,' Hauptmann Haller said. He was, Heydebrand observed, wearing a Knight's Cross and a silver wound badge. He was carrying a black leather suitcase.

'Let me take that, Herr Hauptmann.'

The three of them went with some awkwardness into the guest room. The scent of roses was overwhelming.

Abruptly Heydebrand laughed. 'I hope you like flowers,' he said, putting the suitcase down.

Why should Elisabeth bring anyone here, now of all times? The Hauptmann's impassive face told him nothing.

'On leave?' he asked.

Haller nodded. 'Two weeks,' he said.

'Eastern Front?'

'No. France.'

'Until last month,' Heydebrand told him, 'I'd have said

you were lucky. But all that's changed now. When's the last time you were in Berlin?'

Heydebrand's routine social question did something to the tall captain's face. He seemed to look inward at himself instead of at Heydebrand. Then he turned to the window and gazed at the great sandstone columns of the Brandenburg Gate, the huge chariot of victory atop it silhouetted, black against the twilight.

With his back turned he spoke, his voice flat. 'Not for a long time. 1938.'

That made no sense to Heydebrand. How could an army officer have managed to stay out of Berlin for six years?

'Welcome back to the centre of the universe,' he said. 'Or what's left of it after the face-lifting it's got from the R.A.F. and the Americans.'

Haller had turned back from the window and Heydebrand watched for a reaction to that defeatist remark, but the handsome face was still impassive.

'Have you known Elisabeth long?' Heydebrand asked.

Haller shook his head. 'As a matter of fact, we just met yesterday.'

That surprised Heydebrand too, but he didn't pursue it. Instead he asked: 'Where are you from, Herr Hauptmann?'

It was Elisabeth, finally, who answered that question. 'Heydi, he's from England.'

A full five seconds passed before Freiherr von Heydebrand could be sure that Elisabeth was serious. Then he adjusted his monocle and with a perfectly straight face asked Haller: 'Tourist?'

Freiherr von Heydebrand was carefully pouring cognac into three crystal snifters from a half-full cut crystal decanter. 'Remy Martin,' he said, 'and that's the last of it. After dinner we join the ranks of the schnapps drinkers.'

Haller expected him to make a ceremony of the brandy, first a swirl of the snifter, then a toast, then perhaps an appreciative sip. That would have been in keeping with the young lieutenant's manner. Instead, without even touching glasses, Heydebrand downed his cognac in one gulp.

'Elisabeth,' he said, 'would you promise me something? Unless you want me to go grey overnight, don't do that again.'

'Heydi, if you could have seen your face!' the girl said.

'Good God in Heaven,' Heydebrand said, 'England.' From

his tone of voice, England might have been the moon. 'Say the word e-x-t-r-a-o-r-d-i-n-a-r-y.'

Haller complied. 'Extraordinary.'

'Well, that's settled anyway. Dead giveaway. You're not British, you're American. The British say ekSTRAWdnry. O.S.S.?'

'That's right.' Haller felt himself smiling. Heydebrand's insouciance was contagious.

'I assume you've seen General Beck?'

'He spent the night in Lichterfelde,' Elisabeth said quickly. 'A very satisfactory meeting, Heydi.'

Haller saw no reason to contradict her.

'How is he, Elisabeth?'

'You know what he's like. He wants to be on his own more and more. He insisted I spend the weekend in town. But he is getting stronger.'

'General Beck was convinced the Allies would send someone in,' Heydebrand told Haller, 'but a lot of us reckoned that was an old man's *Wunschtraum* . . . there's a more colourful way of saying that in English, isn't there?'

'Pipe dream,' Haller supplied, glad for the diversion. Once Heydebrand got over the shock of his arrival, there would be some interesting questions.

'As in marijuana pipe,' Heydebrand said. 'That's good.' He poured what remained of the cognac.

'Opium pipe,' Haller corrected.

Heydebrand said: 'Of course, how stupid of me. Opium,' and Haller was instantly alert. It was clear that the lieutenant had a good command of English and that his interrogation had begun.

Strange, Haller thought. He had been so intent on evaluating the conspirators, he had almost forgotten it would work the other way too. But this Heydebrand, behind his carefree pose, showed competence, subtlety. Haller almost wished it wasn't there.

'The reason most of us never really expected you'd come is that we couldn't imagine *why* you'd come,' Heydebrand said carefully. 'They hardly sent you in to help us, Herr Haller. You don't know the situation here, after all. What could you do that we couldn't do better?'

Haller couched his answer in intentionally vague terms. 'All the contact we've had was in Switzerland and Sweden. It was time to send someone in.'

Heydebrand persisted. 'To do what?'

'What we're doing now. Talk. Get a line on the provisional government.'

'To what end?' Heydebrand looked puzzled. 'Ever since Stalingrad, Dulles has been telling our contact in Bern that we'd have to live with Unconditional Surrender. No matter what.'

Haller spoke slowly, choosing his words with care. 'Unconditional Surrender covers a lot of territory. Our options are still open.'

The one advantage Haller knew he had was that his real mission would seem inconceivable to the German. Sitting here in the hot summer dusk in the turn-of-the-century drawing-room on Pariserplatz in central Berlin with Elisabeth and Oberleutnant von Heydebrand, it almost seemed inconceivable to him.

'That's going to surprise some people,' Heydebrand observed dryly. He shrugged. 'But forgive me, Herr Haller. Politics is hardly my strong point. So we'll let that go for now, shall we?'

Once more Haller was aware of the subtlety. If there were others more capable of assessing the nature of Haller's mission, why should Heydebrand give him the chance to formulate his answers now?

'Besides, if I don't get into the scullery, who's going to cook the partridge?'

Elisabeth gasped. 'Partridge? My God, Heydi!'

'I didn't spend my entire leave on Pariserplatz. There's still game to be found on the Schorfheide, provided the Reich Marshal doesn't object to some poaching.'

Elisabeth offered to help in the kitchen.

'If you hunt,' Heydebrand said, shaking his head, 'you ought to eat what you kill, not to mention cooking it yourself. Horcher's own recipe, partridge braised on a bed of sauerkraut. Women shouldn't be privy to such secrets.'

After Heydebrand disappeared in what Haller assumed was the direction of the kitchen, Haller and Elisabeth went out through the french doors into the little walled garden. It smelled faintly of the earth and the gathering night.

'The Schorfheide,' Elisabeth sighed. 'Just sixty miles from Berlin. How I dream of going to the country! Nowhere special – just grass and trees and unpaved lanes. A stream maybe. And birds singing.' Her hand slipped casually into the crook of his elbow as they walked. 'And no air raids. Do you think they'll come tonight?'

The unexpected touch of her hand pleased him. 'I'm sorry. Do I think what?'

'The chief topic of conversation in Berlin. Do you think they'll come tonight?'

'The R.A.F.?'

'Of course. "They" means just two things in Berlin. The bombers – R.A.F. at night, Americans during the day.' Her hand tightened on his arm. 'And the Gestapo always.' She asked suddenly: 'Do you like him?'

'Heydebrand? Yes,' Haller said truthfully, 'I do.'

'He's going to ask me to marry him. He might have tonight, if you hadn't come. Did you ever see so many roses?'

'He's a lucky guy.'

Elisabeth's self-deprecating shrug brushed his arm against her side. 'You don't have to say that.'

'I mean it.'

She did not reply at once. She seemed lost in herself in the darkness, their only contact the touch of her hand. Haller longed to reach her. He knew why, of course. It was because he himself was so alone. But knowing why did not help. The need itself was a danger.

'All along I assumed I'd say yes,' she told him finally. 'Now I don't know.'

'Why not?'

'I'm not sure I love him.'

And Haller saw Berlin in 1938, the New Synagogue ablaze behind the main telegraph office against the cold clear November night, and a girl, with eyes not brown like Elisabeth's but pale blue like Heydebrand's, pleading with him.

'Can anyone ever be sure of that?' he asked Elisabeth.

Her hand left his arm. 'I was once.' She sounded young, and as alone as Haller, and vulnerable. 'But they killed him.'

Ernst Otto Jaeger was waiting on the northbound platform of the Potsdamerplatz station. The station was new, part of the U-bahn network completed shortly before the war, and like most of those along the line that ran under Hermann Goering-strasse to Unter den Linden and north to the Friedrichstrasse Bahnhof, it was said to be bomb-proof.

Although it was not yet 10.30, hundreds of terror raid victims, bombed out and with nowhere else to sleep, were already bedded down on the platform. The scene reminded Jaeger of a film he had once seen, a street in Calcutta in the hot tropical night, the beggars lined up in sleep, shoulder to shoulder near the open Indian sewers.

The train roared in from the tube and stopped with Germanic efficiency so that the doors of the red smoking car opened directly under the smoker sign, where Jaeger was waiting. He found a seat; not many people used the subway at this hour, even on a Saturday night. The train started with a lurch and accelerated into the darkness. He sat smoking moodily, trying to dismiss Monika from his thoughts. But she remained there, like a succubus, to remind him of his own unexpected weakness.

He had thought her asleep when he got up and found a cardboard suitcase containing his old civilian clothing in the hall closet, but she called, just as he was about to leave: 'Try not to be too noisy when you come back.'

She hadn't even asked where he was going. Apparently she didn't give a damn. He had attacked her on the floor like a rapist but it was he who had felt violated. Whatever happened to Germany, he thought sourly, Monika would survive. He was less sure about his own chances.

The blue shirt felt almost weightless, the trousers were a loose fit after breeches and jackboots. It had been another Ernst Jaeger who had worn them last, just as it had been another Monika he remembered from those years, the self-effacing young hausfrau somewhat in awe of him, no less beautiful but certainly less artful in bed. Or on the floor, he reminded himself.

When the train pulled into the Friedrichstrasse station he forced himself to think of Rambow. In Kropotkin Square they had told him Rambow would have the other half of the hundred-mark note by the time Jaeger reached Berlin.

He wondered how soon Rambow could arrange the meeting, wondered how soon after that he should kill Rambow.

Pinpricks like distant stars glittered blue on those lamp-posts still standing, casting faint radiance like the light at the bottom of the sea. A single car went slowly down Friedrichstrasse, its headlights narrow slits. Jaeger's shoes crunched on broken glass on the pavement in front of the Baerenschenke.

The tavern was crowded with shabbily dressed men, dark and alien-looking, like foreigners who had wandered into Berlin by mistake. That was essentially correct, Jaeger knew; they were foreign labourers lured to the capital of the Reich by the promise of steady work and good pay. Once there, they found they couldn't leave. Their terms of conscription were renewed by the Labour Office whether they wanted it or not. Still, they lived better than the slave-labourers who were kept penned like cattle near the armaments factories in Siemensstadt.

Jaeger shouldered his way to the bar. Ripples of silence eddied out from him. The civilian clothing was the best he could manage but he was still the foreigner here – brown hair cropped so close his scalp showed through, pale grey eyes, the too-Aryan well-fed look not of a Berliner and certainly not of a conscript labourer, but of a soldier home from the front.

'Beer,' he said, and the barman, the one other obvious German in the tavern, beefy-faced with rolls of fat like pink sausages on the back of his neck, drew the beer and carefully shaped the stiff creamy head with a wooden wand.

The Baerenschenke was a contact point. The Gestapo would know that, of course. They welcomed such places. Information flowed both ways. Rambow wouldn't be the only Gestapo V-man who came in here.

But Rambow was more than that. He worked both sides of the street. By now he probably couldn't even tell himself where his loyalties lay, if anywhere.

The beefy barman slid the half-litre stein in front of Jaeger, who drank most of it without pausing for breath. Whatever else had changed in Berlin, whatever curtailments and hardships resulted from the terror raids, the beer was as good as he remembered.

By then eddies of conversation had flowed back to fill the void of silence around him. He caught the barman's eye. 'I'm looking for Rambow.'

'Not here.'

'He's expecting me.'

'Your bad luck,' said the barman.

Rambow was of value to both the Gestapo and the Red Underground, and thus had remained alive. But he would wear the hatred of both his masters like a cloak.

'The Director's bad luck too,' Jaeger said.

The beefy face came closer, the eyes showing contempt now that the contact had been established.

'He's already come and gone. Try the East Workers' canteen in the station.'

Jaeger put a five-mark coin on the bar to pay for his beer.

The barman shoved it back at him. 'I don't want your fucking money.'

*

Two levels below Friedrichstrasse the huge waiting-room looked like an oriental bazaar. Jerry-rigged booths had been set up along makeshift aisles like souks for black market buying and selling, for barter. The air was suffocatingly hot, clogged with the stink of bad tobacco and unwashed bodies. A constant drone of talk echoed from the walls and high ceiling. Jaeger heard snatches of conversation in half a dozen languages, none of them German. The place astonished him. It wasn't Berlin. It was another world, half a dozen other worlds. He saw smartly-dressed women with dark avid eyes, who had to be French conscripts; tall fair Danes and Norwegians; swarthy Italians who spoke with their arms and bodies as well as their quick Mediterranean voices; big raw-boned Poles who regarded everyone else with ponderous suspicion. Helmeted, green-uniformed Berlin police patrolled in pairs, marching up and down the oriental aisles.

The East Workers' canteen held down the space near the gateway to tracks 11–15. Alongside the crowded buffet a cadaverously thin man was playing an accordion. Despite the heat Poles and Ukrainians sat at the small tables drinking glasses of some ersatz steaming brew.

Jaeger recognised Rambow at once from the picture they had shown him at Kropotkin Square. He was weasel-faced with nervous, darting eyes and a hairline moustache. Forty, maybe forty-five. He was sharing a table to the left of the track gateway with one of the smartly-dressed women whom Jaeger took to be French, his hand covering hers on the table.

Jaeger found a chair and pulled it over. The girl glanced up at him quickly, glanced away and then back with interest. Down here he would look like a meal ticket.

In a furious voice Rambow asked: 'Who the hell invited you to sit down?'

'Does she speak German?'

'Get lost.'

Jaeger took out his wallet and removed a twenty-mark note. He extended it towards the girl. 'Fifteen minutes,' he said. 'All right?' He held the wallet so that Rambow could see the torn hundred-mark note that was protruding. The girl's hand pounced on the offered money like the claws of a bird of prey. She looked at Rambow, who nodded slowly. She smiled at Jaeger and left the table.

'I just got it this morning,' Rambow said. 'Let's have a look at yours.'

The two halves of the torn hundred-mark note were matched under the table. Rambow seemed unhappy that they fitted.

'You've got to understand,' he said. 'It's getting harder all the time.'

'What is?'

Rambow shrugged his narrow shoulders. 'Any goddamn thing but the black market. That's easy.'

It took Jaeger ten minutes to tell him what he wanted, Rambow's head going from side to side all the while, slowly, his eyes casting furtive glances to right and left – the German look.

When Jaeger finished speaking, Rambow said: 'What makes you think I know this Esser?'

'Julius Esser served time in Oranienburg Concentration Camp. So did you. He got out in 1937. So did you.'

'I never met him.'

'You'd have mutual friends.'

'I don't move in his circles.'

'I didn't ask you to have tea with him. Just set up the meeting.'

Rambow's head moved left, then right. 'When?' he asked.

'That has to be up to Esser.'

'I could see him agreeing to it,' Rambow said. 'Not his friends.'

'Convincing them is Esser's job, not yours.'

'Where?' Rambow asked. 'My people won't budge out of Berlin-East.'

'Berlin-East's all right.'

'You want in on it?'

'No,' Jaeger said. 'But the Gestapo will. You arrange that part too.'

'Jesus!' Rambow said. 'What happens to my people?'

'What do you think happens to them?'

'Jesus,' Rambow said, this time dispassionately.

'A thousand marks,' Jaeger told him.

Rambow's hand crawled on the table, palm up, fingers moving in a come-hither gesture.

'Fifteen hundred,' Jaeger said. 'That's the limit.' Rambow nodded.

He would do it. That was the first part. The easy part.

'Will you look at that, Heydi,' Elisabeth marvelled.

'It's called the sun,' he told her as he hooked back the red damask drapes. 'It comes up every morning – one of the few things that can be relied on these days.'

Two empty schnapps bottles stood on the sideboard and Heydebrand now pulled the cork from a third. He had removed his starched *waffenrock* tunic, his shirtsleeves were rolled up, his face was dark with beard stubble.

They had spent the night talking, Heydi and Elisabeth almost pathetically eager to hear anything about the outside world, like inmates of a maximum security prison receiving an unexpected visitor.

Somewhere around midnight they had abandoned the formal *Sie* for the familiar *du,* and the girl especially had hung on every word Haller said. She seemed as impressed by his mention of places in America and England as she was of his casual references to parachute drops and Moon Squadron pick-ups in Normandy and the Loire valley.

Heydi's interest too seemed genuine, and as the long hours passed Haller found himself relaxing and enjoying the other man's company. True, Heydi had exploited the situation – a leisurely meal, two bottles of schnapps, an entire night of wide-ranging conversation – to make his own assessment of the newcomer. But he was chiefly guarding against an imposter, and there Haller knew he was on firm ground. All he had to do was be himself. Towards morning, whenever Heydi remembered to slip in one of his artless-sounding test questions, Haller was only amused.

The testing had ended an hour before dawn, when the German said: 'My father was a great Anglophile. He spent a year at Cambridge in the twenties. Best year of his life, he said. Balliol College.'

'Balliol's Oxford,' Haller told him dryly.

And Elisabeth, exasperated, said: 'Heydi, will you *please* stop that? You've been doing it all night. It's – it's paranoid. It really is.'

'Was I that transparent?' Heydi asked.

'Just some of the time,' Haller told him, and Heydi laughed.

'Forgive me, then. You have to remember Germany's had eleven years of Nazi rule, and that means seventy million certifiable cases of paranoia. I'll stop now, Elisabeth. I'm convinced.'

Now Elisabeth asked: 'Is that your real name? Richard Haller?'

Haller told her it was. 'Why?'

'I was just wondering. Richard. Do you say it like that?'

'A bit softer on the "ch",' Heydi instructed her. He was hovering over her with the third bottle of schnapps.

Elisabeth held a hand over her glass, shaking her head. She had drunk little; Haller had matched his host drink for drink. 'I'm going to bed, Heydi,' she said.

'How can you sleep in the daytime?' he protested.

'With a delicious feeling of decadence, that's how. Why don't you let Richard get some sleep too?'

'I wish first,' said Freiherr von Heydebrand, pulling himself upright with effort, 'to drink a toast to the President of the United States.'

Elisabeth glanced wryly at Haller. 'And then of course another one to the Prime Minister of England?'

'Of course. Why not?' said Heydi. He swayed; the schnapps sloshed in the bottle.

Elisabeth rose, surrendering herself to his bear-hug but turning to receive on her cheek the kiss intended for her lips.

'Good night, then, Richard,' she said after Heydi had released her. 'Don't let him keep you up until noon.'

'We're brothers,' Heydi said, 'Richard and I. Aren't we brothers?'

'Sure,' Haller humoured him, 'that's it. Brothers.' He had drunk enough to make his head pound.

'Accident of birth. Makes you American, me German. Known you all my life,' said Freiherr von Heydebrand.

Haller decided that he felt very German in the elegant room on Pariserplatz. He bowed over Elisabeth's hand.

She laughed, and as he straightened she brushed her lips lightly against his mouth. 'I'm glad they sent you, Richard Haller,' she said. Then she drifted off in the direction of the guest room.

After she left, Heydi poured three ounces of the kümmel-flavoured schnapps down his throat, three more into his glass. He said: 'Did you know I was prepared to propose to her tonight?' His voice sounded accusatory.

Haller tried to make light of it. 'Well, it had to be a proposal or a proposition. Unless you grow those roses for a hobby.'

'I have decided,' Heydi announced maudlinly, 'that it would be wise to postpone my proposal. In fact, unlike Elisabeth, I may regret that you came here.'

Haller tried to make light of that too. 'When's the last time she saw an American? Or anyone from outside?'

'It's more than that,' Heydi insisted. 'I can tell.'

Haller said nothing.

He could still feel the light unexpected touch of Elisabeth's lips.

Seven

Before the sand-coloured Opel Super Six staff car came to a stop at the corner of Tirpitz Quay and Bendlerstrasse, the rear door opened and the colonel started along the grey stone embankment.

He turned without checking his limping stride, told his driver, 'Two hours, Sepp,' and swiftly climbed the broad stairs to the columned portico of 13–14 Bendlerstrasse.

The last light of day, refracted by the perpetual pall of smoke over Berlin, spanned the sky like a great red dome. Reflected in the water of the Landwehr Canal it was the colour of blood.

Colonel Klaus Philip Schenk, Count von Stauffenberg, limped along the portico, returning salutes with a quick irritable gesture of his handless right arm. A black leather glove covered Stauffenberg's three-fingered left hand, a black eyepatch the socket of his left eye. The limp resulted from his smashed left kneecap. The non-existent right hand was giving him pain now. Dr Sauerbruch had warned him of that. The pain would come and go; it might last for years.

Unless he was luckier than a man had a right to expect, that prognosis, offered by Berlin's most prominent surgeon, was irrelevant. What remained of Colonel Stauffenberg's life could be measured in days, perhaps a week or two, not years.

Inside the huge L-shaped grey stone building that housed the Armed Forces High Command, Stauffenberg proceeded as swiftly as his limp would allow along the hall to Stairway C at the end of the longer wing of the building. He took the stairs two at a time, punishing his left leg, and hobbled along the second-floor corridor to his office. In black letters on the door were the words:

Chief-of-Staff
Home Army

Stauffenberg entered and with a deft tossing motion deposited the briefcase that had been held between his left arm and side on the desk. He looked at his watch. One minute twenty-two seconds from the time he had left the staff car. Not bad, but he thought he could improve on that. The speed of his movements here in the Bendlerstrasse did not matter, but the speed with which the disabled Colonel Staffenberg could function elsewhere would matter a very great deal.

At the Führer's retreat at the Berghof above Berchtesgaden perhaps, from which Stauffenberg had just returned by plane. Or perhaps at Wolf's Lair, the Führer's field headquarters deep in the pine forests of East Prussia.

One thing was certain. It would not be Berlin. Adolf Hitler never even visited his capital any more.

Opposite the window that looked out over the blood-red water of the Landwehr Canal the entire wall of the office was a sliding partition. The interior of the building was constantly changing to meet new requirements of the Armed Forces High Command. Stauffenberg himself wore two hats these days, one as Ordnance Chief-of-Staff, the other as Chief-of-Staff to the Commander of the Home Army, General Fromm.

Stauffenberg banged impatiently on the partition with his maimed left hand.

'Klaus?' a voice called in response. Even though it was Sunday evening, past eight o'clock, Olbricht was in. That did not surprise Stauffenberg.

'Are you busy?'

'Paperwork, Klaus. Come in.'

Stauffenberg slid the partition just enough to pass through to General Olbricht's larger office. It was as cluttered as Stauffenberg's own office was spartanly bare. Three desks – one covered with ordnance maps, one piled high with oaktag folders that almost hid the telephone, one strewn with papers. General Friedrich Olbricht, Deputy Commander of the Home Army, rose from behind that one, a square-built man with a high forehead and round steel-rimmed glasses.

The two men wasted no time on military courtesy. 'What was on his mind?' Olbricht asked.

'The usual. Keep them in the training camps long enough to show them which end of a rifle is which, then send them to the front. He wants two hundred thousand replacements for Army Group Centre.'

'Good God in Heaven,' said General Olbricht. 'That isn't possible.'

Stauffenberg shrugged. 'I'm to return to the Berghof before the end of the month.'

'When?'

'Who can say, with the Führer? The twentieth, the twenty-fifth perhaps.'

Olbricht looked at him. 'We can't be ready by then, can we?'

'We can try,' Stauffenberg said. 'Would you give me a run-through?' He looked at the round door of the safe behind the map-covered desk.

'You could do it blindfolded, Klaus. Don't worry.'

'Not fast enough,' Stauffenberg said, and General Olbricht, with a slow patient shake of his head and a faint smile, locked the door of the office and went into Stauffenberg's part of the large, partitioned room to lock that door too. Then he twirled the three dials of the safe and swung it open. He removed a black leather briefcase from the safe. When he gave it to Stauffenberg the younger man clamped it between his right arm and side. Olbricht then gave him a pair of small steel pliers. Stauffenberg dropped them into the gusseted breast pocket of his tunic.

'Time me,' he said.

Setting the briefcase on the desk he unbuckled the straps. Then he deftly withdrew the pliers from his pocket with the three fingers of his left hand, plunged them into the briefcase and through the brown-paper wrapping of the dummy bomb, and made a snipping motion.

Olbricht looked up from the sweep-second hand of his watch. 'Seventeen seconds,' he said.

'I want to get it down to twelve. I think I could do it in twelve. Try it again.'

He went through the routine once more.

'Fifteen seconds,' Olbricht said.

'Not fast enough.'

But Olbricht replaced the pliers and briefcase in the safe. 'Just keeping it here scares the hell out of me,' he said.

'Can you think of a better place?'

Olbricht admitted he could not.

Stauffenberg smiled; it made him look very young. He was thirty-seven and had recently been promoted colonel. He had thick black hair and eyebrows and the sort of handsomeness that just missed being pretty. The black eyepatch gave him a look of stylised theatrical recklessness.

'All the news from the Berghof isn't bad,' he said. 'After the conference he took me and Keitel aside for a little talk.'

'Who was there?'

'The usual crew. Keitel, Jodl, Bodenschatz. Bormann, of

course. The Führer's adjutant Schmundt. Himmler, Goering.'

The last name drew an exclamation of amazement from Olbricht.

'Sometimes he forgets to play the Last of the Renaissance Men and actually shows up for work,' Stauffenberg said sarcastically. He sat down behind the map-covered desk. 'After the conference we had tea in the big room with the moving window.'

'Speer's masterpiece.'

'Actually, it's pretty impressive. Anyway, I was going to excuse myself. The Führer doesn't mind that usually.'

'Of course not. He likes to see you rounding up cannon-fodder. You and General Fromm.'

General Friedrich Fromm, Commander-in-Chief of the Home Army and O.K.W. Chief of Ordnance, was Stauffenberg's immediate superior.

'Is he with us?' Stauffenberg asked.

Olbricht shook his head slowly, unhappily. 'Mondays, Wednesdays, and Fridays,' he said. 'Just like Rommel in France.'

'We don't need Rommel as much as we need Fromm.'

'I'd rather not hear that on Tuesdays, Thursdays, and Saturdays,' Olbricht said.

Stauffenberg resumed his story. 'After the Führer told me to stay, I hung around near the Speer window. You can see clear down through a cut in the mountains to Salzburg. I admired the view and thought the Führer forgot all about me. He sat at the other end of the room half dozing and listening to Goering laugh at his own jokes. Until Himmler left.'

'I don't follow you.'

'That's what the Führer was waiting for. He left Goering and came over to me. You know that abrupt way he has. The fat Reich Marshal was still laughing, and suddenly Hitler wasn't there.'

'What did Himmler's leaving have to do with it?'

Stauffenberg smiled his boyish smile again. 'Valkyrie. That's what he wanted to talk about.'

'Well, well, well,' said Olbricht. 'Alone?'

'No, I told you. With Keitel.'

'Not Bormann?'

'Just Keitel,' Stauffenberg said. 'Congratulations, General. The Führer's sold on Valkyrie.'

*

A slight toss of Hitler's head had been enough to bring Field Marshal Keitel, Chief-of-Staff of the Armed Forces High Command, hurrying to the Speer window, where Stauffenberg stood with the Führer.

Hands folded in front of his military tunic, as if protecting his groin, Hitler said: 'Shall we go outside, gentlemen? Such a lovely day.'

Keitel on the Führer's right, Stauffenberg on his left, they marched across the big conference room of the Berghof. Moments later the three men stood on the terrace. It offered a wider panorama than the view from the Speer window.

'Nowhere else on earth,' Adolf Hitler said definitively, 'is as beautiful as the Obersalzberg in summer.'

Field Marshal Keitel, silver-haired and fawning in his impeccably cut uniform, nodded earnestly.

'Graf von Stauffenberg, don't you agree?' the Führer asked. Then he laughed. 'But of course you are from Upper Franconia, another beautiful part of the Reich.' He stood at the edge of the terrace gazing across the mountains and through the Alpine cut towards the distant city of Salzburg, dazzling white in the sunshine on the flat plain below the mountains.

'Marshal Keitel,' he said, 'I have come to a decision.' He did not say a world historical decision, as he sometimes did, although he used that tone of voice.

'Yes, my Führer?'

'There are now seven million slave labourers and conscripts in the Greater German Reich, almost two million in Berlin alone. They represent a terrible danger.'

'I, myself, have often thought so,' Keitel said quickly.

'A few weeks ago,' Hitler went on, 'General Olbricht of the Home Army suggested that it might be advisable to update the plans for Operation Valkyrie. I am in total agreement.'

Valkyrie was a contingency plan for swift countermeasures to be taken by the Home Army in the event of an uprising by the seven million slave labourers in the Reich. Since they were worked to death on short rations, such an uprising was inconceivable.

Stauffenberg wondered if Hitler was aware of that. It was true that he saw enemies everywhere these days, but his decision to update Valkyrie could have been more subtly inspired.

The contingency plan for coping with an uprising of slave labourers could, if altered slightly, cope with a putsch by Heinrich Himmler's S.S. Like all dictators since the time of Rome, Hitler didn't trust his Praetorian guard. Besides, under certain circumstances, history might repeat itself. Hadn't he had to crush the abortive so-called Second Revolution of the Storm Troopers ten years ago?

Himmler was far cleverer and no less ambitious than the murdered Ernst Roehm.

'Therefore,' Hitler told Keitel, 'the Home Army is to have the full co-operation of the High Command in preparing Valkyrie to meet current requirements.'

'Absolutely, my Führer,' said Keitel. 'I guarantee it personally.'

Stauffenberg could hardly believe it. The old, all but forgotten Operation Valkyrie was being updated in secret right now. He had spent weeks with General Olbricht doing just that.

They could work openly now.

Hitler had given the operation his blessing.

'My Führer?' Stauffenberg said, aware that Hitler had asked him a question.

'How soon can you present the new contingency plans for my consideration?'

Stauffenberg replied quickly: 'By the end of the month at the latest, my Führer.'

Before the end of the month, Hitler would be dead.

Now in General Olbricht's office, Stauffenberg finished his account of the discussion on the Berghof terrace. 'Keitel invited me to drive to the airport in his car,' he told Olbricht. 'You know Keitel when the Führer's made one of his world historical decisions. He told me that if we needed any red tape cut, just give him a blitz call any hour of the day or night.'

General Olbricht drew the blackout curtains across the window, switched on the overhead light. 'Klaus,' he said slowly, 'it's going to work. For the first time I truly believe that.'

The phone rang on the other side of the partition in Stauffenberg's office, but by the time he could reach it the line was dead. Just as he returned, the ringing began on Olbricht's desk.

'General Olbricht speaking.'

In a moment he held the phone out to Stauffenberg, then thought better of it and cleared a space for the instrument among the piles of file folders on the desk.

'Your adjutant,' he said.

Stauffenberg took the ear-piece in his left hand and leaned over the desk. He heard laughter, voices, the thin distant rhythm of a tango. 'What the devil are you doing back from leave so early? I thought you'd still be busy with a bedful of dirndls in Austria.'

'Not these days. I'm a changed man, Herr Oberst. I hardly left Berlin.'

Stauffenberg laughed. 'Are you calling from a nightclub or a brothel? It's impossible to tell the difference on the phone.'

'I'm home.' Stauffenberg's adjutant sounded offended. 'Celebrating my imminent return to duty with a few friends.'

A Strauss waltz replaced the tango. 'How's Elisabeth?' Stauffenberg asked.

'Right here with me. Why don't you drop by and say hello?'

Stauffenberg detested the sort of frivolous party now apparently under way at the Pariserplatz apartment, and Heydebrand knew it. Thus the casual invitation had to be more than it seemed, and Stauffenberg waited for elaboration.

'We'd really hate you to miss it, Herr Oberst,' Heydebrand said. That was elaboration. It meant some of the conspirators were present.

The phone, both men had to assume, was on intercept, all conversations wire-recorded by the so-called Brown Friend and then selectively transcribed for evaluation at the Prinz Albrechtstrasse by S.D.-Interior, Bureau III of the Reich Central Security Office. There was nothing Heydebrand or Stauffenberg could do about that, except speak circumspectly.

'Don't bother to bring your own bottle,' Heydebrand said. That was further elaboration. It meant, in a word: Trouble.

A young surgeon from the Charité Hospital led Elisabeth across the floor in the final glide of an expert tango and delivered her back to where Haller stood in conversation with the former Reichstag delegate and concentration camp inmate Julius Esser.

The surgeon, whose name was Raffaello Matti and who came from Ascona in the Swiss Ticino, bowed over Elisabeth's hand. 'The loveliest dancer in Berlin,' he said gallantly, 'for the loveliest dance in the world.' He looked at Haller. 'You Germans, I'll never understand it. Precisely what is Hitler's antipathy to every ballroom dance except the Viennese waltz? What can he possibly be objecting to?'

A Viennese waltz was playing now, an old scratchy rendition of *Wiener Blut* that someone had put on the phonograph.

'Bourgeois decadence,' said Julius Esser dryly. 'That gives

us Germans something in common with our former Russian allies.'

Raffaello Matti threw back his head and laughed. He had brilliant white teeth and a sharp-featured dark face under black hair combed sleekly back. He looked Italian but spoke with almost Prussian pomposity. He had studied medicine in Berlin, according to the dossier Haller had seen in Baker Street, and had stayed on to work under Dr Ferdinand Sauerbruch at the Charité.

'Former allies, indeed,' he said. 'But you had best take care who you say that to, Herr Esser. In any case, you'll have noticed how the Nazi ban on dance music is enforced less as the air raids increase. This is hardly the time for martial airs.' He turned back to Haller. 'Don't you agree, Herr Hauptmann? It's rather like what your Minister of Propaganda has referred to as the optics of war. The luxury restaurants and nightclubs were shut after Stalingrad, but they have opened again. Morale, finally, is more important than optical illusion. Joseph Goebbels is a cynic but he is no fool.'

'That's too complicated for me, Herr Doktor,' Haller said, 'and too seditious.' He tempered that with a brief grin. 'I'm just a company commander.'

'Herr Esser will know what I mean,' Raffaello Matti said condescendingly. He bowed over Elisabeth's hand again, kissing air two inches above her knuckles, and went off in the direction of the bar set up on the sideboard.

The party had begun three hours ago, just after six o'clock. Fifty people, perhaps sixty, now crowded the five rooms of the apartment on Pariserplatz.

'It's quite simple,' Heydi had told Haller earlier. 'Invite half a dozen and you get ten times that many. Berlin lives for parties these days. The old Roman notion of eat, drink, and be merry before the barbarians breach the city walls. Except that the barbarians are here already.'

Heydi had introduced the American offhandedly as an old army friend on leave from the Western Front when he bothered to introduce him at all. In addition to Raffaello Matti, Haller recognised three men from photographs he had studied in Baker Street. To these three Heydi had somehow conveyed additional information; they did not know who Haller was but they accepted him without question as a member of the conspiracy.

The first, now talking with Raffaello Matti at the bar, was Wolf Heinrich Graf von Helldorf, a strange, moody man, fifty years old according to his dossier, a Nazi party member since 1926, Berlin Police Chief since 1935. It was said that he owed that appointment to years of whoring around with his old friend Joseph Goebbels. As far as Baker Street knew they were, incredibly, still close.

Helldorf had spoken freely with Haller about the excesses of the regime, always referring to them as S.S. brutality. The S.S., Haller decided cynically, made a fine excuse for the chief of civilian police. As they talked, Haller kept thinking: where were you on Crystal Night in November 1938, friend? What did you think of S.S. brutality then? You had a pretty good thing going before the war, thanks to those excesses, didn't you? Getting rich selling passports and exit visas to Jews who could afford them, wasn't it?

Haller finally dismissed the thought as irrelevant. His decision about the Valkyrie conspirators would not hinge on Count von Helldorf's greed.

The second, now buttonholing Heydi as he hung up the phone, was a far more germane case. Carl Goerdeler, former Lord Mayor of Leipzig and Reich Price Commissioner, had resigned both posts contemptuously when the Nazis tore down the statue of Leipzig's most famous citizen, the Jewish composer Felix Mendelssohn, from outside the Gewandhaus concert hall. He, even more than General Beck, had organised the movement that had gone since 1936 from opposition to resistance to conspiracy. He was a tall, distinguished, grey-haired man whose position as financial adviser to the Stuttgart firm of Robert Bosch gave him the opportunity to travel. A compulsive talker and inveterate optimist, he had spread the anti-Nazi gospel in England and America before the war and in Germany since 1939. The optimism put him in what Milt Green called cloud-cuckoo-land; the compulsive talking put him in jeopardy of his life.

According to Heydi, the Gestapo had an open warrant for his arrest. That it had not yet been served attested to Himmler's patient hope that the loquacious Goerdeler could help widen the Gestapo net.

The third, the former Social Democrat Reichstag delegate and inmate of Oranienburg Concentration Camp, Julius Esser, now asked Haller: 'And what did you think of our Swiss doctor?'

Haller looked at the furrowed brow, the eyes deep-set under beetling black brows, and wondered how much Esser knew. He was only the token socialist in what was, after all, a conspiracy of disillusioned conservatives and army officers.

'He doesn't exactly keep his opinions to himself,' Haller said.

'You can't really tell anything from that,' said Julius Esser. 'It's true that the typical anti-Nazi is easy to recognise – he says "Hitler" for "the Führer", "Nazi" for "N.S.D.A.P.". He prefers French cinema to the execrable extravaganzas of the U.F.A. studios. He detests the House of German Art in Munich, and he reads Spengler and the French lyric poets. He hates Wagner, loves chamber music, abhors parades.'

A bass voice was now bellowing Wagner on the phonograph.

'That's your typical anti-Nazi,' Esser said. 'Easy to recognise – and equally easy to impersonate. Half the people who go around talking that way might be Gestapo V-men, playing *agent provocateur.*'

'Not very subtle,' said Haller.

'No,' Esser agreed, 'but it can get very subtle indeed. Now, the really clever Gestapo plant would act rather less obviously. Take Herr Goebbels' good friend Count von Helldorf over there. Does he say what he thinks, or only what he thinks he should say? On the other hand, the truly dedicated anti-Nazi might overplay the role, to court suspicion of being an *agent provocateur.* Is that why Carl Goerdeler isn't in the Prinz Albrechtstrasse cellars right now? You see, there are no answers, only guesses.'

Esser looked towards the door, his beetling brows raised, the lines etched into his solemn face softening. He bowed quickly to Elisabeth, excused himself with words Haller couldn't hear, and crossed the room to join a newcomer to the party, a boyish-looking colonel who wore an eyepatch.

Eight

At the same moment, Monika Jaeger was showing her identification card to the S.S.-Sturmmann at the ornate red-brick-and-marble entrance of the Reich Central Security Office at 8 Prinz Albrechtstrasse.

Before Reichsführer-S.S. Himmler had appropriated the building for the R.S.H.A., it had been an art school. It was now called, after its address, the Prinz Albrechtstrasse, a name that could strike a German numb with terror.

That reaction was foreign to Monika.

Of the seven main branches of the R.S.H.A., Bureau IV was the *Geheime Staatspolizei*, the Secret State Police – the Gestapo. Bureau IV Section Ib/8 was Student and Youth Affairs, under S.S.-Sturmbannführer Gottfried Ritter. This was where, and for whom, Monika worked, and where she was heading now.

Gottfried hardly seemed a likely S.S. major, let alone a Gestapist. Until early 1943 he had served as Provost of the University of Munich, when his handling of the difficult White Rose affair had brought him to the attention of Gestapo Chief Heinrich Mueller. The student dissidents of the White Rose movement had not only demonstrated the need for a Gestapo Section of Student and Youth Affairs but had inadvertently provided it with a director.

A pale vague professorial man in his early forties with courtly manners and a modest sense of his own importance, Gottfried Ritter had found Monika in the Prinz Albrechtstrasse stenographic pool eight months ago and made her his private secretary. Almost at once his low-key seduction campaign had begun, and she had finally yielded to it – if anyone could be said to yield to a man so passive as Gottfried Ritter – the night before Ernst's unexpected return to Berlin.

After Eugen's I.G. Farben urbanity, Gottfried's ardent unskilled fumblings were just what Monika wanted. One night was enough to convince her that Gottfried would wind up where a man belonged, wrapped around her little finger.

But Ernst's return complicated things. An accommodation would have to be reached. Vague and passive or not, an S.S.-Sturmbannführer could do things for her. Even Eugen, with all his influence, couldn't go near the S.S. luxury shop in the basement of Karstadt's department store. Gottfried had all but promised her guest privileges there.

Still, she had been annoyed when Gottfried phoned. Ernst had made dinner reservations at the Newa Grill, Berlin's latest 'in' restaurant, and Monika had looked forward to it eagerly.

'I'm afraid you'll have to come in tonight,' Gottfried told her on the phone. 'Something's come up that can't wait.'

'It's Sunday night,' Monika complained.

'There are no Sunday nights at the Prinz Albrechtstrasse,' said Gottfried.

Monika weighed the Newa Grill against Karstadt's basement, fried fish from the Baltic or a grudging five-ounce chopped steak against S.S. booty from all over Occupied Europe.

'Half an hour, then,' she said.

The S.S.-Sturmbannführer became the uncertain lover. 'I'll make it up to you, Monika.'

'The office,' she told her husband with an almost genuine *moue* of disappointment after she hung up.

'Is the office also Gottfried?' Jaeger asked.

'Yes, but that doesn't mean what you think it means.'

Jaeger shrugged. 'I was just curious. One thing I've learned, you never argue with the Gestapo.'

Now at the Prinz Albrechtstrasse Monika followed the familiar third-floor corridor that led to Gestapo Section Ib/8. Only every second bulb in the ceiling was illuminated and despite Gottfried's contention about Sunday night, the Prinz Albrechtstrasse was quiet – a few S.S. men on the ground floor, a clerk on the staircase who returned Monika's greeting with a furtive glance in her direction and a nod before hurrying down. The third-floor corridor was deserted.

Perhaps she had imagined the furtive glance, but as she approached the office Monika began to feel uneasy. Eight months working for Gottfried and he had never called her in on a Sunday night before. Had he sounded nervous? She didn't think so, but even if he had, Ernst's unexpected return to Berlin could account for that.

The door was shut but not locked, which should have indicated Gottfried's presence in the office. Strict R.S.H.A. procedure – unoccupied offices were to be locked at all times.

Unlike the parsimonious illumination in the corridor, the office blazed with light. It was a two-room suite, the large outer office consisting of a waiting-room with three chairs and a low table on one side of a wooden divider, and filing cabinets and Monika's desk and typewriter table on the other. The two windows, shattered in an air-raid last month, were boarded over. Light gleamed behind the pebbled glass panel in the door to Gottfried's inner office.

Monika paused there. She was going to call his name, decided on his title instead. 'Herr Sturmbannführer?'

No answer.

She tried the door, opened it. A portrait of Heinrich Himmler stared down at her from the wall with the eyes of a crotchety fanatic. Gottfried wasn't there. She saw his meerschaum pipe in an ashtray on the desk, thought she could faintly smell the aromatic Dutch tobacco he purchased at

Karstadt's. She returned to the outer office and sat at her own desk, tapping her fingernails impatiently on its surface. She could, she thought, catch up on some work while waiting. Her files, thanks to the holiday with Eugen, were not up to date; the quarterly Sipo A-card index of known enemies of the regime had arrived during her absence and she had still not co-ordinated it with the Residence Inquiry List or the monthly Secret Register.

But she was too annoyed to work. What right had Gottfried to send for her and not even be there when she arrived?

She got up and went into the ante-room, where she leafed through the current issue of *The Black Corps*, the weekly S.S. newspaper. From somewhere in the building the faint shrill ringing of a telephone startled her. She really would have to get used to having Ernst home, she told herself. His return had made her more tense than she'd cared to admit. He would have to understand that there was more to life, more to her life, than sharing her bedroom with a handsome stud who happened to be her husband.

She searched through her purse for cigarettes, found none. Anger replaced annoyance; she'd been here fifteen minutes already and still no sign of Gottfried. She decided to phone Ernst to come for her. Perhaps he hadn't cancelled the Newa Grill reservation yet.

When she got through to Block Leader Binnicker the one-legged old man told her with a touch of malice that her husband had gone out a few minutes after she had.

Ten more minutes passed. Monika promised herself she would find a way to punish Gottfried. It was almost 10.30 now, too late for the Newa Grill even if Ernst had been home.

She used the phone again, this time to call the duty-desk. After identifying herself she asked: 'Has Sturmbannführer Ritter left the building?'

'Not unless he did so without signing out,' an amused voice replied. Gottfried Ritter was not the sort to leave the Prinz Albrechtstrasse without signing out.

Monika hung up and heard footsteps in the corridor. She got to her feet quickly. Better to let Gottfried find her on the point of leaving rather than waiting for him with dutiful patience.

She opened the door and there, facing her, one hand still out to grasp the knob, his black S.S. uniform tailored to perfection, its leather accoutrements gleaming, the silver S.S. runes on the right collar patch and the silver oak leaf and two pips of his rank on the left, stood S.S.-Gruppenführer and Gestapo Chief Heinrich Mueller.

'Frau Jaeger, isn't it?' he said.

He was a wiry little man not quite Monika's height. Under close-cropped greying hair his otherwise pleasant face was marred by expressionless eyes of a washed-out blue that flicked from side to side before fixing on Monika's face.

He did not wait for her to step aside but walked directly at her so that she had to edge to one side of the doorway. He marched through the ante-room to Gottfried's office without taking any further notice of her until he was seated at Gottfried's desk.

'Frau Jaeger!' he called.

Only her deep tan hid the fact that the blood had drained from Monika's face. Himmler she had seen in person perhaps half a dozen times, and the Reichsführer-S.S. inspired no terror in her. Himmler commanded the police and the whole vast S.S. apparatus with a bureaucratic efficiency hampered by a simplistic racist zeal that even Hitler might have found excessive. Gestapo Mueller, his nominal subordinate, controlled the Gestapo from a position of absolute, uncontested power because ideology meant nothing to him and power everything.

He ran his empire from behind a wall of anonymity so strictly preserved that few men could describe his appearance. Yet his name was the most feared in Berlin.

He also ran the Gestapo cellars.

All this passed through Monika's mind as she stood before the little man seated at Gottfried's desk, and it didn't help when she tried to convince herself she had nothing to fear from Gestapo Mueller.

He told Monika to be seated and leaned towards her, his arms folded on the desktop.

'That's no Wannsee suntan,' he said.

'No, Herr Gruppenführer. I was – abroad.'

'In Spain and Portugal with the I.G. Farben Director of Procurement,' Mueller said. 'We know that.' He had an odd way of speaking, in quick snorting bursts, as if he suffered from a breathing problem.

His pale eyes flicked from side to side and found her eyes again. 'Sturmbannführer Ritter is to be congratulated for his taste. Your husband is in the army?'

'Yes, Herr Gruppenführer.'

'No children, I believe? The Reichsführer-S.S. would consider that a dreadful waste of such splendid breeding stock. I myself am more concerned about another sort of waste. It would be a pity to damage such obviously – superior equipment. I sincerely hope that will not be necessary, Frau Jaeger. You are quite lovely.'

Monika's heart was pounding. The word damage was no euphemism. Himmler often dealt in euphemisms; Mueller rarely.

'So lovely, in fact, that I wonder at your settling for a man like Sturmbannführer Ritter. Are you happy with your work here at Bureau IV?'

'Yes, Herr Gruppenführer,' Monika said quickly.

'But your personal life is somewhat complicated at the moment?'

Monika did not know how to answer that question. 'I never let it interfere with my work,' she said finally.

Gestapo Mueller laughed. 'The effect, I assure you,' he said, 'would go unnoticed here if you did. In any event, we are now in the process of simplifying things for you. Tell me, have you ever visited the cellars?'

Monika shook her head swiftly from side to side.

'You had the opportunity, of course?'

'I was invited once,' Monika said. 'I didn't go. I'm . . . not like that.'

'You disappoint me, *gnädige* Frau. Not like what?'

Another question Monika did not know how to answer. She tried: 'I don't . . . enjoy such things, Herr Gruppenführer.'

'But what on earth has enjoyment to do with it?' Mueller snorted. 'No one enjoys sharpened interrogation, I assure you. Not even those who administer it, despite what you may hear on the outside.'

Sharpened interrogation *was* a euphemism, and coming after Mueller's use of the word damage it had the desired effect. Once at the zoo Monika had seen a mouse introduced into the cage of a boa constrictor. The mouse had made one frantic rush around the glass perimeter of the cage and then settled in a corner to await its doom. Such fatalism on the part of the tiny creature had made no sense to Monika until now.

Whatever Mueller wanted from her he would get. To offer resistance would be insane.

'The will of a man undergoing sharpened interrogation,' he told her, 'can often be broken more swiftly if he suffers his ordeal before witnesses. For a certain type of man the ideal witness is a woman. It is, finally, a question of pride. That type of man surrenders to avoid the ultimate degradation – to be broken totally in the presence of an attractive woman.'

Gestapo Mueller drew back the black sleeve of his tunic and looked at his watch.

'Sturmbannführer Ritter has been unexpectedly intransigent,' he said, and stood. 'Shall we pay him a visit, *gnädige* Frau?'

The room was small and windowless, its whitewashed walls brilliantly lit by bulbs set in small wire cages in the high ceiling. One Gestapist, a short bespectacled man with enormous shoulders, was leaning against the far wall smoking a cigarette. His shirtsleeves were rolled up over thick forearms and he wore a black rubber apron. He came away from the wall and rigidly to attention when he saw Mueller and Monika in the doorway.

Mueller raised a negligent hand. 'Carry on,' he said, his words intended for the second Gestapist, who stood in the exact centre of the room. Slender and dark-haired, he also wore a black rubber apron. His hands were raised to shoulder level because that was the level of Sturmbannführer Gottfried Ritter's bare feet.

Gottfried hung suspended from the ceiling by his arms, the arms fettered behind his back so that when the second Gestapist had tugged the loose end of the rope hanging from the pulley to raise Gottfried off the floor, Gottfried's shoulders had been immediately dislocated.

Now the slender, dark-haired Gestapist, still holding Gottfried's feet, walked in a small circle, twisting the rope from which Gottfried hung.

'A moment, please,' said Gestapo Mueller. 'Turn him this way. So, like that.' He shouted: 'You! Ritter!' and slowly Gottfried Ritter's head came up. He saw Mueller and he saw Monika. He was naked, his narrow chest pumping like a bellows. His shoulder blades protruded outward, the flesh around them blue in the harsh white light. His mouth opened and from it emerged a bubbling sound, like coffee perking.

Monika knuckled her eyes in a childlike gesture. *Make them stop, please, please make them stop, I'm afraid.*

Her knees buckled. She would have fallen but Mueller caught her with unexpected gentleness. 'Try to control yourself,' he told her softly, not angrily, concern in his voice. 'This shouldn't take long.'

She slumped into Mueller's arms, turning her head away from Gottfried. With an impatient gesture Mueller summoned the bespectacled Gestapist. Mueller on one side and the Gestapist on the other, they supported her.

Fingers that smelled of tobacco tilted her chin up.

She opened her eyes and looked directly at Gottfried's face.

Mueller raised his hand and nodded. The slender Gestapist, still holding Gottfried's feet, walked again in a small circle, twisting the rope from which Gottfried hung. The rope made a creaking sound. It resisted him so that he had to trudge more slowly for each new circle, his jackboots pushing hard against the cement floor. Soon the rope resisted his efforts entirely. With all the twisting it had shortened somewhat. He now held Gottfried's feet at the level of his own head.

Mueller made a chopping motion with his hand.

The slender Gestapist stepped back quickly.

The rope jerked and spun, unwinding itself. Gottfried seemed to leap from side to side. From his throat came a hoarse bellowing sound that oscillated with the motion of his body.

Monika saw his face and then the back of his head, his face and then the back of his head, his rib-cage and twisted shoulders, his back with his arms attached the wrong way, his rib cage again, his meagre buttocks, his genitals flapping between his thighs, his meagre buttocks again, his penis distending, the backs of his knees, his feet jerking spasmodically.

The spinning stopped, the rope swayed, Gottfried swayed.

The rope hung taut, Gottfried hung flaccid, loose and boneless, sacklike. Then he shuddered.

He had an orgasm.

Monika awoke in a small room, its single window high on one wall looking out on daylight, the usual portrait of Himmler on the opposite wall looking down at her disapprovingly.

Memory surfaced – a heavy woman with a mannish haircut carrying her up a flight of stairs, the glint of glass and metal, something stinging her arm, a dizzy floating sensation, hard strong hands stripping off her clothing while she floated further away from herself and yet closer to the core of her being, where she could recall Gottfried hanging like that not with terror but with a sick excitement that was worse than terror.

She lay perfectly still under the sheet that covered her. It was very hot in the small room. If she moved, if she made any sound, she was afraid someone would hear her, would enter the small room, would make something bad happen to her.

She shut her eyes and saw Gottfried dangling and instantly opened her eyes and saw Mueller standing in the narrow doorway. His arm rose in what might have been a careless approximation of the German greeting.

Monika sat up and realised she was naked. She drew the sheet to her throat. Mueller's washed-out eyes flicked this way and that, then caught and held her eyes.

He said: 'Did you know that Sturmbannführer Ritter suffered from a bad heart?'

Monika did not know that. She did not even know where she was. She only knew she was terrified.

She could feel her nipples tautening against the coarse fabric of the sheet. Mueller's eyes flicked there and back to her face.

'I want you to do something for me.'

Monika would do anything if it would get her out of this room, away from Gestapo Mueller.

'Do you by any chance know Sturmbannführer Ritter's wife?'

Once Gottfried had sent Monika to his apartment in Dahlem. He had forgotten his pipe and Dutch tobacco. Monika remembered Frau Ritter as a dowdy woman with bleached hair and cultural pretensions. She had served Monika tea, real tea from Karstadt's, and tried to involve her in a discussion of some book or other. Alfred Rosenberg's *The Myth of the Twentieth Century*, that was it. Frau Ritter had not liked the book.

'I met her once,' Monika said. Her own voice surprised her; it sounded quite normal. Recalling the scene in the dark clutter of the Ritter apartment had, for the moment, distracted her from the terror of last night.

Mueller's voice brought it back. 'Under what circumstances?'

'The Sturmbannführer sent me to their apartment to get something.'

'Splendid,' said Mueller. 'That is what you will do now. The poor woman has been phoning about her husband. A natural concern. But nothing is wrong, you understand. The Sturmbannführer was called to Munich on business. When she asks you, tell her that. The problem is that on learning of her husband's death a woman often behaves quite unpredictably. Therefore, she is not to learn of it until after your visit.'

Monika gasped. 'He's dead?'

'His heart. I thought I told you.' Mueller snorted, took a handkerchief from his pocket, carefully unfolded it, blew his nose. 'In the locked drawer of Ritter's desk in his study you will find a small black notebook. You will bring that, and whatever other papers you find, to me. The fact that you have the key should convince Frau Ritter that her husband sent you. If you can think of some additional reason for your visit, all the better.'

'His pipe tobacco,' Monika suggested. 'A fresh tin of his pipe tobacco.'

'Excellent, Frau Jaeger. He asked you to get those things before he left for Munich last night and he expects you to have them when he returns tomorrow . . . Frau Epp!'

In a few seconds a heavy woman with a mannish haircut entered the room carrying Monika's clothing neatly folded over one arm.

When the woman left, a change came over Mueller. He became attentive, solicitous of Monika's comfort. 'You slept well despite the spartan accommodation, I hope? I often sleep here myself when work keeps me late. Perhaps you'll join me for breakfast? China tea? Ceylon? Or do you prefer coffee?'

Shortly before noon Monika sat in a swaying U-bahn car clattering through the dark tunnel south towards the suburb of Dahlem. Breakfast had been a feast – fresh rolls and real butter, cheese from Holland, succulent ham and liverwurst, all the strong dark coffee she could drink. Mueller had played the earnest host, exuding heavy Bavarian charm. He had not mentioned Gottfried once.

Stauffenberg pivoted away from the window and limped angrily back across General Beck's dining-room to confront the three men seated at the table drinking ersatz coffee.

'What exactly do you know about this Rambow?' he demanded.

'Herr Oberst, be reasonable,' Julius Esser said. 'I can't very well refuse.'

Stauffenberg stalked towards the window, turned, came back. 'You haven't answered my question.'

'He's a Communist, or he was. He spent four years in Oranienburg,' Julius Esser said.

'Why did they let him go?'

Esser shrugged. 'Why do they let anyone go? Why did they let me go?'

Stauffenberg accepted without further discussion the fact

that the Gestapo was unpredictable. 'We don't need Rambow,' he said. 'We don't need the gutter rabble he claims to represent.'

Julius Esser spoke slowly, choosing his words. 'You don't see beyond a bomb, a few battalions of the Home Army taking over Berlin, a few hours of military activity that – '

'What else is there?' Stauffenberg cut him off rudely.

'The future, if we succeed,' Esser said softly. 'The entire political spectrum from conservative to centrist to Social Democrat to Communist, all of us working together for the new Germany. And if we don't demonstrate a certain faith now, a willingness to co-operate – '

'There won't be any future if we make one irretrievable mistake today.'

'I'm not asking you to look months ahead, only days,' Esser's voice was patient, his brow furrowed. 'You don't really think the S.S. will roll over and play dead, do you? Hitler hasn't been running the country for months. He's too busy being Gröfaz. Himmler controls the Reich by default and Goebbels is master of Berlin. Even if your bomb kills Hitler, how long do you think you'll hold the Wehrmacht against that pair without popular support?'

'Popular support? From a Communist swine like Rambow?' Stauffenberg said contemptuously. 'Don't make me laugh.'

'Klaus, listen to me,' Ludwig Beck said. The retired general looked frail, the civilian suit he wore hung loosely on his frame, and his voice was low and dispirited, but for the first time Stauffenberg stood still, and he listened.

'We all know that only the Wehrmacht has the power to overthrow the regime, that the two absolute requirements are the death of Hitler and a swift takeover of the machinery of government here in Berlin. But then? Afterwards? You are thinking tactically, Herr Esser strategically. If the population of Berlin stands idly by, the S.S. will inevitably mount a counter-putsch. And the S.S., Klaus, has more guns and tanks in the Berlin area than you have at your disposal in the Home Army. We have to hope that a show of support for us in the streets will dissuade them. If there is any chance that a meeting between Herr Esser and the Communists will accomplish this, that meeting must take place.'

Somewhat subdued, Stauffenberg looked at his adjutant. 'Heydi?' he said.

But Freiherr von Heydebrand would not be drawn into the

argument. 'I'll take Herr Esser there tonight if that's what you want.'

'I want your opinion.'

'I have no opinion,' Heydi said.

'That comes as a surprise,' Stauffenberg observed sarcastically. 'Especially after last night.'

Despite the difference in their ranks Heydebrand and Graf von Stauffenberg were on easy terms. Although aware of his shortcomings, Heydi admired and respected the older man. Even in the Prussian atmosphere of the Bendlerstrasse Stauffenberg was considered impatient and arrogant. But what his fellow officers failed to see was that, like most perfectionists, he was even harder on himself than on others.

Their friendship had been tested last night, and not over Esser's resolve to go ahead with the meeting in Berlin-East. Heydi was certain that Stauffenberg would defer on that to General Beck.

He would not defer to anyone on the subject of Richard Haller.

For twenty minutes he had listened to the American, asking an occasional question but not once interrupting peremptorily, an uncharacteristic attitude for Graf von Stauffenberg. Then he said: 'I don't know what they expect to accomplish by sending you here, Herr Haller, but you can't expect me to believe that nonsense about sitting down to discuss peace terms. Whether we succeed or fail, the Allies will dictate the peace. You know that as well as I do. When you're ready to tell me the real reason they sent you in, I'll listen.'

Heydi had been dismayed. As Elisabeth had presented Haller to him, like a gift, so he had presented Haller to Stauffenberg.

'Good God, Klaus,' he blurted. 'What's the matter with you? He risked his life coming here. He risks it every day he stays here.'

Stauffenberg's voice was cold. 'Let's hope that he doesn't risk yours, Herr Oberleutnant.'

Now in Lichterfelde Julius Esser was saying: 'I've got to meet with them. Believe me. I don't know this Rambow, but I do know the people he represents.'

'The people he claims he represents.'

Esser brushed that aside with a wave of his hand. 'Franz Jacob was active in the transport union before 1933 and Anton Saeftkow knew Rosa Luxembourg in the old days. I had no idea they were still alive.'

'Which indicates how much good they'll do us,' said Stauffenberg.

General Beck pushed back from the table slowly and stood. 'Klaus, we all know that if any one individual could bring down the regime single-handed, it would be you.' Beck's thin-lipped scholar's face looked for a fleeting instant almost mischievous. 'But since that unfortunately isn't the case, we must each of us be permitted to perform his role. The consensus is that Herr Esser should go to Berlin-East tonight, I believe?'

Julius Esser nodded. So, reluctantly, did Heydebrand.

At that moment a loud crashing sound came from the basement.

Despite his limp it was Stauffenberg who reached the stairs first.

'You're in luck.' Elisabeth told the Liebermanns five minutes earlier. 'It's right here in Lichterfelde, a twenty-minute walk. A man will come for you tonight.'

The Liebermanns' few possessions had been packed in a small carton.

Frau Liebermann's round face suddenly puckered. She began to cry.

'*Schatzchen*, what is it?'

'N-nothing,' Frau Liebermann managed.

'That we must always be on the move? But what else can we do? Surely you are aware of the risk these brave people take, hiding us?'

'It isn't that,' Frau Liebermann said. 'I'll always be grateful. You know that.'

'Then what?' Professor Liebermann asked patiently.

'You put them up there and thought I'd forget,' Frau Liebermann accused her husband.

She indicated a shelf behind the cold furnace. It was bare except for a second, larger carton.

Professor Liebermann sighed elaborately.

'I can't just leave them,' Frau Liebermann protested. 'How can you expect me to do that?'

Elisabeth looked her question at the Professor.

'A tea service for eight, Fräulein Lauterbacher. Fine old Dresden china.' He gazed at the ceiling helplessly. 'For two years. Everywhere.'

'It's all I have left from the old days,' Frau Liebermann told him.

Professor Liebermann spoke to himself ruefully. 'Nice try, Lorenz.' He went behind the furnace, where he had to stand on tiptoe to reach the heavy carton. He began to ease it forward on the shelf. Up on his toes like that, the weight was more than he had expected, more than he could manage.

The carton fell with a crash.

Stauffenberg came downstairs quickly, Heydi right behind him.

'Who are these people?' the colonel demanded of Elisabeth.

'They're leaving tonight,' she said.

The Liebermanns stood together in front of the furnace, the Dresden tea service forgotten. The woman was trembling.

'I asked you who they were.'

Elisabeth looked at Heydi, but his craggy face was expressionless. She was unaware of the tension between the two officers, unaware that the last thing Heydi wanted now was another argument with Stauffenberg.

'What difference does it make?' she said. 'They're leaving here, and so are we.' Elisabeth had already packed Beck's clothing; he would be staying in the big Stauffenberg house at Wannsee until Valkyrie-Day.

Stauffenberg's glance took in the two cots, the bare shelves, the small carton tied with twine. 'They're Jews, aren't they?' he asked. It wasn't really a question.

Elisabeth did not deny it.

'How long have they been here?'

Once more Elisabeth looked at Heydi, who stood at the bottom of the stairs, his eyes averted.

'A few days. Only a few days, Klaus,' Elisabeth said.

'Your noble gesture might have cost the general his life, you little fool,' Stauffenberg told her furiously.

'My uncle knew – '

'Your uncle's a sick man. You're supposed to be looking after him.'

A third time Elisabeth looked at Heydi. His face was granite.

'And today?' Stauffenberg wouldn't let it go. 'If any of us had been followed here today? With these Jews down here?'

Frau Liebermann was crying softly; her husband's face was pale and set, his arm around her shoulders. Elisabeth realised that neither of them understood. Consumed by fear, they were sure the two officers had come to arrest them.

Still, Professor Liebermann stepped forward and tried

pathetically to protect Elisabeth. 'The Herr Oberst must understand,' he said, 'that this young lady had no idea . . . she believed she was sheltering refugees from the East . . . Aryans, you understand, from the General Government in Poland . . .' His voice trailed off. He waved his arms vaguely as if trying to gather the threads of a logic that had eluded him.

'It isn't what you think,' Elisabeth tried to reassure him. 'Nothing's changed.'

Stauffenberg's gloved left hand chopped at air in an impatient gesture as his voice overrode Elisabeth's. 'You heard the lady,' he said harshly. 'Nobody's going to hurt you, Israel.'

In 1938, long before the deadly round-up of Germany's Jews had begun, all male Jews were ordered to add the name Israel before their first names, all female Jews, Sarah. They had swiftly become epithets of contempt.

'You Prussians!' Elisabeth cried out. 'Both of you – rotten stinking Prussians! You're no better than the vermin you're trying to overthrow!'

Nine

By 10.45 that night the gravediggers from the Nikolai Cemetery, both of them Old Fighters in the early street-brawling days of the N.S.D.A.P., were singing the Horst Wessel Song for the third time in the dingy little bar they frequented on Prenzlauerstrasse in Berlin-East.

'Die Fahne hoch, die Reihen dicht geschlossen!' they sang at the top of their voices and glared in red-faced truculence at the other patrons of the *lokal*, as if daring them to complain.

It was the official marching song of the Party, and a few of those so challenged, far from complaining, joined in.

'Die Strasse frei den braunen Bataillonen!

'Die Strasse frei dem Sturmabteilungsmann!' they sang.

A huge man with sleeves rolled high on his tattooed arms scowled fiercely at the grey-eyed man with cropped brown hair who stood at the bar next to him drinking schnapps.

'Every night,' said the huge man. 'Every fucking night. Not only can't the shitheads carry a tune, but the arsehole who wrote those words was a pimp who got himself shot in a fight over a goddamn whore. Probably syphilitic,' he said.

Jaeger didn't know if the huge man meant that Horst Wessel had been syphilitic, or the whore.

'He's buried over there,' said the huge man. 'Right across the street, under the north wall of the cemetery.'

'Who?' Jaeger asked, not really listening.

'The celebrated Party martyr, Horst Wessel,' the huge man shouted, 'that's who.'

'Es shau'n aufs Hakenkreuz voll Hoffnung schon Millionen,' sang the gravediggers.

'The swastika? Hope?' the huge man repeated the words of the song. He placed both hands flat on the bar, shifted his weight, raised one leg, and gave vent to the loudest fart Jaeger had ever heard.

'My name's Drunkenpolz,' he told Jaeger. 'Yours?'

'Hiedler,' Jaeger said.

'Let me buy you a beer to wash down that schnapps,' Drunkenpolz offered.

'Why?'

'Because you're not singing, that's why. It's the best beer in Berlin, I absolutely guarantee it. From the Friedrichshain brewery on the other side of the cemetery. I ought to know,' said the huge man. 'I'm the brewmaster there.'

Jaeger accepted the beer. Every now and then he made some small appropriate response to Brewmaster Drunkenpolz's monologue of seditious complaint. He wondered what was keeping Rambow, but even that didn't hold his attention long. He thought of Monika and he thought of Kropotkin Square in Moscow, Comrade Cell and the Director briefing him about the wife he no longer knew, and then he saw Monika a few hours ago coming out of the steamy bathroom wearing a towel like a turban on her head and nothing else as she crossed the room to sit on the edge of the bed, her bronzed back to him while she loosened the towel and began to rub her streaky wheat-blonde hair dry.

'Well?' Jaeger had said.

'Well what?' She half turned towards him, her weight on one arm on the mattress, her firm breasts displayed with an indifference that itself was ostentatious.

'You know what,' Jaeger said. He wanted her at that moment and the need disturbed him; it implied weakness.

Monika's damp hair fell across her eyes; she looked at him through it. She had awakened Jaeger when she came home at 6.30, and he was still in bed an hour later. 'Do you intend to sleep your whole leave away?' she asked.

'I expect to be out all night,' Jaeger said.

Monika burst out laughing.

'Official business,' he told her.

'So – you can stay out all night tonight on so-called official business when you haven't even been reassigned yet, but you refuse to believe me when I tell you that's what I was doing *last* night. That's good, Ernst. That's really good.'

'Where were you?'

'Must we go through that again?' Monika asked wearily. 'I told you. At the Prinz Albrechtstrasse.'

'Doing what?'

'Working. What else?'

'With Gottfried?'

Five seconds passed before Monika answered. 'Ernst, I told you I don't want to talk about it any more.'

'What kind of idiot do you think I am? Tell me you didn't spend the night with Gottfried.'

'I already told you. Five times since I got home.'

'I don't believe it.'

'Believe anything you want, then.'

Jaeger's rage had mounted ever since her return home. It was directed not so much at Monika as at himself, at the unexpected weakness tearing at him, the tough, competent cold-storage agent consumed by an irrational bourgeois jealousy.

Neither of them spoke for a while. He watched her slip into a silk kimono, deep blue with a golden dragon on the back.

'Let me fix you something to eat before you go out,' she offered in an attempt to end the argument.

But the kimono rekindled his rage. It was nothing she could have afforded to buy for herself.

He caught her wrist and forced her down across the bed. 'You're more in character on your back than in the kitchen.'

'Yes? You must know, you know so much. Are you going to screw me or beat me? Have you decided yet? Or would it make you late for your official business?'

Her scorn made him feel foolish and clumsy. He released her. 'Monika, I – '

'Gottfried Ritter died last night.'

'What?'

'I saw Gottfried die last night. In the Gestapo cellars. Now will you leave me alone?'

Jaeger's face had become masklike. He realised he was holding his breath. He was no longer the husband irrationally jealous of the beautiful wife he hardly knew, the lithe blonde stranger who had learned to make love like a sexual dialectic.

He remembered the briefing on Kropotkin Square in Moscow.

In complete control of himself, he began his contrite apology.

Now in the *lokal* on Prenzlauerstrasse in Berlin-East he heard Brewmaster Drunkenpolz say: ' . . . ruptured eardrums, both of them. What kept you out?'

'Essential industry,' Jaeger said.

The red-faced Alte Kämpfer had stopped singing. They banged their litre steins on the bar, and the barman slid them across and under the taps to refill them. Drunkenpolz turned slowly and Jaeger saw Rambow standing there behind him. The weasel-faced little man jerked a thumb towards the door and when Drunkenpolz reached into his pocket said, 'I'll take care of that. Get going. You're already late.'

After the brewmaster left, Rambow said: 'I didn't know you knew him.'

'I don't. Who is he?'

'Anton Saeftkow's muscle. I once saw him get under a piano and lift it on his back. A concert grand.' Rambow ordered a small beer.

'It's all set?' Jaeger asked.

Rambow looked insulted. 'I'm here, friend.' He sipped beer and made a face. 'Not that I'm wild about it. Saeftkow and Jacob, both of them. Jesus.'

'What about Esser?' Jaeger asked.

'What about him?'

'Is he coming alone?'

'I didn't ask him and he didn't tell me.'

Jaeger shrugged. Esser himself would be enough.

Rambow finished his beer. 'I'd better get a move on. Saeftkow's not taking any chances. He won't go in there without me.'

'Why you?'

'He trusts me,' Rambow said.

The two officers marched along the eastern side of Horst Wesselplatz and from there along Prenzlauerstrasse to the cemetery, where they turned their steps north along the wall, jackboots ringing on the pavement.

By day, except for one remarkable distinguishing feature, it would have been somewhat difficult to recognise them as members of the feldgendarmerie, the military police. Field caps, field-grey tunics, iron grey breeches, jackboots – all were standard issue. Subtle distinctions like collar tabs and shoulder straps in feldgendarmerie orange, or the small police-style national emblem of eagle and swastika surrounded by a wreath of oak leaves sewn on the upper left sleeve, might have been missed by day. Even the silver-grey embroidered lettering that spelled out *feldgendarmerie* discreetly on the left cuff might have gone unnoticed.

The one remarkable feature was the gorget they wore. It was this nickel-plated accoutrement, the size and shape of half a dinner plate, suspended from a flat-linked chain around their necks to hang down over their chests, which prompted line troops to refer to the feldgendarmerie as chained dogs. If any doubt about their identity lingered, it was dispelled by the bold lettering of the word *feldgendarmerie* on this small ornamental breastplate.

Doubt, at night, was impossible. The lettering on the gorget, brushed with radioactive paint, glowed in the dark.

'That's the place, over there across the street,' one of the officers told the other after they had proceeded two blocks north of the cemetery.

Unlike other areas of the city, this section of Berlin-East north of the River Spree had suffered little air-raid damage. It was almost as if R.A.F. Bomber Command had magnanimously decided that the huge Friedrichshain and Bötzow breweries flanking the cemetery should, unlike the armaments plants further west, continue full production. Smoke from the breweries' great stacks hung in the night air, smelling heavily of malt.

The block which the officers had reached, however, contained some ruins, and the building pointed out by the first feldgendarmerie officer had received one of those freak hits that sheared off its front wall while apparently leaving the structure intact. In the moonlight it looked like a stage set for a play that Bertolt Brecht might have written.

'Two advantages,' said the first officer when he heard the surprise in his companion's voice. 'It's been condemned as unsafe, so there won't be any squatters. And it was hit recently enough so that the former tenants haven't removed all their stuff yet.'

'What's the advantage of that?' asked the second feldgendarmerie officer, who was the taller of the two and whose orange collar tabs bore the two stripes of a captain.

'Looting is punishable by death,' the lieutenant explained. 'People have learned to keep clear of a recent ruin . . . Here comes Sepp.'

A BMW 326 staff car with a single Notek blackout headlight mounted on the left front fender came slowly along the street, went by, turned out of view along Prenzlauerstrasse.

The lieutenant looked at the luminous dial of his watch. 'Right on time.'

The BMW 326 would, and did, again pass the small apartment building with the sheared-off front five minutes later. By then the two feldgendarmerie officers were approaching it from the other direction.

'What time is it?'

'12.45.'

'He's been in there a long time.'

The lieutenant shrugged. 'They have a lot to talk about.'

The two officers reached the north-eastern corner of the cemetery.

'Not according to your colonel.'

'Maybe he's right. Maybe it is risky.'

'But necessary?'

'*I* think so,' said the lieutenant.

'And bringing me? I didn't think he'd go for that.'

The lieutenant laughed shortly. 'Why not? Since you're here he might as well get some use out of you.'

From a heap of rubble that once had been a building Jaeger watched the two officers march by on the opposite side of the street, the lettering on their gorgets glowing eerily. They had passed the building with the sheared-off front a second time and were now heading back. It was no coincidence.

The BMW staff car had been no coincidence either.

Jaeger knew that the feldgendarmerie patrolled neighbourhoods in an apparently random nightly pattern. But the odds were very long against this place and this time being part of that pattern.

Rambow had said nothing about the military police. Rambow, as far as Jaeger knew, would have no contact with them. Yet they had made their appearance on the scene before the Gestapo.

Jaeger looked at his watch. Ten minutes before one.

Although the arrival on the scene of the feldgendarmerie worried him, the fact that the Gestapo had not yet arrived had the opposite effect. The longer the meeting lasted, the better. He knew Saeftkow and Jacob from the old days. Given enough time they would win Julius Esser's confidence; they were Party professionals who had, in the years before Hitler, learned how to deal with Social Democrats. Part of the trick was letting a man like Esser convince them of the need for a united Left. They would have done that by now. Esser might hold back a few facts, but he would tell them enough.

It was quite possible that Esser had marching powder, in a hollowed tooth perhaps, quite possible that after their arrest Esser would kill himself rather than face the Gestapo cellars.

It was unlikely that Saeftkow and Jacob would. For Communists in Berlin in 1944 survival was everything – even survival in Plötzensee Prison or a concentration camp. The war wouldn't last for ever and that the Red Army would reach Berlin before the Anglo-Americans seemed certain.

Besides, Saeftkow and Jacob would not be betraying their own people. They would only be betraying the reactionary elements represented by the Social Democrat Julius Esser.

They would talk at once.

Jaeger heard a car. He expected the BMW but this was a heavier vehicle, its engine louder. It came into view, a Horch 850 limousine with spare wheel mounted at the front of the running board.

Unless Jaeger was mistaken, a car from the Prinz Albrechtstrasse motor pool. The big eight-cylinder Horch was much favoured by the Gestapo.

The danger, of course, was not that Saeftkow and Jacob would themselves harm Julius Esser, nor that the intermediary Rambow would, nor even that Esser would reveal more than necessary. The danger was that Saeftkow or Jacob, or more likely Rambow, was a Gestapo informer.

That had been Stauffenberg's original objection to the meeting and it still made sense to Haller. Stauffenberg himself made sense to Haller, and he had to keep reminding himself that their instant and intense dislike of each other signified nothing beyond the dislike itself. Besides, had he been in Stauffenberg's shoes he would have been as mistrustful of the American agent as Stauffenberg was.

His eager acceptance by the others had simplified his assignment in practical terms but complicated it emotionally.

The reverse was true in the case of Stauffenberg.

Stauffenberg was the driving force behind the conspiracy, obviously. Stauffenberg alone might make its betrayal necessary. If he thought only in terms of Stauffenberg, it was easy. It would be no hardship to betray an arrogant staff officer like Graf von Stauffenberg. It was, after all, the Prussian militarism he epitomised that was the enemy. That, and Nazi barbarism.

And the others? He would try not to think about them. Stauffenberg was a professional and so was he.

Haller even explored the possibility, Byzantine though it was, that Stauffenberg, suspecting Rambow to be a Gestapo V-man, might have sent him with Heydi on purpose.

To let him have a good look at betrayal before he was guilty of it himself.

But no, that was too Byzantine, even for Graf von Stauffenberg.

Or was it? Sending Haller into Berlin in the first place hadn't been too Byzantine for Baker Street, after all.

'Here comes Sepp again,' Heydi said.

Haller looked, and grasped the German's arm, turning him so that the glowing letters on their gorgets would not be seen from the street.

It wasn't the BMW coming back. It was a larger car, engine switched off suddenly, coasting silently to the kerb before the bombed-out building, its rear door opening and three men emerging on the run.

The only one who might give them any trouble on the drive back to the Prinz Albrechtstrasse in the big Horch limousine, Gestapo Oberwachtmeister Egon Kraske decided five minutes later, was the big hulking brute with the tattooed arms. Kraske dismissed the others as a trio of intellectuals; they would go like baggage.

When they reached the pavement Oberwachtmeister Kraske gave a sign to Lutze, who instantly brought his Luger down hard on the hulking brute's skull, caught him under the arms as he collapsed, and dragged him towards the Horch where the driver Dieckhoff helped bundle him inside. Like the rest of the operation this went without a hitch. Kraske was proud of his squad; they had an almost instinctive response to orders. Sometimes Lutze even seemed to anticipate Kraske's thoughts.

Thus it was Lutze who said '*scheiss*' under his breath – it was precisely what Kraske was thinking – when they saw the two chained dogs striding across the street, the glowing letters on their gorgets heralding them.

Kraske had already had one run-in with the feldgendarmerie. He found himself wishing, not for the first time, that there wasn't such a multiplicity of law-enforcement agencies in the Reich, their jurisdictions overlapping, their prerogatives jealously defended, their rights insisted on. Most deferred to the Gestapo, a commendable deference from Kraske's viewpoint. But try telling that to the Security Department with their own little fiefdom inside the Prinz Albrechtstrasse or to Goering's special Luftwaffe police or to the S.S. Death's Head units, just to name a few.

Or to these chained dogs now approaching.

'You will all remain perfectly still!' the taller of them ordered. 'Which one of you is Esser? Hurry, speak up, we don't have all night.'

The shorter feldgendarmerie officer covered the group near the Horch with an Erma-38 sub-machine gun held at the level of his hip. Lutze said '*scheiss*' under his breath again; it was again what Oberwachtmeister Kraske was thinking. But Kraske was also thinking of his previous run-in with the chained dogs. The jurisdiction in that instance had been complicated, the feldgendarmerie had ultimately prevailed, and Kraske had received a severe reprimand from his superior officer. He said now: 'Herr Hauptmann, I'm certain we can arrive at – '

'Are you Esser?' the captain demanded. 'You're under arrest.'

From the pocket of his tunic he drew a paper and unfolded it. He read from the warrant in a bored monotone the date and time of issue, the place – it was the Bendlerstrasse, no less – and the charge, something about black market dealings with the enlisted men's canteen.

Kraske laughed, engagingly, he hoped. 'So, a black marketeer too,' he said. 'I'm hardly surprised.' He drew himself to his full height – Kraske was not a big man – and stiffly executed the German greeting as he clicked his heels and said: 'Heil Hitler! Gestapo Oberwachtmeister Kraske at your service, Herr Hauptmann.'

The captain returned a far lazier version of the greeting and a far more casual 'Heil Hitler,' then asked: 'What are you doing here?'

'R.S.H.A. Bureau IV Ia flying squad!' barked Kraske.

The captain gave him a long scathing look. 'Section Ia? What is this, anyway? Esser's no Marxist.'

'As to that I wouldn't know,' said Kraske. 'Our orders are to arrest the lot of them.'

'You wouldn't know. Naturally,' the captain said sarcastically. He held out his hand. 'Your identification, sergeant, if you please.'

Oberwachtmeister Kraske stared for an instant at the letters glowing in the dark, then produced his black leather Gestapo disc. The captain gave it the briefest of glances and made an irritable brushing motion with his hand. Kraske returned the disc to his pocket; the lieutenant shouldered his submachine gun.

'Why are you here?' the captain asked, his tone of voice indicating that no reason could possibly be satisfactory.

'Illegal assembly,' said Kraske promptly.

The captain laughed, an ugly sound laden with menace. 'No doubt to plan the bombing of the Prinz Albrechtstrasse.'

'As to that,' Kraske replied with pompous uncertainty, 'I wouldn't know. My orders are to take them in.'

At that moment the BMW staff car came along the street, its single headlight spilling a faint glow on the pavement. The captain waved his arm and the staff car drew up in front of the big Horch.

'At your orders, Herr Hauptmann,' a deep voice called from the car.

The captain told the driver to stand by. He sounded annoyed, and Kraske knew the annoyance was not directed at the driver but at him. The captain clearly felt Oberwachtmeister Kraske had already taken too much of his time.

Kraske unhappily recalled a clerk he knew in the R.S.H.A. administrative section, Bureau I, telling him that a prejudicial account of his previous run-in with the chained dogs had been inserted in his personnel file.

'Well then,' the captain said, 'do your duty, sergeant. Take them in. All except this man Esser, of course.'

'My orders are to take all of them in.'

'I countermand those orders, sergeant,' said the captain, returning to his earlier, bored tone of voice.

Naturally, a captain of feldgendarmerie had no authority to countermand orders given to Kraske at the Prinz Albrechtstrasse. But he *was* an officer, and obviously a Prussian. The sergeant licked his lips and did some quick thinking. He could invite the captain back to the Prinz Albrechtstrasse, of course, to unsnarl the jurisdictional dispute; or he could volunteer to take his prisoners to the Bendlerstrasse to do the same. On his other run-in with the feldgendarmerie he had tried the former approach.

That had worked so poorly he would likely spend the rest of his career as an Oberwachtmeister.

'And while we're at it,' said the captain, 'let me have a look at your warrant for Esser's arrest.'

Kraske glanced at Lutze, who was studying the pavement. 'The Herr Hauptmann will understand that in such cases,' Kraske said, 'the warrant does not specifically name – '

The Herr Hauptmann cut him off with that brushing motion of his hand again. 'Yes, yes, all right, you make take the others, then. We have no objection to that, have we, Herr Oberleutnant?'

'No, sir,' said the lieutenant.

'Who are they, while we're at it?' the captain asked. He hardly sounded interested.

'Who *are* they?' Kraske repeated.

'The others,' the captain told him with a sigh.

'As to that,' Kraske said in his most pompous and insecure voice, 'I wouldn't know.'

The captain exchanged a significant look with the lieutenant. It seemed to say: spare me these non-commissioned idiots.

'It is an open warrant, Herr Hauptmann,' Kraske explained. 'A very normal sort of warrant in such a . . . '

'Show it to me,' snapped the captain, and Kraske said:

'Unterwachtmeister Lutze, you will show the Herr Hauptmann the warrant.'

Lutze did so, but the captain handed it back without bothering to read it.

'Now, which one is Esser?'

There was no reply and the captain raised his voice: 'Julius Esser will identify himself!'

One of the prisoners shuffled forward and said, his voice barely audible: 'I am Esser.'

'In the car – move!'

Esser looked first at the captain, then at Oberwachtmeister Kraske, as if trying to determine which of them might let him survive the night. He edged closer to Kraske.

'I said, in the car!' The captain shoved him and Esser stumbled towards the staff car, caught his balance, and looked back hopefully at Kraske. Kraske looked at Lutze, who shrugged.

The captain addressed Kraske: 'Your name again, sergeant?'

'Oberwachtmeister Egon Kraske, Herr Hauptmann.' Kraske clicked his heels.

'Section Ia, is it? You are to be commended, sergeant, and I will in fact mention it to the appropriate authorities.'

By then Esser was in the staff car. The lieutenant, a thumb hooking the strap of his sub-machine gun, joined him on the rear seat.

Kraske heard the lieutenant say: 'One move, you war-profiteering son of a bitch, and I'll spill your guts all over the upholstery.'

The driver emerged and hurried around the BMW to open the front passenger door for the captain, who turned his back on Kraske and took the half dozen steps to the car, where he turned and said 'Heil Hitler' with a wave of his arm.

'Heil Hitler,' said Oberwachtmeister Kraske.

Jaeger watched the BMW staff car drive off at a sedate speed, as if its occupants were out for the night air and had no particular destination.

For the first several seconds Jaeger should have been able to tell how far the departing car had driven, thanks to its *Nachtmarschgerät* tail-lights. Developed first for night convoy traffic, they soon proved their value in blacked-out cities and became standard issue on all Wehrmacht vehicles. The apparatus consisted of two pairs of square lights, sufficiently dim for blackout purposes and so spaced that at distances up to 25 metres all four squares were distinct, at 25 to 50 metres they showed as two red rectangles, beyond 50 metres as one long bar of red.

But Jaeger could not ascertain how far the BMW had gone because the driver had switched off the apparatus just as the car started to move. Thus the rear licence plate, its large letters and digits centred below the four squares of light, could not be seen.

And even that didn't seem to disturb the Gestapists, now loading Saeftkow and Jacob into the Horch. Idiots! Jaeger thought.

The two men masquerading as feldgendarmerie officers were Army, of course – otherwise how would the equipment have been available to them? They had handled themselves impressively, the captain especially. Jaeger recalled how his voice had slid so easily from a contempt that bordered on pity to an arrogance that did not quite descend to caricature.

Jaeger watched the Horch limousine pull away. Despite Esser's escape the night had not been a failure. A lot would depend on how much Saeftkow and Jacob had managed to pry from him and Jaeger assumed it would have been enough.

He could consider the first part of his mission accomplished.

For a troubled moment he wondered if Comrade Cell had chosen him for the next part more because of Monika's position at the Prinz Albrechtstrasse than for Jaeger's own dedication and skills. Except for Monika, Jaeger might be rotting in a P.O.W. camp somewhere east of Moscow right now.

Instead of gratitude he felt resentment. Was that another form of jealousy? Irritably, he brushed the thought from his mind.

At least he had a weapon he could use at the Prinz Albrechtstrasse now.

On a scrap of paper he scrawled *WH–IA–2473*. The WH was the Wehrmacht-Army designation, IA signified Prussia and specifically Berlin, 2473 was the matriculation number. The series of letters and digits was the licence number of the BMW staff car.

Jaeger heard a sound, cautious footsteps; saw a figure coming slowly along the street. He allowed Rambow to come abreast of him and then stepped suddenly into view.

'Jesus!' Rambow swore. 'You scared the hell out of me.' He waited, but Jaeger said nothing. Rambow asked: 'What about the fifteen hundred marks?'

'How much do you get from the Gestapo?' Jaeger asked.

'That has nothing to do with our agreement.'

'I was just curious,' Jaeger said.

'They don't pay me a goddamn thing,' Rambow told him. Jaeger could believe that. Rambow's release from Oranienburg was payment enough. What Rambow's co-operation with the Gestapo bought was the rest of his life.

'When do I get the money?'

'You don't think I carried it on me tonight, do you?'

'Then when?' Rambow persisted.

'I'm afraid it won't be fifteen hundred the way things turned out,' Jaeger told him.

'What are you trying to pull on me?'

'What are *you* trying to pull? You gave them your own people, not Esser. Esser was the important one.'

'I couldn't help that,' Rambow whined. 'You saw what happened, didn't you?'

Jaeger nodded reluctantly. 'The feldgendarmerie – a hell of a coincidence, wasn't it? Your bad luck. You'll get a thousand.'

Rambow laughed. He suddenly seemed to feel better about things. 'Coincidence, my arse,' he said. 'What could the feldgendarmerie want with a has-been politician like Esser?'

'I don't know,' Jaeger admitted after a brief silence in which he seemed to consider the question.

'You disappoint me,' Rambow said. 'They were ersatz.'

Again Jaeger waited a beat. 'Esser's people?'

'Well what do you think? All of a sudden a nobody like Julius Esser brings the army out.'

'I thought you said they were ersatz.'

'Ersatz chained dogs, sure. But still army.' Rambow had now become condescending. 'You don't think civilians could get hold of those gorgets, not to mention a staff car, do you?'

'No, that's true,' Jaeger admitted.

'I could deliver them to the Prinz Albrechtstrasse cellars,' Rambow said. 'Is that worth anything to you?'

'Could be.' Jaeger's voice was thoughtful.

Rambow said: 'I figure it's worth another thousand. At least.'

'Maybe. How would you go about doing it?'

'Somebody checked that staff car out of a motor pool somewhere in Berlin,' Rambow told him. 'I've got the licence number, that's how.'

The question of the timing of Rambow's death, which Jaeger had put out of his mind for the time being, had now been answered by Rambow himself.

As a loose end, as someone who could identify Jaeger by sight, Rambow had to be eliminated eventually. But now he could also finger whoever had signed out the BMW staff car. Jaeger wanted to be the only one who could do that.

Rambow saw the motion of Jaeger's hand and brought his own hand down. He was still reaching for the Walther 7.65 PPK tucked into one side of his belt when Jaeger drove his hand hard at the V-man's belly.

It was no mere blow of Jaeger's fist. The three-inch blade of the knife slipped in and ripped upward, then slashed sideways right and left under Rambow's rib cage.

Rambow died less than ten seconds after Jaeger had decided to kill him.

Part Two

THIRD ENCOUNTER

Ten

We missed Friday the 13th by one day that July of 1944, but as it turned out Thursday the 13th was plenty bad enough.

Milt Green talking – this is where I do my second bit part, more or less flat on my back and not liking it. The place was called University College Hospital, where I had the second bed from the window on the north side of the ward, giving me a view of dirty grey sky above what they told me would be Grafton Street if I could see it.

Thursday the 13th was my sixth day there counting the previous Saturday when they brought me in, bleeding all over the ambulance and the emergency room or casualty ward or whatever they call it in London, and starting to bleed again when they put me prematurely on a stretcher for the trip upstairs. A nursing sister named Eunice fed this to me piecemeal when I began showing interest in things, which was Monday. Mostly I began showing an interest in Eunice, a good healthy sign of my eventual recovery.

Sister Eunice had flaxen hair and eyes like blue saucers. Twenty-five, maybe, with one of those soft creamy complexions they get from all that mist in Cornwall, where Sister Eunice came from. The piecemeal intelligence was that my left arm, in plaster from shoulder to palm, was broken in three places, that my three broken ribs had caused some lung haemorrhaging, and that my face, victim of various bruises, contusions and lacerations, would eventually assume its original appearance, whether for good or bad Sister Eunice refused to say. She had a nice brisk manner, a nice brisk bosom and behind, and a way of making every man in the ward – an even dozen of us – think she made her rounds just to see him. The rest of them, of course, were all wet on that score.

After lunch on Thursday Sister Eunice told me: 'You had a visitor yesterday.'

'No I didn't,' I said.

'I mean you might have done. If they'd permitted it.'

'Male or female?' I asked.

'Female,' said Sister Eunice.

There were a few girls in London who I liked to think would be if not crushed at least disturbed by my disappearance.

'Did she have a name?' I asked.

'I rather imagine she did. Don't most people?'

'Funny. Very funny,' I said.

'Open,' said Sister Eunice and popped a thermometer into my mouth, thus terminating my end of the conversation, or trying to.

'She said she'd return today.'

'Will they let her come up?' I asked.

'Put that thermometer back, Major Green,' said Sister Eunice. 'Of course they will. Otherwise, why would she bother to come back? *I* rather think it's too soon.'

'You're jealous,' I said.

'The thermometer,' she said.

I put it back and mumbled something around it.

Sister Eunice blushed prettily. 'Major Green!' she said, but she wasn't really offended.

I mumbled something else.

Sister Eunice's saucer eyes got saucy. 'Well, by next week they just might give your bed to someone who really needs it. Let's wait and see, shall we?'

We were both half serious, and half was enough for now. Sister Eunice removed the thermometer.

I spent the next couple of hours as a captive radio audience. The bed closest to the window was occupied by a retired schoolteacher from Liverpool named Mr Musgrove, and Mr Musgrove had a small radio which he played whenever he was awake. Mr Musgrove was the victim of an earlier flying bomb attack that had hit Marylebone while he was visiting his daughter there. Mr Musgrove had a smashed pelvis and was slightly hard of hearing. The radio kept blatting away. Sister Eunice said it was mildly against the regs, which meant it was all right with staff unless any of the rest of us complained.

I suffered in silence. Mr Musgrove's favourite BBC news

reader was Bruce Belfrage, but he'd listen to Howland or Priestley too. Mr Musgrove was a great listener to the news. I wanted to get away from it.

'Were you aware,' he asked me once, 'that they read in evening dress?'

'Who?' I asked.

'Belfrage and the rest.'

'What for?' I asked. 'Nobody can see them.'

'That is how things are done,' said Mr Musgrove.

Mr Musgrove also liked a radio comic named Tommy Handley, a fellow Liverpudlian with one of those friendly Midlands voices, and a character called Colonel Chinstrap who always brought the house, or at least Mr Musgrove, down when he said, 'I don't mind if I do,' in response to the offer of a drink.

Mr Musgrove would laugh every time and wheeze and say, 'It's original with him, you know. "I don't mind if I do." ' And again the laugh and the wheeze.

I wouldn't have minded a drink myself. Stuck in a hospital bed without any prospect of one, I didn't find Colonel Chinstrap's catch line much to my liking.

The bed to my right was occupied by a grizzled docker with a bitter face named Peters who had caught it when a buzz bomb dropped on the Upper Pool docks. They'd amputated his right leg at the hip and he lay there most days staring sullenly up at the ceiling. I made a try or two at talking with him but it was no good. I might as well have been another radio he couldn't help listening to.

I drifted off to sleep that Thursday afternoon until teatime. They don't let you sleep then, not at University College Hospital. Tea is part of the treatment, like it or not. It was lousy tea.

I woke to the rattle of crockery and the sound of voices, Mr Musgrove's earnest reedy one and another I didn't recognise. Then I realised it was the docker, Peters.

When the tea lady wheeled her cart down to our end of the ward they became silent.

'Must I?' I asked the tea lady. It was our daily routine; I think she looked forward to it.

'There's a good boy. One or two?'

She meant sugar.

'None,' I said.

'Milk?'

'Nope. Black as the La Brea Tar Pits.'

That always broke her up. It must have sounded very exotic. The La Brea Tar Pits, for the record, are in California, they contain dinosaur bones, and I've never been within a thousand miles of them.

After she returned for the crockery, Mr Musgrove immediately resumed his conversation with Peters, talking across me. For once the radio was off. I settled back and shut my eyes and heard the reedy sound of Mr Musgrove's voice and Peters's deep bass drifting past me to join the sound of traffic outside the window.

Then suddenly I tuned in.

'You really ought to read it, my dear fellow,' Mr Musgrove was saying.

'I ain't much for reading,' Peters said.

'Nevertheless, remember the name. *Truth.* And truth is what it prints. People like Sir Ernest Benn.'

'I heard of Benn,' said Peters. 'He's the bloke what knows who got us into this war.'

'Precisely,' wheezed Mr Musgrove.

There was a silence. Then Mr Musgrove said: 'One mustn't underestimate them. They're clever.

'Clever, my arse,' said Peters. 'Filthy little buggers.'

'Oh, but they *are* clever. Got their hands into everything, haven't they? Clothing, food, furniture, tobacco. The black market, not that I patronise it, of course. But just you try buying anything on the black market and – '

'Where would I get the bloody money?' Peters interrupted bitterly.

' – you'd see what I mean. The East End. One finds them concentrated there, of course. They're clannish. Always have been, no matter where you find them. No use for anyone else. The ghetto is a misconception, you know. No one forces them into it. It's their own choosing. Sir Ernest Benn says – '

'Dirty buggers,' Peters said.

'One has only to read the casualty lists,' said Mr Musgrove. 'One never sees their sort of names there, does one?'

Peters grunted sullenly.

'One hesitates to say,' Mr Musgrove said, 'that Hitler is right, but in this one instance I'm inclined to wonder. *Not* that I favour genocide, you understand.'

'What the bloody hell is that?' Peters asked.

'But they really must be dealt with once and for all,' said Mr Musgrove, ignoring the question. 'They have altogether too much power. International Communism, Wall Street – and that is only the tip of the iceberg, dear me, yes . . .'

I lay there, my eyes shut, listening, disbelieving. I wasn't dumb enough to think that old Adolf had invented anti-Semitism all by himself, and I'd bumped into my share of it here and there in England, not to mention the States. But here they were, both of them victims of Nazi bombs, mouthing the straight *Mein Kampf* line, Peters with the sullen complacency of an uneducated bigot and Mr Musgrove with the casually vicious prejudice of a failed intellectual.

And me pretending to sleep and telling myself with despair that this war wasn't going to solve anything.

The worst part of it was that otherwise Mr Musgrove was a pretty nice old gent.

'Hello.'

It was a soft contralto voice, somewhat husky. I hadn't heard her footsteps, but I noticed that Mr Musgrove and Peters had stopped talking.

'Major Green? Major Milt Green?' she said, soft enough not to wake me if I was asleep. I opened my eyes.

Rounding the bend towards thirty, I thought. Hair light brown and sort of curled in at the level of her shoulders. Pretty face, pink-cheeked, a dimple in the chin, no make-up. Below that, a very dark grey dress padded at the shoulders and not shaped to the waist. This year's style, the lean military look. She was a bit too plump to carry it off.

The two-buck word for the kind of smile she showed when I opened my eyes is tremulous. I did not smile back. I was still thinking of Mr Musgrove and Peters. I must have looked like hell, bristling at her through black and blue marks fading to a rich yellow brown and a week's beard stubble.

'You *are* Major Green?'

'If its about why I'm A.W.O.L., miss, honest, I can explain,' I cracked. I was going to try on a grin when she said:

'I'm Gillian Bennett.'

No grin, no comment. Nothing. I just waited. I'd asked Sister Eunice about Harry Bennett. They hadn't got him here. It was possible he'd gone to a nearby hospital, maybe the Middlesex, in a different ambulance, but I didn't think so. I just had that feeling you get.

'Harry's dead.'

I said I was sorry. Nobody ever thought of the right words.

No matter what you say at a time like that, you wind up feeling inept.

'Less than two days after I got back from America,' Gillian Bennett said, no self-pity in her voice. It was just the statement of a fact that seemed to surprise her. 'We hadn't seen each other in four years, and I came back, and now he's dead.'

With the sort of voice you might use to wonder how come it's raining if the weather bureau said it was going to be sunny today.

'If there's anything I can do,' I offered. That was part of the formula, socially approved, but I felt stupid saying it. What the hell could I do, flat on my back, one wing broken in three places, and three broken ribs?

I measured my small portion of grief against Gillian Bennett's larger one and wished she hadn't come to see me.

'As a matter of fact there is,' she said in that soft voice. Mr Musgrove had given up trying to eavesdrop on us. He fiddled with his radio and found Ann Shelton singing *Lili Marlene.* 'May I sit down?'

Ordinarily I like *Lili Marlene*, bathos and all. Ever since the Eighth Army brought it back from North Africa, the Tommies and G.I.s owned it as much as any German *schütze.* But coming after Mr Musgrove's anti-Semitic diatribe it bothered me. When I said, 'Yeah, sure, sit,' my voice was less than inviting.

Gillian's antennae were out enough so that she stiffened a little, but she peeled off snow-white gloves and sat on the edge of the bed. 'Is this all right?' Her hands were small and pale.

'Yeah, sure. Now what's it all about?' I asked. That came out somewhat better but still didn't sound like I was overflowing with sympathy. The mattress sagged to the right, where Gillian was sitting. A single knife-point of pain nicked my taped ribs to remind me they were broken.

'It's hard to explain,' Gillian said, sounding more American than British. 'No matter how I try to explain it, it's going to sound foolish. He's dead, after all. But maybe that's why.'

'Well, why don't we try it out?' I suggested.

A shade irritably? Maybe. Mr Musgrove was humming along with Ann Shelton in that reedy voice of his.

'Last Friday night, or early Saturday morning actually, he phoned you. At least I assume it was you he phoned,' she said quite calmly, 'because the call resulted in an appointment with you on Saturday.'

'It was me he phoned,' I admitted.

'He was excited about it in the morning. Just a cup of coffee and he was off. Harry's like a bulldog when he gets his teeth into something.'

She said that in the present tense. Our eyes met; hers filmed over, dark brown honest eyes on the brink of tears.

'Why did Harry die?' she asked me.

There is no answer to that question, or other questions like: why Harry instead of me? Or, why did we enter Grosvenor Square exactly when we did? Or, wouldn't Harry still be alive if a taxi happened to be outside his club after lunch? Or, why did that particular buzz bomb expend its fuel supply precisely where it did?

You can go nuts asking questions like that.

She said: 'That isn't what I meant to say at all,' and began to cry.

I said there-there and went pat-pat to her hand, and saw Mr Musgrove watching us again. I almost wished Sister Eunice would come by on her rounds and tell her she was not supposed to upset the patient.

She blew her nose, a forceful unladylike honk in a wisp of lacy handkerchief. 'What did Harry want?' she said. 'When he called you. When you had lunch with him.'

'We were working on – a project together,' I said vaguely. 'Harry had some ideas on the subject.'

'Something was bothering him.' Those honest brown eyes looked at me and she asked: 'There was something he wanted to do, wasn't there?'

'Who knows what he wanted to do about it?' I asked irritably.

That made me feel guilty. Until then I never realised you could tell a lie by asking a question.

I knew, all right.

'About what?' she asked quickly.

Four years apart was a long time. I had no idea if she knew that Harry worked for Baker Street. 'I'm terribly sorry, Mrs Bennett,' I said a bit pompously, 'but Harry worked for one of those organisations that came under your Official Secrets Act.'

While she was mulling that over she rummaged in her large black purse and came up with a flat manila envelope. From that she withdrew a photograph and handed it to me.

'Do you know who this man is?' she asked.

'Where'd you get that?' I asked right back.

It was an eight-by-ten of Dick Haller, of course.

*

She told me about the two planeloads of passengers in Lisbon and Harry showing her Dick Haller's picture.

'Whoever he is,' she said, 'I know this much. He went to Germany a week ago, and Harry had something to do with that. And he didn't like it one little bit.'

I kept looking at Dick Haller's picture.

'He's a US Army officer,' Gillian said.

I returned the glossy photograph to her and said nothing.

'Major Green, please don't treat me like a child. You know who he is, don't you?'

'Yes, I know who he is.'

'And you know why he was sent in, don't you?'

'I can't answer that. I'm sorry.'

'But Harry didn't go for it.' She was sounding American again. 'Is the man in the picture going to die? Is that what was bothering Harry? He isn't dead already, is he?'

That thought seemed to alarm her.

'You told me where the plane was going, Mrs Bennett. It was going to Berlin. How would I know if he's still alive?'

'Was he a friend of Harry's?'

I said more than I should have. 'He's a friend of mine.'

'What did Harry want to do that was so important he died for it?'

'I wouldn't attach any cause and effect to that, Mrs Bennett.'

'You wouldn't. I do. Because if Harry hadn't got so worked up that he had to see you he'd be alive right now.'

It was like one of those questions you couldn't ask without driving yourself nuts.

'Does it need doing, what he wanted to do?'

I remembered approaching Grosvenor Square with Harry last Saturday still not decided about seeing that cryptographer I knew.

For a crazy moment I thought that Harry dead was luckier than Dick Haller alive.

Nobody should be ordered to make the kind of decision Dick Haller had to make.

That led to a crazier thought. Could I get through to Allen Dulles, the O.S.S. chief in Bern, if I tried? Or was it already too late?

'Can *you* do it, Major Green?' Gillian asked.

'What?'

'Can you do what Harry wanted to do before he died? Can you finish it for him?'

That was why she'd come to see me. That was what was

going to sound foolish no matter how she tried to explain it.

If we do it, I recalled asking Harry, *what happens to Dick Haller?*

Mr Musgrove's radio squawked and a flat calm BBC voice said that an unknown number of buzz bombs had got past the Spitfires off the coast and were streaking towards London through Bomb Alley over Kent and Sussex.

Outside, the siren on Tottenham Court Road began to wail, and in a few minutes we could hear distant thuds, none of them close enough to rattle the windows.

'There's nothing I can do to help you,' I told Gillian Bennett.

She was polite. Hoped I'd feel better. Sorry she'd been so much trouble. Trite phrases to keep her disappointment and anger under control.

She went. The minute she was gone I wished she was still there. Sister Eunice came.

'Argument?' she asked.

'No. Why?'

'You look perfectly dreadful. You shan't be seeing her again, I suppose?'

'Yes, I will,' I said. I had to see her again.

When Sister Eunice wandered off to the far end of the ward Mr Musgrove spoke to me.

'Lovely girl,' he said.

'Who, Sister Eunice?'

'I meant your visitor.'

I nodded. He cleared his throat and wheezed: 'Tell me, have you ever heard of a magazine called *Truth*?'

I just looked at him for five seconds. 'Tell me,' I said then, 'can a son of a bitch like you manage to lie there in bed and still go fuck himself?'

And I stared at the ceiling and wondered what Dick Haller was doing right at that moment.

Eleven

Haller was waiting for Elisabeth at a boulevard café on Kurfürstendamm across the street from the U.F.A. Palace theatre. The marquee advertised *Request Concert* and on the enormous billboard above the rotunda he could see, three times life size, a soldier in field-grey playing the organ in a bombed-out church. A crowd of shabbily dressed Berliners milled on the pavement waiting to enter the theatre. Pedestrians plodded listlessly through the heat of the afternoon along the broad, smashed street, its shattered shop windows boarded over, one building in five a gutted ruin. A double-decker bus, its once bright red paint rusted and grime-covered, lumbered around a bomb crater and stopped near the corner puffing like a fat man who has just run an obstacle course. A dozen or so passengers pushed their way aboard through an equal number struggling to leave the bus. Elisabeth was not among them.

The small tables were jammed together in the shadow of the awning outside the café, crowded with Berliners who had survived the last R.A.F. raid and were trying not to think about the next.

On the corner where the bus had stopped stood a concrete pillar, its four silent loudspeakers brooding over the scene. The café patrons glanced at it frequently, fearfully, their loud garrulous talk and sudden bursts of nervous laughter wartime Berlin ersatz for conviviality.

'Another weissbier?' asked the waiter, an old man in a wrinkled mess jacket soaked through with sweat.

Heller looked up indifferently. 'All right, Reinhard. Why not?' he said.

The old man passed a damp rag over the table. 'If the Herr Hauptmann will permit me, the young lady was already here. She stayed almost an hour and left just before the Herr Hauptmann arrived.'

'Why didn't you tell me sooner?' Haller asked the waiter irritably.

But it was himself he was angry with. What good would it have done to see each other one last time? It would only make it harder for himself, and for Elisabeth.

Already they had spent most of the time since Tuesday together. He could no longer convince himself, as he had at the beginning, that his motives were professional, that he needed Elisabeth as cover for his reconnaissance of Berlin. In three days he and Elisabeth had allowed themselves to become disturbingly dependent on each other. Through him, she was escaping vicariously from the intolerable prison of the city. And he was escaping from the intolerable pressure of his mission. The burdens of their private realities had bound them together in something more complex than love. And more reckless.

It should never have started, he knew, and this final rendezvous was only one more indefensible indulgence. He thought he had convinced himself not to come. Then he had come after all, an hour late.

'One doesn't intrude, Herr Hauptmann,' the waiter said diffidently.

'Did she leave a message?'

The old man shook his head. 'Perhaps I should not say this, sir. The young lady seemed to be crying when she left. Does the Herr Hauptmann return to the front soon?'

Haller did not reply. All that remained was a brief meeting with the contact man here in Berlin, a quick visit to the Swede to pick up his civilian clothing and Swiss papers, a flight to Lisbon, then the flying boat to England. By Saturday he could be making his report to Baker Street.

The tactical details of Valkyrie were sound, the leader as ruthless as he was brilliant. If it had been a Moon Squadron operation in Occupied France Haller would have confidently turned over to the conspirators the necessary materiel.

From his experience in France Haller had known he would need a wedge to gain entrance to the inner councils of the conspiracy. His Monday night heroics in the rescue of Julius Esser had supplied that wedge.

Even Stauffenberg's hostility to the American was muted after Heydebrand reported to him at the Bendlerstrasse Tuesday morning. Heydi recounted the events of the night before in elaborate detail and with evident self-satisfaction, almost smugness. The outcome justified his own faith in Richard Haller.

The one-eyed colonel was stuffing papers into an already bulging briefcase with his gloved left hand while his adjutant spoke. 'All right,' he said, 'where is this paragon of yours?'

Heydi cleared his throat. 'As a matter of fact he's down the hall in my office.'

'Naturally,' said Stauffenberg.

'Well, since we'll be in Zossen for the day, I thought . . .'

'You want him to see General Olbricht, don't you?'

The colonel and his adjutant would be leaving in a few minutes for Zossen, the secret Armed Forces High Command communications centre eighteen miles south of Berlin. The Guard Battalion of the *Grossdeutschland* Division, which would play a vital role in Berlin in the hours immediately following the assassination, had lost its commanding officer to the Western Front, and Stauffenberg had three good prospects to replace him – a tank commander who had distinguished himself at the battle of Caen, a lieutenant colonel of infantry who had served with Kesselring in Italy, and a major who had escaped from a Russian P.O.W. camp. A Personnel officer at Zossen knew all three men and Stauffenberg wanted to see him before interviewing them.

'General Olbricht could brief Richard, yes,' Heydi said.

'Richard, is it?' Staffenberg said, shaking his head. 'Very well, go get him.'

Moments later Stauffenberg told Haller: 'You'll be briefed on the tactical aspects of Valkyrie by the Deputy Commander of the Home Army in a few minutes, Herr Haller. And then of course you'll return to England and personally convince your good friend Winston Churchill to convince his good friend Franklin Roosevelt to scrap the Casablanca doctrine and offer us a nice plate of cream-covered peace terms after we succeed. Isn't that right?'

Haller's response to Stauffenberg's sarcasm was carefully worded. 'I see it this way, Herr Oberst. Your success will dissociate the military from the Nazis and provide a basis for the continued existence of Germany as a nation.'

'The alternative?' Stauffenberg asked.

'There's talk of turning Germany into an agrarian buffer zone between East and West after the war.'

Stauffenberg ignored that possibility. 'When will you leave here?'

Haller said he hoped he could leave by the end of the week. It was obvious that Stauffenberg hoped so too.

The colonel braced his briefcase with his right arm and buckled it awkwardly. 'I have one question for you, Herr Haller. If the Allies want Hitler dead, why haven't they tried to do the job themselves?'

Haller countered with the obvious. 'Why hasn't the Wehrmacht sent a commando team to kill Churchill?'

'Come now, you know what I mean. It's no secret that the Führer spends almost half his time at the Berghof above Berchtesgaden. Your air force has been pulverising the Reich, but I don't have to tell you not a single bomb has fallen on the Berghof. Strange, isn't it?'*

* Milt Green with a comment. Stauffenberg's assertion, with the suspicion it implied, is accurate. The Allies knew the exact location of Hitler's Alpine retreat above Berchtesgaden. They did not bomb it until 25 April 1945, more than ten months after the events narrated in these pages and less than three weeks before the war ended. And only then because they erroneously believed it to be the headquarters of the non-existent Nazi Alpine redoubt.

The phone buzzed and Heydi picked it up. 'Sepp's outside with the car,' he said.

'Tell him five minutes.' Stauffenberg crossed quickly to the sliding partition between his and General Olbricht's office.

Haller spent two hours with the Deputy Commander of the Home Army. From his Baker Street dossier Haller knew the bespectacled, fifty-six-year-old Olbricht to be a deeply religious man who had always abhorred the Nazis.

He was, as Haller had hoped, eager to talk.

Notwithstanding the suicidal nature of Stauffenberg's mission, Olbricht's role would be as crucial. It was Olbricht who would order the troops to march in Berlin.

For the first three or four hours after the assassination everything would depend on the Guard Battalion stationed here in the capital – fewer than a thousand men to hold the strongpoints until panzer units loyal to Stauffenberg could reach the city.

Loyal to Stauffenberg, that was the way General Olbricht put it. Once again Haller was reminded that the impatient, arrogant colonel was clearly in command.

Loyalty to Stauffenberg on the part of the Guard Battalion itself was out of the question. Its officers and non-coms were dedicated Nazis. But for a few hours they could be expected to follow orders coming down the chain of command from the Bendlerstrasse. Their fanatical allegiance to Führer and Fatherland would help the conspiracy.

General Olbricht was a professional, the *coup d'état* he outlined a professional plan with every chance of success. Traffic control at the Brandenburg Gate and Alexanderplatz, a cordoning off of the Wilhelmstrasse area, occupation of the main radio station in Charlottenburg, of the post and telegraph office . . .

It could all work, given luck.

Except for one unforeseen element. Except for Richard Haller himself.

Now on Thursday afternoon at the café across the street from the U.F.A. Palace theatre Haller knew with a sinking feeling that his evaluation was completed, his mission all but accomplished. It did not help to remind himself that Baker Street had experts who could see beyond the next few days, the next few weeks and months, to a Europe released at last from the murderous tyranny of German militarism. A German militarism that had made Adolf Hitler inevitable.

Richard Haller told himself he had no right to resist what he had to do.

Of what significance were a few more months in a war that had already killed thirty million people? Right and wrong, good and evil had been shelved for the duration. Short-sighted morality was absurd, as unprofessional as it was self-indulgent.

Orders were orders, weren't they?

Befehl ist Befehl. The words rang with a finality in German that they lacked in English.

He saw Elisabeth then, coming along the crowded Kurfürstendamm. She wore a bright yellow dress and her dark hair hung free, swinging as she walked. He was on his feet and hurrying towards her by the time she saw him and waved and began to run. She flung her arms around Haller's neck, her face flushed, her brown eyes shimmering with tears.

He held her close, breathing the fragrance of her hair. 'I thought I'd never see you again,' he said.

'I was afraid you'd already . . . gone away. Or that something terrible happened to you. I had to come back, darling. I had to.'

The old waiter Reinhard beamed approvingly at the Hauptmann of Grenadiers on leave in Berlin kissing his girl.

First rule of survival behind enemy lines: never allow yourself to become vulnerable.

Second rule, if you couldn't follow the first: never let the enemy know you have become vulnerable.

Richard Haller had learned, and taught, both rules in Occupied France. He knew that a mission's success depended on getting in, doing the job, and getting out fast.

By Tuesday noon Haller had all the facts he needed to pass judgement on Operation Valkyrie.

He then convinced himself that he had to explore the terrain.

In France a walk-through had occasionally been necessary when the Resistance Fighters were themselves strangers to the area. But if, as was usually the case, the Underground knew the region better than he did, such reconnaissance was superfluous to the mission and dangerous to himself. Haller evaluated personnel and planning, not geography. The need to evaluate the latter usually meant that the personnel were wrong for the job.

This, obviously, was not the case with Operation Valkyrie.

Still, Haller spent Tuesday afternoon and all day Wednesday exploring the terrain.

Another rule he had learned and taught in Occupied France: when you have to move openly among the enemy, make sure you blend with the scenery. Useful corollary: in city streets a couple are less obtrusive. The single man must always pretend business, the couple could be out for a harmless stroll. Early Tuesday afternoon Haller got General Beck's permission for Elisabeth to accompany him.

All absolutely professional, he assured himself.

Checkmark at the Brandenburg Gate. A motorised platoon of the Guard Battalion could indeed direct the flow of traffic along the East–West Axis.

Checkmark at Wilhelmstrasse. Two platoons could seal off the northern entrance to the government quarter.

Another checkmark at the Propaganda Ministry. Two platoons could guard its exits while Propaganda Minister and Berlin Gauleiter Joseph Goebbels, the only top Nazi virtually certain to be in the capital on Valkyrie Day, was placed under arrest.

Walking arm in arm, and then hand in hand, with Elisabeth. To blend with the scenery, of course.

Late Tuesday afternoon they found the café on Kurfürstendamm, two Kriegsmarine officers vacating a table in the shadow of the green awning the instant they arrived. The old waiter came over at once.

The wicker chairs stood side by side at the small table, facing the street. Haller looked at Elisabeth as she watched the flow of life along the busy, damaged thoroughfare, her face flushed from their walk and the heat of the afternoon, her eyes eager to take in everything.

The waiter cleared his throat. 'If the Herr Hauptmann is ready to order?' The old man was smiling tolerantly. He suggested Berliner weissbier – such a hot day.

Haller nodded and returned his attention to Elisabeth and at that moment something perverse and dangerous stirred inside him.

He wanted to become involved, wanted to see Germany not as Baker Street saw it but as Elisabeth saw it.

Despite the first rule of survival, never to become vulnerable. Despite the supplementary rule, never to let the enemy know you have become vulnerable.

To see Germany as Elisabeth saw it was breaking the first rule.

Breaking the second was unavoidable. The enemy was himself.

That she could have come through twelve years of Nazism uncorrupted amazed him. Elisabeth Lauterbacher was twenty-three. She had been a child of twelve when the senile President Hindenberg appointed Adolf Hitler chancellor in January 1933. That same year Joseph Goebbels became Minister of Propaganda and Public Enlightenment, and the campaign to control the thoughts and actions of seventy million Germans began.

Elisabeth was thirteen in June 1934 when Hitler used Heinrich Himmler's élite S.S. to purge the Storm Troops and thus win the loyalty of the army, thirteen years old when congratulations poured in from all sides because the Führer had unleashed one group of fanatical killers against another in the name of law and order. She was barely fifteen when the Nuremberg Laws that changed the status of Germany's half million Jews from citizen to subhuman were decreed.

By the time she was eighteen and a member of the Faith and Beauty branch of the League of German Girls, Adolf Hitler had sent the Condor Legion to win a fascist Spain for Franco, scrapped the Treaty of Versailles, used the Wehrmacht to erase the Austrian border, the S.S. to open Germany's first concentration camps at Dachau, Buchenwald and Sachsenhausen, the Ministry of Education to expel non-Aryans from German schools, the police to organise the Crystal Night pogrom against the Jews, and the law courts to make the Jews pay billions of marks for the damage their existence had caused. The Führer also, by the time Elisabeth was eighteen, had so terrified the Western democracies that Prime Minister Chamberlain could return from Munich to London with the assurance that he brought 'peace in our time'.

Elisabeth was not yet nineteen on 1 September 1939 when the German invasion of Poland began the Second World War.

She reached young womanhood during the years of Adolf Hitler's greatest triumphs, when the strength of his will was the destiny of the Reich, when he could do no wrong, when field-grey and Luftwaffe blue and S.S. black ruled the Continent from the English Channel to the gates of Moscow. By then the propaganda machinery of Joseph Goebbels had convinced the blond and blue-eyed Aryans they were more than men and hardly less than gods, *Ubermensch.* The concept inevitably implied its opposite, the *Untermensch*, six million Jews to be shipped in cattle cars to the death camps at Auschwitz, Birkenau, Treblinka and Maidanek, not of course that such camps existed, and as many millions of Slavs to be worked to death as slave labour in the Reich, not of course that their working conditions were really so bad.

And when the military triumphs of the first three years of the war gave way to disaster? When Dunkirk became Stalingrad, when the propaganda and enlightenment of Joseph Goebbels and the terrorism of Heinrich Himmler coalesced, when field experience in Poland and Russia taught the Nazis how to deal not with the *Untermensch* but with their own people, when arrest of kin made dissidence unthinkable and 'subversion of oneself' – even defeatist remarks in a diary – was a high crime punishable by death? What could a German do but mind his own business and hope, somehow, to survive?

Elisabeth could hide Jews in Jew-free Berlin. Punishment if caught – death.

Elisabeth could say, when Haller admired her courage: 'Courage? To rebel against a regime that holds its people by brute force? Germany is as much an occupied country as France or Poland.'

Haller knew it wasn't that simple. He also knew that the danger he faced was not just Elisabeth. It was what Elisabeth stood for – the faceless good Germans, millions of them, silent, powerless, fearful, not corrupted but victimised, not masters but slaves.

What Elisabeth stood for, and what Baker Street had decided to ignore.

He put Elisabeth on the train to Wannsee early that Tuesday evening and returned alone to the apartment on Pariserplatz. Heydi returned from Zossen an hour later, greeted him brusquely, went to the sideboard and poured two tumblers of schnapps.

'Well?' His voice was impatient, almost hostile.

Haller raised an eyebrow. 'You were right,' he said mildly. 'Olbricht was very helpful.'

Heydi emptied his glass while Haller sipped at the harsh corn liquor. 'So I heard. And you decided to go over the terrain.'

'That's right,' Haller said, wondering how the lieutenant knew.

'And?'

'I think it can work. Goebbels is the key, isn't he?'

'Very perceptive of you,' said Heydi sourly. 'The Guard Battalion would stop taking orders from the Bendlerstrasse in a minute if Goebbels countermanded them. That's obvious.'

The young lieutenant's craggy face was red, the sabre scar on his cheek a livid slash as he screwed his monocle into place and stared at Haller.

'You took Elisabeth with you,' he said flatly.

Haller's face registered surprise.

'No mystery, hero. We dropped Stauffenberg off at Wannsee on the way back.'

Heydi went to the sideboard again, drained the schnapps bottle into his tumbler, opened another bottle and topped the glass off.

'Elisabeth's through with me,' he said. 'I'm nothing but a lousy Prussian as far as she's concerned. Is it true that American women lead their men around by the nose? That's what I've heard.'

'No more than anywhere else, I guess.'

'If you snapped your fingers she'd jump into bed with you, you know.'

Haller sighed. He wondered how much Heydi had drunk before he got home. 'That's nonsense,' he said.

'Is it, hero? I know what I'm talking about.'

'Cut it out,' Haller said defensively, feeling vaguely guilty about Elisabeth, about Heydi. It was a manageable guilt, compared to the other one.

'You remind me of someone,' Heydi said. 'I finally figured out who. An army medic from the Russian Front on study leave at the University of Munich when Elisabeth was a student there. They were in love,' Heydi removed his monocle. 'It's obvious you remind Elisabeth of him too.'

'You've had too much to drink,' Haller said. 'Why don't you sleep it off?'

'He was condemned to death by the People's Court and executed. Last year in Munich.'

'Oh Jesus,' Haller said.

He saw that his glass was empty; he had not been aware of drinking.

On Wednesday afternoon Haller and Elisabeth were back at the café on Kurfürstendamm. The waiter Reinhard greeted them like old friends, beaming at them, ushering them to the same table.

They were earlier than the day before. Haller had planned little reconnoitring, only around the Alexanderplatz station where Elisabeth met him. They found the area a virtual wasteland, the main post office on Königstrasse almost too severely damaged to function, the wide once-fashionable Unter den Linden a no-man's land of tree stumps, shattered buildings, bomb craters.

Checkmark for Berlin-East. The Guard Battalion command post at the Armoury at the eastern end of Unter den Linden could effectively divide the city in half.

It was all stalling anyway, Haller finally admitted to himself. Two days of exploring had only confirmed what he already knew. Operation Valkyrie was a masterful plan. If Baker Street wanted it to succeed he doubted that they could come up with any improvements.

At the café Reinhard waited as he had the day before, and finally cleared his throat.

'If the Herr Hauptmann is ready to order, may I suggest . . .'

Impulsively Elisabeth asked: 'You wouldn't have some red wine by any chance?'

Reinhard made a don't-you-know-there's-a-war-on face.

'From the South Tyrol perhaps?' Elisabeth asked eagerly. 'A Sankt Magdalener, tasting of sun on the terraces over the Adige?'

Reinhard's face softened. 'I myself am from the Tyrol,' he said. 'The lady is a connoisseur.'

He returned in a few moments with a bottle of Sankt Magdalener, drew the cork and poured the red wine reverently.

'What was all that about?' Haller asked as the waiter went to serve another table.

'I thought he sounded South Tyrolean. My mother was born there, in Bolzano. The other side of the Alps,' Elisabeth said, her voice wistful, as if it were the other side of the moon.

'Then that makes you half Italian.'

'Better not tell the people there,' Elisabeth laughed, 'that you consider them Italian. They're Tyrolers. To them Italy's still part of the Ausland.'

Haller raised his glass. 'To the South Tyrol then.'

'To . . . where you come from.'

The wine tasted, as Elisabeth said, of terraced vineyards and the southern sun.

'Heydi once told me most languages don't have a word like

"Ausland". A single word to stand for the rest of the world, everywhere that's not your country and so must be strange and inferior. That's very German, isn't it?'

Haller asked her: 'What's the trouble between you and Heydi?'

'I guess I didn't know him as well as I thought I did. He's – well, he's the kind of German we're talking about, who needs an Ausland to ridicule and hate.'

'That doesn't sound like Heydi.'

'Let's not talk about it.' Elisabeth finished her wine and held out her glass. 'May I have some more?' She sounded like a little girl then, ingenuous and vulnerable. 'In school they taught us almost nothing about the Auslanders except of course that we were so much better than they were and that they envied us terribly. Hitler once said there's more culture in a single Beethoven sonata than in the entire history of America. It was the same at the university in Munich. Worse. I knew a boy who played the guitar and sang folksongs. "Waltzing Matilda" – is that American?'

'Australian.'

'He was singing that in the back room of a student restaurant in Munich, an Italian restaurant where you could . . .'

Elisabeth's voice stopped.

'What is it?'

'That man there.'

Haller followed her eyes. A fat man was just passing their table. His face had a porcine look, greedy and self-satisfied.

He reached out for her hand. 'What about him?'

'It's nothing. He reminded me of someone else.' Elisabeth's hand was cold in his as she resumed her story. 'They had a back room where my friend sang and played the guitar. He was denounced for singing that song. Because it was from the Ausland. And because it told of a man who was free to wander around the countryside like our own Wandervögel did before the First War. He was forbidden to play the guitar after that, or sing. The Gestapo. Can you imagine anyone being forbidden to sing in public because he sang about a man who wandered alone and thought himself free?'

Haller saw the tears, bright on her cheeks. 'That was two years ago,' she said. 'The first time he returned on study leave from the Russian Front. He was a medic. When he came back last year they killed him . . .'

Twelve

Munich, the third Monday in February 1943, lay under a fresh blanket of snow. Early in the morning she went walking with Stefan in the Englischer Garten, their footprints the only ones on the snow-covered paths, the stately baroque buildings along Leopoldstrasse barely seen through the winter-bare trees, Stefan so handsome in his peaked cap and field-grey greatcoat that she wished they were back in his room on Türkenstrasse behind the university.

The night before, they had been together there. The first time. She had expected some drastic change in herself, something profound, metaphysical even.

The only change was that she loved Stefan more.

He had been gentle and . . . beautiful. Beautiful was the only word she could think of, and she smiled as they walked through the Englischer Garten. Beautiful. Better not tell him that. She did not think a man would like to be thought of as beautiful.

'Why are you smiling?'

'Darling,' she said.

'What?'

'Just darling.'

They left their footprints in the snow beside a rushing stream and there was a place they paused where, even in winter with the beech and chestnut trees bare, no buildings of the city could be seen. They could have been walking thirty miles south in the foothills of the Alps. Stefan kissed her.

'Maybe,' she said against his lips, 'maybe it will snow tonight too and I'll have to stay with you again.'

That was the way it had started last night, innocently on Stefan's part. By the time they had finished talking the trams had already stopped running. Elisabeth shared a room with two other girls on the northern edge of Schwabing, too far to walk through the snowstorm.

She had been less innocent than he; she knew the streetcar schedule and hadn't mentioned the time until it was too late.

'I can't tonight,' he said uneasily.

She knew that Stefan attended secret meetings once or twice a week. Though he was studying medicine he had joined the circle of students around Professor Huber. Philosophy,

Christian existentialism . . . Because man has free will every individual is accountable to mankind. He tried to explain that to her once. It was, in Germany in 1943, a dangerous idea.

Professor Huber and Hans and Sophie Scholl and Stefan Held, her Stefan. Secret meetings to prepare the mimeographed leaflets that appeared mysteriously in public places, that were stuffed at night in letter boxes, that were found sometimes by university students on their desks. Always under the heading White Rose. The White Rose leaflets.

Is not every German alive today secretly ashamed of what Germany has become?

The German who contributes money or scrap metal or even old clothing to the war effort betrays mankind.

The guilt of those in black who slaughter Jews is shared by the entire nation if its people turn a blind eye.

Hitler cannot win the war. He can only prolong it.

For a year the Gestapo and the Security Department of the S.S. had combed Munich to find the origin of those leaflets.

The search had narrowed to the university.

Professor Huber, the Scholls, her Stefan. She was sure of it.

He mistook her fear for disappointment. 'A study group,' he told her. 'Professor Huber, the usual dry philosophy. Sometimes I wonder why I bother. Philosophy's not much help on the Eastern Front.'

'Then don't go.'

'It's at my place tonight.'

She didn't ask if she might come. She knew what the answer would be.

A few minutes later they left the Englischer Garten by the Veterinärstrasse gate, walking fast. If they didn't hurry they would be late for the monthly speech by the Gauleiter of Bavaria. Attendance was compulsory.

Gauleiter Paul Geisler, an Old Fighter from the street-brawling days of the N.S.D.A.P., was a caricature of the ugly Bavarian, the beer belly, bull neck, and bullet head, the bristles of hair protruding from nostrils and ears, the rumpled brown Party uniform, the expression on his face at once greedy and self-satisfied. He reminded Elisabeth of a pig rooting in a barnyard.

She sat in the assembly hall between Stefan and Hans Scholl, Hans a medic on study leave from the Russian Front too.

The Munich Gauleiter flag hung at the rear of the stage, silver eagle and wreathed swastika on a red background. Party functionaries sat in ranks behind Geisler. Fifty or so S.S. men in black stood in pairs around the hall.

At first the Gauleiter droned the usual soporific platitudes which Elisabeth herself could have recited. Duty to Führer and Fatherland. You men in field-grey know what it is to serve, if necessary to die. A great privilege to be young in these times . . . Exhortation to greater sacrifice in order to assure greater victory . . . Honour and obedience, two sides of the same coin. In the words of the S.S. motto: My honour is loyalty . . .

Elisabeth had heard the speech a hundred times, from streetcorner loudspeakers, from radios, at meetings of the League of University Students, at Faith and Beauty outings, at the Labour Service camp near the Swiss border.

Suddenly it changed.

Geisler hunched his shoulders, crossed his arms on the lecturn, thrust his bullet head forward. 'As for you girls, to sit in the lecture halls of the university and study German culture is not enough. You have healthy bodies. Let the professors propagate Aryan ideas; you girls should be propagating Aryan children. As your mothers could tell you, it is an automatic process which once started needs no further help from you. There is no reason why each girl student should not, for each year of education presented to her by the Reich, present a child in return to the Fatherland.'

A low murmur went through the audience, Geisler silencing it with a chopping motion of his hand.

'The Reichsführer-S.S. has already made plans for the generation that comes after you – Aryan settlements in the East, from the Gulf of Finland to the Sea of Azov – and he relies on you girl students to provide breeding stock.

'Of course,' Geisler continued, 'this diverting little act which nine months later produces a child for Germany requires, shall we say, a certain amount of co-operation. It requires, however briefly, the assistance of a man.

'For many of you girls, I can see that will present no problem. For others . . .'

Geisler had to hold up both hands for silence. 'For others less fortunately endowed, for those among you who ordinarily might experience difficulty in finding a mate, I will be happy to supply one.' The Gauleiter of Bavaria was leering then, playing to his audience – not the assembled students but the pairs of S.S. men standing around the hall, their faces mirroring the expression on his.

'An S.S. man whose antecedents I can vouch for and who,

while performing his duty, will provide you with the thoroughly enjoyable experience . . . the thrust of S.S. steel between your legs.'

Stefan sprang to his feet and she heard him shout over the angry roar that came from the audience: 'We've heard enough from that brown-shirt swine!'

Hans Scholl stood quickly, then a few others, then scores. Soon field-grey rose like a wave in the assembly hall.

Was it because of last night? Geisler's foul words, Geisler's coarse leer, turning beauty into ugliness? Would Stefan otherwise have been the ringleader?

A sea of field-grey rolled down the broad centre aisle.

Gauleiter Geisler at first looked disbelieving, and then he looked frightened.

S.S. black and army field-grey were exchanging blows.

Before the students could reach him, the S.S. hurried Geisler from the hall through a side door.

The tide of field-grey flowed outside and along Ludwigstrasse to Marienplatz, the heart of Munich.

For five hours windows were smashed, official cars overturned, the S.S. chased from the streets. What had begun as a spontaneous protest against the Gauleiter's speech became the first – and last – student uprising in the Third Reich.

Two weeks prior to the Geisler speech at the University of Munich, the survivors of the German Sixth Army under Field Marshal von Paulus staggered out of the rubble that once had been the city of Stalingrad to surrender. The date was 1 February 1943.

An army of 300,000 men had been wiped out in two months. The myth, the self-destructive myth of Wehrmacht invincibility, was shattered in the frozen ruins of a city on a bend in the Volga River. Fear replaced the myth. Montgomery already had broken the strength of Rommel's Afrika Korps at El Alamein, the first thousand-bomber R.A.F. raids already had struck the German heartland. The Third Reich had sown the wind. The terrible whirlwind of retribution was gathering strength in East and West.

Many in the Hitlerite hierarchy, Geisler among them, responded with an even more fanatical adherence to doctrinair National Socialism, an even more fanatical belief in the myth of the Aryan future.

That had been one reason for the Gauleiter's speech. There was another.

Five days after the speech, at five o'clock on the afternoon of Monday, 22 February, Elisabeth Lauterbacher sat on a hard straight-backed chair in a large room on the second floor of the Königsbau section of the Residenz, the Munich palace of the old kings of Bavaria.

The Königsbau now housed the Munich offices of the Gestapo.

One Lukas Möllinger, a Hauptwachtmeister in the Gestapo, had been interrogating her for more than two hours. Möllinger was a heavy man in black leather jackboots, black whipcord breeches, and a grey whipcord jacket bulged by his broad shoulders. He had an unexpectedly high tenor voice.

The room was square, carpeted and curtained in deep blue, its walls a stark white. Whatever opulent period furniture it once had contained had been replaced by the drab furnishings of an interrogation room – in this case two long tables, a few hard chairs, a small desk in one corner, two standing lamps. The Gestapo had learned that opulence distracts, simplicity encourages concentration. Even the usual photographs of Führer and Reichsführer-S.S. were absent. Such photographs could break the subject's train of thought.

For two hours Möllinger seemed intent on breaking neither the subject's train of thought nor the subject herself. The interrogation was mild. No coercion had been threatened, let alone applied. It had, until five o'clock, hardly been an interrogation at all.

Patiently Möllinger had discussed with Elisabeth the latest White Rose leaflet, which had appeared three days before in Munich.

The leaflet called Stalingrad a disaster and said a quarter of a million German youths had perished because Adolf Hitler had personally refused the Sixth Army's request to retreat before encirclement made retreat impossible.

The leaflet demanded self-determination for the German people and the removal of the Nazi Party.

The leaflet declared Adolf Hitler the enemy of the German people.

The Scholls and Stefan had not deposited these broadsheets surreptitiously at night in mailboxes around the city, nor had they left them on desks in a few lecture halls at the University.

Hans Scholl and Stefan brought the leaflets in two suitcases from Stefan's room on Türkenstrasse to the University. Inside the main building Hans' sister Sophie joined them as they climbed the stairs to the top floor that looked out over the interior courtyard.

It was early morning, the courtyard and corner staircases crowded with students. Hans and Stefan opened their suitcases and emptied them over the railing. The thousands of leaflets they had mimeographed in Stefan's room fluttered down over the courtyard.

Ordering all gates closed and locked, the university beadle telephoned the Gestapo. Less than an hour after they had climbed the stairs, the Scholls and Stefan went meekly into custody.

From their behaviour, it almost seemed they wanted to become martyrs.

At five o'clock on the afternoon of the 22nd, three days after their arrest, Möllinger abruptly changed his tactics. Faintly Elisabeth could hear the tolling of the Town Hall clock from the nearby Marienplatz. Möllinger looked up from the leaflet on the table between them.

'It's over by now,' he said.

That wasn't a question. Elisabeth said nothing.

'Their trial before the People's Court,' Möllinger elaborated. 'Did you know that Chief Justice Freisler himself flew here from Berlin to preside?'

Elisabeth felt a sudden uneven pounding of her heart. In another time and another place, Roland Freisler would have been known as a 'hanging judge'. The only reason he was not so called now was because execution in the Third Reich meant not the noose but the headsman's axe.

'You have it in your hands to save them,' Möllinger told Elisabeth. 'The White Rose traitors are obviously not just the three students Hans and Sophie Scholl and Stefan Held. We want the others.' He stood, stretched his broad shoulders until they creaked, went to the high window, parted the drapes and looked out. He let the drapes fall into place again. Like opulent decoration, the Gestapo had learned, a view distracts.

'Religious Catholics baffle me,' Möllinger said. The Scholls were converts; Stefan had been born into a Catholic family in Swabia. 'I have always considered martyrs and suicides close relatives. Yet the Catholic makes saints of the first and refuses burial in sacred ground to the second. Can you explain that? Can you explain why your lover Stefan Held *wants* to be beheaded?'

It was not cold in the room but a chill gripped Elisabeth.

'You can't? Do you suppose,' he asked, his tenor voice rising, 'it is because they know they have failed to draw attention to themselves in any other way? That, of course, is precisely why the suicide kills himself.' Möllinger asked: 'Who else was involved in this with them, Fräulein Lauterbacher?'

Elisabeth shook her head. 'I don't know.'

'Were you?'

'No.'

Möllinger nodded. 'I want to believe you. Do you know why?'

Elisabeth looked at him mutely.

'Because I find it inconceivable, my dear Fräulein, that a niece and godchild of Colonel-General Beck, former Chief-of-Staff of the German Army, would be a party to treason. I find it equally inconceivable that she would not save her lover's life if she could. I will ask you again. Who else is involved? No? You don't wish to save your lover's life? You now believe he deserves to die, perhaps? That is commendable, Fräulein Lauterbacher.'

'It's not true! I . . .'

'You have only to supply the names of their confederates and our friend in the swallow-tailed coat will have whetted his axe for nothing. You know of course that the White Rose leaflets appeared in cities as far from here as Nuremburg and Ulm? So, there are couriers.'

'I don't know anything about that.'

'But you know about the leaflets?'

'The whole university . . .'

'I mean the writing of the leaflets. How much of the writing of the leaflets is the work of Professor Huber?'

'I don't know.'

'Then you know that some part of it is?'

'I don't know that either. You're trying to confuse me.'

Möllinger's lips curled upward slightly. 'My dear Fräulein Lauterbacher, to confuse you is one technique at my disposal. What we call "sharpened interrogation" is another. Do you perhaps know the meaning of the term?'

Elisabeth's head moved up and down quickly.

'Let me give you some idea of what you have been spared as the niece of General Beck. Out of respect for the old gentleman.' Möllinger was then standing behind Elisabeth. His voice had become softer, his breathing louder. 'Basic tool, the lash. Not very imaginative, perhaps, but reasonably effective.

Twenty-five blows on the loins usually render a male subject unconscious; women can withstand far less. I myself don't approve of flogging. Nor of the burning of the extremities with a soldering iron, nor the rubber truncheon which is rather like the lash except that it breaks bones.'

Möllinger's voice was softer still, his tone cajoling, as if it was important that Elisabeth understand his likes and dislikes among the techniques at his disposal. One grey whipcord sleeve appeared abruptly to her left, one thick-fingered manicured hand placed flat against the table. Elisabeth sat absolutely still, her shoulder hunched, her own hands clasped on her lap.

'The little press we use to crush testicles, designed specially for that purpose, naturally does not apply here.'

She could now feel the warm exhalation of Möllinger's breath against her cheek; it smelled faintly of peppermint.

'But there are sharpened matches to be driven under the fingernails, pliers to yank the fingernails out, the metal band to be tightened about the subject's head.

'I,' Möllinger injected a personal note, 'have always preferred electricity in these modern times. Electrodes attached to anus and vulva, for example. You would be amazed at the contortions the human body can perform when sufficient voltage passes through it. Or, the electrodes can be placed here.'

Möllinger's left hand closed on Elisabeth's breast. With his right hand he grasped her hair and yanked her upright, knocking over the chair. He turned her towards him, forcing her back against the table and thrusting one knee between her legs.

She struggled to break free, her head turning frantically from side to side, her body twisting. Twice he struck her backhanded across the mouth.

He stepped back as suddenly as he had attacked her. She slumped against the table and tasted blood in her mouth.

'Sometimes with an attractive young woman,' Möllinger said calmly, 'we use the natural approach. Elsewhere, my dear Fräulein Lauterbacher, it would be called rape.' He righted the chair. 'Now, I would like to ask you certain questions again.'

At that instant the telephone on the desk in the corner of the large room rang.

Even more obviously than a view, an interruption distracts the subject of an interrogation. Further, when the interrogation has been sharpened, the interruption gives the subject a respite. The Gestapo therefore avoided unplanned interruptions.

Möllinger looked at his wristwatch. The timing had been perfect. Not only had he got nowhere with the girl, but for her he was now the enemy, the brutal sadistic Gestapo torturer. It was going precisely according to plan.

'Yes? Möllinger speaking. He isn't really?' Möllinger's voice rose shrilly. 'This is hardly the time for . . . Insists? What right has . . . Of course I realise she is a student. What does he imagine the Scholls are, or Stefan Held?' Möllinger asked in disgust, then listened for a full minute without interrupting. He slammed the receiver down and when he looked at Elisabeth his eyes were filled with contempt.

Elisabeth was seated again. Her lips were bruised and swollen; blood trickled down her chin.

Möllinger tossed her a white linen handkerchief. 'You're bleeding,' he said. 'Clean yourself up. Quickly. And comb your hair.' Möllinger shook his head. 'Apparently,' he said while Elisabeth patted her swollen lips with the handkerchief, 'the university administration finds it necessary to go over my head to protect a vicious little whore like you.'

A moment later the door opened and Gottfried Ritter, Provost of the University of Munich, entered the room.

A slender man with greying hair and courtly manners, Gottfried Ritter was a popular figure with the students. Before rising to the post of Provost he had lectured in contemporary European – which came to mean German – history. As a lecturer he drew large audiences who came to hear his parenthetical and daring jibes at the Party, jibes which somehow the authorities seemed to tolerate. As Provost he had a reputation for fairness and compassion. It was said of Gottfried Ritter that he had taken the road of internal migration; that is, he absorbed himself in his work as a means of avoiding, or at least minimising, contact with the excesses of the regime.

He could not avoid such contact now. He took one look at Elisabeth and told Möllinger: 'Get her coat. She's leaving here with me.'

'I'm afraid that is not possible, Herr Professor. Our examination of the witness had hardly begun.'

Removing his rimless glasses and staring hard at Möllinger, Gottfried Ritter said: 'Either she walks out of this building with me, right now, or I call Berlin.'

The Provost's trick with his glasses was well known at the University. Removing them, he could stare anyone down. Gottfried Ritter was extremely nearsighted.

Möllinger averted his eyes. 'I sent three of them before

Freisler today, Herr Professor. There are others. Fräulein Lauterbacher can lead me to them.'

Ritter went to the desk, picked up the phone. 'Is there a physician in the building, operator?' he asked. 'Put me through to him at once. This is Dr Gottfried Ritter speaking. Authorisation, Sturmbannführer Troost. Bureau IV liaison to the University, correct.'

'Troost?' Möllinger asked. 'Troost sent you here?'

The question was ignored. 'You assaulted the girl. The resident physician will establish that.'

'The difference between assault and sharpened interrogation ought to be apparent even to you, Herr Professor.'

'It is assault if no physician is present.'

'A detail honoured more often in the breach.'

'Sturmbannführer Troost tells me you have a reputation for – how did he put it? – impatience. Or was it recklessness? Hello? Who is this, please? Dr Ott, of course. Gottfried Ritter speaking. I didn't recognise your voice, Werner. How is Jutta? And the children? Splendid, splendid. Yes, one night next week. Absolutely. It has been too long.'

Gottfried Ritter watched Möllinger remove Elisabeth's loden coat from where it had been draped over the back of a chair. The conversation with Dr Ott never progressed beyond small talk and soon Ritter hung up.

'That was wise of you,' he told Möllinger.

The Gestapist stared at him appraisingly, then shrugged. 'A word of advice, Herr Professor. It is foolish to make enemies at the Königsbau. You wouldn't be the first educator accused of obstructionism.'

Ritter helped Elisabeth on with her coat. 'If you find it necessary to resume this dialogue, you know where I work. Are you ready, Elisabeth?'

He took her arm in a firm grip and together they walked to the door. To Elisabeth the office then seemed enormous. She did not dare look back. She knew Möllinger was watching them and in another instant his shrill voice would order them to halt.

Gottfried Ritter opened the door and they went out, his hand still on her arm, guiding her.

And Möllinger sat at his desk and smiled. It had gone faultlessly – the two hours of desultory examination, the sudden pressure and unexpected brutality, the girl's obvious terror, then Gottfried Ritter rushing to the rescue like the hero in a Karl May cowboy story. Even their exchange of threats had sounded convincing, Ritter the moralist keeping a tight rein on his outrage, Möllinger the bested bully getting off a parting shot.

For a man new to Gestapo work Gottfried Ritter showed considerable promise.

In another hour students would occupy every table in both rooms of the Lombardi Restaurant in Schwabing, but now, at a few minutes before six, seats could still be had. Ritter found them a corner table in the low-ceilinged back room. He helped Elisabeth off with her coat and sat across the red-and-white-checked tablecloth from her. He lit the stub of candle protruding from the neck of a wax-encrusted Chianti bottle and caught the waiter's attention.

'A pitcher of the house wine,' he asked.

Elisabeth recognised a few students. They seemed far more interested in her companion. The Provost of the University may not have been the last person they expected to see here, but he was close.

He poured the wine, sampled it. 'A young Santa Maddalena,' he said approvingly, 'from the vineyards near Bolzano in the Alto Adige.' His use of the Italian, not the German, names for the wine and the South Tyrol where it came from ordinarily would have surprised Elisabeth. But nothing about Gottfried Ritter could surprise her now. This unassuming, scholarly man had matched the Gestapo strength for strength, and his moral courage had prevailed in the Königsbau itself.

Elisabeth would not allow herself to think what might be happening to her at this very moment except for Dr Ritter's intervention. But there was something else she could not stop thinking about. What was happening to Stefan?

'My family used to take their holidays there when I was a child,' Dr Ritter was saying. 'Before Hitler. It seems a thousand years ago, Germany at peace, the ruinous inflation over, the Nazis only a handful of streetcorner bullies in Munich and Berlin . . . ' Dr Ritter shook his head, the candlelight glittering on his spectacles. 'But I didn't bring you here to talk about that.' The nostalgia had gone from his voice. In its place was the cold self-assurance with which he had faced down the Gestapist Möllinger.

'Listen to me, Elisabeth. There are things you must understand. The Gauleiter's speech was an intentional provocation ordered by the Königsbau. To bring the White Rose students out of hiding. What the boy Stefan Held and his friends did was brave. And as stupid as it was brave. I saw Stefan the day they took him. He knew exactly what he was doing and so did the Scholls. They all knew what the outcome would be – their own execution, Elisabeth. In the pathetic expectation that it would cause a spontaneous uprising of students throughout the Reich. They will be beheaded. That is all that will happen.

'No, don't interrupt. These things must be said.' He paused; she accepted the stern tone, the even sterner judgements, as she would have accepted them from General Beck. Gottfried Ritter had earned the right to use that tone and make those judgements.

She thought he was staring at her intently. She couldn't be sure; her eyes had filmed over with tears.

'Stefan Held has now or will shortly become a statistic like a million Jews or a million Slavs, or those in field-grey who have given their lives for the Führer. *Only* a statistic, Elisabeth. The Third Reich manufactures its own martyrs. Stefan Held will never find his place in that select group.'

Elisabeth was crying then. 'Stop, please . . . It isn't fair . . . Stefan, what he did was brave and noble and . . . '

'And irredeemably foolish,' Gottfried Ritter cut her off harshly. 'Of what use is a heroic gesture today? We are living in a graveyard, Elisabeth. Conquest interests Adolf Hitler less than annihilation, power less than destruction, a new world order less than Götterdämmerung. If there is to be a future, if Germany and Europe are to rise from the ashes of war, young men like Stefan Held are needed. The ultimate courage, now, is a kind of cowardice. To survive the butchery, to get through alive somehow, anyhow, no matter how cravenly. It is a tragedy that your Stefan refused to accept that. God knows I tried to tell him. And failed,' Gottfried Ritter said. 'He wouldn't listen. I don't want to fail you as well. Or those others whose names I don't know, those others whose acts of defiance would destroy not the Third Reich but themselves.'

The room had grown more crowded, most of its tables occupied. Elisabeth had not touched her wine. Willi Graf and Alexander Schmorell came in, friends of Stefan. Both wore field-grey, both looked grave. Graf saw Elisabeth, took a step in her direction, but Schmorell stopped him. He had recognised Gottfried Ritter.

Elisabeth was with the enemy.

How mistaken they were, she told herself. And then she wondered: were they among those others who would destroy not the Third Reich but themselves? Both were on leave from the East, as Stefan was. Graf, who had been imprisoned briefly before the war for anti-Nazi activities, was grim and outspoken. Schmorell, a rangy outdoor type with unexpected wit, kept his thoughts to himself.

Both, Elisabeth recalled, disappeared for days at a time. Had those disappearances coincided with the distribution of the White Rose leaflets? Were they the couriers Möllinger had referred to?

They sat in the opposite corner of the room, pointedly ignoring Elisabeth.

They were wrong about Gottfried Ritter, she thought. If only she could explain that to them, make them see. Would they listen to Ritter?

And not just Willi Graf and Alexander Schmorell. She could name every one of the dozen students in Professor Huber's study group.

Should she tell Dr Ritter what she knew about them? To save them from themselves? Would Stefan approve of her doing that?

'Listen to me, Elisabeth. They're not finished with you at the Königsbau. They'll call you back, and the next time my intervention would change nothing. You must withdraw from the university, leave Munich. At once. Do you understand?'

'And do what? How can anyone hide from the Gestapo?'

'If you are guilty of nothing more than associating with Stefan Held, you must go to your uncle. General Beck's name will be enough to protect you.'

'How can I leave Munich while Stefan – '

'That is over for you,' Dr Ritter told her coldly. 'Stefan Held is finished. We must be concerned with survivors.'

Elisabeth shook her head. What did he mean, finished? There was time, something would happen, they had just taken Stefan before the People's Court this afternoon, perhaps her uncle could intercede . . .

She saw a pimply-faced boy whose face was familiar talking earnestly with Willi and Alexander. Zechlin, that was his name – except for Sophie Scholl, the only civilian in the group that met with Professor Huber.

Alexander Schmorell got up and crossed the room. His bow to Dr Ritter was perfunctory. He found an empty chair at a nearby table and placed it next to Elisabeth. He took both her hands and held them hard.

Across the room, Willi Graf was on his feet. He tapped a

spoon against his wine glass. Gradually the room became silent.

'I have just been informed,' he began, and then his eyes found Elisabeth and for a while he could not speak. 'I have just been informed that Hans and Sophie Scholl and Stefan Held were taken directly from the Munich Law Courts, where a verdict of guilty of treason was handed down this afternoon . . .'

Graf's deep voice faltered. He couldn't stop looking at
Elisabeth felt herself drawn against Alexander Schmorell,
Stadelheim Prison, where the sentence of death by beheading was carried out half an hour ago.'

Elisabeth felt herself drawn against Alexander Schmorell, his big arm around her shoulder. Graf's words echoed in her head without meaning. How could it be true? How could Stefan be dead?

Graf was still talking, and it took Elisabeth a while to understand the words, as if he spoke some foreign language she hardly knew. Ask you all . . . stand . . . a moment of silence for our comrades . . . fallen today for Germany.

Willi Graf himself was standing. The boy Zechlin stood at his side.

No one else.

Alexander Schmorell said something to her in a soft urgent whisper. Gottfried Ritter was looking at her, his spectacles catching the candlelight so that she could not see his eyes.

Again Alexander's urgent whisper. This time she understood. If you stand. If they see you standing, the others will rise too.

Somehow she found the strength to push her chair back and get up. Alexander Schmorell did not help her. It was important that she do it herself.

When she was standing, her head high, there was a single instant when every pair of eyes in the room was watching her.

Then, and only then, Alexander Schmorell stood.

The gesture came to nothing. Elisabeth, Willi, Schmorell, the boy named Zechlin. No one else.

In five brief hours of open revolt the students of Munich had expended their capacity to act. Now for five long days they had been living again under the numbing terror of the police state.

'Troublemakers!' a voice shouted.

And another: 'That's all they were, troublemakers.'

'Traitors!'

The cry was taken up. 'Traitors! Traitors!'

The Third Reich manufactures its own martyrs. Stefan Held will never find his place in that select group.

Stefan was dead, had died for nothing.

Dr Ritter was right.

Gottfried Ritter then, seventeen months before his death, watched Elisabeth leave quickly with the soldiers, Graf and Schmorell, and he could foresee everything that was to come – almost everything.

The girl would come to him tomorrow, and she would talk. Perhaps he would have to give the Gestapo Graf and Schmorell. He regretted that, but it would earn him what he needed, a full measure of Gestapo trust.

The war was lost, and the death wish of Adolf Hitler would be fulfilled. Would anything remain, after Götterdämmerung?

If the Gestapo put Gottfried Ritter in charge of student affairs, there might be hope.

An occasional scapegoat like Graf and Schmorell to placate the Prinz Albrechtstrasse. So that others like them, scores and hundreds of others, would survive.

Anti-Nazi youths today, the leaders of Germany tomorrow. Gottfried Ritter's hand-picked leaders for the next generation. They would owe him their lives. With their gratitude assured, they would serve Gottfried Ritter as he built the new Germany.

The one thing he did not foresee was his own fatal visit to the Prinz Albrechtstrasse cellars.

'Don't you see? I led him to them. Graf, Schmorell. Even Professor Huber. In April Gottfried Ritter went openly to work for the Gestapo. And in April they were tried before the People's Court and executed. All I wanted to do was help them. And I killed them.'

Thirteen

The Elisabeth who could accuse herself of that on Wednesday afternoon and the Elisabeth Richard Haller saw twenty-four hours later hardly seemed the same person. For Thursday's

Elisabeth, any emotion that mortgaged the present moment was unthinkable.

Reinhard brought Sankt Magdalener without being asked and she watched with grave delight as he uncorked it, as if right before her eyes on the crowded Kurfürstendamm he was reproducing the miracle of the loaves and fishes. She selected pedestrians at random and invented life histories for them that somehow suited the face, the walk, the attire, her observations trenchant but never cruel. She watched the audience come out of the theatre across the street, steps slow, eyes downcast, as they merged with the passers-by. Only then she became solemn.

'In there,' she said, 'on the screen, for an hour and a half, they live in a world where Germany will win the war. Then they come out, and they're back in this world.'

It was the only world she knew, and if those others could escape it in the magic of a reel of film, she could escape it through Haller. 'What's it like where you live? Where you lived before the war?'

The café terrace was crowded, the level of conversation loud. Haller could have said, in a normal tone of voice, 'I was born in Richmond, Virginia,' and no one but Elisabeth would have heard. He said: 'I didn't really live anywhere.'

'Everybody lives somewhere.'

'Everybody but a petroleum engineer. That's what my father was. Texas, and then the Dutch East Indies, the Middle East. Arabia.'

'Good God,' Elisabeth said. 'You've been to Arabia?'

'I was just a kid. Then I got shipped off to school in Switzerland. After that I wandered around the States a while as a roughneck. That doesn't translate, does it? Someone who works in the oil fields. Then I decided I needed an education.'

'In what?'

'Languages, international relations. I was going to make a world where people ended the stupidity of war. Permanently. It didn't exactly work out that way, did it?'

They talked, the afternoon light faded, a new audience was admitted to the temporary celluloid future across the street. They sat close, side by side, her head on his shoulder.

Reinhard brought a second bottle of Sankt Magdalener.

'What will you do when all this is over?'

'You don't let yourself think about that in my kind of work.'

'Couldn't you try now? Please?'

'Indulge myself,' he said after a while. 'Find a place away

from everything, try to figure out who I am. Do some more wandering maybe.'

'Where?' She spoke the one word with a child's eagerness.

He was the Ausland, the outside world beyond the fortified borders of the Reich, beyond the reach of Goebbels's propaganda and Himmler's terror, all the world she had never known.

'I don't know,' he said. 'New Mexico maybe. The Maine woods. Northern Ontario. Pure self-indulgence anyway, at least until my separation pay runs out. Then I guess I'll do what everyone else does. Make all the usual mistakes. Get a job I don't particularly want, settle down for no real reason – '

'No, you would never do that,' Elisabeth said earnestly. 'Where is Ontario, please?'

He laughed and turned his head and kissed her.

He knew it would be very easy for her to fall in love not with him but with what he stood for.

And him with her? What was his excuse?

'Speaking of self-indulgence,' he said lightly, drawing away from her, 'I'm starving. Where would you like to have dinner?'

'I would like to have dinner,' Elisabeth said promptly, 'at the Newa Grill. It's the best restaurant in Berlin, but we'd never get in.'

Reinhard had come over to refill the wineglasses. 'Begging your pardon,' he said, 'but the young lady is mistaken.'

'You mean we *can* get in?'

'No, I mean in thinking the Newa Grill is the best restaurant in Berlin. Does the Hauptmann perhaps know the Hasenheide in Treptow, just across from Karstadt's?'

Haller shook his head. 'That's on the other side of town,' he said.

Reinhard set his tray on the table. He scrawled something on a card. 'And more than worth a U-bahn ride if you know the headwaiter. I absolutely guarantee you the best meal in Berlin. Pre-war quality.' He handed the card to Haller. 'Just ask for Fritzi and give him this. Twenty marks would also be in order. He's my brother-in-law.'

Haller looked at Elisabeth. 'Why not?' she said.

The Hasenheide consisted of several small rooms on street level in what once had been a posthouse, the dark-panelled walls decorated with antlers and mounted boars' heads, the heavy oak tables close together and rubbed daily to an almost marble smoothness.

Fritzi, his face dewlapped and lugubrious as a bloodhound's, wore a grey Bavarian jacket with green felt lapels. He looked sceptically at Haller's collar tabs and even the Knight's Cross seemed to make no impression. Captain was hardly an exalted rank at the Hasenheide; at the bar Haller could see two majors and a colonel waiting, and among the Wehrmacht brass at the tables sat an occasional S.S. officer.

'And when Karstadt's closes in half an hour,' Fritzi said, 'it will be worse. My regrets, Herr Hauptmann,' He was already looking past Haller's shoulder to a civilian with a scrubbed pink face and a Golden Party Badge in his lapel. 'Should you care to reserve for some time next week . . .'

Haller produced the card Reinhard had given him, folded a twenty-mark note next to it, and gave both to Fritzi. The change they produced in the lugubrious Bavarian was startling. With legerdemain he made the card and banknote disappear. 'The wine cellar,' he said, his head bobbing up and down. 'The wine cellar without a doubt. If the Herr Hauptmann and his lady will be so kind? I did not understand you were a gourmet.'

He ushered them through two candlelit rooms and down a tightly spiralling stone staircase. Elisabeth paused suddenly, her back stiffening, as she reached the bottom. A moment later Haller knew why.

The situation in the bar and upstairs dining-rooms was reversed. For every field-grey tunic in the wine cellar Haller saw a dozen black S.S. uniforms.

Five minutes later, at their corner table under a grape arbour, Elisabeth said, 'I'm all right now, really. It just happens. You see the S.S. and you want to run.'

A latticework of wood held wine bottles on three walls of the cellar room; the fourth, broken by the staircase, repeated the upstairs motif of antlers and boars' heads. A waitress in dirndl skirt and lacy low-cut bodice had appeared, to be waved away by Fritzi.

'If the Herr Hauptmann and his lady will permit me to surprise them?'

Haller had agreed at once. It would give Elisabeth time to get over her fright. And she had. Now she would let nothing, not even a room full of S.S. officers, spoil the night for her.

She looked like a little girl with her nose pressed against a plate-glass window. 'My God, right here in Berlin.' She tilted her head. 'That table there. It's venison, I swear they're eating venison. With red cabbage and dumplings.'

Fritzi himself came with the champagne bottle, the waitress trailing behind with a silver urn.

'Piper Heidsieck,' Fritzi announced grandly. 'And with the wine, smoked salmon from the Loire.'

The dirndl-clad waitress brought the smoked salmon, paper-thin slices overflowing two large plates, while Fritzi unfastened the wire and worked the cork from the bottle. Elisabeth watched him, her dark eyes aglow with delight in this place and this moment and this ridiculous dewlapped sentimental Bavarian who said, 'With my compliments, Herr Hauptmann. I was a cavalier myself once.'

It was Haller, then, who lost the mood of the evening. All around them in the wine cellar sat S.S. officers, Himmler's fanatical henchmen. Had that one there with the weak chin done a tour of duty at Auschwitz or Treblinka? Had that thin-lipped one in earnest conversation with a blonde wearing three strands of pearls around her plump well-fed throat helped raze the Warsaw ghetto and murder its survivors? Had the Adonis in the far corner ordered American P.O.W.s in Normandy to their knees, hands fettered behind their backs, before dispatching them with a bullet in the nape of the neck?

'What's the matter?' Elisabeth asked.

It was not difficult sitting among them, their silver accoutrements gleaming on black, their faces complacent, their women ostentatiously dressed, to tell himself that Baker Street was right.

They were Germany.

'Please tell me,' Elisabeth persisted. 'Is it something I did?'

Across the room Fritzi stood on a chair. 'Meine Herren und Damen,' he said, and waited for the babble of conversation to subside. 'Meine Herren und Damen, it has been announced that British terror bombers are approaching Berlin. May I suggest that you remain at your tables?' The dewlapped head-waiter laughed nervously. 'The wine cellar here is as safe as any shelter in the city, and the food is far better.'

Across the street in Karstadt's basement, where the S.S. and its favoured friends did their shopping, the last few customers heard the news on the police band of the shortwave radio owned by the manager of the fine foods department. The R.A.F. was late tonight. It wasn't until 9.47 that the announcement came.

'Achtung, Achtung! Enemy bombers in two waves are approaching the capital. The first is following a line south from Stettin along the Oder River, with Berlin-East the probable target. A second wave, detected by radar in the Brandenburg-Schwerin area, is now nearing the Spreewald. Its anticipated primary targets are Treptow and Neukölln. Achtung, Achtung . . .'

S.S.-Gruppenführer Mueller's chauffeur Bäuerle stood laden with packages while Monika made her final selections. Gestapo Mueller himself was in the S.S. barbershop down the hall. Half a dozen customers remained in the delicatessen, four in S.S. black, two women. None of them seemed alarmed.

'How much time have I?' Monika asked Bäuerle.

'The sirens won't sound for perhaps ten minutes, gnädige Frau.'

Monika's eyes flicked hungrily over the neatly arranged shelves again. It was still hard for her to believe. Lieber Gott, she told herself, this was paradise!

On display for sale to the S.S. and its friends in Karstadt's basement was the culinary booty of Occupied Europe.

From the French section Monika had already selected a tin of *foie d'oie au naturel*, not *pâté* and not from Alsace but the real thing from les Landes; a crock of *confit de canard*, the succulent breast of duck packed in its own fat; two tins of artichoke hearts and one of white asparagus. From the Danish section, a tinned ham and another tin of tiny prawns. From the Russian, a fifty-gram jar of Beluga caviar, Malossol grade.

Would Ernst believe that she was entitled to shop here as a Gestapo employee? She doubted it; he was no fool. Then in return for working Sunday night at the Prinz Albrechtstrasse? He might accept that. And if he didn't? What could he do about it anyway?

Or about Heinrich Mueller?

Heinrich had not slept with her yet, but it was obvious he would. If the dapper little Gestapo Chief's appetites were not as vigorous as Ernst's, all the better. Her show of pleasure would come effortlessly. The horror of Sunday night had receded to an oddly titillating memory of danger, as if somehow she were not looking back on it but looking forward to it.

It had already receded by the time she got the black notebook from Gottfried's widow.

She had, with understandable curiosity, flipped through the

notebook. More than two hundred names and short biographies, all of them of young people no more than twenty-five, all university students or former students. Nothing odd about that – Student and Youth Affairs, after all, had been Gottfried's work. Some sort of a letter code following the names, but there was hardly anything odd about that either. Cryptic notations were not the exception but the rule at the Reich Central Security Office.

The reward for getting the black notebook was here in the packages weighing down Bäuerle's arms. And there would be more, much more. She was hungry for anything Heinrich Mueller had to offer.

Strange, he was such an anonymous little man. Faceless was the only word she could think of. Just trying to recall what he looked like, only half an hour after he had left for the barbershop, was difficult. She could see the polished shoes, the lightweight grey suit, the cropped hair, but she had no real image of Mueller's face.

The faceless bureaucrat, the relentless professional, the very mention of whose name terrified people.

That was danger, and she hungered for that too.

She was back in the French section. 'And a tin of those,' she told the clerk after a moment's thought.

'*Quenelles de brochet*, gnädige Frau?'

Monika nodded.

'Then may I recommend the sauce Nantua as well?'

Monika took both, and the clerk began to tally her bill.

Suddenly Heinrich was at her side. He had a way of doing that, appearing out of nowhere. His face gleamed and from it came the scent of an expensive aftershave lotion.

'Are you planning to open a restaurant?' he asked her with a thin smile after a glance at the laden Bäuerle. 'Put all that on my account,' he told the clerk.

'Your name, mein Herr?' It was typical of Heinrich that the clerk would not know his identity.

When he saw Mueller's identification, the clerk stiffened. 'Jawohl, Herr Gruppenführer! We'll have the order delivered, of course?'

Mueller shook his head. 'Take the groceries to the garage and wait there,' he instructed Bäuerle. 'It appears we are to be inconvenienced by an air raid.' He turned to Monika. 'Shall we go across to the Hasenheide? The food is good and the wine cellar quite safe.'

*

Conversation and laughter were louder than before. The faint ululating wail of the sirens could be heard along with the first distant volleys of the anti-aircraft guns at the Friedrichshain flak towers to the north. Soon there was a distant rumble, another, a third – R.A.F. bombs, perhaps a mile away. Glassware and crockery rattled. Then came a prolonged sound as of heavy fabric ripping, and the explosion that followed shook the room. The electric lights dimmed, went out, came back on. Conversation and laughter halted, resumed. Three more tearing sounds followed the first, and three more crashing explosions. The next thudded further off. The Friedrichshain flak was continuous now, a steady rattling.

The woman with the three strands of pearls around her plump throat was crying softly. Her thin-lipped S.S. escort said something to her, his face bloodless and furious.

Elisabeth grasped Haller's hand. He returned the pressure of her fingers, thinking at first that she was afraid. But she said: 'That woman over there, do you know her?'

'The one who's crying?'

'No, the tall blonde with the man in the grey suit. A little more to your left.'

Haller turned slowly to look where Elisabeth had indicated. Half a dozen tables away he saw the wheat-blonde hair and the deeply tanned face. Whoever she was, she was gorgeous. And she did look familiar.

'She's been staring at you ever since they came downstairs,' Elisabeth said.

Haller saw the man in the grey suit offer her a cigarette, saw her cup his hand in hers to accept flame from his lighter, saw how the wings of wheat-blonde hair fell on either side of her hands, and then he remembered.

The Junkers tri-motor from Lisbon, the brief stopover at Barajas airport outside Madrid.

Had they talked?

He watched the woman blow a plume of smoke. Her cigarette lit, she was staring at him again.

They had talked, all right. She had approved of the work he was doing, taking mail from London via Lisbon to Germany for distribution to British P.O.W.s, and his response had been a glacial Swiss rebuff. He could recall the exact exchange.

'You don't like Germans, do you?' she had asked.

He responded: 'Do you know any reason why anyone should?'

Now she saw him in the uniform of a German army officer.

*

'Please? I'm sorry, Heinrich. What did you say?'

She had just remembered where she had seen that good-looking captain before, or at least thought she remembered. But how could a man be a Swiss diplomat one day and a Wehrmacht officer a week later? It hardly made sense.

'Your interest is obviously elsewhere,' Gestapo Mueller told her dryly.

Then a pair of giant hands seemed to rip canvas directly over their heads, the room shuddered with the explosion that followed, and plaster dust sifted down from the ceiling.

Maybe, Monika thought, she was mistaken. She almost had to be mistaken. But he certainly looked like the same man.

'Who the devil is he?' Mueller snapped at her. 'That captain you can't take your eyes off?'

'I – I'm not sure,' Monika said.

'I find what you're doing unseemly,' Mueller said coldly. 'Rude, in fact.'

Monika knew she had been staring rudely, and she knew what Mueller's real objection was. Her behaviour might draw attention to himself, and Gestapo Mueller's passion for anonymity surpassed even that of the Führer's secretary, Martin Bormann.

She knew it had gone too far now for her to back out. Tell him.

But if she was wrong, she would appear still more ridiculous in his eyes.

Monika asked him: 'Does the R.S.H.A. ever send agents abroad masquerading as neutrals – Swiss perhaps?'

Mueller smiled at the naïve question. 'Naturally we do. And so do the British and Americans. Lisbon, for example, is full of such agents.'

'Does the Wehrmacht?'

'Military Intelligence,' said Mueller, 'has been totally discredited, the Abwehr absorbed into R.S.H.A. Bureau VI under Schellenberg. But you know all that.'

The air was ripped apart again and another high-explosive bomb shook the wine cellar.

Finally, Monika told Gestapo Mueller about the stopover at Barajas airport. He listened without interruption, his face impassive, then looked around the room, saw the thin-lipped S.S. officer seated nearby and beckoned him.

'Standartenführer Dreher,' the thin-lipped S.S. officer introduced himself to Haller and sketched the suggestion of a bow to Elisabeth. 'Are you assigned here in Berlin or on leave, Herr Hauptmann?'

'On leave,' Haller said.

'May I see your papers? Strictly a formality, I assure you.'

Haller had seen the man in the grey suit signalling the thin-lipped Dreher, had seen them in whispered conversation, Dreher clearly deferring to the civilian.

Obviously the girl had told him about the chance encounter at Barajas airport.

He had to assume his army I.D. card, leave warrant, and ration book would pass for the real thing, at least here in the restaurant. But if the paper and ink were subjected to careful analysis?

Not that the S.S. would have to go to such lengths.

If they simply phoned the Normandy headquarters of the 67th Regiment of Grenadiers, Richard Haller was a dead man.

And they would phone. It was what he would have done in their place.

'Your papers, Herr Hauptmann,' Dreher repeated impatiently. He said something else, but the ripping sound of a five-hundred-pound bomb hurtling to earth drowned out the words.

The room shuddered, lurched. Just as the lights went out Haller saw Standartenführer Dreher lose his balance, grasp the edge of the table.

Other tables had overturned. A dessert cart at which Fritzi had been preparing crêpes was ablaze with a blue alcohol flame that spread along the linen cloth. Black uniforms milled in confusion. The plump-throated woman was screaming soundlessly, her mouth a wide O of terror. The shock-wave had left Haller temporarily deaf.

He grabbed Elisabeth's hand, elbowing Dreher aside. He pulled her past the flaming cart, past overturned tables, to the bottom of the staircase.

Up the stairs. Two tight spiral turns in darkness, and then into the first of the interconnecting rooms. Or what remained of it. The far end of the room was a sheet of flame. Ceiling beams were down, one plaster wall had buckled inward, leaving a gap that opened on darkness. People rushed towards that, shoving, struggling. Haller could still hear nothing.

He dragged Elisabeth towards the smashed wall. Soon they were pressed in on all sides, borne forward by the mob.

Forward and outside.

In the light of the flames now leaping up the façade of the

building Haller could see a bomb crater in the middle of the street, water gushing from a burst main. On the west side of the street through roiling smoke loomed Karstadt's. To the east was the Hasenheide park, the heath from which the restaurant took its name.

Haller and Elisabeth ran for the park. Anti-aircraft searchlights were crisscrossing the sky and two green parachute flares faded and winked out. Bombs thudded distantly as Haller's hearing began to return.

They plunged into the darkness of the heath.

Fourteen

After the Friday meeting of the R.S.H.A. bureau chiefs Heinrich Mueller returned to his office. As usual, the luncheon meeting had left him with a headache.

Even the unvarying seating arrangements had contributed to his annoyance. Kaltenbrunner presiding blandly at the head of the narrow rosewood table under the Fritz Erler portrait of the Führer. On one side the Security Department chiefs, Ohlendorf of Bureau III, Interior, and Schellenberg of Bureau VI, Exterior and Counter-espionage. And on the other side Mueller himself and Chief of Criminal Police Artur Nebe. It might have been a diagram of the Reich's security hierarchy.

Or a diagram of the battle lines within the R.S.H.A. No matter what the bone of contention, they always ended up aligned the same way. The S.D. on one side and the Sipo – his own Gestapo and Nebe's Kripo – on the other. And Director Kaltenbrunner squarely in the middle, too weak-willed to stop the internecine warfare.

Mueller almost wished the R.S.H.A. had a real head, not this unimaginative Austrian lawyer who only relayed orders from Himmler. But no, things were better as they were. Gestapo Mueller did not need another strong personality to deal with.

The bone of contention this Friday, 14 July, was the plot to assassinate the Führer.

The S.D. wanted to move against the conspirators at once with what evidence they now had. The two police chiefs wanted to widen the net before closing it. Mueller was not certain what Artur Nebe's motives were for waiting. Very likely, he decided, the same as his own.

Mueller himself thought the conspirators might succeed, no matter what the R.S.H.A. did. Backing the wrong side could be fatal.

Besides, the information obtained from the Communists Jacob and Saeftkow was suspect. It was not even a question of thieves falling out. Jacob and Saeftkow were no part of the plot. Most of the names they had cited were already known. Goerdeler, for instance, had been talking his head into a noose for years. As for the socialist, Julius Esser, the Communists might have denounced him simply to settle an old political score.

Artur Nebe had, before the luncheon meeting, assured Mueller that Esser himself would shortly be taken, quite possibly later this afternoon – the Criminal Police thus correcting last Monday night's Gestapo blunder.

Nebe hadn't crowed over it. And more important, he hadn't told Kaltenbrunner and the others. But Mueller still didn't like it.

If Esser were taken and the S.D. found out, it would strengthen their hand, enable them to move against the conspirators. And who knew where that would end? It could even trigger a confrontation between the army and the S.S. Mueller had no wish to find himself caught in that. He devoutly hoped the war would end first. He had reason to believe he could emerge from Germany's defeat not only in one piece but in a position of power. Mueller had plans. He also had Gottfried Ritter's notebook.

The S.D. chiefs had been stalled another week and the ambitious Ritter, of course, was dead.

Mueller pushed open the door to his office. In the waiting-room he saw an army major reading the current issue of *The Black Corps.* The major did not look up when Mueller passed him to enter the small middle room of the three-room suite.

'What's on for this afternoon?' he asked his secretary.

'Panzinger at three, then Krause,' said Barbara Hellmuth without consulting her calendar. 'Then you're due at the Reichsführer-S.S.'s office at four, Herr Gruppenführer, so you may have to scrub the rest of your schedule.'

Panzinger would present his final report on the interrogation of Jacob and Saeftkow, a report which Mueller had intentionally deferred until after the luncheon meeting. Krause should have the Swiss legation's answer about the courier who had flown in from Lisbon with the P.O.W. mail last Friday.

Himmler, Mueller assumed, would put him on the carpet for Monday night's fiasco. He wished Himmler had stayed in Berchtesgaden.

'Who's the soldier boy?' he asked Fräulein Hellmuth.

Again she did not consult her calendar. 'Major Ernst Otto Jaeger, former N.S.D.A.P. Guidance Officer with General Busch's headquarters on the Eastern Front, now awaiting reassignment, Herr Gruppenführer.'

'Has he an appointment?' Mueller asked, puzzled. He usually spent the half-hour after the Kaltenbrunner lunch on the cot in the cubicle next to his office. Often with three aspirins.

'No sir. But his wife is Frau Monika Jaeger of Section Ib/8.'

'Oh,' he said with a level look at Barbara Hellmuth. 'That Jaeger.'

Mueller immediately discounted the idea of a jealous husband.

'What does he want?' he asked, intrigued.

Mueller sent for people; people did not drop in on him. Yet Jaeger had.

Fräulein Hellmuth handed him an envelope. 'He said you would understand, Herr Gruppenführer.'

Mueller opened the envelope, found a single sheet of paper with two capital letters printed on it. KZ. The abbreviation for *Konzentrationslager*, concentration camp.

Mueller crumpled the sheet of paper, tossed it in the direction of Fräulein Hellmuth's wastebasket. He was in no mood to play guessing games and was about to tell her to send Jaeger on his way. Then he stiffened.

True, KZ was the accepted abbreviation for concentration camp.

But KZ had once, in what to Mueller seemed another lifetime, had a different meaning.

Mueller stood at the window, his back turned as Jaeger entered the large corner office. Soon he would turn abruptly to confront his guest, the bright sunshine back-lighting his own face, obscuring it, but transfixing the expression on his guest's face like a bug pinned to a specimen board. It was one of many ploys Mueller used to dominate an interview.

Mueller realised he was stalling. The letters KZ had badly shaken him. He had thought that part of his life buried until he himself was ready to resurrect it.

Heinrich Mueller, then a very junior member of the Munich Police Department, had become an expert on Communism in the early 1920s in much the same way Adolf Hitler had become an expert on National Socialism. Which is to say, accidentally.

Munich in those days was a madhouse of political parties of extravagantly right- and left-wing orientation. Reichswehr Corporal Adolf Hitler, attached to the political department of Headquarters IV, was ordered in 1919 to infiltrate one of those lunatic fringe political groups. Less than a year later he changed its name to the National Socialist German Workers' Party and became its Führer.

Heinrich Mueller was given a similar assignment by Bureau IV of the Munich Police, the infiltration of the Communist Party. After the overthrow of the short-lived Red Republic, the party had gone underground. Mueller was eventually responsible for a long report – it was still considered definitive – on the structure of the Communist Party beginning with the Spartakus League in Berlin and ending with the Central Committee in Moscow.

Mueller remained a great admirer of Razvedupr, the Russian Secret Police. That admiration was no secret. Such Gestapo routines as middle-of-the-night arrest and many of the techniques of sharpened interrogation came straight from Kropotkin Square.

Admiration was one thing; involvement was another. Mueller, in the twenties and early thirties, had become involved.

The strength of totalitarian power lies in the complete identification of propaganda and terror.

The concept of racial antagonism is as crucial to Nazi doctrine as the concept of class antagonism is to Communism.

We are not that different, my dear Mueller.

The over-riding question is: who will win? It would be not only foolish but suicidal to back the wrong side. The verdict of history is not yet in.

You would be wise to co-operate with us, Mueller.

The words spoken to him so long ago by *Kamerad Zelle.* Comrade Cell. KZ.

Now Mueller turned and raised his right arm in a lazy parody of the German greeting. Major Ernst Otto Jaeger returned it stiffly. Heil Hitlers were exchanged, Mueller's a bored monotone, Jaeger's barked. Mueller saw a wiry man of somewhat more than middle height with light brown hair cropped almost as short as his own. The grey eyes had a strange bruised look to them. They made Jaeger look like a failed intellectual.

Mueller had seen the type in the S.D. often enough. Dangerous men with a taste for cruelty.

Jaeger did not seem the least awed by where he was or with whom. He stood at ease in his meticulously pressed field-grey. Mueller glanced at the ribbons on the left breast of the tunic.

'Knight's Cross, and the order of frozen beef,' he said, referring to the Eastern Front combat ribbon. 'Frau Jaeger can be proud of you. Sit, won't you, Herr Major?'

Jaeger selected the deep, black leather armchair near the dead fireplace; Mueller crossed to the swivel chair behind the heavy oak desk. The armchair looked comfortable but was not. One tended to sink into it too deeply, awkwardly, feet leaving the parquet floor.

The cushion sighed under Jaeger and he at once brought his weight forward and sat on the edge of the chair.

Mueller observed that with both approval and annoyance. He said: 'In what way can I help the husband of our valued Frau Jaeger?'

'Monika has nothing to do with this,' Jaeger said.

Mueller's annoyance increased. 'Then I fail to see why you are taking up my time.'

Jaeger stood. 'In that case, I won't, Herr Police General.' The use of that title rather than Gruppenführer, Mueller realised, was no accident. Jaeger was telling him he had come to see a professional police officer, not an S.S. fanatic. The man was clever and, to all appearances, fearless.

'Sit down,' Mueller commanded.

Jaeger chose a straight chair near the west window; now each of them had back-lighting. 'To answer the Herr Police General's question,' he said, 'there is no way I know that you can help me. But I can help you.'

'Really?' said Mueller with a condescending smile.

Jaeger said: 'WH-IA-2473. What does that mean to you?'

'A licence plate, of course. Wehrmacht, Berlin registration. What of it?' Mueller demanded irritably. Jaeger, not five minutes in his office, had somehow reversed their roles. It was not Mueller, but the army major, who was shaping the interview.

'On Monday night, or more precisely at 1.37 Tuesday morning, a BMW staff car bearing that licence plate left the vicinity of the Nikolai cemetery in Berlin-East,' Jaeger said. 'In it were two feldgendarmerie officers and the former Social Democrat Reichstag delegate Julius Esser.'

Mueller forced his face to remain impassive. 'Is that a fact?' he asked in a lazy voice.

'A fact,' Jaeger said, 'which an incompetent Gestapist named Kraske should have observed for himself.'

'And just what were you doing there at that hour Tuesday morning?'

Mueller wished he could see Jaeger's face more clearly against the back-lighting. He wanted to watch the self-assurance crumble.

Jaeger said: 'I had a certain interest in the success of the operation, Herr Police General.'

That frank answer, so recklessly given, startled Mueller. 'What operation?' he asked, although the answer was obvious. He wanted time to think.

'The arrest of Esser along with the Communists Saeftkow and Jacob, which I set up. Naturally the people I represent wanted to learn the outcome.'

'What people?' Mueller asked.

'A mutual acquaintance from the old days,' Jaeger said, and his cool tone of voice, finally, was too much for Mueller.

'In ten minutes I can have you in the cellars,' he shouted. 'They are not perfect, down there. Sometimes they make mistakes. In an hour you could be dead.'

'Is that what happened to Gottfried Ritter?' Jaeger asked.

Mueller's head was pounding furiously. He reached for the phone.

Before he could pick it up Jaeger said: 'Wait, Herr Gruppenführer.' Mueller was now not the professional policeman but the S.S. officer. 'You could send me to the cellars. If you allowed yourself the luxury of believing Germany will win this war.' Jaeger paused. 'Or the luxury of believing that Comrade Cell will spend the rest of his life in Moscow.'

They stared at each other. Mueller's hand left the phone.

'When I saw Comrade Cell earlier this month,' Jaeger said, 'he spoke of you as a friend. He has not forgotten your help eleven years ago with the *Antifa* cells, and the Thaelmann affair.'

Mueller said nothing.

'But eleven years is a long time. Let me refresh your memory, Herr Gruppenführer. After the Reichstag fire, when the Party had to go underground, the *Antifa* cells were organised to infiltrate industry and the government. Sixty per cent were compromised almost at once and the remainder in jeopardy. However, a report on their activities somehow disappeared from police headquarters on Alexanderplatz and resurfaced twenty-four hours later at the Moabit criminal court. During those twenty-four hours the report was photographed at the Soviet Trade Delegation here in Berlin. And certain changes, of course, were made. As a result, the *Antifa* network continued to function for another decade. Comrade Cell remains grateful for access to that report.

'It was some months earlier that Ernst Thaelmann was arrested and sent to Moabit prison to await trial. He was, you will recall, head of the Communist Party in Germany. He was also a rival of Comrade Cell. Arrangements were made for Thaelmann's escape from prison. Unfortunately the turnkey who was to release him committed suicide. Ernst Thaelmann, far from being rescued, was sent to Buchenwald. Comrade Cell remains grateful for the – suicide.'

Jaeger stood, approached the desk. 'As I said, he thinks of you as a friend. You are going to need that friendship.'

Jaeger held up a hand; Mueller had been about to speak. 'The Anglo-Americans and the Russians have already agreed that when the Reich surrenders, the matter of war crimes will be considered by a tribunal of the victors. Before such a court what chance would the man responsible for, among other things, the Final Solution to the Jewish Problem have?'

'It was Himmler and Eichmann who . . . '

'It was Himmler at the top, Eichmann at the administrative level. And you in between, Herr Gruppenführer.' Jaeger placed his hands on the edge of the desk and leaned over it. 'Comrade Cell will follow the Red Army into Berlin – six months from now, certainly within the year. Your co-operation now will ensure his continuing gratitude. Not that even Comrade Cell could protect you from an Allied tribunal here in Germany. But a grateful Comrade Cell could offer you a new life in Russia. If you co-operate with me.'

Mueller could not speak at once. He now saw clearly for the first time what all those in the *Führerlexikon*, the Who's Who of the Third Reich's leadership, were beginning to see. Their own death.

'What is it you want?' he asked.

He was prepared to be reasonable, but when Jaeger told him what he had come for, Gestapo Mueller shook his head.

Mueller could be as coldly logical as Jaeger, as patient as Comrade Cell.

They were stalemated. Mueller would accept no intermediary. When the time came he would himself deliver the guarantee of his own future to Comrade Cell.

The future, any future at all for himself or his fellow conspirators, seemed highly unlikely to Freiherr von Heydebrand that afternoon.

Heydi replaced the phone on the desk in what passed for his office at the Bendlerstrasse – a tiny cubicle walled off by fibreboard in one corner of a large second-floor room. There was space for desk, chair, a small file, and Heydi himself. The room lacked the luxury of a window and Heydi thrust his sweating face in the flow of warm air from the electric fan on the desk. He could hear hammers pounding nearby, East Workers from the barracks in Siemensstadt labouring around the clock to keep the huge Armed Forces High Command Headquarters functioning despite the air raids. It was a question of cramming more and more people into less and less space. Much of the shorter wing of the Bendlerstrasse was no longer usable, and every day Heydi saw new faces, new configurations of offices, new confusion. Heydi had started out last month in a pleasant office with a view over the Landwehr Canal. He was now working in a closet.

The phone call from police headquarters on Alexanderplatz, logged in by Heydi at 16.27 hours, 14 July, had seemed inconsequential at first. A Meister Adolf Rall, a sergeant-major at the Alexanderplatz, had called to clarify the role of the police riot squad in the event of a run-through of Operation Valkyrie. Heydi had obfuscated in answer to Rall's questions. Meister Rall had not used the identification code.

No, Heydi said, he could not inform Rall of the date and hour of the run-through. Rall didn't think Berlin's two million slave labourers would announce their intention to revolt, did he? An effective rehearsal must begin without prior notice.

Dumb question, Heydi thought, and then told himself not to take out his hangover on Meister Rall. And not to drink himself to sleep every night, while he was at it.

At whose disposal would Meister Rall's superior officer place the riot squad?

An even dumber question to ask of the Bendlerstrasse liaison officer, especially since the answer was available at the Alexanderplatz, where Rall was calling from.

Valkyrie, Heydi said, was a Home Army exercise. Did that answer the Meister's question?

Apparently not, because Meister Rall then asked: 'Could you give me some estimate as to how many hours after X-hour the police will be at the disposal of Military District III?'

Heydi spent a moment wondering what sort of dummkopf made sergeant-major these days. Then suddenly he became alert. The words 'estimate', 'hours', and 'disposal', spoken in that sequence, represented the police half of the identification code.

Heydi responded with the words 'informed', 'home', and 'operation' by saying irritably: 'I've already informed you that the Home Army will take immediate charge of the operation.'

And the cautious Rall finally got to the purpose of his call. 'My apologies then, Herr Oberleutnant,' he said, 'but I don't want to make any mistakes. You see, I'm a temporary replacement for Vogel, who has fallen ill.'

Vogel was Julius Esser's code name, fallen ill a euphemism for arrested by the Criminal Police.

'How serious is it?' Heydi asked.

'Well, you know Vogel. He has the constitution of a horse.'

That meant the opposite of what it seemed. They were not holding Esser at the Lehrterstrasse prison or in Moabit, where his escape might have been arranged. They had brought him straight to the Gestapo cellars.

It could take hours, or Esser could hold out a day or two. But in the end they would break him.

Experts had hidden Esser, a couple named Jellbach who ran the Uncle Emil organisation, but Heydi could guess how he had been captured. The Jellbachs had searched frantically but without success for Esser's wife and since Monday night over Esser's head had hung the deadly Gestapo weapon of arrest of kin. Esser, trying to find his wife himself, must have walked into a Kripo trap.

And now? Heydi stared bleakly at the walls of his tiny office. Julius Esser was no army officer and at least he had no knowledge of the tactical details of Operation Valkyrie. But he could name every key member of the conspiracy.

In the Gestapo cellars he *would* name them. Himmler, before long, would have them all.

Heydi reached listlessly for the phone to call Stauffenberg's office down the hall. By now the colonel would have finished interviewing the candidates for command of the Guard Battalion – the vital post that no longer mattered at all.

The phone rang just as Heydi touched it.

'Oberleutnant von Heydebrand,' he said.

'Heydi?' It was Stauffenberg, and the colonel sounded exuberant. 'Come on in here, will you? It looks like we're on our way at last.'

Heydi found Stauffenberg and Police Chief Helldorf standing near the teletype machine, Helldorf in civilian clothing. For an instant as the colonel turned Heydi saw his face in profile, the eyepatch not visible from the right side. Stauffenberg looked boyish, and as exuberant as his telephone voice. The black eye-patch, when he faced Heydi, only served to point up his jauntiness.

'Take a look at this,' he said, making room for Heydi in front of the teletype.

FÜHRER HQ BERGHOF 14 JULY 1625 HOURS. MARSHAL KEITEL VERY URGENT TO COLONEL GENERAL FROMM, GENERAL OLBRICHT, COLONEL COUNT STAUFFENBERG, OKW BERLIN. TWO HUNDRED THOUSAND REPLACEMENTS OVERDUE ARMY GROUP CENTRE. FÜHRER DEMANDS RECTIFICATION. SEND RESPONSIBLE OFFICER BERGHOF NOON SATURDAY 15 JULY FÜHRER CONFERENCE.

For once Stauffenberg seemed unselfconscious about his missing right hand. He pointed the pinned sleeve at Heydi. 'That's it,' he said. 'Less than twenty-four hours.'

Heydi held back his bad news. With the arrest of Julius Esser speed seemed their only hope now. The Führer's eagerness to throw two hundred thousand untrained replacements at the Red Army juggernaut, ironically, would supply it. Heydi wanted an objective answer to his question. 'Can we be ready that soon?'

'I don't see why not,' said Stauffenberg. 'A bomb's waiting for us at the Obersalzberg.'

Heydi knew that. Major General Helmut Stieff, Chief of Organisation Branch, O.K.W., would deliver on demand a bomb to kill Adolf Hitler. The bombs – he had hidden a small supply at both the Obersalzberg above Berchtesgaden and the Führer's East Prussian field headquarters near Rastenburg – were of British manufacture. Intended for the Dutch Underground, they had been captured by the Abwehr. They had passed into General Olbricht's possession and Olbricht had assigned Stieff as their custodian.

The British bombs were a curiosity at first, thanks to their chemical-mechanical fuses; all it took to activate them was the shattering of a small vial of acid, which then ate through a wire holding a hammer over the percussion cap and the plastic explosive itself.

They were ideal briefcase bombs, and no others like them could be had in Germany.

'It's not the bomb I'm worrying about, Herr Oberst,' Heydi said, addressing his commanding officer formally in Helldorf's presence.

The bad feeling between Heydi and Stauffenberg over Richard Haller had not lasted. They had worked together too long and too closely for that. Stauffenberg thumped his adjutant's chest with his gloved left hand and laughed. 'I tend to worry when I'm hung over too,' he said. 'Your eyes are an interesting shade of crimson, lieutenant. Remember, you have to have patience with a girl like Elisabeth. That's what Nina says.'

Nina was the Countess von Stauffenberg.

'I meant,' Heydi said, 'can we activate Valkyrie on such short notice?'

The teletype message had almost made him forget Rall's phone call. Now he related it briefly.

They spent a few moments discussing Julius Esser as if he were already dead. Then Stauffenberg said: 'You've answered your own question, Heydi. With Esser in their hands we have to strike tomorrow.'

Helldorf seemed less sure of that. 'It's odd,' he said. 'Himmler could have moved against us any time in the last six months. He knows who we are, but . . .'

'So you keep saying,' Stauffenberg cut in.

'I never told you how I knew. You wouldn't have cared for my source. Artur Nebe,' Helldorf said.

Stauffenberg's single eye narrowed. 'That bastard spent most of 1942 commanding an Einsatzgruppe in Russia slaughtering Jews.'

Helldorf looked away. His own record was far from clean and all three of them knew it.

'I'm not saying he's trying to make amends. He went much too far for that. The plum of course was Moscow; he was going to be police chief there. Himmler gave him the Einsatzgruppe as training.'

Stauffenberg waved his gloved left hand impatiently. 'Never mind all that. What's Nebe been telling you?'

'That even Himmler wants to wait and see which way the

wind's blowing. Like Nebe himself. Or Gestapo Mueller, for that matter. Only the S.D. remains completely loyal to Hitler.'

'So?' Stauffenberg said.

'So it doesn't have to be tomorrow, Klaus. Himmler and the Gestapo aren't ready to move against us.'

'But *we're* ready. We only need four hours from the time the bomb goes off, to get our panzer units into the city. The Guard Battalion can give us those four hours.'

'Maybe,' Helldorf said.

'Well, can't it?'

Stauffenberg remained impatient; Helldorf became angry. 'I thought you invited me to sit in on those interviews. I thought you wanted my opinion.'

'We did,' Stauffenberg said.

'And you ignored it.'

'Nobody ignored it. Olbricht and I disagreed with you, that's all.'

Helldorf shrugged, his brief flare of anger spent. 'It's your Guard Battalion,' he said.

Stauffenberg was pacing: to the window, back to the door, then across to the teletype to re-read Keitel's message.

'Transportation's already arranged,' he told his adjutant. 'We fly Rangsdorf–Berchtesgaden at 08.00 tomorrow. This is it, Heydi.' Then he returned his attention to the police chief. 'Wolf, believe me, he's the right man for the job. His membership in the N.S.D.A.P. is irrelevant, he's a career army officer first. He'll follow orders. He's spent his whole life following orders.'

'Befehl ist Befehl,' Helldorf said softly. 'Half the population of Germany will regret those words before we're finished.'

'He'll follow *my* orders,' Stauffenberg said confidently. 'For the first few hours anyway, and the first few hours are all we'll need from Major Ernst Otto Jaeger.'

Fifteen

Befehl ist Befehl. Orders are orders.

A most convenient excuse, Dr Raffaello Matti told himself as he entered his office in Berlin's huge Charité Hospital at dusk that evening. If you happened to be German.

Hardly any excuse at all if you were born in Ascona in the Ticino and still carried a Swiss passport.

Raffaello Matti removed his surgical smock and put on a fresh white shirt. Through the open window he could hear the frantic bellowing of cattle from the veterinary college across Lutsenstrasse. A frown settled on his handsome, saturnine face. The improper treatment of animals offended him. The oafs who practised veterinary medicine these days, if Raffaello Matti had his way, would be lined up against a wall and shot.

Shutting the window and drawing the blackout curtains, he sat down at his desk. He felt as helpless as those poor dumb brutes, so maltreated across the street, must feel.

Raffaello Matti was trapped, the victim of his own convictions.

As a founder of the medical section of the Association for Authoritarian Democracy, he couldn't return to his native Switzerland. The Association, a National Socialist front organisation, had been guilty of certain excesses and outlawed since 1939. Raffaello Matti would be arrested the moment he crossed the frontier.

And how much longer would he be safe in Berlin?

As Medical Director of the Circle of Friends of Heinrich Himmler, he was in a prestigious position, on an equal social footing with Berlin's leading bankers, industrialists, and insurance executives. Why, only last week he had dined with the younger Krupp and Count von Bismarck at the latter's Charlottenburg townhouse.

The Circle of Friends of Heinrich Himmler acted as a connecting link between economic and political power brokers in the Third Reich. The advantages for an industrialist were obvious: the allocation of slave labour often depended on membership in the Circle. The advantages for Himmler and the S.S. were less obvious but more considerable: the Circle of Friends donated unreceipted funds for activities Himmler could not otherwise have financed.

Such as medical experiments in the concentration camps.

Raffaello Matti administered those funds. The dangerous nature of the experiments at Auschwitz and elsewhere didn't trouble him, the subjects of the experiments being only Jews, Slavs, and gypsies. Raffaello Matti believed, as he had in Switzerland, that medical experimentation, however perilous, if properly carried out on subhumans, would eventually benefit mankind. A better understanding of typhus and infectious hepatitis, of survival at low temperature or simulated high altitude, of the effects of mustard gas and the techniques of bone grafting – all these would prove immensely valuable, even if doctors like Mengele, Brandt, Gebhardt and the others lacked the scientific detachment Raffaello Matti would himself have brought to the experiments.

Raffaello Matti also served as an S.D. V-man, an *agent provocateur* for the Security Department of the S.S.

His *modus operandi* was simplicity itself. He was Swiss, he was a surgeon, and he had worked here at the Charité under Dr Ferdinand Sauerbruch, certainly no friend of the regime. That he stayed on in Berlin could be attributed to a selfless desire to serve not the Nazis but the German people in their time of travail. Raffaello Matti spoke out openly against the futility of war and even, lately, against the government. Others of like mind confided in him. The rest was simple. Or had been until it became apparent that Germany would lose the war.

Six months ago Raffaello Matti had sought a way out. He found it through a Swedish businessman named Lindstrom who was a conduit to the American O.S.S. in Bern – a conduit that presented no danger to Raffaello Matti unless the Swede was compromised.

Raffaello Matti, devout Nazi, had become Allen Dulles's man in Berlin. In the understated terminology of the spy trade, a double agent, supplying both the S.D. and the American O.S.S. with information about the conspiracy to kill Adolf Hitler. The supply was plentiful. Ever since operating on General Beck last March, he had enjoyed uncritical acceptance among the conspirators.

Playing both ends against the middle, Raffaello Matti might yet manage to survive.

It was ironic that the Americans, those most decadent and mongrelised of people, might ultimately be the ones to save him.

Raffaello Matti was studying Mengele's report from Auschwitz on the latest results of the high altitude simulation experiments – unfortunately, a number of the subjects had died prematurely due to their generally run-down condition – when the soft buzz of the telephone interrupted him.

'Dr Matti speaking.'

'Herr Doktor, I hope you'll remember me.' The man gave his name; it meant nothing to the preoccupied Raffaello Matti. He wanted to return to Mengele's interesting report.

'We met last Sunday night at Freiherr von Heydebrand's,' the caller persisted, and Raffaello Matti was on the point of cutting him off with the suggestion that he phone his receptionist for an appointment when the man said: 'This won't take long, but it is important, Herr Doktor. Von Gruening recommended that I see you.'

Raffaello Matti's long graceful fingers closed tightly on the telephone receiver. Von Gruening was the O.S.S. half of his identification code.

'Ah yes, Gero von Gruening,' he responded carefully. 'Of course I'll be pleased to see you. Would this evening be convenient?'

His caller was downstairs now in the lobby of the administrative wing.

'It's the second floor, room 201,' Raffaello Matti told him.

'Five minutes, then, Herr Doktor.'

At that moment in his comfortable office on Herrengasse in the Swiss capital of Bern, Allen Welsh Dulles was also awaiting a visitor. The Herrengasse office was safe and he knew the visitor would make certain he was not under surveillance. The blackout would help him; the stolid citizens of Bern often complained that the blackout imposed on their neutral country by Nazi Germany was of benefit only to secret agents.

Allen Dulles, O.S.S. chief on the Continent, was in 1944 fifty-one years old. He had grey hair and a grey moustache and, behind his round silver-rimmed glasses, the sparkling eyes of a scholar doing the work he loved best. The expression on his face, usually open and benign, was troubled now. A billiard pipe was clamped between his teeth and aromatic smoke filled the large, clublike room.

Dulles had been more dismayed than surprised by the cipher that had arrived from London not an hour ago. O.S.S. and its British counterpart, S.O.E., were composed mostly of amateurs, after all. Well-meaning and even talented amateurs did not make the best intelligence officers. Sooner or later, for them, emotion replaced reason. They fell victim to their own propaganda and began to do the wrong thing for the right reason.

Allen Welsh Dulles was a professional. A lawyer by training, he had served the government on and off since the First World War. He had attended the Versailles Peace Conference in 1919, spent four years as chief of Near Eastern Affairs in the State Department, served as legal adviser to the disarmament conferences in Geneva in the 1920s and early 1930s. Dulles had known those conferences would not prevent another world war and by November 1942 he was back in Switzerland. He quickly established contact with anti-Nazi Germans like Goerdeler and Beck. Given the opportunity, he believed they could overthrow Hitler and put an end to the war.

That possibility had made London and Washington uneasy. They were increasingly inclined to replace reality with rhetoric, to thunder about Unconditional Surrender. Dulles, with his logical mind and legal training, was the first to admit the strength of their arguments.

But he couldn't dismiss from his mind the hundreds of thousands of casualties a total military conquest of Germany would entail. Nor could he forget the millions perishing in the Nazi death camps.

The cipher he had received from London might make it possible to end the slaughter, and Allen Dulles knew it was enough to tip the balance for him.

Dulles refilled his pipe and thought briefly and without bitterness of the fact that, except for this Major Green, Baker Street had by-passed him, and then there was a soft knock at the door.

Dulles's visitor towered over him as the two men shook hands. Not quite six and a half feet tall, the German was bean-pole slender and extremely near-sighted. Even his thick glasses did not restore normal vision. It was why, although only in his early forties, he had never served in the armed forces.

'I came as soon as I could, Allen.'

'It's good to see you, Hans Bernd. Sit down, won't you? Drink?'

Dulles poured brandy for both of them and wasted no time on small talk. 'How soon can you get back in?'

'I can always find an excuse if it's important enough,' Hans Bernd spoke fluent, accented English.

'It's important enough.'

Dulles told him about the cipher he had received from London.

'My God,' Hans Bernd said, 'you mean they're trying to *stop* it?'

'I'm afraid so.'

'That's monstrous. They can't do that.'

'Oh, but there's a strong chance they can.' Dulles spoke matter-of-factly. Only his eyes suggested the anguish he felt. 'The agent is one of the best we have.'

'I'm to deliver a message to him, is that it?' Hans Bernd said. 'Calling him off?'

Dulles puffed his pipe. For a while he did not speak. 'I'm afraid it's not that simple,' he said then. 'He doesn't take orders from me. *And* I was by-passed. That was no accident. I'm very much afraid, Hans Bernd, that I have no way of establishing acceptable contact with him.'

Hans Bernd shook his head, pursed his lips and exhaled a long breath. 'Then what can I do?'

Allen Dulles stood. 'Get in as soon as you can,' he said. 'And unmask him.' Dulles had almost said, 'Betray him.' Was there a difference? Richard Haller was merely obeying orders.

'I understand,' Hans Bernd said.

Dulles led his guest to the door. 'Make sure you understand this. No limits, Hans Bernd. No restrictions. His mission must be terminated.'

'Of course I remember you, Herr Hauptmann,' Raffaello Matti said, extending his hand. His face, sharp-featured but handsome, wore a worried smile.

Haller shook the hand, suppressing his distaste. Fifteen minutes, he told himself, a quarter of an hour with this renegade Swiss surgeon and it would all be over.

It was crucial, he knew, that Matti was an agent not of the Gestapo or the Criminal Police but of the S.D. Baker Street had made an astute choice. While the other services were busy covering their own tracks and looking for ways to survive the inevitable defeat, only the S.S. Security Department remained fanatically loyal to the Führer. Give the S.D. the details of Operation Valkyrie and they would move swiftly to crush it. Give the same information to the Gestapo or Kripo and it might well end up in a conspirator's wastebasket.

Haller looked steadily at Raffaello Matti, whose large dark eyes shifted to the window and back. Haller wondered what was distracting him.

'Butchers,' the doctor muttered under his breath. 'Damn butchers.'

Then Haller recognised the muffled sound that came through the closed, curtained window. It was the frightened lowing of cattle. Raffaello Matti was that most grotesque of Nazi stereotypes, one who could not stand cruelty to animals.

On the wall behind the desk Haller could see medical diplomas from Zürich and Berlin and signed photographs of a dozen Nazi luminaries. Raffaello Matti saw where he was looking. 'I treated all of them in my time,' he admitted with some faint vestige of pride, 'even the Führer. Polyps on his vocal chords.' The surgeon's eyes returned to the curtained window as the faint sound was repeated. He winced and switched on the radio on his desk, tuning in a brass band playing Blechmusik, then turning the volume up.

'May I inquire how you know Gero von Gruening?'

Haller ignored the question. 'I have some information you are to convey.'

Raffaello Matti misunderstood. 'You must realise I have to wait for von Gruening's friends to contact me. It may take a certain amount of time.'

'I don't mean von Gruening's friends.'

'But I was given to believe . . . the identification code . . . I'm afraid I don't understand.' Raffaello Matti offered the smile of a man pathetically eager to ingratiate himself but painfully unaware of how to go about it.

'My information is for the S.D., Herr Doktor. It concerns a plot to assassinate the Führer.'

Haller would remember, afterwards, that it took Raffaello Matti a full ten seconds to adjust to that, ten seconds to accept or at least resign himself to a duplicity beyond his comprehension, to a captain of grenadiers who knew the O.S.S. identification code yet wanted to pass information not out of Germany but into the Prinz Albrechtstrasse.

And in the time it took, in those ten seconds the Swiss Nazi needed to adjust his thinking, in those ten seconds that stretched, that hung suspended in the sound of the brassy Bavarian music coming from the radio, Richard Haller knew he could not go through with it.

'I won't pretend to understand,' Raffaello Matti said then.

Haller looked at him blankly. After a while he said: 'I'm not asking you to understand. I'm telling you to deliver the information.' His words seemed disconnected, without meaning to himself. He brushed the sleeve of his field-grey tunic across his forehead. The room was suffocatingly hot.

'For a friend of Gero von Gruening,' Raffaello Matti said, 'believe me, I would do anything. The S.D. will have your information half an hour after you leave here.'

Raffaello Matti waited, eager to please his new masters.

Haller tried feverishly to think. He had come here prepared to give Matti, give the S.D., the whole story of Valkyrie. Not just the names of the conspirators – the Gestapo and S.D. had known those for months. But the information the S.D. needed if they were to move despite the Gestapo's reluctance. The tactical details of the putsch itself, chapter and verse.

Finally he said: 'A small clique of ambitious Wehrmacht officers, discredited politicians, and unscrupulous Prussian aristocrats, plans to assassinate the Führer. We want you to disclose their identities to the S.D. Colonel General Ludwig Beck, former Army Chief-of-Staff. Carl Goerdeler, former Lord Mayor of Leipzig. General Friedrich Olbricht, Deputy C-in-C, Home Army, and the Home Army Chief-of-Staff, Colonel Count von Stauffenberg. The Social Democrat politician Julius Esser, and Berlin Police Chief Helldorf. I'll repeat the names for you, Herr Doktor,' Haller said carefully. 'Beck, Goerdeler, Olbricht, Stauffenberg, Esser, Helldorf. These are the ringleaders, self-serving traitors who must be destroyed without mercy.'

'Yes, yes, to be sure, Herr Hauptmann.' During Haller's recital of the names, Raffaello Matti had quickly lost interest.

'You have their names? Beck, Goerdeler . . .'

'I have all their names, I assure you, Herr Hauptmann.'

'Repeat them,' Haller insisted. 'I must be certain.'

Raffaello Matti repeated the names.

Moments later the Swiss doctor saw his guest out. Then he returned to his desk, wondering why the O.S.S. thought it so important to tell the S.D. who the conspirators were. He shrugged. If the Americans were so ridiculously naïve, so be it. The information would indeed be in the Prinz Albrechtstrasse, as promised, within half an hour.

A lot sooner than that. The Prinz Albrechtstrasse already had it.

Twenty minutes later Richard Haller was walking swiftly along Mittelstrasse towards the Prussian State Library. He had only to see the Swede, to pick up his change of clothing and identification papers. Tomorrow he would be in Lisbon, the following day in London. Presenting his assessment of the conspirators.

Totally inept, all of them, their *coup d'état* doomed to fail.

Haller would be guilty only of bad judgement and there was nothing about that in the code of military justice.

Silhouetted against the low moon, the first building past the intersection on the north side of Mittelstrasse was a ruin. So was the second. Both, Haller was sure, had been undamaged on his previous visit to the Swede.

The third building stood intact, and the fourth. Haller walked faster.

All that remained of the apartment block where the Swede had lived was its façade, a baroque false front for shattered masonry, a few blackened beams, and remnants of furniture. Precariously perched in one window on the ground floor was a bathtub. A large sign was nailed across what had been the entrance. In German, Polish, and French it told Haller that the punishment for looting was death.

He searched for the notice board usually posted outside a new ruin and found it to the left of the official warning against looting. He struck match after match, burning his fingers.

Otto, call Helga. All well.

Where is Frau B. Schmidt? Reward.

Three other messages tacked to the board, scrawled in pencil. Hope, despair, uncertainty.

Nothing about the repairing of watches, nothing from the Swede. Nothing for Haller.

Right or wrong, he had made his decision. And an R.A.F. bomb had stranded him in Germany.

That Friday night, 14 July, Gestapo Mueller's phone rang at an inopportune moment. Only his deputy Krause knew that Mueller was spending the night in his isolated lodge on the western edge of the Grünewald pine woods. Mueller wanted Krause's information badly enough to get out of bed and answer the phone. Krause, however, had come up with a blank, the Swiss legation insisting that the P.O.W. mail courier who had flown into Berlin a week ago was no longer in the Reich. Either they were lying or Monika had been mistaken. Mueller assumed they were lying. Even the cautious Swiss now accepted Germany's defeat as inevitable. Mueller returned to the bedroom and watched Monika roll over languidly and stub out her cigarette.

That Friday night, 14 July, Monika had no need to feign passion. Heinrich made love aggressively, selfishly, but even so the weight of his lean hard body excited her. Not because of what he did but who he was. There was nothing Gestapo Mueller could not do for her, if she pleased him. She remembered how Berlin had made her want to scream when she returned a week ago. How quickly that despair had passed! She wondered how many others like her could be found, who wished the war would never end.

That Friday night, 14 July, in the big villa in Wannsee twelve miles south-west of Berlin, Stauffenberg ended his conference with General Beck and went outside to sit on the dock. The night was breathlessly hot even on the lake but the air had cleared enough for the low moon to shine through. Countess Nina, visibly pregnant, had seen their five children to bed and by ten o'clock had joined her husband, bringing the portable phonograph and his favourite recording of Beethoven's Archduke Trio. They listened to the music and the water lapping against the pilings. Countess Nina wished she could see her husband's face more clearly in the moonlight. He almost seemed the real Klaus again, relaxed and serene like in the old days before he had been maimed, the terrible tension of the past few months gone. They sat side by side and when he reached for her hand she said, 'It's going to be soon, isn't it?'

Elisabeth, that Friday night in her room on the second floor of the villa, heard their soft footsteps on the path as the Stauffenbergs returned from the lake shore. For a long time after the house was silent she lay awake staring at the pale rippling reflection of moonlight on the ceiling. She tried to make her mind go blank and, when she couldn't, tried to think of other things. That she must apologise to Klaus and Heydi for her outburst in Lichterfelde, that she should make certain her uncle got more rest, that she ought to discuss with Countess Nina the possibility of extending the Emil network here to Wannsee. But it kept coming back, she couldn't help it. He was the world she would never know, the life she would never live, like the flickering unreal images on the screen in the Kurfürstendamm theatre, the screen blank now, the interlude over, the memory of it already fading as the crowds shuffled out to the bleak reality of the bombed streets. He was gone.

Ernst Otto Jaeger, that Friday night, was unaware that Monika was not at home. Jaeger spent the evening at the Invalidenstrasse barracks in Berlin-Moabit, where the Guard Battalion was billeted. A few hours with the four young company commanders, all of them Hitler Youth graduates, convinced him that when the time came they would follow any orders he gave them. At midnight, with the U-bahn no longer running, Jaeger decided to spend the night in Moabit. In the morning he would agree to the Bendlerstrasse request and cut his leave short to assume command of the Guard Battalion immediately. Once his file had been brought to the attention of Colonel Stauffenberg the rest had fallen into place exactly as Comrade Cell had predicted. Stauffenberg, something of a martinet, recognised a good officer when he saw one.

That Friday night, a few miles outside Karlsruhe along the Basel-Berlin line, the express train was shunted to a siding in a beech wood during an R.A.F. attack on the city. It remained there five hours. Hans Bernd Gisevius knew he would be lucky to reach Berlin by noon Saturday. It might be much later than that. Freight trains would have priority over the so-called express. So would cattle cars taking French Jews across the Reich to the death camps.

And in London that Friday night, Milt Green found the converted stable in Chenies Mews where Sister Eunice lived. It was after midnight and Milt Green was staggeringly but not obliteratingly drunk. He remembered. He remembered, all right. They needed the bed at University College Hospital, that part had been easy. Discharge granted, and good luck to you, major. He had got Gillian Bennett's address from the duty officer at Baker Street. He wanted her to know what he was doing. It was important that she knew, almost as if her knowing could, finally, answer one of those questions that could drive you nuts. Together they found the cryp at home, and Milt Green, his left arm in a cast, his legs rubbery, entered a dream in which Gillian stayed at the cryp's place while they went to Grosvenor Square, and the dream became a nightmare in which Milt Green was going to tell the cryp to forget it, he'd changed his mind, only Milt Green said nothing as he watched the cryp disappear into the code room to kill Milt Green's friend Dick Haller because Milt knew there was no other way Dick could be stopped, no control once Dick went in, no provision made to abort the mission, and after a while the cryp emerged from the code room and they cut back to the cryp's place where Milt Green proceeded to get very drunk and he either did or did not take Gillian Bennett home before pounding on Sister Eunice's door in the middle of the night.

Sister Eunice in a robe, furious at first, then full of concern as she let him in, and it must have been the look on his face that made her ask those questions they always asked, the ones that could drive you nuts, and instead of answering he suddenly heard noises like a grown man makes when he cries.

Sixteen

Above the Berghof, fluttering in the updraughts from the valley floor, flew the Führer Standard with its gold-wreathed swastika and four eagles, indicating that Adolf Hitler was in residence. He had, in fact, been in residence at the Obersalzberg on this Saturday, 15 July, for almost two weeks, an unusual state of affairs. It was hoped among the faithful that this sojourn in the place he loved above all others would inspire the Führer to produce the military miracle that would prevent the Anglo-American breakthrough in Normandy and contain the Red Army onslaught on East Prussia. The inspiration and the miracle, thus far, had not been forthcoming, and Hitler had remained secluded in the large white three-storey chalet despite the glorious Alpine summer. Even the daily ritual of the promenade to the teahouse had been dispensed with.

That he was in residence would have been obvious even without the Führer Standard on its tall flagstaff. All morning and into the early afternoon Mercedes and Opel staff cars had laboured up the steep, switchback road from Berchtesgaden, and by 12.30 the parking area between the post office gate, the greenhouse, and the garage was full.

At 12.35 the S.S. chauffeur who had driven Colonel Graf von Stauffenberg and his adjutant up from the airport was directed to the overflow parking area between the massive yellow stone barracks and Speer's architectural studio. As they had already shown their identification at the outer and inner perimeter gatehouses, they were free to walk unescorted the length of the three-hundred-yard paved path that led to the Berghof itself.

Major General Helmut Stieff, Chief, Organisation Branch, Army High Command, met them when they had covered half the distance. Stieff was a short, slightly hunchbacked man. Because congenital deformity disturbed the Führer, Stieff, although a member of the entourage that had moved from East Prussia to the Obersalzberg two weeks ago, was rarely permitted in the same room with Adolf Hitler.

Stieff would never have the opportunity to use one of the time bombs in his custody.

Unlike congenital deformity, a wound received in action against the enemy met with Hitler's consummate approval. Graf von Stauffenberg's eyepatch, missing right hand, and maimed left hand not only made his appear heroic but were a measure of his loyalty to Führer and Fatherland.

They might even have helped blunt the fury of an Adolf Hitler tirade. Stauffenberg had invited one; he had, after all, failed to produce the replacements for Army Group Centre. But there would be no carpet-chewing today.

Stieff spoke quickly as they walked down the path. 'They're giving you fifteen minutes at 1.30. Professor Hoffmann will be there.'

'Why Hoffmann?' Stauffenberg asked. Hoffmann was the Führer's official photographer.

Stieff smiled a tight nervous smile. 'Publicity shots. The disabled colonel reporting not just to the Führer but to the Party and Reich leadership. They'll all be there, Klaus. Himmler, Bormann, Keitel. Even Goering.'

Stauffenberg looked at Heydi.

'Good God in Heaven,' the young lieutenant said softly. 'The whole lot of them.'

The presence of O.K.W. Chief-of-Staff Keitel they had counted on, and probably Bormann, but not Himmler and certainly not Goering. Of the top leadership that would leave only Joseph Goebbels, and arrangements had been made to place Goebbels under arrest in Berlin in the first hour of Operation Valkyrie.

'Are they running on schedule?' Stauffenberg asked.

'Five minutes behind. You'll be in there by 1.35 at the latest.'

The hunchbacked Stieff was carrying a worn, bulging black leather briefcase that almost exactly matched the one tucked under Stauffenberg's arm. They accomplished the switch where the path dropped more steeply between the stands of larch and beech trees to the lawn of the Berghof itself.

Stieff accompanied them up the broad outside staircase and through one of the twin archways of the main entrance. Their boots clattered on the terrazzo floor in the long dim hallway. The door ahead to the left gave on the waiting-room, telephone exchange, and rest rooms; the larger double doors to the right on the main conference room, the one with the so-called Speer window.

Stieff left them in the waiting-room. It was crowded – army brass for the most part, a few Luftwaffe and Kriegsmarine officers, all of whom outranked Heydi. S.S. bodyguards in the white Berghof livery passed among the guests with trays of canapés and wine. It was very hot in the room and the air was blue with tobacco smoke. Heydi's mouth was so dry suddenly that it would have been difficult to talk. He found an armchair in a corner and picked up a magazine and shook his head no to an S.S. servant and found the magazine incomprehensible. Even the photographs made no sense. He sat in the corner of the room and looked at his watch and saw after he thought a great deal of time had passed that it was only 1.05. Half an hour to go. Stauffenberg, amazingly, had entered into light social conversation – Heydi saw his smile, heard his laughter – with a fat Luftwaffe general. After a while someone opened the door to the hall and left it open so that air would flow between it and the two windows on the opposite wall. Heydi could almost breathe. He realised he was holding the magazine upside down. He righted it; the lines of print ran off in odd directions and made no more sense than before.

Stauffenberg, still totally self-possessed, bowed slightly to the Luftwaffe general, clicked his heels, and crossed the room to the door that led to the telephone exchange, the briefcase, Stieff's look-alike briefcase, still clamped under his arm. Again Heydi looked at his watch. It was then 1.14. Exactly eight minutes later the colonel emerged from the telephone exchange and stood in front of Heydi's chair until Heydi also stood.

Stauffenberg spoke softly; what he said was lost in the babble of conversation. He looked at Heydi's face impatiently and repeated the words.

'The call went through.'

Heydi's knees were shaking. For the first time in his adult life the sang-froid in which he took such pride had deserted him. 'Jawohl, Herr Oberst,' he said, the words possibly apposite but the voice one he did not recognise.

'Get a grip on yourself,' Stauffenberg said, his own voice ice. 'Listen to me. You'll stay here. General Olbricht will call back. Blitz call, 1.45. Our excuse to leave. You understand?'

The colonel was going over familiar ground, wisely, to strip the fear from Heydi. 'You'll take the call. I'll be inside. You'll come for me.'

Stauffenberg spoke as though to a small child or a drunkard or an idiot, and it worked. Heydi felt offended but better. His head had cleared. His knees no longer shook. 'I know all that,' he said irritably.

Stauffenberg nodded in approval. The gloved left hand patted Heydi's shoulder. Then he said: 'This you don't know. There was no reason to wait. I want them moving in Berlin even before we leave here. I gave Olbricht the codeword. Valkyrie has started.'

Conversation flowed around them as Heydi sank back into his chair. The risk Stauffenberg had taken was huge. To move prematurely could be suicidal. If something went wrong and they had to abort the operation in Berlin, what then?

In the balance against that risk was the element of surprise. The first few hours after the death of Adolf Hitler, even the first few minutes, would be vital. The sooner the operation began, the better – the sudden declaration of a state of martial law, the alert of the Krampnitz armoured troop school, the Döberitz infantry school, the Potsdam and Lichterfelde cadet corps, the crucial movement by motor convoy of the Guard Battalion from Moabit to the Armoury on Unter den Linden, the conspirators already going into position when the first news hit the capital like a shock wave . . .

Besides, what could go wrong?

At 1.30 S.S.-Sturmbannführer Otto Guensch, Hitler's adjutant, made his way through the crowded waiting-room to tell Colonel Stauffenberg of a slight delay. He would be expected in the conference room in precisely ten minutes.

The proximity of the deed had an unexpected effect on Heydi. He was as calm, suddenly, as Stauffenberg himself.

Jaeger was called from the Guard Battalion officers' mess to the communications room at 1.25. He scanned the paper as it emerged from the chattering teletype.

> GUARD BATTALION ORDERED IMMEDIATELY TO MILITARY DISTRICT III BERLIN HEADQUARTERS UNTER DEN LINDEN 1.
>
> FIRST PRIORITY: BLOCKADE GOVERNMENT QUARTER, CONFINE ALL PERSONS IN BLOCKADED AREA INDOORS.
>
> SECOND PRIORITY: REMOVE ALL UNAUTHORISED MILITARY AND ALL SS PERSONNEL FROM BLOCKADED AREA.
>
> THIRD PRIORITY: OCCUPY PROPAGANDA MINISTRY, FOREIGN MINISTRY, HITLER YOUTH LEADERSHIP KAISERDAMM 45, SCHWANENWERDER AND LANKE RESIDENCES OF REICH MARSHAL GOERING.
>
> FOURTH PRIORITY: OCCUPY WINTERFELD-

STRASSE TELEPHONE EXCHANGE, ORANIENBURGERSTRASSE MAIN TELEGRAPH OFFICE, RINGBAHNSTRASSE CENTRAL POST OFFICE.

FIFTH PRIORITY . . .

Jaeger turned away from the machine.

Had Monday night accomplished nothing?

He became aware that Lieutenant Bleiner, the communications and N.S.D.A.P. Guidance Officer, was addressing him. Bleiner, a tall young Austrian, seemed calm. 'It's an exercise, Herr Major,' he explained to the new commander. 'A rehearsal for a state of martial law in the event of an uprising of the slave labourers.'

'I'm aware of that,' Jaeger snapped angrily, and immediately regretted it. Whatever happened, he would need all the help he could get from the poised Bleiner.

'An exercise,' the Austrian continued, 'unless of course the slave labourers are already in the streets.'

If Hitler was dead? What then?

Kropotkin Square had been explicit on that point. The putsch in Berlin must still be stopped. If it succeeded, Comrade Peresypkin was convinced, the conspirators would make peace with the West and prevent the Red Army from reaching Berlin. Historical necessity dictated that that must not happen.

Jaeger, at all costs, had to control the situation. It would take a minimum of four hours for Stauffenberg's armoured units garrisoned outside the capital to enter Berlin. Until then, everything was in the hands of the Guard Battalion.

In Jaeger's hands.

Jaeger had to give the city to the one man who, as much as Adolf Hitler himself, would fight on until the bitter end.

'Get me the Bernau motor pool,' he told Bleiner, and moments later he was arguing over the telephone for the immediate dispatch to Moabit of 350 tons of motor convoy capacity. That much was not available, emergency or no emergency. He could have 270 tons.

It would be enough. The Guard Battalion would be deployed in the heart of Berlin in less than an hour.

Where Ernst Otto Jaeger, the most dedicated of Communists, would place it at the disposal of that most dedicated of Nazis, Joseph Goebbels.

At 1.35 in the Berghof a white-uniformed member of the

Leibstandarte Adolf Hitler appeared in the waiting-room doorway.

'Achtung! Achtung! The Führer!'

Every man in the room stood instantly and rigidly to attention.

Jackboots thudded in the hallway.

S.S.-Sturmbannführer Otto Guensch, staring straight ahead, marched past the door. Behind him goose-stepped two pairs of the magnificent specimens of the Leibstandarte Adolf Hitler; behind them S.S.-Gruppenführer Hermann Fegelein, Eva Braun's brother-in-law, alongside General Wilhelm Burgdorf, the Führer's army adjutant; then Field Marshal Keitel matching strides with Hitler; then the fat Reich Marshal in a glittering white and gold uniform of his own design, marching unhappily in step with Heinrich Himmler in his black S.S. tunic; then more of the Leibstandarte Adolf Hitler.

The hallway emptied, the sound of boots on tile receded, and Heydi was certain every man in the room could hear the thud of Freiherr von Heydebrand's heart.

Soon through the window came the roar of automobile engines.

The Führer, without warning, had left. He was known to do that occasionally, breaking off a conference or cancelling an appointment at the last moment, claiming that the irregularity of his schedule, as much as the Leibstandarte Adolf Hitler, was his bodyguard.

Conversation resumed in the waiting-room. For another moment Heydi stood where he was, unable to think, unable to move.

Where was Stauffenberg?

When the first half dozen six-wheeled Krupp personnel carriers arrived outside the Invalidenstrasse barracks, Jaeger straddled an NSU motorcycle, kicked the starter and raced off. In five minutes he would be at the command post on Unter den Linden. Not a mile from 20 Hermann Goeringstrasse, Goebbels' home address. The Propaganda Minister invariably lunched there.

Stauffenberg stood in a cubicle in the Berghof rest room, briefcase under his right arm. swiftly unfastening the buckles with his maimed left hand as he had so often practised.

In exactly three minutes he would appear at the double doors of the conference room, the chemical fuse of the bomb activated, the acid eating at the wire.

As the day was hot, the acid would work more swiftly. They had estimated twenty minutes. Fifteen would do it now, possibly less.

Fifteen minutes to deliver and position the bomb, receive the blitz call from the Bendlerstrasse, motor down the switchback road to the airport . . .

His maimed left hand grasped the pliers, groped in the briefcase, felt the rectangular shape of the bomb.

In fifteen minutes plus the few seconds it would take him to plunge the pliers through the wrapping and snip the vial of acid, Adolf Hitler would be dead.

He spread the pliers.

And heard running footsteps.

'Klaus!'

Heydi's voice.

Jaeger stood for a moment outside the grey sandstone Armoury at Unter den Linden 1. Traffic flowed across the bridge from the Lustgarten and along Berlin's showpiece boulevard, civilian cars for the most part, a surprising number of them despite the shortage of fuel and the damage to the roadway, total war no more than Goebbels' optical illusion, the luxuries of life still available to the privileged. The streets were crowded with Saturday afternoon pedestrians strolling unconcerned past the uprooted linden trees, the bomb craters, the debris.

It was 1.42. Jaeger turned to enter the command post.

Stauffenberg and Heydi entered the Berghof telephone exchange at 1.45. The operation had begun in Berlin twenty-three minutes ago.

'I'm expecting an urgent call. Colonel von Stauffenberg.'

The Signal Corps sergeant manning the switchboard nodded. 'I remember, Herr Oberst. It hasn't come through yet.'

Headquarters, Military District III, was in Potsdam, the Armoury at Unter den Linden 1 hardly more than a communications centre. Jaeger went inside, found the duty officer, and identified himself.

'What are your orders?' he asked the duty officer.

'To serve as a command post for the Guard Battalion, Herr Major.'

'Nothing about the traffic out there?'

'Only to await your orders, Herr Major.'

'Stop all traffic entering Unter den Linden from here to the Brandenburg Gate. I want Pariserplatz totally cleared. What's the matter with you, man? You should have done that before I got here. My convoy will be passing through Königsplatz any minute now. How many have you on duty here?'

'Headquarters Company and a platoon of feldgendarmerie.'

'Muster your chained dogs, then. Hurry, man. All traffic out of Pariserplatz.'

Jaeger went back outside. Thus far, he had done no more than implement the teletype's First Priority.

'Your call, Herr Oberst. Booth two.'

'Stauffenberg speaking. Yes?'

'Herr Oberst, this is the office of General Olbricht, Deputy Commander of . . . '

Stauffenberg did not recognise the voice.

'Put him on. Hurry!'

'I was instructed to inform you to return to Berlin at the earliest – '

'Put the general on!'

Half a minute passed.

'General Olbricht speaking.'

And Stauffenberg told him: 'The situation regarding the reserves for Army Group Centre remains unchanged.'

Which meant: Abort Valkyrie at once.

The teletype message Jaeger had received sent only the Guard Battalion, *Grossdeutschland* Division, into immediate action. Other, stronger military units stationed farther from the heart of the capital had been placed on alert. Valkyrie General Order Number One, which was to follow, would command them to march on the city.

The half-hour interval between the issuance of the two orders was provided as a fail-safe device. If something went wrong, the conspirators reasoned they could call off the mission of Major Jaeger's command without arousing too much suspicion.

General Olbricht, on receiving Stauffenberg's signal to abort, should have phoned the Invalidenstrasse Barracks and Berlin Headquarters, Military District III, with instructions for Major Jaeger to return to Moabit, ending the rehearsal of phase one of Operation Valkyrie.

Olbricht, however, replaced the phone on his cluttered desk at the Bendlerstrasse and did nothing for two full minutes.

That something had gone wrong at the Obersalzberg was a certainty, but he had no way of knowing until Stauffenberg returned by plane to Berlin what the problem was.

Had Stieff failed to deliver the bomb? Had the bomb been defective? Had the bomb exploded, the Führer somehow escaping with his life? He had to assume that Stauffenberg had somehow acted impetuously, prematurely. Was Stauffenberg himself now in jeopardy? But how could that be? He'd answered the phone, hadn't he?

Olbricht in those two minutes was paralysed by indecision.

He wished Stauffenberg was there to tell him what to do.

The phone rang.

Stauffenberg, thank God! It had to be Stauffenberg.

It was General Fromm, Commander-in-Chief, Home Army, Olbricht's superior.

'Just what the goddamn hell is going on?' Fromm shouted. He was, like Rommel in France and others, privy to the conspiracy. He had, like Rommel and others, neither betrayed it nor joined it.

'Herr General, I can explain . . . '

'I want to know who ordered the Guard Battalion to Unter den Linden!'

Olbricht said that he had.

'On what authority?'

'It was thought, Herr Generaloberst, that a rehearsal of phase one of Operation Valkyrie would be in keeping with Field Marshal Keitel's directive relevant to . . . '

'But you didn't see fit to inform me?'

Olbricht did not reply at once. Fromm, calmer now, asked: 'Are you intending to issue General Order Number One?'

Olbricht realised then that Fromm was nervous, his uncertainty masked by bluster. If the putsch was under way, Fromm did not want to get caught on the losing side.

Olbricht said: 'Only the Guard Battalion exercise was planned for today, Herr Generaloberst.'

There was a long pause. 'Is it your intention to return the Guard Battalion to Moabit then?'

'I was on the point of issuing those orders when you called, sir.'

Olbricht thought he heard Fromm sigh.

'In future, no order relevant to Operation Valkyrie is to be issued without my authority. Is that understood?'

'Should the situation for which Valkyrie is . . . '

'Should *any* situation relevant to Valkyrie arise, you will consult with me.'

The next time, if there was a next time, to issue the Valkyrie Orders prematurely would be unthinkable.

Jaeger looked westward down the length of Unter den Linden. Already the feldgendarmerie were deployed, directing traffic, sealing all entrances, ordering pedestrians off the street.

He raised his field glasses and focused on the Brandenburg Gate at the far end. The first half-dozen Krupp personnel carriers skirted the great triumphal arch and pulled to a halt. The troops, steel-helmeted, carrying sub-machine guns, piled out into Pariserplatz.

Jaeger looked at his watch. 1.52. Time to move. He beckoned to the nearest feldgendarmerie uniform.

'Find the duty officer,' he ordered. 'Tell him to make sure communications are kept open to Pariserplatz. I'm going down there to take personal command.'

Pariserplatz was the hub of activity now. Pariserplatz was also the entrance to Hermann Goeringstrasse, where Goebbels should now be.

Jaeger straddled the NSU motorcycle. Just then the duty officer himself came running from the building, followed by Bleiner.

'Apparently that's it for today,' the Austrian said. 'Everybody goes home. The Bendlerstrasse's just cancelled the operation.'

Seventeen

The optics of war: Propaganda Minister Joseph Goebbels drove his own small, unpretentious Volkswagen to the Propaganda Ministry every morning, invariably arriving just before 9.00.

Sunday was no exception, and on Sunday Goebbels timed his arrival with the route march of a Hitler Youth unit just then parading through Wilhelmplatz.

The optics of war: The flunkies who served in the Propaganda Ministry had exchanged their brown cutaways for field-grey.

The optics of war: Goebbels never smoked in public. The Führer disapproved of smoking. But the Propaganda Minister's fingers were tobacco-stained. He smoked two packs a day.

The optics were apparent to Berlin Police Chief Wolf Heinrich Count von Helldorf as his open, chauffeur-driven Mercedes-Benz 320 pulled up outside the eighteenth-century palace at 8-9 Wilhelmstrasse on the north side of Wilhelmplatz at exactly 9.00 on Sunday morning, 16 July. The Hitler Youth on their route march had stopped in their tracks to gaze in awe at the dark little man in the double-breasted grey civilian suit who emerged from his Volkswagen and saluted their colours with a stiffly out-thrust right arm before hurrying across the portico and into the palace. The orthopaedic shoe almost hid his limp. Whether the limp resulted from a congenital clubfoot, as rumour had it, or from a childhood attack of polio, as Goebbels himself claimed, not even his old friend Wolf von Helldorf knew for certain.

Helldorf crossed the pleasant, sunlit square. Like Goebbels, the police chief wore civilian clothing; he hoped to get away before noon and spend the hot summer Sunday at Wannsee with the Stauffenbergs.

The head usher, a dignified old man who had looked so correct in his brown cutaway and looked so ridiculous in field-grey, showed him upstairs. The french doors that led to the balcony had been thrown open and sunlight streamed into the second-floor office, gleaming on the vast marble desktop and the globe to one side of it.

Goebbels rose, and the two men shook hands. Goebbels' broad thin-lipped mouth smiled; his dark eyes did not.

'We don't see much of each other these days, Wolf,' he said. The deep voice, even after all these years, surprised Helldorf. Goebbels was barely five feet tall and didn't weigh a hundred and ten pounds.

'I'm lucky if I can keep it down to eighty hours a week,' the police chief said. 'That doesn't leave much time for socialising.'

Helldorf, since joining the conspiracy, had tried to avoid his old friend. Their contact, in the past year or so, had been restricted to chance meetings at the Comradeship Club. Helldorf could even wonder, with conscience-serving hindsight, if they ever really had been friends.

Goebbels was unquestionably the most intelligent of the Nazi brass and, with the possible exception of Hitler himself, the most dedicated. But in the Propaganda Minister's case dedication did not signify fanatic belief in Party ideology. In private, Goebbels could poke fun at the concept of the master race while his propaganda apparatus was busy promoting it, thereby making the fanatical Himmler's chosen work of genocide easier. Goebbels could even be charming, and charm was not a prominent personality trait among his colleagues.

But even more than Hitler, Goebbels equated ideology with power. Stripped of what Goebbels regarded as non-essentials, the programme of the N.S.D.A.P. was the will to power and the concomitant destruction of whatever stood in the way of that power. Such an ideology, Helldorf knew, could turn on itself.

In defeat a Hitler or a Goebbels would not stop until he brought the undeserving world down with him.

Joseph Goebbels, failed intellectual, unsuccessful poet, magnificent orator, inventor of the science of propaganda, loving husband and father, compulsive woman-chaser, was the most complex man Helldorf had ever known.

'What was that business yesterday all about, anyway?' Goebbels asked after a few minutes of small talk.

The question did not surprise Helldorf. Goebbels' caustic tongue made him unpopular with the military; he would have had no satisfactory answers from them.

'What business?' Helldorf said, wanting time to think. It was a mistake.

'This isn't November 1938,' Goebbels told him dryly. 'You weren't out of town, my friend. So you could conveniently return the next morning claiming you would have arrested every brownshirt arsehole who set fire to a synagogue or smashed a shop window. Yesterday you were right here in the capital of the universe, my friend.'

November 1938 *had* been the turning point for Helldorf. He wondered now just how much Goebbels knew about that. And what he might, under certain circumstances, do about it.

'Oh, you mean the troop movements.'

'That's terribly bright of you,' Joseph Goebbels said.

'From what I could learn, it was a training exercise for something the Bendlerstrasse calls Operation Valkyrie, a contingency plan to deal with an uprising of the slave labourers.'

'Or of the S.S., whichever comes first,' Goebbels cut him off, the dry Rhenish accent very pronounced. 'Did it occur to you that such an exercise could be a cover for a *coup d'état*?'

'That's – preposterous,' Helldorf said.

He had almost said paranoid.

'I would have thought so too, my friend. But with a reasonably healthy amount of self-protective paranoia, I tried a little experiment. As you know, I have a direct line to the Berghof. I tried to call Keitel. I couldn't get through.'

'Keitel,' Helldorf said lightly, 'has been known to avoid you.'

'Wolf, don't be obtuse. It wasn't Keitel I couldn't get through to. It was the Berghof itself.'

Helldorf knew that the operation called for that. Colonel General Fellgiebel, Chief of Communications, would have blocked the signal circuits after the call from the Bendlerstrasse to Stauffenberg. Apparently Stauffenberg, in the confusion following Hitler's departure, had neglected to call him off.

Goebbels lit another cigarette off the stub of the one he was smoking. 'Tell me, Wolf, what precisely is the role of the Berlin police in this Operation Valkyrie?'

'Strictly a minor one. When a state of martial law is declared, I take orders from the Bendlerstrasse. It's mostly a question of keeping my men off the streets.'

'Who in the Bendlerstrasse?'

Either Olbricht or Stauffenberg would have been the truthful answer. But both men served under Fromm. Helldorf decided to equivocate.

'General Fromm,' he said.

'Of course, General Fromm.' Goebbels blew three perfect smoke rings, jabbing his index finger through each of them in turn. 'If I asked you to name the membership of a small group of dissidents whose figurehead leader is General Ludwig Beck, could you supply those names?'

'Yes,' Helldorf said at once. 'I could.'

'Would your own name be among them?'

'If you ask that question seriously,' Helldorf said, 'then there is no possible answer that would satisfy you.'

Goebbels laughed; Helldorf did not.

'If, as Gauleiter of Berlin, I asked you to arrest them? Would you do that?'

'Yes,' said Helldorf. 'But getting evidence to convict them would be something else again.'

'Evidence,' said Goebbels, rising to his feet, 'is whatever

Freisler and the People's Court say it is.' He stubbed his cigarette out. 'Don't worry, I'm not going to ask you to arrest them.'

'Am I supposed to ask why?'

'It's really quite simple. There are three possibilities, my friend. First, the plotters are arrested before they act. Second, they are arrested after they act. Third, they continue to do what they have been doing for years – that is, talk. In the first two cases, who would emerge as the most powerful man in Germany?'

The answer was easy. Helldorf said: 'Himmler.'

He knew that Goebbels abhorred the Reichsführer-S.S.

'And in the third case? Who would emerge – or rather, remain – the most powerful man in the Reich?'

That answer was easy too, but Helldorf did not give it. With Hitler devoting his time to the conduct of the war, Joseph Goebbels, as Gauleiter of Berlin and Minister of Propaganda and Public Enlightenment, Joseph Goebbels, the most eloquent and visible of the N.S.D.A.P. leadership, had already achieved that position.

Goebbels went to the door, his limp more evident then.

'As the war follows its inevitable course,' he said thoughtfully, 'certain things must be done to Germany. The Führer knows what those things are. So do I. Himmler doesn't. His racial fanaticism clouds the issue for him.' Goebbels opened the door. 'Keep them talking, Wolf. Only talking. I depend on you.'

Returning to Alexanderplatz, which had borne the brunt of last Thursday night's raid and was now, on Sunday morning, crowded with Organization Todt rescue squads and swarms of Russian P.O.W.s attacking with pick and shovel the rubble that had been the huge Berolinahaus office building, Helldorf recalled Goebbels' final speech and he suddenly felt chilled. The Propaganda Minister's choice of words – he was a man who always chose his words with precision – was no accident.

Certain things must be done. Not *for* Germany but *to* Germany.

If seventy million Germans had proven themselves unworthy, the leader and his spokesman showed their other face. Perhaps it had always been there, behind the dream of the Thousand Year Reich, the dark and terrible secret they had hidden even from themselves.

Not the ruthless will to power but the compulsive need to destroy. Behind the conqueror's mask, the face of the suicide.

And the annihilator.

*

Richard Haller approached police headquarters on foot, fifteen minutes before Helldorf returned there from the Propaganda Ministry in his chauffeured Mercedes.

Alexanderplatz, once the busy traffic hub of Berlin-East, looked like the epicentre of an earthquake. Even the worst of the damage in London, the blocks of desolation around St Paul's, where yellow ragwort and fireweed grew among the twisted girders and crumbling walls, was nothing compared to this. Not one of the buildings enclosing Alexanderplatz had escaped damage. Great piles of rubble made the square impassable to vehicular traffic and the long ragged columns of Russian P.O.W.s picking their way between the bomb craters and wrecked cars and trucks would soon be digging in the ruins for survivors they did not want to find.

South of the zone of total devastation, police headquarters itself stood, most of its windows shattered, the dingy brick façade chipped and scarred, the wide stone steps in front broken away from the building and tilted like the deck of a ship suspended in a stormy sea.

Haller paused there, knowing that everything had changed and nothing had changed.

It had taken almost six years, and the war, and the plot to assassinate Hitler, and the decision reached in Baker Street, to bring him back there.

It had taken thirty-six hours spent in a small room in a gasthaus on Mittelstrasse. Haller had found the place on Friday night, not two hundred yards from the ruins of the Swede's apartment building. He had not left the gasthaus until this morning. Shaving gear, a toothbrush, and enormous meals instead of the meagre fare his ration coupons entitled him to were provided by the landlady, who had a son Haller's age serving in the East. She was both solicitous of the captain's welfare and saddened because he spent that summer weekend of his leave in a solitude she could not comprehend. Haller himself could comprehend it, could comprehend finally the warning given by the colonel in charge of the Special Training School at Beaulieu in the New Forest, a former Jesuit seminarian as legendary as he was irreverent. When you're operating behind enemy lines with no possibility of control, you're alone, more desperately alone than anyone in the world. Well, the colonel had amended with a hard grin, Jesus was alone like that when he went off into the wilderness to wrestle with temptation. A time may come when you have to go off into the wilderness and make like Jesus. And temptation, of course, is simply the enemy inside yourself. When that time comes, you'll find out who you are.

For Haller, that weekend, the wilderness had been the four walls of the small room in the gasthaus on Mittelstrasse and the enemy the Richard Haller who, as a twenty-four-year-old graduate student at the Institute for International Affairs in Geneva in November 1938, had decided to see Hitlerite Germany for himself.

He did not stay long. He had planned on a month. He was back in Geneva in ten days.

In the café on the Rue des Etuves in Geneva in November 1938 when he returned, they saw the stiff way he moved and the bruises on his face, and they asked, 'What the hell happened to you?' and Richard Haller after a long silence said, 'There was some rioting.' And they looked at his eyes and they asked, 'Where's Linde, didn't she come back with you?' and after an even longer silence Richard Haller said, 'No, she's still in Berlin.'

Linde was Sieglinde Meier, tennis partner, skiing companion, occasional bedmate, twenty-one, blonde, blue-eyed, her appearance as anomalous as her name. Sieglinde Meier was Jewish.

Seeing Germany for himself meant going in with Linde to convince her father to leave before it was too late. In November 1938 a Jew with enough money could still buy his way out.

Moritz Meier, portrait painter, for whom the elder Krupp, Fritz von Thyssen, and even Dr Hjalmar Horace Greeley Schacht had sat, considered himself a German who happened to be born Jewish.

He had no reason to leave. He was certain what he called the Brown Madness would pass. The Germans were as cultured as any people in the world, Berlin had been his father's home and his grandfather's, so he had to call himself Israel-Moritz, so what? So there had been the boycott of Jewish shops in retaliation for the Jewish propaganda campaign abroad against Nazism, so what? So a few shop windows were broken by the Brown Rabble, what could you expect from such human garbage? His friends Krupp and Thyssen and Schacht would stop them when the time came, his friends who pulled the strings for the Bohemian corporal from Austria who couldn't even get into architecture school, they were just giving him a little rope, so what? So Jews had been dismissed from the career civil service, there really were too many, as Schacht had said. And the legal profession and the universities, the same, a certain type of Jew had a way of calling attention to himself, it was unfortunate but true. I, myself, Herr Haller, was born a Jew but I'm the first to admit it. So my passport is marked with a J, so what? So I need an identity card that says I'm Jewish, there's something wrong with an identity card? We Germans and Jews understand each other, young man, and if a certain rectification is necessary, I am a patient man unlike you Americans, no offence.

Moritz Meier, portrait painter, friend of Krupp and Thyssen and Schacht, lapsed Jew, patient man, standing at the dining-room window on a bleak cold day early in November 1938, a letter in his trembling hand, the letterhead that of the REICH CHAMBER OF FINE ARTS, the signature that of Adolf Ziegler, President.

'What is this? What is this?' Moritz Meier speaking those words over and over again.

First Linde and then Haller read the letter.

. . . apparent on the basis of your September 1938 submissions to the Reich Chamber that your work stands irremediably apart from the cultural ideals of National Socialist Greater Germany. Therefore, effective on receipt of this letter, your membership in the Reich Chamber of Fine Arts is terminated and you are proscribed from pursuing any and all professional and extraprofessional activity in the field of fine art.

'What is this? What is this?' He answered his own question: 'A mistake, a bureaucratic blunder.'

He phoned the Ruhr but could reach neither Krupp nor Thyssen. Nor could he get through to the office of Reichsbank President Schacht for an appointment.

For two days he did nothing.

'He'll agree to leave now,' Linde predicted to Haller. 'His eyes are open now.'

The third day after he received the letter he left the big townhouse in Charlottenburg and was gone all day. He returned that night with a strange smile on his round red face.

'*Shul*,' he said. 'I went to *shul*, can you imagine? The first time in twenty years. So there's a law against it? You'd be amazed the number of people who remember they're Jews.'

That was 8 November 1938.

The next night, 9 November, was Crystal Night.*

*

* Milt Green with a comment. *Kristallnacht* was also called The Night of Broken Glass. Two days earlier, Ernst vom Rath, Third Secretary of the German Embassy in Paris, had been assassinated by a young Polish Jew. It

Opposite the main telegraph office, flames leaped from the windows of the New Synagogue. A mob of torch-bearing Brown Shirts, some of them drunk, some brandishing horse-whips, charged down Artilleriestrasse to the University Clinic, where a dozen old Jews had brought their rabbi, bleeding profusely from a scalp wound. The prayer shawls they still wore fluttered in the wind as they battered at the clinic door in vain. Sparks shot into the cold night and smoke swirled in the head-light beams of two S.A. trucks parked facing the clinic.

It was almost midnight when Haller and Linde got there, Haller driving Moritz Meier's Opel. He braked to a stop behind one of the Storm Troop trucks and grabbed Linde's arm as she opened the car door.

'You can't go out there.'

She broke away from him and was on the street running.

Haller waited ten seconds, literally unable to move. One big Jew somewhat younger than the rest stood in front of the injured rabbi, arms spread wide, long coat flapping in the wind, trying to protect him as two S.A. men darted close with torches, thrusting them at the rabbi's long white beard. The big Jew swung his arms awkwardly, knocking down one Brown Shirt. The other one, calmly, like setting fire to a haystack, held his torch under the big Jew's face. His prayer shawl caught fire, and then his hair. He ran three strides, screaming, head trailing flame, and then he fell, rolling and burning, pounding himself with great desperate blows. Finally he lay still, the flames subdued. An S.A. man kicked him methodically – head, chest, groin – boots thudding against flesh.

A second Jew, a frail old man, had been stripped naked. Shivering, he was down on all fours, a Brown Shirt lashing his welted back with a horsewhip as he scuttled frantically over the cobblestones licking S.A. jackboots.

A third Jew tried to run. He almost made it to Moritz Meier's car, panting, gesticulating wildly. Felled by a blow from behind, he lay against the kerb. Two S.A. men loomed

---

was the excuse the Nazi regime had been waiting for. Goebbels' propaganda machine whipped the street mobs to a frenzy against the Jews. The S.A. since the Roehm Purge in 1934 restricted to ceremonial functions, was unleashed. In fifteen hours, 177 synagogues in Germany and Austria were demolished, 7,500 Jewish-owned shops destroyed, and thousands of Jews molested and beaten, some fatally. As 9 November was also the holiest of Nazi holy days, commemorating Hitler's 1923 Beer Hall Putsch, the N.S.D.A.P. leaders could claim they were busy elsewhere and had nothing to do with the slaughter. Even Berlin Police Chief Helldorf was conveniently out of town. His role in the pillage, rioting, and mayhem remains equivocal.

over him, smiling as they unbuttoned their flies and urinated.

By then Haller was out of the car and going after Linde. She had been stopped by a pair of Brown Shirts in front of the S.A. trucks.

'Better get out of here, Fräulein,' one of them said. 'This is no business of yours.' He was a short dark man who looked more Jewish than Linde did. Sieglinde Meier looked like a Himmler stereotype of good Aryan breeding stock.

'Get out of my way.'

The second S.A. man was paunchy and middle-aged. He took her arm with almost the same restraining gesture Haller had used in the car. 'Fräulein,' he said in a patient, totally reasonable voice, 'you have to understand they are only Jews.'

Linde shook his hand off and spat in his face.

'I'm a Jew, you stinking son of a bitch!' she screamed and ran in front of the headlights to find her father.

They caught her before she could reach the clinic door. Haller got the dark one turned around and put him out with a savage left hook that did not move six inches but had all the weight of his shoulder behind it. The paunchy one yanked the horsewhip from his broad leather belt and laid it twice, three times, across Linde's back. Haller got the whip away from him and used it once, the rhinoceros hide welting the pale face from hairline to jaw, the S.A. man crying out, and then Haller was held from behind and hit. He broke loose once before they swarmed all over him, dragging him down. Only the first four jackboots smashing against his ribs hurt. He thought he saw Linde standing with her father and then Moritz Meier stood alone in his prayer shawl, and then they dragged him to the truck.

Where he was allowed to watch five of them raping his daughter.

Haller went up the tiled steps and into police headquarters. The walls inside were scabrous, faded green paint peeling away in long strips. Some of the shattered windows had been boarded over, giving the gloomy, high-ceilinged rotunda a disused look. The police wore the same old-fashioned spiked helmets they had worn in 1938, the green and white police flag still hung adjacent to Nazi red, white, and black, the information desk on its platform at the far side of the rotunda still loomed with unsubtle Prussian menace over those who came before it, the fat, ferociously scowling duty sergeant in his green uniform might have been the same one Haller had seen in November 1938.

'The Herr Hauptmann wishes?'

In a properly deferential voice. At least that was different from 1938, when Haller had presented himself, his face bruised and swollen, before the same desk, a nervous American assistant consul at his side.

'I want to see Count von Helldorf.'

– This man is an American citizen, said the nervous assistant consul. He wants whatever information you can give him about a Jewish girl named Sieglinde Meier.

'Does the Count expect you, Herr Hauptmann?'

– Your papers! Surely you are not Jewish yourself?

'He'll see me.'

– Passport, visa, all in order, said the nervous assistant consul. Mr Haller is not Jewish.

'As the Herr Hauptmann says. Count von Helldorf is expected back shortly. Staircase B, if you please, sir.'

– What is Mr Haller's interest?

– Fräulein Meier was the victim of a brutal assault the night before last, Haller said. She's been missing since then.

– The night before last. Of course. And was Mr Haller also the victim of a brutal assault?

– Mr Haller has been persuaded, said the nervous assistant consul, not to press charges.

– The disposition of all cases relevant to the events of 9 November, said the sergeant in a bored voice, is in the hands of the Gestapo.

Haller had gone there to the Prinz Albrechtstrasse, where he was treated with that exaggerated courtesy that borders on contempt. The case against the Jewess Sarah-Sieglinde Meier – the Sarah had been mandatory for all Jewesses since August – was still pending. The Jew Israel-Moritz Meier had been released.

Haller found Moritz Meier in the attic studio of the house in Charlottenburg. His canvases had been slashed, their frames broken. Moritz Meier himself was neatly dressed, his polished shoes dangling three feet off the floor and just above the surface of his paint-smeared tabouret.

Haller called the police. It was an instinctive reaction and a naïve one.

They kept him forty-eight hours at the Lehrterstrasse prison. The interrogation was not sharpened, but neither was it subtle. Haller could leave Germany at once, the victim of an unfortunate set of circumstances. Or he could be held as a material witness in the mysterious death of the Jew Israel-Moritz Meier. The eventual disposition of that case could take months.

If he'd stayed? If he'd tried to brazen it out? Crystal Night was the watershed. Until then the Nazis had shown some regard for world opinion. In the second week of November 1938 it might have gone either way.

Haller convinced himself then, after forty-eight hours in Lehrterstrasse, that he had done all it was humanly possible to do. He returned to Switzerland on the Berlin–Basel express.

He never heard from or of Linde again.

Now Haller was seated on a long bench in the second-floor corridor that served as an ante-room outside the office of the chief of police. At a desk in a makeshift work area enclosed to waist height by raw pine boards sat a homely woman pounding a Continental Silenta typewriter. Haller shared the bench with a dozen sweating police officers, their old-fashioned spiked helmets on their laps, their uniforms too heavy for the hot summer morning.

When Helldorf entered the corridor the dozen officers rose as one from the bench, coming swiftly to attention. Helldorf himself had the easy bearing of a man accustomed to authority. Dark hair, straight nose, sensuous mouth, all were as Haller remembered from their previous meeting. But it was the remarkable intensity of Helldorf's eyes that struck him now. Haunted was too mild a word. They looked like the eyes of a man who had contemplated suicide and decided it wasn't worth the bother.

Those eyes took in the rigid line of policemen and then saw the American. 'So, Hauptmann Haller,' he said, 'this is a surprise.' He motioned Haller towards the door of his office. 'Fräulein Braun, no interruptions, please.'

Haller found himself in a vast room with five windows, all admitting sunlight. It appeared that for the Berlin Police Chief, despite the air raids, there was still window glass to be had. The furnishings were substantial – a large desk, a swivel chair in which Helldorf seated himself, a dark leather armchair for Haller, banks of filing cabinets, a wall of leather-bound books, on the wall behind the desk a life-size portrait of Heinrich Himmler in S.S. black, and on the opposite wall a huge flagged map of the city.

'So,' Helldorf said again in that peculiar German way that

can give so much meaning to such an insignificant word. He busied himself with the radio on his desk, as Raffaello Matti had done. Even the police chief could not be sure that a microphone had not been planted in his office. He tuned in on a military band.

'We assumed you had left Berlin by now, Herr Haller.'

'I couldn't. That's one reason I'm here.'

Haller explained about the Swede.

Helldorf briefly studied the flagged map on the wall. 'Mittelstrasse, that would have been last Thursday's raid.' He picked up the phone. 'Fräulein Braun, I need some information on a possible air raid casualty. Yes, the usual – morgue, hospitals, first-aid stations, and in this case the Swedish Embassy. Name, Axel Lindstrom. A Swedish national residing at Mittelstrasse 17. Yes, that's right. As soon as possible, Fräulein Braun.'

And, when he hung up: 'We could have your answer in as little as ten minutes, or possibly never. The body could be buried in the rubble.' Helldorf leaned forward. 'You said that was one reason you were here.'

'I'd like whatever information you can give me on a Sturmbannführer Gottfried Ritter, R.S.H.A. Bureau of Student and Youth Affairs.'

'That's easier,' Helldorf said at once. 'The man is dead.'

'Dead?'

Helldorf tilted his swivel chair back, clasped his hands behind his head. 'The death certificate says heart failure. My source at the Prinz Albrechtstrasse says he died in the cellars there.' Again Helldorf leaned forward. 'Could you tell me what your interest in the dead man was?'

Haller thought that over. 'It wouldn't serve any useful purpose,' he said then.

Helldorf smiled fleetingly. 'It might tidy things up for me. I'm a policeman, Herr Haller. It might tell me why he was killed.'

'It might,' Haller agreed. 'And it might complicate things for me.'

Helldorf seemed to accept that. 'Does your interest end with Ritter's death?'

'Not necessarily. There's his staff, after all. Has someone moved up to replace him?'

Helldorf shook his head. 'The Bureau of Student and Youth Affairs was basically a one-man office, and it would have been difficult to find a replacement for Gottfried Ritter. He was an educator, not a Gestapist. He had his V-men, naturally, and the use of Bureau IV investigators when necessary, but his was hardly a normal Gestapo operation. My source tells me that Mueller himself will be taking over the bureau. The permanent staff consisted of just two people. Ritter and his secretary, a Frau . . . ' Helldorf frowned, and then he brightened. 'Frau Jaeger, that was the name.'

'Then she's what's left of the staff now?'

'And for what it's worth,' Helldorf said with a nod, 'I can tell you this. Frau Jaeger was more than just Ritter's secretary. They were having an affair.'

It was, Haller told himself, probably not worth much if Gestapo Mueller himself had taken over the bureau.

'And there is one other thing, Herr Haller, one other curious aspect to the situation. Last Sunday, when Ritter died, Frau Jaeger spent the night at the Prinz Albrechtstrasse.'

Haller grinned. 'Is there anything you don't know?'

'I told you, I'm a professional. It's my business to know what's going on.'

'You said Frau Jaeger spent the night. Working?'

'You mean, was she interrogated along with Ritter? I doubt it. She's still employed there, at any rate.'

'I'd like to meet this Frau Jaeger,' Haller said. 'Could you arrange that?'

Helldorf thought. 'I could. I don't advise it. It would mean using people I don't entirely trust.'

'Then, could you find out where she lives?'

'Now that's a simpler . . . ' The buzz of the phone interrupted the police chief. 'Yes? Yes, I see. And would you call the R.S.H.A. now, Fräulein Braun? Personnel. I want the address of a Frau Jaeger employed by the Gestapo Bureau of Student and Youth Affairs. J, a, e, g, e, r – that's correct.'

Helldorf hung up and shook his head slowly. 'The Swedish Embassy has already made arrangements to ship the body of Axel Lindstrom back to Stockholm,' he told Haller.

The American's face remained impassive; he had been prepared for that.

Moments later Helldorf was on the phone again. He said 'yes' twice and 'Would you repeat that, please?' and then he thanked Fräulein Braun. When he hung up this time his face was anything but impassive.

'Either there are two Major Ernst Otto Jaegers in Berlin,' he said, 'or Frau Jaeger is the wife of the new commander of the *Grossdeutschland* Guard Battalion.'

*

Elisabeth breast-stroked back to the dock, climbed the ladder, and removed her bathing cap, fluffing her dark hair before she spread her towel and stretched out in the hot noon sun. The Wannsee was glass-smooth, its surface reflecting the blue of the sky. It could almost have been a pre-war Sunday, the band playing at the boathouse where the Havel River flowed into the lake, a few sails gliding against the green backdrop of Peacock Island across the water, the air so clear it was hard to believe that, hardly a dozen miles from the Stauffenberg villa, the shattered buildings and rubble-choked streets of Berlin lay prostrate under the same sky.

Elisabeth closed her eyes and surrendered to the sensuous warmth of the sun, to the lilting Lehar melody drifting across the water from the boathouse. She shut out the distant drone of traffic along the Avus autobahn; only those with S.S. or Party connections could still obtain petrol for the luxury of a Sunday drive, and Elisabeth would not let such thoughts spoil her mood.

This would be a lazy Sunday, a decadent, selfish summer Sunday – an hour or so in the sun, and then a walk along the lakeshore with Heydi to the boathouse where they would dance on the terrace and . . .

Where was he now? London?

Stop that, Elisabeth told herself. But if she only knew he'd got out safely, just knowing that would have helped.

Did he have a wife or a sweetheart there, in London? In America maybe?

You must stop that, Elisabeth Lauterbacher. You must stop it right now.

How did they spend a summer Sunday, in London?

A motor detached itself from the drone on the Avus and approached along the lakeshore drive.

He's safe. He has to be safe.

A car door slammed, footsteps crunched along the gravel path, clattered on the planking of the dock. A shadow came between Elisabeth and the sun.

A deep voice said: 'It *is* Elisabeth? Good Lord, I've stayed away from Berlin too long.'

Elisabeth opened her eyes and sat up. He was tall, as ridiculously tall and gawky as she had remembered. He needed a shave and his suit was so rumpled she was certain he had slept in it. Behind the thick glasses his eyes stared at her with frank pleasure.

How long had it been? Two years? Three?
He grasped her hand and she got to her feet.
'Hans Bernd,' she said, 'how wonderful it is to see you.'

Eighteen

While Jaeger packed his suitcase, Monika sat at the dressing table brushing her long, sun-streaked blonde hair and watching him in the mirror. She was wearing an off-white silk blouse knotted at the waist to reveal two inches of tanned midriff above her straw-coloured slacks.

'Very efficient,' she observed. 'Are you in such a hurry to leave?'

Jaeger did not reply.

'You amuse me, Ernst, you really do. Cutting your leave short to go back on duty.'

'I'm not going anywhere. It's right here in Berlin.'

'Then why are you moving out?'

'I told you. The Guard Battalion's on twenty-four-hour alert. I'm expected to sleep with my men.'

Monika laughed. 'I could have sworn you weren't the type.'

'Funny,' Jaeger said. 'Very funny.' He sat on the edge of the bed and lit a cigarette. The ersatz tobacco smelled harsh and sour.

'Why don't you put that thing out and smoke a real one?' Monika reached into a drawer and tossed him an unopened pack of Gauloises.

Jaeger pocketed it and continued smoking the ersatz. 'Where'd you get those?' he asked.

'Karstadt's.'

'Karstadt's. Well, well, well.'

'You didn't expect me to say the corner kiosk, did you?'

'That's impressive,' Jaeger said.

'Yes? What is?'

'Obviously Gottfried Ritter wasn't the only one.'

'Ernst, when will you learn? There are two kinds of people in Germany. The sheep who let things happen to them and those who make things happen.'

'The war won't last for ever,' Jaeger said.

'Now what's that supposed to mean?'

'That when this is over your sheep may be the survivors.'
'Remind me to worry about that when the time comes.'
Jaeger shrugged. It would be unwise to pursue that particular line of conversation. And quite pointless. The Monikas of the world would always survive, accommodating themselves to red revolution as effortlessly as brown.
He said lightly: 'You're prettier than Nero anyway.'
'Prettier than . . . oh, I see.' Jaeger had risen and approached the low bench on which she sat. 'If that's an invitation and you can actually spare the time, the answer is yes. The answer is always yes, Ernst. Provided there are no strings.'
Her frank rejection of fidelity made her, if anything, more desirable to Jaeger. He accepted that, as he accepted her terms; they were preferable to the bourgeois weakness of jealousy.
When he reached around her to cup her breasts in his hands she leaned back and turned her face into the rough fabric of his breeches and he was annoyed that his body responded so quickly to her. Drawing away, he caught a handful of hair and forced her head back until she slid from the bench to her knees, her throat arched, amused contempt in her blue eyes.
The phone rang then.
'Let it ring,' Jaeger said hoarsely, and knew at once that he had made a mistake. Now that he had enjoined her not to, Monika would have to answer the phone to show her indifference.
'Did you ever know a woman who could just let the phone ring?' She was on her feet, cool, unruffled, as if he hadn't touched her. 'Yes? Frau Jaeger speaking. *Good* morning, Binnicker.'
Block leader Binnicker, the one-legged guardian of the door, Jaeger thought sourly, remembering their first meeting. Half his time for the rest of the tenants, half for Monika.
'Oh, is it afternoon then?' She was looking at Jaeger, now seated on the edge of the bed. 'No, I don't know anyone by that name. Should I? Is that a fact? . . . Ernst dear, could you light a cigarette for me? On the dressing table . . . Of course I'll speak to him . . . You're a dear, Ernst, thank you . . . Hello? Yes, hello, Hauptmann Haller.'
Bitch, Jaeger thought.

In the small inelegant lobby, too crowded with overstuffed, unused chairs and fleshy tropical plants in majolica jars, Haller stood at the porter's desk, the phone in his hand. The woman sounded charming, far more than the situation warranted, as if she liked nothing better than an unexpected visitor shortly after noon on a hot summer Sunday.

'Then they told me he was dead,' Haller was saying. 'It was something of a shock, Frau Jaeger. I know it's foolish, but somehow at the front you never think of people dying in Berlin. Was it an air raid?'

'His heart,' Frau Jaeger said. 'Quite sudden, the poor man. I believe Binnicker said you were friends?'

'Not exactly friends. I was his student and . . . well, this is difficult to explain. I was doing some work for him, not exactly academic. Then, after the White Rose affair in Munich, he went to work at the Prinz Albrechtstrasse and I went to the front.'

'What do you mean by not exactly academic?'

'That's what's difficult to explain. Not academic and not finished either. When they told me you worked for him I thought perhaps I should see you.'

'Why don't you come up now and have a drink with us?'

'Well, if you're sure I'm not intruding.'

'As a matter of fact, I'm about to become a grass widow. My husband was just leaving to go on duty when you called. So your timing couldn't possibly be more admirable, Hauptmann Haller.'

Bitch, Jaeger thought again.

'Have you time to stay for a drink?' she asked him. Her back was turned; she was scowling at her image in the mirror as she deftly touched her eyelashes with a tiny brush. Her question had been asked with obvious indifference. Jaeger had never come closer to hitting her since the day of his return to Berlin.

'I wouldn't want to postpone your grass widowhood,' he said, then mimicked her: ' "Your timing couldn't possibly be more admirable, Hauptmann . . . " Hauptmann who? What was his name?'

'Haller. Hauptmann Richard Haller.' With the tip of her little finger Monika touched something to her eyelids, giving them a faint bluish sheen. Then she removed her blouse. 'Something more Sundayish,' she said, and went to the closet.

The major was dressed in walking-out uniform, the Knight's Cross with oak leaves at his throat going one better than

Haller's own Knight's Cross. He was not quite Haller's height, hair light brown, grey eyes, firm mouth and jaw. Haller came to attention, clicking his heels. 'Haller, Richard, Herr Major.'

'Jaeger, Ernst Otto, Herr Hauptmann. Won't you come in? My wife is applying a few last-minute touches. Women,' said Jaeger.

'Women.' Haller nodded understandingly as he entered the apartment. It was luxuriously furnished, although eclectic; the Persian carpet, the Rosenthal china displayed behind glass, the heavy marble slab of a chessboard cocktail table with intricately carved ivory pieces set for a game that would never be played, the Empire desk, the tapestried chairs – Haller decided the place had been furnished piecemeal.

'On leave?' Jaeger asked after they sat in matching wing chairs on either side of the small marble hearth.

'Most of a week still to go.'

'Then?'

'Back to France.'

'Where did they decide you were a hero?' With a gesture, Jaeger indicated the Knight's Cross at Haller's throat.

'El Agheila. Fifth Light Division,' Haller said.

'The Afrika Korps,' Jaeger said. 'Forty-one, wasn't it?'

Haller nodded. 'April forty-one. But nobody called us the Afrika Korps then. Just Rommel and the Fifth Light, and a month after they gave me this the Fifteenth Panzer joined us.'

'Do you think Rommel's tactics will work in France?'

'Impossible,' Haller said. 'The armoured thrust, then the so-called Panzer corridor, its walls strengthened by infantry . . . those are offensive weapons.'

'And we're not on the offensive.'

'Not at the moment,' Haller said.

'Not these days,' Jaeger said.

'Not this year,' Haller said.

They smiled at each other.

Ignoring Monika's array of bottles on the sideboard, Jaeger found some korn in the cabinet below and poured two glasses. Tall, rangy, blue-eyed, blond, Hauptmann Haller looked every inch the mindless *Ubermensch*, yet he could reduce Rommel's panzer tactics to a few cogent phrases with a cynicism that matched Jaeger's own. There was a brain behind the Aryan façade.

'Pros't,' Jaeger said, raising his glass.

'Pros't, Herr Major. And let me apologise for barging in on your Sunday.' Hauptmann Haller spoke a precise but colloquial German with no discernible regional accent.

'Not at all,' Jaeger said. 'You know, your accent eludes me. I'm usually pretty good at identifying them.'

'Yours is easy, begging the Herr Major's pardon,' Haller said. 'Absolutely no doubt about where you're from.' As he spoke, Jaeger was aware of an odd thing – the precise, accentless German seemed to take on character, the faintest suggestion of a singsong nasality. 'Born and bred a Berliner,' Haller said. 'Weren't you?'

'That's right, and now I suspect I've placed you. It's Swabia, of course.'

Haller nodded. 'Ever been there?' And, when Jaeger shook his head: 'Freiburg, to be precise.'

'The Black Forest,' Monika said from the bedroom doorway. 'I've always wanted to go there myself. Pour me one of those, would you, Ernst?'

Jaeger watched Haller rise, an expectant smile on his handsome face. The bedroom doorway was to his right, and he had to turn to see Monika as she entered the room.

Seeing her, the captain froze – the smile pasted on his face, his arm outstretched to take Monika's hand, his head beginning to swoop in a bow for the formal cursory hand-kiss.

And Monika? Jaeger had never seen such a swift change pass over her face. Or anyone's. From mild curiosity to – what? Malicious delight was all Jaeger could think of.

The tableau lasted perhaps two seconds.

Haller completed the bow. 'Frau Jaeger, a pleasure.'

'The pleasure, believe me, Herr Hauptmann, is mine.'

Heydi stood at the doors that opened on the rear terrace of the Stauffenberg villa and looked down across the sloping lawn to where Elisabeth lay stretched in the sun.

Heydi had taken little part in the discussion and would, he suspected, take even less in the decision. Too junior, and possibly – at least from Stauffenberg's viewpoint – too emotionally involved. Heydi had not kept his admiration for the American a secret, after all.

'It makes me want to take a razor to my own throat,' he heard Hans Bernd Gisevius say. 'I was the one who kept them informed.'

'You kept Dulles informed,' Stauffenberg corrected him, 'and Herr Richard Haller wasn't Dulles's idea. Heydi!'

Heydi turned away from the french doors. 'Herr Oberst?'

'Where is the American?'

'I don't know.'

'You don't know? I thought he bunked at your place.'

'He was in and out Friday morning. I haven't seen him since.'

Helldorf spoke then. 'He came to see me this morning.' The police chief did not sound happy. 'Klaus, he can't leave Germany now. His Swiss papers were destroyed in Thursday's raid.'

'That doesn't change anything.'

'No, not for you. It might for Haller.'

'How? He can still blow us wide open. He just can't get out afterwards.'

Helldorf shook his head. 'Listen to me, Klaus. You're a military man, I'm a cop. You deal in logistics, in men as interchangeable parts. I deal in human beings.'

Stauffenberg thrust his gloved left hand out. 'And I'm maimed and bitter and I trust no one,' he said softly. 'Is that what you're trying to say?'

Helldorf sighed. 'I'm trying to say if Haller intended to betray us he would have done it already.' Gisevius was about to speak but Helldorf waved him silent. 'No matter what kind of signal Allen Dulles received from London, Hans Bernd. Haller has something else on his mind. Something more important to him than getting out. Something with no possible bearing on Valkyrie.'

'What is it?'

'I don't know the details yet. I want to find out.'

'And how long would that take? We can't afford to wait.'

'No? I waited ten years before I knew that Hitler had to die. How long did you wait, Klaus?'

'I fought in Russia,' Stauffenberg said, his voice cold. 'I saw what men like your friend Artur Nebe did there. It didn't take me ten years. I wasn't spending my off-duty hours chasing after whores with Dr Goebbels.'

Helldorf's face went white. He said: 'All right, maybe I deserved that. But it's finished now. And this is just beginning. Because whether we succeed or fail, it won't be long until they're here in Germany – Richard Haller's people. We'll have to account to them. That's what I've been trying to tell you.'

'You mean apologise for not letting them betray us?'

'The man I saw this morning is not interested in betraying us. Believe me.'

'Then what is he interested in?' Stauffenberg demanded.

'A Gestapist named Gottfried Ritter.'

'Ritter? Who is he?'

'He *was* head of the Bureau of Student and Youth Affairs. He died last week in the Prinz Albrechtstrasse cellars.'

'I suppose you got that the usual way?'

'Yes, from Nebe,' Helldorf admitted.

'Did Nebe say why he was killed?'

'He didn't know. But he knew this: Mueller has taken over the bureau himself. Oh, and there's a secretary. Haller wanted to meet her. You'll know the name, Klaus,' Helldorf said slowly. 'A Frau Major Jaeger.'

Stauffenberg looked at him. 'Coincidence?'

'It's the same Jaeger. I checked that.'

'I mean that his wife works for the Gestapo.'

'Possibly. According to Nebe, Jaeger himself isn't known at the R.S.H.A.' Helldorf shrugged. 'Of course, I didn't approve of Jaeger in the first place, so maybe I'm biased. But for all we know, his wife might be his direct line to the Gestapo. In which case Haller could be our good fortune.'

'Haller? What are you suggesting?'

'You don't trust him. I don't trust Jaeger. Put them together where we can watch them. Where they can watch each other. Reassign Hauptmann Richard Haller to the *Grossdeutschland* Guard Battalion.'

Stauffenberg limped to the window and back. He massaged the stump of his right wrist with his gloved left hand. 'We've already given Richard Haller too much rope. Tell me, who would his contact here in Berlin be? If he wanted to turn over a blueprint for Operation Valkyrie.'

Helldorf thought for a moment. 'It depends on how much Allied Intelligence knows about the R.S.H.A. If they knew, for instance, that Nebe is my source inside, or that the Gestapo is sitting on the fence until . . .'

'Never mind who he wouldn't go to,' Stauffenberg said impatiently.

'They know. Dulles told them,' Gisevius said. 'Haller's contact would be with the S.D. Specifically a V-man named Raffaello Matti.'

'Matti? The Swiss doctor?' Heydi whistled. 'To listen to him, you'd have thought . . .'

'Pick Matti up,' Stauffenberg told Helldorf. 'Find out if Haller's seen him. At least we'll know where we stand.'

'If he has?'

'If he has,' Stauffenberg said, 'then Haller's won and we have lost. And this discussion, gentlemen, is quite irrelevant.'

'And if Haller hasn't seen him?'

'Then you'll keep him in a nice quiet place where Haller *can't* see him.'

Stauffenberg turned to face his adjutant. 'As for Herr Richard Haller himself, you will find your American friend, Heydi. And you will, in the words of Mr Allen Dulles of Bern, terminate his mission.'

Monika sat on the Persian carpet, arms folded on the edge of the cocktail table, long legs tucked under her, back to Ernst, face tilted up towards Hauptmann Haller on the sofa. Perhaps the pose was a bit too kittenish. She wasn't certain if she meant it more for its positive effect on Haller or for its negative effect on Ernst. Did it really matter? She hadn't enjoyed herself so much in ages.

Every now and then she'd glance over her shoulder at Ernst, and the perplexed look on his face was almost as delicious as the danger. But the danger was the best part – the uncertainty, the not knowing – a strange shivery excitement like sexual foreplay.

What would happen after Ernst left? What would the man who called himself Richard Haller do?

She chattered like a magpie, her small talk calculated to frustrate Ernst and needle Hauptmann Haller. Hot, she said, a real old-fashioned Prussian heat wave, isn't it? Beastly climate, positively ghastly. I bet the Black Forest's a delight now, the mountain air, the cool shade of the pine forests. It *was* Freiburg, Herr Hauptmann? Another drink? Ernst's korn if you really prefer it, but we actually have, believe it or not, some good Scotch whisky. Dimple. That odd-shaped bottle over there. You never saw one like that, not in Swabia, did you, Herr Hauptmann?

Except for the mention of the cheap grain spirits he drank, she did her best to exclude Ernst from the conversation. She wasn't sure how much he had sensed when she'd entered the room. That she and the captain had met before? Probably. That both were shocked at meeting now? Possibly.

There were silences, and twice Ernst tried to fill them as if searching for an excuse to stay. A dreary mention of a Marshal Guderian, whom both men seemed to respect; an even drearier one of that military alert yesterday. She interrupted both attempts with more inconsequential, empty-headed chatter, the second time rudely.

'Must you, Ernst? Is that all you ever think about?' She stretched and assumed a more languid pose. 'The funniest thing happened in the Adlon lobby the other day. You do know the Adlon, Herr Haller? Everybody goes there, simply everybody. Anyway, I ran into Emmy Goering. Getting so fat I hardly recognised her. But here's the delicious part – her escort was General Galland. Full dress Luftwaffe uniform complete with Knight's Cross with oak leaves, swords, and diamonds. He's very handsome if you like your men sleek and glowering. I've always had a preference for the Nordic type myself.' A dazzling smile for Hauptmann Haller. 'So anyway, there she was, clinging to his arm, positively clinging, and she . . . '

Ernst looked at his watch, lunged to his feet, went into the bedroom and returned with his suitcase.

He exchanged heel-clicking bows with Haller and was, finally, at the door. Monika joined him there.

'Enjoy yourself,' she said.

'What?'

'Sleeping with your battalion, dear.'

At that moment the air raid siren on Potsdamerplatz began to wail; a moment later the Skagerrakplatz siren at the other end of Bellevuestrasse echoed it.

'You'd better finish your drinks in the cellar,' Jaeger said.

'Afraid?' Monika asked him.

'Of course. Berlin terrifies me after the Eastern Front.' He stood in the open doorway, waiting. 'Well, come on. Or I could take you to the Potsdamer station. It's safer.'

'And full of grubby refugees.'

'Hurry up, will you?' Jaeger said impatiently. 'I'm already late.'

'Then why don't you just run along, dear? I'm sure the Herr Hauptmann can take care of me.'

Jaeger glared at her and slammed the door.

Monika returned to the so handsome and so thoroughly ersatz army captain.

'You know,' she said, 'for a man who couldn't find any reason why anyone should like us Germans, you certainly wear that uniform well.'

*

The woman was wearing a beige dress of some lightweight nubby fabric a shade lighter than her tanned skin. Tall, elegant body, sun-streaked blonde hair and, as she sat again, arms folded on the edge of the chessboard cocktail table, that reckless smile.

'Do you want to go?' she said. 'It doesn't have to be the cellar. There's a deep shelter at the Hotel Esplanade across the street.'

'It's up to you.' Haller shrugged.

'Are you fatalistic then? I am. Or is it a matter of principle with you?' The early warning sirens wound down and in the silence that followed she very deliberately said: 'They're your bombs, after all.'

Haller made himself look bewildered for a moment. Then he laughed abruptly. 'Because you know I've been in Lisbon, is that it? Don't be ridiculous, Frau Jaeger.'

He removed his wallet, placing it on the cocktail table between the rows of black and white pawns. Not that it would prove anything. Naturally his papers would be in order. He wondered if he would have to kill her.

But then his search for Gottfried Ritter's list would be over. And he had to have it.

The list was everything now.

'I'm sure they are very pretty papers,' she said, 'almost as pretty as the Herr Hauptmann himself. I'm equally sure they would not tell me who you are.' With her fingertips she slid the wallet back across the chessboard table, careful not to overturn the carved ivory figures. 'Check, Herr Haller. Your move.'

'I was on Abwehr assignment in Lisbon. Swiss cover. That's all there is to it, Frau Jaeger.'

'Is that why you ran out of the Hasenheide last Thursday night?'

'A lot of people were getting out of there in a hurry. The woman with me panicked. Don't make a big thing out of it.'

'The Abwehr,' the woman said, 'what's left of the Abwehr, is now part of Schellenberg's Bureau VI.'

'Of course it is. So what?'

'Did you notice my companion at the Hasenheide?'

'No, not particularly,' Haller said. That was the truth; the man had been nondescript, a face in the crowd.

'You want me to believe you work for Bureau VI and don't know Heinrich Mueller when you see him?' The woman flashed her dazzling smile. 'Of course, Heinrich is quite thoroughly . . . ordinary. But he's also quite knowledgeable. So I asked him a question. A Swiss courier one week, a Hauptmann of Grenadiers the next, was that possible? It might have been before the Abwehr became part of Bureau VI. It no longer is.'

In one graceful movement the woman rose. 'Check again, Herr Haller. And it would be checkmate if I telephoned my office and let them know you're here. But you wouldn't let me do that, would you? Tell me, if I were not the woman whose cigarette you lit at Barajas airport, what *would* you have done?'

Haller said: 'That's an academic question now, isn't it?'

'Not exactly academic, as you yourself said. Why did you claim to be a former student of Gottfried Ritter?'

'Assuming you weren't the woman at Barajas?'

'You're learning, Herr Hauptmann. Let's play by those rules for a while, just for fun.'

'As a student in Munich I worked in the Provost's office. Dr Ritter was compiling a list of dissident students. I helped him.'

Outside, the sirens shrieked, short peremptory blasts.

'The red alert,' the woman said calmly. 'They've reached the city. But perhaps I don't have to tell you. Perhaps they brief you on things like that – where you come from.'

Haller heard the *crump-crump* of flak guns and distantly and then closer the drone of approaching bombers. The woman went to the window, her figure framed in the bright rectangle of sunlight.

'Sometimes you can see them from here. If they're going for . . . there they are!'

Haller went to her side. Her hands were flat on the sill; she was leaning out, her throat corded as she looked up.

High above, so high that it seemed to move slowly against the brilliant blue of the sky, Haller saw the first formation of B-17s flying a tight, perfect V. Tiny puffs of flak punctuated the blue. Twenty thousand feet, Haller guessed, maybe twenty-five. A second formation followed the first, coming serenely, inexorably. No bombs fell.

'Sometimes they do that,' the woman said. Her calm voice had a brittle quality then, the words like dry twigs you could take in your fingers and break. 'Trial run, even two trial runs. They fly in along the East–West axis, guided straight to the heart of the city by Minister Speer's super-highway. The Americans prefer clear weather and daylight, the British clouds and night. Which are you?'

The flak guns were firing almost continuously now.

'Girls operate those guns,' she said. 'Teenagers. And Russian

P.O.W.s.' Her voice was calm, too calm, and when she turned to Haller her eyes had a wild look. 'The Russians don't mind. Why should they? A man who works for the I.G. Farben once told me the Anglo-Americans want to hit the cities, the people. Terror raids, isn't that so? Isn't it? Not the ball-bearing works at Schweinfurt and not the panzer factories at Friedrichshaven, not the armaments plants. Because if you destroyed those before your army reached German soil you'd give the Reich to Russia, wouldn't you? That's what he says, my I.G. Farben friend. He called it squabbling over the corpse before it's quite dead . . . They're coming back.'

The B-17s appeared again, this time from the north-east. They spawned tiny motes, silver in the sunlight. A whining sound decreased in pitch and increased in volume, ending in a jolting roar.

A flash brighter than the sunlight shot along the cobble-stoned street, then dissolved in a dark mushroom of smoke. Concussion buffeted Haller and suddenly although he could not hear the sound he knew the woman was screaming, he could see the scream in her eyes and on her mouth as he dragged her away from the window. Bottles flew from the side-board. The glass-fronted cabinet displaying white and gold china leaned forward, swayed, came down with a crash Haller did not hear.

The next stick of high explosive bombs fell farther to the west and as he led her to the sofa he remembered the brittle voice, the calm ironic words.

The cities, the people . . . not the armaments plants because if you destroyed those before your army reaches German soil you'd give the Reich to Russia, wouldn't you?

Goebbels' propaganda, of course, with the necessary touch of truth to make it believable.

And it was true, wasn't it? The terror raids were intentional, payment in kind. The Germans, all seventy million of them, goose-stepping over a prostrate Continent, terror-bombing England, turning their backs on the cattle cars crammed with Jews for the death camps, didn't they deserve what they got?

Wasn't that one explanation for the Baker Street decision that had sent him here?

Squabbling over the corpse before it's quite dead . . .

The knowledge hit him like the shock wave from a high explosive bomb.

Not just the Baker Street decision. The Moscow decision.

Wouldn't Russia have its contacts too? Wouldn't Russia know of Operation Valkyrie?

Wouldn't the Soviets, their land laid waste, their cities pounded to rubble, their people victims of the *Einsatzgruppen* murder squads – wouldn't they reach the same decision?

Wasn't there a Russian agent here, right now, somewhere in the bomb-shattered capital of the Reich, working towards the end that he himself had rejected? Someone he had never, and would never, meet?

With a sweeping motion of her arm the woman sent the ivory chessmen flying from the table. 'How long?' she cried. 'How long will it be until we are all wiped out like that? Can you tell me? Do they know, where you come from?'

'I come from Freiburg, Frau Jaeger.'

'I wanted the war to last for ever, can you blame me? Every day the final day, every night the last night, and then in the morning the reprieve.' Tears made bright tracks on her cheeks. 'Nothing else mattered, nothing. Just to take what they were so eager to give me. Just to live.'

She swayed, would have fallen; he caught her.

'Those stinking foul fucking brown-shirted shits!' she cried. 'With their names in the *Führerlexikon* and their pricks between the legs of any woman who rolls over on her back for them! Is it a list you want? A list of students, in a black notebook? Names, addresses, biographies, coded commentaries? Is that what you were sent here to get?'

'Where is it?'

Her eyes were wide, white showing all around the irises. She was laughing. He slapped her face twice, not hard. 'Where is it, Frau Jaeger?'

She stared past him, seeing nothing. Or everything.

'The one place you can never get it. Mueller has it. Gestapo Mueller. He killed Gottfried Ritter to get it. What are you waiting for? You're going to kill me, aren't you? Why don't you get it over with?'

He left her there, in the midst of the debris in the cluttered room, her head down, her blonde hair dropping in wings on either side, the way of life she had made for herself collapsed into a nightmare world, the miracle of the deliverance no longer visible along the dark cthonic tunnel of her fantasy.

Not the list, no. That was finished too. But she had given him something – the purging need to pity not only her but all the faceless, nameless ones like her who had only wanted to survive.

Part Three

THE VALKYRIE ENCOUNTER

Nineteen

Since his villa in suburban Zehlendorf was bombed out some weeks before, Police Chief Count von Helldorf had taken a suite of rooms at the Excelsior.

On Anhalterstrasse near the railroad station, the big hotel was closer to the Prinz Albrechtstrasse than to Helldorf's own office in Berlin-East and its location made contact with Artur Nebe a simple matter. The Excelsior had further merit, for Helldorf or anyone else influential enough to get a room there. Although it had been hit earlier in the month – half its rooms remained uninhabitable – it was still the safest hotel in the city. From the lower lobby an underground passage led directly to the deep shelters of the Anhalter station.

Shortly before ten o'clock on Monday night, 17 July, Helldorf stood over the large mahogany table in the sitting-room of his suite studying a government Printing Office *Umgebungskarte*, a map of the city of Berlin and its environs. On it a police draughtsman with a sense of humour had superimposed in India ink eight small but overblown nudes in positions as lewd as they were improbable.

Helldorf's green whipcord uniform blouse clung damply to his back and shoulders in the heat of the night as he switched the radio on, went to the door and let Artur Nebe in.

S.S.-Gruppenführer Artur Nebe rarely wore the black uniform and he was not wearing it now. In his rumpled grey suit he looked like a door-to-door salesman who'd had a hard day.

He preceded Helldorf into the room. 'Think the R.A.F.'ll give us a break tonight?'

'They neglected to inform the Alexanderplatz,' Helldorf said.

Beginning yesterday afternoon Berlin had sustained its worst bombing of the war. The R.A.F. had come over at midnight, which was late for them. American Flying Fortresses had returned this morning and again this afternoon. That was unusual; they rarely made the milk run and the lunch attack on the same day. In the three raids three thousand heavy bombers had dropped more than fifteen thousand tons of high explosive and incendiary bombs on the city. Fires still raged in Siemensstadt, Pankow, and Wedding. Even with the windows shut and the blackout curtains drawn both men could taste the grit in their mouths, and their eyes were bloodshot and smarting. Helldorf's twelve thousand uniformed police could not cope with the aftermath; too many streets remained blocked; neither Organization Todt convoys nor the gangs of slave labourers could get through.

'What happens if they're still pounding us like this when Stauffenberg gets the call from Wolf's Lair?' Artur Nebe asked.

General Stieff had already sent word to the Bendlerstrasse that Hitler had left Berchtesgaden for his headquarters near Rastenburg in East Prussia.

Helldorf shook his head. 'We'll learn the hard way whether a paralysed city helps or hinders a *coup d'état*.'

'It had better help,' Nebe said. 'We can't afford another fiasco like Saturday.'

Helldorf went to the makeshift map table. 'I've got this anyway,' he said.

Leaning over the table, Nebe rewarded the police draughtsman's sense of humour with a broad smile. 'They look like something out of the *Kama Sutra*,' he said.

Helldorf jabbed at the map, his finger touching each of the eight nudes in turn. 'Eight small towns, none with a population of ten thousand. And it suddenly occurred to me they had one thing in common.'

Nebe raised an eyebrow.

'Whorehouses,' Helldorf told him.

'Whorehouses?'

'Not one of those towns is big enough to support a whorehouse but they all have them, all duly licensed in the past few months. The Waffen-S.S. needs its recreation.'

'My God,' said Artur Nebe softly. 'Himmler's secret bases. Even I couldn't find out where they were.'

'You don't have a dirty enough mind,' Helldorf said.

'You'll block the roads into Berlin?'

'With Organization Todt heavy trucks. That ought to give Stauffenberg the time he needs. We estimate there are ten thousand Waffen-S.S. at those bases.'

'They must keep the girls pretty busy,' Artur Nebe said.

Helldorf's mouth moved in a bitter imitation of a smile. 'The police should be doing more, you know. I don't need a thousand men to set up those barricades. But Stauffenberg won't have it. He says it's a matter of psychology. The Berliner is a rare creature, he says.'

'Well, that won't get any argument from me.'

'A pragmatist,' Helldorf went on, 'who didn't vote the Nazis into power but has since made peace with them, hoping he'll outlive them. A cynic who opposed the Nuremberg laws against the Jews but was the first to buy sequestered Jewish businesses. A romantic whose heart goes out to the *schütze* in field-grey but who spits on Prussian police green.'

That evaluation hit too close to home for both men and for a while they stood in uneasy silence, which Artur Nebe broke.

'You've made your own peace with yourself, haven't you?'

Helldorf stared down at the map. 'About the Jews? I was a trader, I bought and sold. I'll tell you something, Artur. The day after Crystal Night, when I got back to Berlin, I walked the length of Friedrichstrasse and went home and loaded a Luger. I was going to shoot myself.'

'What stopped you?'

'Ludwig Beck,' Helldorf said. 'He'd resigned from the army that August and he was already lining people up. He just walked in on me. Walked in and took the goddamn gun out of my hand and said, help me kill those swine instead.'

He looked up. Nebe met his eyes. 'Who'll take the gun out of my hand?' Nebe asked.

Helldorf could say nothing. No word, no rationalisation, no person, could help Artur Nebe. No act of contrition, no heroics, no God, nothing.

S.S.-Gruppenführer Artur Nebe, Chief of Criminal Police, had spent a year in Russia commanding an *Einsatzgruppe*.

Helldorf did not expect him to survive Operation Valkyrie, whatever the outcome. He sensed that Nebe had no intention of surviving it.

'Have they finished with Julius Esser?' Helldorf asked.

'And learned nothing new. Just the names. It was all Esser knew.'

'It was all the American told Raffaello Matti,' Helldorf said.

'That's odd, isn't it?'

'Perhaps. I already gave Stauffenberg my opinion on the subject of Richard Haller. He had a change of heart. It happens.'

'It happens,' Nebe agreed quietly. 'Where's the American now?'

'Last I knew, holing up in a gasthaus in Mittelstrasse. Though he may not be there any more. That block caught it badly last night.'

'And?'

'If you mean, am I going to render him harmless, to use Himmler's favourite euphemism, the answer is no. He's Heydebrand's problem, not mine. Of course, in a way he's yours too. That business of Gottfried Ritter. What have you found out?'

'Well, I can't exactly ask Mueller why he tightened the screws until Ritter died, can I? It will take time.'

'We don't have time.'

The radio suddenly went silent. Outside, the Anhalter station siren wailed the early warning.

Heydi stood with Elisabeth on the flat roof of the small apartment building on Pariserplatz. The tarred surface was still sticky from the day's heat and even at 10.15 the green dusk light lingered in the west. On the edge of the roof stone statues of forgotten Prussian warriors, their backs turned, looked out across the city with sightless eyes. To the north block after block of roofless houses stretched out towards the red-rimmed horizon. Fires still raged in the suburbs beyond Moabit.

The early warning had just sounded.

Heydi turned to Elisabeth, his gunbelt creaking, the holstered Walther heavy at his side. He had worked late at the Bendlerstrasse, coming off duty half an hour ago.

'I try to blame them,' he said, his arm sweeping the northern horizon. 'The Americans, the British.' His monocle reflected the red glow; he looked as sightless as the statues of forgotten Prussian warriors. 'I can't blame them,' he said. 'But they're just making it harder for themselves. With every raid, morale gets stronger, not weaker. You see it chalked on bombed-out buildings all over the city. "Our walls have broken, but not our hearts." The Berliner is the world's number one pig-headed stubborn bastard.'

'Well, that certainly makes you a Berliner, Heydi.'

'My dearest Elisabeth, for the third time, nothing's bothering me.'

Elisabeth had come in from Wannsee late that afternoon to get the guest-room ready for her uncle. General Beck had decided to move into the city to await Valkyrie Day. He was, to use Heydi's words, one pig-headed stubborn bastard too. Still weak from his operation and, though he denied it, she could tell the pain had returned. But they needed him. Politicians like Goerdeler and staff officers like Olbricht did not fully trust one another. All of them trusted General Beck. He might even be able to bring Olbricht's vacillating chief, General Fromm, over to the conspirators. For six years Beck alone had held the frayed cloth of the conspiracy together.

Heydi said: 'Come on, I'd better get you downstairs.'

'You're not coming back up here, are you?'

'I want to watch.'

It wasn't that unusual. For every Berliner who spent his nights in a public shelter even when no early warning sounded, there was a diehard like Heydi who refused to take shelter at all.

'Morbid curiosity,' he said. 'Also typically Prussian, Elisabeth.'

She bit her lip, remembering. *You're nothing but a rotten Prussian.*

His comment had been pointed, the peace between them tentative, his hurt still there under the surface.

It was unfair to blame him for the ugly scene in Lichterfelde. Heydi was his own man in all ways but one. His absolute, relentless devotion to Klaus Stauffenberg.

When they entered the stairwell he lit his flashlight; the power had been out all day. They followed the beam down the steep flight of steps.

Soon Heydi was lighting candles in the drawing-room.

He comes from England, Heydi

Tourist?

Heydi blew out the match and took her in his arms then, his lips brushing her cheek, her mouth, his hand lightly tracing the curve of her breast. After a moment she drew back.

'I believe,' he said lightly, 'that the British say: a penny for your thoughts.'

'He's not British, he . . . oh God, Heydi. I can't get him out of my mind. He won't go away.'

'That's clear enough even to a thick-skulled Prussian like me.'

'Please, Heydi. Don't do that to yourself.'

'I'm not doing anything to myself. Nor, apparently, to you either.'

'Heydi, I'm sorry. I just need a little more time. You're a dear sweet . . . '

He pulled her towards him again, this time with almost brutal strength, his mouth hard against hers for an instant before she turned her head to one side.

'I can't make him go away!' she cried.

And Heydi said: 'He didn't, Elisabeth. He's still here in Berlin. He never left.'

'That's impossible. He . . . '

'He's right here in Berlin. Doing what he came to do. And maybe, just maybe, I can't blame them for that either.'

'What are you talking about?'

'Your American tin god. They sent him here to betray us to the Prinz Albrechtstrasse.'

'That's not true! You want me to hate him!'

'What do you think's been driving me crazy all day? I'm supposed to stop him.'

'To . . . stop him?'

Heydi said nothing.

From the direction of the Brandenburg Gate the short frantic blasts of the red alert shattered the silence.

Twenty

That their second meeting took place in an interrogation room in the deep Gestapo cellars pleased Jaeger. The muted sounds of bombs and flak, the occasional dimming of the unshielded lightbulbs, the unseen bombers dropping random death no more nor less capricious than history unless you saw history through Marxist eyes – none of it could have been any better had Jaeger set the scene himself.

Here, where it should have been everything, the black uniform Mueller wore was nothing, the talisman of the S.S. runes without magic, the terror of the Gestapo cellars of less consequence than the strength of their thick walls to withstand a direct hit. The message of historical necessity was clear.

They had been talking for ten minutes, ever since the red alert. Now Jaeger said: 'Nazism, the failure of Nazism, makes Marxism inevitable. If you don't understand that, you are as good as dead. A suicide.'

'I find this easier to understand,' Mueller said. 'If I order it, you will not leave this building alive. People die in air raids, Herr Jaeger. Up there they are dying right now.'

'Yes, you could arrange that quite easily. Or it could just happen. Pray to whatever gods you believe in that it doesn't. Because you need me,' Jaeger said. 'You don't believe the Brown Revolution was an accident, do you? There are no historical accidents, only misunderstandings. The Brown Revolution leads inevitably to Red, Nazism to Communism, Hitler to Comrade Cell. You could have joined us, twenty years ago; you almost did. You have that chance again. It is your one way to breast the tide of history.'

'What do you want?' Mueller asked.

The question was rhetorical and Jaeger considered that a hopeful sign even though Mueller did not follow through with the answer. 'I assume you are making your own preparations,' Jaeger told him. 'Certain records which will find their way to Kropotkin Square after the war – is that correct?'

'I have some things they would like to get their hands on, yes.'

'May I offer a word of advice? Comrade Cell will need a cadre of middle-level functionaries. Therefore a certain number of civil servants who made the same mistake you did twenty years ago will be allowed to atone. He will expect you to supply names.'

'Noted,' Mueller said. 'I appreciate the suggestion.'

Neither man spoke for a while.

It was Mueller who broke the silence, Mueller who said: 'Then why not the Ritter list too?'

'I'll tell you why not.' Jaeger was pleased that Mueller had brought the subject up. Mueller was learning. 'The names of the future leaders of Red Germany are on that list. And its future enemies. The Ritter list cannot wait for the end of the war. Too many things can happen between now and the surrender. The list must be delivered to Moscow at once.'

'You can do that?' Mueller asked, surprised.

'Obviously I can,' Jaeger said with a show of impatience.

'Otherwise, would I be here? It's quite simple, I assure you – Comrade Mueller.'

Jaeger had no way to deliver the list to Moscow, nor did he need to. He only needed to get it from Mueller. The failure of Operation Valkyrie would result in a bloodbath. Mueller would play his role in that. Jaeger, like his mentor Comrade Cell, understood the momentum of terror. There was the risk that Mueller might surrender the Ritter list to that bloodbath. Jaeger himself would surrender half of it, the names of those who would resist Soviet domination as strongly as Nazi. The other half he would destroy.

'Well?' Jaeger said.

Mueller brushed the black sleeve across his brow. He was sweating. 'I don't know,' he said.

Jaeger shrugged. Mueller was closer than he had been at their first meeting. 'You have some time. Not much, but some. And you should know this, Comrade Mueller. If you were to wait for the Nazi surrender and deliver the Ritter list to Comrade Cell yourself, it would be taken from you and you would stand in the dock as a war criminal. That is one option open to you. The other is a bureau of your own in Kropotkin Square. Choose one, Comrade Mueller.'

Heydi stood near the edge of the roof, tilted the bottle of kümmel-flavoured schnapps, and drank.

Overhead, twin-engine R.A.F. Mosquito bombers darted in and out among the probing searchlights and bursts of flak, sowing signal flares for the heavy Lancasters following ten minutes behind. The sweeping columns of light and the brilliant red and green of the flares, if you did not know their purpose, were quite beautiful.

Heydi saw one of the Mosquitoes caught and held by a searchlight beam, the plane peeling off frantically to the left, the column of light moving with it, holding it. Flak burst closer and suddenly the Mosquito dived, one engine trailing smoke. Half a mile to the north, flame blossomed in the dark streets of the city.

Heydi brought the bottle to his lips again, the harsh alcohol searing his throat. More than half the schnapps was already gone.

'Got the bastards,' he said aloud, and could not hear his own voice. 'Got the bastards!' he shouted, and rocked on the edge of the roof, three storeys above the street, clutching the stone arm of the statue of Frederick II of Prussia.

He shoved himself back from the parapet, his hand touching the smooth leather of the holster at his side. Standard issue Walther P-38 Parabellum. *Para bellum.* For war.

For Richard Haller?

The Mosquitoes whined off, the flak subsided, the signal flares glowed, the searchlights swept their allotted sections of sky, awaiting the Lancasters.

Heydi threw the empty schnapps bottle from the roof.

Their faces cadaverous in the light of a green signal flare drifting imperceptibly down, three men pushed past Haller and ran hard for the entrance to the Interior Ministry shelter. Two wardens with pinpoint flashlights motioned them inside as Haller continued walking west along Unter den Linden.

'Hey you! Soldier! What's the matter with you? Get your ass in here!'

Haller ignored the shouting warden, heard the heavy metal door clang shut. He was alone then in the eerie green light, the stumps of linden trees casting long shadows as the flares drifted down, and he began to walk faster, testing the vertigo. They had shaved some hair, taken half a dozen stitches above his left ear. The nurse at the State Library first aid station, a big Silesian girl who looked more Polish than German, had not argued strenuously when Haller had demanded his uniform. They had been bringing casualties in all day.

The vertigo came in waves, Haller's head pounding dully with every step. But it was nothing he couldn't cope with and he'd already lost more than twenty-four hours. Heydi and the others would know by now that his route out of Berlin had been cut; Chief Helldorf would have told them. Heydi would be eager to find a place for him in Operation Valkyrie.

He heard the high distant drone of the Lancasters and as he entered Pariserplatz the guns in the Tiergarten flak towers opened up.

The Lancasters had done a pretty good job on the gasthaus in Mittelstrasse last night. When he returned there in the afternoon after his fruitless visit to the Jaeger woman, a block leader wearing the Party brassard was just coming out.

'Fifth one today,' the block leader said.

'What?'

'Fifth one today, Herr Hauptmann. Died for Greater Germany. Heil Hitler,' said the block leader.

Haller found the landlady in the kitchen seated at the table staring at a small battered parcel wrapped in brown paper. A pot was bubbling on the stove and Haller smelled turnips.

'I can't open it,' Frau Gallenkamp said. She looked up at Haller, tears running down her round, apple-cheeked face.

Haller waited awkwardly. The pot boiled over; he went to the wood-burning stove and moved it.

'Sometimes they make mistakes,' Frau Gallenkamp said. She reached out tentatively to touch the battered parcel, drew her hand back. 'Maybe it isn't Werner, they can make mistakes, can't they?'

Two of Frau Gallenkamp's permanent boarders came in, look-alike old men who worked at the nearby Marine Museum. They saw the parcel and shook their heads. 'Your Werner?' one of them said.

'It's a mistake!' Frau Gallenkamp cried.

The two old men exchanged identical glances; they clucked their tongues.

'I tell you it's a mistake!' Frau Gallenkamp insisted.

Now the two old men exchanged thin, knowing smiles.

The word in German for what Haller saw then was *Schadenfreude* and it had no equivalent in any other Western language. No equivalent was needed elsewhere. *Schadenfreude* meant a feeling of pleasure at another's misfortune, not the sick enjoyment of the sadist who inflicts pain and not the understandable relief expressed by the notion 'there but for the grace of God go I'. *Schadenfreude* meant a simple, uncomplicated enjoyment of misfortune, any misfortune but your own.

'I'll open it for you, Frau Gallenkamp,' one of the old men offered.

'Get out,' Frau Gallenkamp cried. 'Get out, both of you.'

The two old men exchanged glances again and left Haller alone in the kitchen with the woman.

'Schnapps,' she said after a while. 'In the cupboard, Herr Hauptmann.'

He poured two ounces and she took the glass in both hands and drank. She blew her nose. 'Would you open it, please?' she said. 'Did I tell you he looks like you, my Werner? There's a strong resemblance.'

Haller reached for the parcel.

'Wait,' Frau Gallenkamp said. She opened her handbag and showed Haller a photograph. Werner was thin, he had blond hair, he was grinning self-consciously at the camera, the visor of his garrison cap tilted back rakishly. He looked nothing like Haller.

'You see?'

Haller nodded.

'Open it now. A mistake, I'm sure of it.'

Haller looked at the parcel. They didn't keep you guessing, anyway, he thought. The words DIED FOR GREATER GERMANY were stamped in blue ink under the address. Haller unfastened the twine and removed the brown paper, revealing a cardboard box. He waited.

Frau Gallenkamp's voice then was querulous. 'Well, open it, open it, what are you waiting for?'

Haller removed the contents and put them, one by one, on the table. An Iron Cross Second Class, a signet ring with the initials W.E.G., a few tattered letters, a thin volume of the poems of Stefan George, its pages uncut, a dog-eared Western novel by Karl May, a photograph of a girl wearing blonde braids and smiling up at the young lieutenant in the snapshot Frau Gallenkamp had shown Haller, another photograph of Frau Gallenkamp herself.

'He was such a great reader,' she said after a while. 'I sent him the Stefan George for his birthday. Always trying to improve himself, he was. Twenty-two. Twenty-two in April.'

She went to the stove, moved the pot; went to the cupboard, got an onion and a meagre slab of bacon, a small sack of flour.

'Bacon dumplings,' she said brightly. 'A feast. A feast, Herr Hauptmann. My Werner loved bacon dumplings.'

Her hands worked swiftly, efficiently, as she diced the bacon and set it on the stove in the black iron pan.

Haller was going to say he had only returned to pay his bill; he said nothing. The bacon spat and crackled in the pan.

'You could eat a dozen of them, a big boy like you.'

Soon the dumplings were poaching in a large black pot, Frau Gallenkamp standing over them, her back to Haller.

'Please, can you stay tonight?' she said. 'Just tonight, Herr Hauptmann?'

They were in the cellar that night with the other boarders when the high explosive bomb struck just outside, the concussion collapsing the front wall and lifting the roof off the house like a giant hand taking the lid from a box.

When he regained consciousness at the first-aid station they told Haller he was the only survivor. No *Schadenfreude* in that, only a despairing numbness; half the air raid casualties brought in that night were dead on arrival.

Elisabeth was in the drawing-room when the first wave of Lancasters came over. Candlelight flickered on the gilt mouldings and made the cloud-frescoed ceiling seem to move; the steel roller blinds, framed by red damask, had been lowered. Elisabeth sat in a Louis Quinze chair, gripping its arms, seeing again Heydi's old-young face, hearing his voice.

Your American tin god. They sent him here to betray us to the Prinz Albrechtstrasse.

A lie, a monstrous lie. It had to be. Except . . .

The flak was pounding continuously now. The first explosion sounded far off, the next closer, the third shaking the room, shaking Elisabeth, shaking her belief that Heydi had lied.

Sometimes his candour was embarrassing. 'The penniless aristocracy,' he'd once told her. 'All we have left is honour. It doesn't buy much these days.' Or another time, mock-ponderous-Prussian: 'Only the cynic can be completely honest these days, only the cynic knows that truth is deceit enough for any man.

Not that he was really cynical. 'Every romantic tries to convince himself he's a great cynic.' Who had told her that? Klaus Stauffenberg, long ago, before he had been maimed – Klaus Stauffenberg, as incapable then of arrogance as Heydi was of lying.

I was going to make a world where people ended the stupidity of war. Permanently. It didn't exactly work out that way, did it?

Haller, at the café on Kurfürstendamm, across the street from the impossible future on the theatre billboard, the dying soldier playing the organ in a bombed-out church.

'No, please, it can't be!' Elisabeth cried, and she was up out of the chair, her hands over her ears, and suddenly he was there holding her. She hadn't heard him come in.

'Heydi, oh God, Heydi.'

'Easy now, it's going to be all right.'

Not Heydi.

She was crying; she didn't want to think, had done her thinking, had let it destroy whatever she had left, like the theatre audience coming out to the desolation of Kurfürstendamm.

He kissed her, his mouth gentle on hers, and she clung to him. His face was scratchy, he hadn't shaved. When he held her off at last at arm's length, not speaking, just looking at her, she saw the bandage on his head. His uniform was soiled, one sleeve ripped at the shoulder.

She wanted to say, you're here, you're here, that's all that matters.

Heydi was on the roof, with a bottle and a gun.

She swayed towards him, for one moment longer needing the strength of his hands, and then she was pounding his chest with her fists. 'Bastard! Rotten stinking bloody murderous bastard! You came here to betray them, didn't you? Didn't you? My uncle, Heydi, all of them – you want to get them killed. That's why you're here, isn't it?'

The savage hatred in her voice stunned him so that when she broke away and began to run he stood an instant, mute. Then he started after her, calling her name as she opened the high double doors to the dining-room and went through. Raffaello Matti, he told himself, that was the only explanation, it had to be Matti even though he did not understand how it could have happened.

Three candles on the long refectory table, flickering in the rush of air as she passed, her shadow leaping on the wall. A single candle in the kitchen, reflected from white porcelain, a drawer slamming shut, Elisabeth whirling then, one arm high, candlelight glinting on the blade of the knife, Elisabeth crying out and hurling the knife away, hurling herself past him, the back hallway, the stairs, Haller lurching after her into the darkness, the vertigo taking him then so that he had to grip the banister to keep from falling before he could follow her up to the roof, the metal door banging open on Walpurgis night, the signal flares close now, the sky a vast dome of green and red cut by the searchlight beams, the puffs of flak bursting above the statues of dead Prussian warriors on the edge of the roof where Heydi stood silhouetted against the flames.

She went to Heydi, stood next to Heydi, and by then Haller had expended what little reserve of strength he had. He walked towards them slowly across the sticky tarred surface of the roof wondering if he could ever make them understand, and he saw Heydi's hand bringing the gun up and Heydi taking the trained deadly stance, legs apart, torso in profile, arm extended, and he knew there would be no time to make them understand, no answer to 1938 or to anything, just the guilt and the weariness punctuated by death.

*

Heydi held the double-action Walther P-38 already primed, chamber loaded, hammer down, as he sighted along his extended arm and the barrel of the pistol. All that remained was to squeeze the trigger, Haller not a dozen strides away now, so that when the steel-jacketed 9mm bullet ripped into his chest it would slam him back halfway to the stairwell door.

And Heydi waited a single beat longer, long enough for Elisabeth to drag down on his arm even as he knew he would not have done it, could not do it because the war had not done to him what it had to Klaus Stauffenberg.

Twenty-One

First Sergeant Andreas Pflaum, red-faced, panting, his field-grey uniform sopping wet, flung himself down in the barracks square, Moabit District Headquarters, and lit an ersatz cigarette. It had no taste that he could distinguish from the dust clogging his nostrils and gritty in his mouth, and Sergeant Pflaum crushed it out in disgust with a calloused palm. He looked at his watch. 3.15 and, unless he was sunstruck in this goddamn heat, it was Tuesday, 18 July.

Pflaum had, since shortly after lunch, put the 160 men of Two Company, *Grossdeutschland* Guard Battalion, through close-order drill. This for the benefit of the ape-shit battalion C.O. and his new Exec. who, naturally, weren't watching. Through the dust, settling now a full minute after Two Company had gratefully taken ten, Pflaum could see the mess-hall window, dark curtain drawn against the heat. It was hot all right, fucking Africa hot and Pflaum could almost believe he was back there in the desert.

Guzzling beer, more than likely, the C.O. and his new Exec. Pflaum sighed, raised his canteen, drank lukewarm water. The close-order drill had been his own idea; Pflaum was bucking for another stripe. Somewhat less shit to take from the Hitler Youth junior officers of the battalion if he made Oberfeldwebel.

Pflaum got to his feet and walked slowly among the sprawled figures of the men of Two Company, all of them drenched with sweat as Pflaum was, all covered with dust as Pflaum was, to where they had stacked their Mauser Kar bolt-action rifles in threes, buttplates to the ground of the barracks square, the parched ground itself chewed by the hobnailed boots of the company.

Its enlisted men overtrained, Pflaum reflected sourly, and of course those Hitler Youth farts who passed for company commanders had no experience at all. What the battalion got for serving permanent guard duty in Berlin, like a police riot squad gone stale in a riot-free city. They did look smart on parade, though, at least Two Company did. Pflaum saw to that and at that moment saw Oberleutnant Schlee, C.O., Two Company, enter the barracks square with that stiff walk he had, like someone had shoved a rifle up his ass all the way to the gleaming white Hitler Youth teeth in the beardless pink Hitler Youth face.

Pflaum got the company back on its feet, ordered the Mausers unstacked. This was done with lethargy and groaning. It was over 90° in the shade, if you could find any.

'Double-time them,' suggested Schlee in his high Hitler Youth voice.

Pflaum did so. Soon he was choking on the dust, his coughing unheard in the constant thud, thud, thud of 160 pairs of hobnailed boots.

Naturally the new Exec. had to show up on the hottest fucking day of the hottest fucking July in Pflaum's memory. Fucking officers. The Exec., if anything, looked more ape-shit than the C.O. himself. A real S.S. type if Pflaum ever saw one.

The mess-hall, the coolest place in Moabit District Headquarters, was still more than hot enough. Through the closed window could be heard the pounding of hobnailed boots. The long dim room with its trestle tables smelled of cabbage and ersatz coffee. Jaeger had undone the top two buttons of his field-grey tunic, but sweat still matted his chest hair and the glass of beer he drank was tepid.

'Well, what do you think?' he asked the new Executive Officer of the Guard Battalion, who had appeared at lunchtime with a freshly cut set of transfer papers.

'I think von Schirach and Axmann had your company commanders too long,' the Exec. said dryly, thus echoing the sentiments of Sergeant Pflaum outside. 'They're over-indoctrinated, Herr Major. Very sound on the iniquity of the Versailles Treaty, the superiority of the master race, the necessity of *Lebensraum*, the *Führerprinzip* and, last but not least, the privileged destiny of Greater German youth – to die for the Führer. Too bad they don't have combat experience.'

Jaeger laughed. 'I couldn't have put it better myself.' He banged his empty glass on the bare wood of the table and in a few seconds the fat mess sergeant lumbered towards them to thump a fresh pitcher of beer on the table. Jaeger filled both their glasses. He grew serious. 'After you get outfitted at supply, I'll go over the Valkyrie Orders with you. We're the linchpin, as you'll see. If the Bendlerstrasse calls us out you'd better know those orders cold.'

'No problem,' the Exec. said. 'But don't tell me you believe that crap about an uprising. The East Workers are too busy dying of starvation.'

'Sure, but that's not the point. The point is that I expect to be bouncing all over Berlin on a motorcycle during the exercise, which would leave you in charge of the C.P.'

Both men drank their beer thirstily. 'Welcome aboard, if I didn't say so before,' Jaeger said then. 'I still can't get over it. Your predecessor was a relic of the First War and I thought I was stuck with him. Then, when I met you on Sunday . . . '

'Is that how I got here?' Haller asked.

'No, that's the funny thing. It just occurred to me then that I could use a man like you and forty-eight hours later here you are.'

'The Bendlerstrasse,' Haller said gravely, 'moves in mysterious ways. I thought I was on my way back to the Western Front.'

Jaeger said: 'Hang around a while. The Anglo-Americans will meet you more than halfway.'

'If the Red Army doesn't get here first.'

'Yes,' said Jaeger, 'there is that.' He refilled their glasses, the tepid beer foaming and overflowing.

'I hope Frau Jaeger's feeling better,' Haller said, his tone of voice almost making a question of it.

Jaeger's eyes grew hard. 'There's nothing wrong with Frau Jaeger.'

'Sorry, Herr Major. People can get unnerved by an air raid, that's all I meant.'

'Sunday? How long did you stay?'

'I don't know. Not long. An hour or so.'

'She seemed perfectly all right to me last night. What was that business about Reinhard Ritter anyway?'

'Gottfried Ritter,' Haller corrected.

'Yes, of course. Gottfried.'

'I was his student before the war. Modern European History.' Haller drank, put his glass down.

'And when you learned he was dead you went to see my wife?'

'You probably know the feeling yourself,' Haller said. 'You're at the front and you see men dying all around you, but when someone from a saner time buys it that's different. Do you know what I mean?'

'That it's a different kind of death, a death somehow with meaning? Yes, I know the feeling. Did you know Ritter well?'

'I wouldn't say well, no.' Haller seemed to mull his reply over. 'All right, here it is, Herr Major,' he said. He sounded embarrassed. 'I didn't exactly keep my nose to the grindstone. Too much screwing around, among other things. I would have got thrown out except for Ritter. He was that kind of man.'

'Too much screwing around, was it?' Jaeger said. 'Women would find you attractive, wouldn't they?' His laughter was almost unforced. 'My wife certainly did, that was obvious.'

Haller said stiffly: 'I regret anything I may have done to give the Herr Major that impression.'

Jaeger waved a negligent hand. 'Not your fault. Monika sometimes amuses herself by flirting. But perhaps you know that. I believe you and my wife were already acquainted?'

Haller sounded embarrassed again. 'Strangely enough, sir, when I first saw Frau Jaeger I thought for a moment that I did know her. Tall, blonde, with those stunning legs and that gorgeous pair of . . . ' Haller cleared his throat. 'That is to say, Herr Major, she reminded me of a woman I . . . spent some time with on my last leave. But I quickly realised Frau Jaeger was not that person.'

Jaeger made himself smile. 'Oh, was that it?'

So Monika reminded Haller of some tart he'd screwed on his last leave? Not very flattering. And not very convincing. Unless – Jaeger felt a sudden twist of jealousy. Unless Monika *was* the tart Haller had screwed on his last leave.

He kept the smile in place. Perhaps he was wrong. It would not do to show the despised bourgeois jealousy in front of his new Exec. There would be plenty of time later to wring the truth out of Monika.

'Well,' he said, 'I hope she was helpful?'

'You mean about Ritter, Herr Major?'

Jaeger said that was what he meant.

'We just reminisced about him. I felt I owed that to his memory,' Haller said earnestly.

'How did he die, anyway?'

'He had a heart attack.'

'Frau Jaeger told you that?'

'Yes, she did.'

Jaeger shoved back from the table, went to the window and parted the heavy curtain. Outside, double-time slowed to quick-time and Pflaum could be heard bellowing cadence.

Jaeger let the curtain fall. 'R.I.P. Sturmbannführer Gottfried Ritter,' he said.

SUPREME HEADQUARTERS RASTENBURG 18 JULY 1545 HOURS MARSHAL KEITEL VERY URGENT TO COLONEL GRAF STAUFFENBERG O.K.W. BERLIN PROCEED RASTENBURG WITH FINAL REPEAT FINAL ARRANGEMENTS TWO HUNDRED THOUSAND REPLACEMENTS ARMY GROUP CENTRE READY FOR FÜHRERCONFERENCE 1300 HOURS THURSDAY 20 JULY.

At 5.00 that Tuesday afternoon General Ludwig Beck still had not left Wannsee. He thought Heydi was being too cautious insisting that they travel the dozen miles into Berlin along back roads. He wasn't a fugitive, after all. Not that he expected a Mercedes-Benz six-wheeled touring car escorted by motorcycle outriders racing along the Avus, but still this slipping along back roads in the old soft-topped Skoda struck the former chief of staff as unseemly for the man who would become head of state in the provisional government.

Beck was seated at the window of his room overlooking the lake when Elisabeth came in with his dress uniform. The old man's eyes misted over when he saw it – field-grey tunic, gold oak leaf on carmine collar tabs, gold braid shoulder straps with the three silver pips of a Generaloberst, iron grey trousers with the wide general staff officer carmine stripe along the seams. He hadn't worn it since 1938.

He smiled at Elisabeth and felt a wrenching stab below his ribs.

'Uncle, are you all right?'

'Of course I am,' Ludwig Beck said testily. 'A little twinge, that's all. I confess to a certain amount of nervousness, my dear.' He shook a tablet from the small bottle on the bedside table and swallowed it without water. Morphia. Ten minutes, fifteen, he told himself, his face expressionless as the pain struck again.

Elisabeth had placed the freshly ironed uniform on the edge of the bed.

'I do believe I'll try it on,' General Beck said.

Elisabeth smiled. 'After all the work I went to pressing it, you'd better.'

She left and Beck stood a moment longer looking down at the uniform. He heard a car crunching along the gravel driveway as he removed his shirt. Heydi? No, the young lieutenant wasn't due until later. The pain had begun to recede. It was there, a reminder of the death awaiting him, but he could cope with it now.

Five minutes later he stood before the dressing-table mirror. The uniform was beautiful, and a disaster.

The collar fitted loosely and made his scrawny neck look like a rooster's. The tunic was far too wide for his emaciated frame, the trousers three sizes too large. He looked like a senile veteran of the First War dressing for Remembrance Day.

He unfastened the gold buttons of the tunic slowly, his fingers lingering on the carmine stripe down the front. Then he laid the tunic carefully on the bed, removed the trousers, and put on his civilian clothing.

Elisabeth knocked at the door and entered. She looked from her uncle to the neatly folded uniform.

'I decided it would be more . . . appropriate to appear as a civilian,' Ludwig Beck said.

Elisabeth bit her lip. How much weight he had lost! His body skin and bones and that thing growing inside him.

'We've had enough of general-staff officers strutting around in gold braid,' Beck told her. 'It was a foolish idea.'

'Herr Goerdeler's downstairs,' Elisabeth said after a while.

'Well, of course he is. What kept him, anyway?'

'He's come to say goodbye, uncle.'

'To what? What the devil are you talking about, child?'

'Count von Helldorf's with him. He found out the S.D. plans to arrest Herr Goerdeler in the morning.'

General Beck clamped his thin lips and said nothing. The head of state of the provisional government too ravaged by disease to wear his uniform, the chief of government soon to be a fugitive with a price on his head. They had waited too long, had let history pass them by. But how could it have been otherwise?

A changing of the guard, Ludwig Beck thought, the younger generation taking over. It was all in Klaus Stauffenberg's hands now. As, Beck was honest enough to admit, it had been for some time.

He went downstairs with Elisabeth.

'Why now?' Goerdeler said. 'What made them wait until now?' The frustration was clear in his voice. Carl Goerdeler was by choice a man of action who had been reduced by necessity to talking. Only the Wehrmacht could accomplish a *coup d'état*, and they would take no orders from a civilian. Goerdeler had spent years pleading, cajoling, exhorting other men to act in his place. And now, almost on the eve of Valkyrie . . .

'Himmler's a cautious man, Carl,' Helldorf said. 'The warrant for your arrest is a sop to the S.D., no more. If anything, a hopeful sign. Himmler still wants to see which way the wind is blowing. He's not at all convinced we won't succeed. The problem, of course, is you. You'll have to go into hiding.'

Goerdeler stood with his back to the room, staring out at the lake. 'Like Esser did?'

'It's not for long,' Helldorf told him. 'This time Thursday it will all be over.'

Goerdeler turned from the french doors and forced himself to smile. 'You're right, of course. After so long I can hold out for two more days. But I can't stay here. The S.D. knows who all my friends are.'

Helldorf frowned. 'Ordinarily, I'd have suggested the Charité. Wrap you in bandages, give you ersatz papers, a bed in the hospital, we've done it before. But it's no good now. Raffaello Matti blew that one open when we worked him over at the Alexanderplatz.'

Beck smiled a thin frigid smile. 'You didn't pass it on to Himmler, did you?'

Helldorf ignored that. 'What Raffaello Matti told us he could have told the S.D. We can't chance it.'

There was a silence. Then Elisabeth said: 'I can hide you, Herr Goerdeler.'

They all looked at her.

'The Emil network,' she said. 'When we go in tonight. '

General Beck shook his head. 'I won't have you exposed to the danger.'

'It's no more dangerous than what I've been doing ever since I came to Berlin. We've been hiding Jews for months.'

Goerdeler's voice became animated then. 'I rather like the

notion, Elisabeth. I'm sure you could impose on them to hide one Aryan politician.'

The one-legged block leader Binnicker was supervising a crew of a dozen East Workers when Jaeger entered the lobby at 8.00 that evening. The doors to the street stood open and the East Workers were carrying what was left of the lobby furniture out to the rubble-strewn street. Jaeger saw his distorted reflection in the mirror on the far wall of the lobby. His face was shiny with sweat and dark patches stained the armpits of his tunic. The heat of the day seemed, if anything, more oppressive now.

'Influence,' Binnicker said after greeting him. 'Sometimes a little influence helps. Next week, the O.T. told me, if that soon. What can an old cripple, even a veteran of the Argonnerwald, do?'

Two East Workers stumbled by under the weight of a heavy oak tabletop.

'Move, get along there, move it!' Binnicker shouted at them, his ferocious scowl fading when he turned back to Jaeger. 'Influence,' he said again, nodding his head. 'Perhaps the Herr Major would convey my thanks to his wife?'

Ten minutes later over a glass of korn Jaeger was telling Monika, 'You've got a friend for life downstairs.'

'You mean Binnicker? There have to be some advantages working for the Prinz Albrechtstrasse.'

Most of the damage to the apartment had been repaired. Even the china cabinet stood in its accustomed place, although minus its glass doors and half the set of Rosenthal. Monika wore her Japanese kimono and when she passed between Jaeger and the evening light at the window to refill his glass he could see that she was wearing nothing under it.

'I'm surprised to find you in,' he said. She stood over him with the glass and he could see the tips of her breasts through the fine blue silk.

'Why? Where else would I be?'

Jaeger said nothing.

'On a hot night like this,' Monika added.

The desire Jaeger felt for her then infuriated him. He hadn't told Haller the truth that afternoon; this was his first visit to Bellevuestrasse since Sunday. Visit, he thought, and that infuriated him too. His own apartment.

He drank the korn in one swallow. 'Eaten yet?'

'Yes, but I could make you something.'

Jaeger shook his head. 'I'm not hungry. Too hot, and I was swilling beer all afternoon with the new battalion Exec.'

Monika settled herself on the sofa, arranging the blue silk around her legs, momentarily exposing smooth tanned thighs.

'You know him,' Jaeger said.

Monika looked puzzled. 'Who?'

'My new Exec.'

'How in the world would I know him?'

'He's Hauptmann Richard Haller,' Jaeger said.

Monika leaned forward, brushing her long streaked blonde hair away from her face. 'Well now,' she said. 'The handsome captain himself. Just how did that happen? Was it your idea?'

'Of course not,' Jaeger told her irritably. 'He was assigned to the battalion.'

'Is he a good officer?' Monika asked. Jaeger got the impression she was taunting him. 'The perfect Aryan soldier, no doubt?'

'He'll do,' Jaeger said shortly.

'I'm sure he will.'

'What the hell is "the perfect Aryan soldier" supposed to mean?'

'Only that he looks the part so, Ernst dear.'

Jaeger got to his feet and poured himself another glass of korn. 'I gather you had a nice long talk on Sunday.'

'Did he tell you that?'

'How the hell else do you think I knew?'

'You don't have to snap at me.'

'How long did he stay?'

'An hour, maybe less. Really, Ernst. Would you please stop interrogating me?'

'What's his connection with Gottfried Ritter?'

'Suddenly,' said Monika, 'everybody's interested in poor Gottfried.'

'What was Haller's interest?'

'Nothing special. He just . . . what difference does it make to you?'

Jaeger was standing in front of the cocktail table, looking down at her. 'You talked. For an hour. About what?'

'The war. The way they bomb the population centres. The usual things you say to a stranger in an air raid.'

'Haller told me you went to pieces.'

Monika's head jerked up. 'Is that so surprising? With bombs falling right outside? I had a bad moment, yes. I . . . got over it.'

'With Haller's assistance, no doubt.'

'For God's sake, Ernst. I thought we were talking about Gottfried Ritter.'

'How long have you known Haller?'

'I never met him before Sunday.'

'You mean to tell me he just walked in, a total stranger, for a nice, sentimental chat about Ritter? I don't believe you.'

'No? What do you want me to tell you? That he swept me up in his arms and carried me inside and made passionate love to me while the bombs were falling? Is that what you'd rather hear, Ernst? That I make a gift of myself to every handsome officer who comes knocking at the door? Why don't you go back to your battalion and ask Hauptmann Haller if he enjoyed fucking his commanding officer's wife?'

Jaeger's right hand moved three inches, sloshing the contents of his glass into Monika's face. She came off the sofa trying to claw him. He hit her, a ringing open-palmed blow just below her ear. She teetered back and would have fallen but he caught the wide blue sleeve of the kimono, dragging her around the low table.

The sash at her waist came loose and he saw her then as he had on his first day back, the deep tan hardly faded, the flawless skin of her throat and breasts almost as dark as the aureoles and taut nipples, no tan she ever got in Berlin, the healthy bronze colour flowing over the supple belly down to the pubic triangle. He picked her up then as that first day he had lifted her from the bath, but when he sank with her on the sofa she tried again to claw his face and he struck her hands aside and hit her, four times, very swiftly on either side of her jaw with his open hand. He saw her lip split and he went wild then; she had it coming, all the time he was on the Eastern Front, all the nameless Berlin desk soldiers, all the gifts in the apartment he couldn't afford.

She made a sound, a choking whimper, when he broke her nose, and he could see the terror in her eyes when she gagged on the blood.

The terror stopped him.

He felt then as if he himself had been beaten. He raised his hand in a weary pathetic attempt to comfort her, and she misunderstood. She thought he was going to hit her again.

The terror made her talk.

Twenty-Two

Wednesday dawned grey and hot, and by then the Organization Todt heavy rescue convoys flowed through Berlin's streets like blood through the arteries of a moribund patient miraculously brought back to life. By noon half the city's telephone exchanges had been restored and more than half its electricity. Those few fires that remained were under control.

Top priority went to the government quarter delineated by the streets Dorotheen, Friedrich, Koch, Anhalter, Saarland, Bellevue, Lenné, and Hermann Goering. By late Wednesday afternoon essential services in the Wilhelmstrasse district had been restored to better than ninety per cent capacity.

The area delineated by those streets also was marked for top priority by Stauffenberg and Olbricht. Operation Valkyrie could not succeed unless Jaeger's *Grossdeutschland* Guard Battalion controlled access to the district.

No U.S.A.A.F. bombers appeared over the city on Wednesday the 19th.

At 10.00 p.m. that evening, O.T. engineers in a Henschel repair truck were dispatched to repair a burst water main outside a bombed-out apartment building near the Post Check Office on Dorotheenstrasse. Part of the problem was discovered to be in the basement of the condemned building itself, and two engineers entered it to shut off the intake valve. They smelled kitchen odours – boiled cabbage, they thought – and at first did nothing about it. If victims of the terror raids had decided to occupy the basement of a condemned building, what difference did it make? The poor bastards had to live somewhere, didn't they?

Still, orders were orders. The O.T. engineers filed a routine report in triplicate. One copy would reach the Prinz Albrechtstrasse the next morning.

Berlin licked its wounds and waited in the heat.

A sand-coloured four-door Tatra staff car bearing white licence plates with the WH army designation pulled up alongside the raw pine shack at the edge of the tarmac at Rangsdorf Airport south of Berlin at 6.25 a.m. Thursday, 20 July. On the tarmac stood a vintage two-engined Heinkel III bomber that had been converted to a transport. A relic of the mid-thirties, it would need three and a quarter hours for the flight to Rastenburg in East Prussia.

Sepp climbed immediately and gratefully out of the car, leaving the three officers inside. General Helmut Stieff's ersatz cigar made the air in the small car all but unbreathable.

After a minute the driver was joined by Oberleutnant von Heydebrand. The two men leaned against the fender and watched a fuel truck cross the tarmac to the Heinkel. Then Sepp looked up at the windsock hanging limply above the shack.

'Can you believe this goddamn heat?' he said. 'Every day it gets worse.'

In the back seat of the staff car the weather was also being discussed.

'What's your estimate now?' Stauffenberg asked.

'At these temperatures?' Stieff considered. 'Maybe no more than ten minutes.'

Stauffenberg nodded and pulled the bulging black leather briefcase closer on his lap. In it was a thick sheaf of papers containing plans for forming a dozen new front-line divisions by scraping the bottom of the barrel of the *Ersatzheer*, the Replacement Army.

In the briefcase also, wrapped in brown paper inside a dirty shirt, was the bomb.

According to Stieff, perhaps ten minutes would pass from the time Stauffenberg used the electrician's pliers to break the glass vial of acid until the wire was eaten through, the firing pin struck the detonator cap, and the two 20-gram priming chambers set off the 975 grams of brownish, waxy-looking hexite.

Also according to Stieff, the ensuing explosion, contained by the reinforced concrete walls and ceiling of the bunker in which the Führerconference took place, would kill everyone in the room.

At 6.55 the four men left the Tatra staff car and climbed aboard the Heinkel III. Five minutes later they were airborne.

At 9.30 the valet Linge appeared with an unopened half-litre bottle of Fachinger mineral water, a lemon, the one-page press summary prepared by Reich Press Chief Dr Dietrich, and the Armed Forces High Command Situation Report. Linge was earlier than usual. But Mussolini would arrive by armoured train today. The afternoon conference had been moved forward to 12.30. The fat, despondent Duce after that.

Linge's white-gloved hands opened the Fachinger, poured it, cut a sliver of lemon and dropped it into the glass. Linge did not speak. 9.30 was too early for talk, Linge knew. He bowed out.

Get Dr Dietrich's press summary over with first. Reading glasses, now that Linge was gone. Couldn't be seen wearing them, but even the special type, bold and large, blurred these days.

He sat up in bed, a narrow camp bed in the small underground room lit now by the overhead electric light. The ventilator shaft fan purred and thumped. His stomach grumbled. Flatulence. Dr Stumpfegger said not enough exercise. Morell knew better. Complete exhaustion of the intestinal system brought on by overburdened nerves. Morell's injections worked. Stumpfegger was a fool.

Terror raids, said the press summary. All they gave him these days. American bombers from west and south, severe damage to residential areas of Munich, Koblenz, Saarbrücken. The population suffered losses. Not Berlin this time. He liked it when they hit Berlin. He hated Berlin. When he rebuilt it after the war, he would rename it. Germania. The Berliners deserved what they got.

He read again: the population suffered losses.

They had it coming. For their weakness, their inadequacy. He had been prepared to give them the world if they were strong enough to take it.

Not strong enough. Let them die, in terror. A vision of cities burning, women and children running, screaming, human torches. He smiled. Club Foot Dwarf was always badgering him to visit the bombed-out cities. For morale. Even Obese Renaissance Man made such visits. But not him. The citizens of the Reich had proven themselves inferior, like the Wehrmacht. Unable to overcome the subhuman Slavs, the mongrel Americans, the undernourished British.

They had let him down. They were not good enough. Did they deserve better than the mental defectives? Or the gypsies? Or the Jews?

The Jews, against him from the beginning. The Reich was Jew-free now, like most of Europe. The gypsies couldn't be coordinated into the life of Greater Germany. So they died too. The mental defectives ate food that could be put to better use. He would have eliminated them all, but the Evangelical

Church had been too outraged, and the Catholics. Pious idiots!

Seventy million Germans? No stomach for a fight and when things go wrong they cave in. Only the fittest deserved to survive.

He sipped the Fachinger water, cool and bubbly.

Should have known it from the beginning. All against him. In Vienna at the architecture school. Insufficient faces. What did faces have to do with architecture? A clever excuse, no more. Could Speer draw faces? Then 1923, marching in Munich. A few shots from the police and they broke and ran. His followers. So he had to run too. And Roehm in 1934. Homosexual traitor, plotting against him. Wiped out, with the whole sick S.A. crew. The Wehrmacht? No better. Worse if anything because he had given them the power he took from Roehm. He gave them that and Austria, then Czechoslovakia. And for what? For an ungrateful weakling like Ludwig Beck to resign.

Weakness was a convenient excuse. Like the surrender at Stalingrad when he ordered them – ordered them – to fight to the last man.

All of them weak, or traitors. Der treue Heinrich fainting at the sight of a few hundred Jews, women and children, being shot, but quite capable of ordering the deaths of millions of others. Maybe Himmler meant well, but his weakness was insufferable.

Fat Renaissance Man, unable to destroy a few squadrons of R.A.F. fighters. He could have had Britain.

Club Foot Dwarf and his optics of war, Club Foot Dwarf who whored around Berlin with his friend the police chief. Berlin, a whore of a city.

They would all get what was coming to them.

Sometimes in a quick flash he could see it, the Apocalypse, all the Reich burning, a sea of flame from the Baltic to the Brenner Pass. He could feel the excitement in his loins.

He crumpled Dr Deitrich's press summary, tossed it away, took the Armed Forces High Command Situation Report from the tray Linge had left. The bold capitals of the Führer-type blurred, came into focus.

In Normandy, a town called St Lô abandoned to the Americans. Ten enemy tanks destroyed, and sixteen aircraft. In the past two nights, thirty British four-engined bombers shot down over northern France. Reprisal attacks on London through the nights of 18 and 19 July. Enemy convoy destroyed off the Channel Islands.

In Italy, enemy forces advancing on Livorno. Harbour destroyed. (Could see the harbour in flames, the Italians running, their clothes afire, their screaming mouths becoming blisters and charred flesh. Nice.) Enemy attacks broken on the shore road, west of Ancona. Of course, that was Kesselring. Good man so far, but he would falter sooner or later, they all did. Talk here at Wolf's Lair that Kesselring should replace Keitel as Chief-of-Staff, O.K.W. Ridiculous. Keitel was loyal as a dog if not very bright. None of them was very bright. All of them abused his trust, sooner or later, as Kesselring would falter, sooner or later.

Kill them all if he had his way.

Eastern Front. Red Army attacks halted on the River Bug. Heavy fighting in the vicinity of Brest-Litovsk. Two hundred and fifteen enemy tanks destroyed so far this week. In the lake district north and north-west of Vilna, attacks repulsed, breakthroughs sealed off. Temporarily. Army Group Centre urgently needed the replacements the Bendlerstrasse had refused to send.

That Colonel Stauffenberg flying in today. Probably with more excuses. A count, wasn't he? Aristocratic swine, all of them.

Will ram briefcase of aristocratic swine down throat of aristocratic swine if he hasn't brought the goods from the Bendlerstrasse.

'Linge!' he shouted.

Linge's head appeared instantly at the door.

'Weather?'

'Hot, my Führer.'

'Hot? Is that all you ever say?'

'Hot and humid, my Führer.'

'Get me Burgdorf.'

Linge bowed out of the doorway. General Wilhelm Burgdorf, the Führer's army adjutant, soon appeared, rigidly offering the German greeting.

'They have prepared the Conference bunker?'

'Yes, my Führer. It is hot.'

'I know that.' Voice hoarse, exasperated.

'I mean there is some difficulty with the ventilation system in the bunker, my Führer.'

'Idiots! Do they expect me to put on a pair of overalls and repair it? Must I do everything myself?'

'It is doubtful that the repairs can be accomplished by noon. May I suggest that the Führer consider using the guest barracks instead? It is above ground.'

'I know that.' Voice hoarse, more exasperated.

'I mean to say it would be cooler there, with the windows open. The map-room could be made ready in an hour.'

'And the mosquitoes?'

'Will be bad, my Führer.'

Mosquitoes in the guest barracks or the stink of the sweat of dead-animal-eaters in the underground bunker.

'Prepare the guest barracks.'

'Jawohl, my Führer.'

'And get me Morell.'

'Jawohl.'

Morell came, administered injections. A clear fluid from the testes of a nonagenarian Bulgarian peasant. Strength.

Over his bulletproof vest Adolf Hitler donned the field-grey tunic he had vowed to wear until the war was won or he was dead.

He went upstairs and outside to feed Blondi, the Alsatian bitch yelping ecstatically as he approached the run.

He taunted Blondi with the horsemeat, finally surrendered it. Blondi licked his hand.

It was already very hot, even in the gloomy shade of the tall pines. S.S. men patrolled Security Zone A, marching in pairs on either side of the barbed wire. A mosquito whined at his ear.

It was 10.15. The Heinkel 111 was just then landing at Rastenburg airport three miles away.

Twenty-Three

The Volkswagen KdF, Sepp behind the wheel and at his side a Lieutenant Colonel Streve, drove past the still, algae-covered water of Moysee and along the narrow road through the pine forest to the Security Zone C checkpoint. Streve had met the Heinkel to facilitate their passage through the checkpoints. In the cramped back of the car were Stauffenberg and the hunch-backed General Stieff, the latter calmly chatting with Streve while Stauffenberg showed his papers.

Heydi had stayed behind at Rastenburg airport. His job was to phone Wolf's Lair just after 1.00 with an urgent call for Stauffenberg, giving the disabled colonel an excuse to leave the underground conference bunker after activating the bomb.

Stauffenberg got his first surprise after they had cleared the checkpoint. Streve said: 'At least you won't have to pretend you're a mole, Herr Oberst.'

'I beg your pardon?'

'The conference has been moved above ground to the guest barracks near Reichsleiter Bormann's quarters.'

Stauffenberg felt himself tense at Stieff's side. Nine hundred and seventy-five grams of hexite, detonated underground in a concrete bunker, would kill everyone in the room. What it would do above ground in the guest barracks was anyone's guess.

Streve noticed Stauffenberg's tension. He said: 'No possibility of an enemy air raid, I assure you. They still haven't learned the location of Wolf's Lair. Besides, the barracks' walls are reinforced with eighteen inches of concrete.'

Stauffenberg began to feel better. He shifted the weight of the briefcase on his lap. His relief did not last beyond the Security Zone B checkpoint. There, Streve said:

'I trust you're prepared, Herr Oberst?'

'Of course I'm prepared.'

'Keitel will ask you to be brief. It's a busy schedule.'

'I'm aware of that.'

'Yes, but I was instructed to tell you the conference has been moved forward to 12.30.'

To the left of the road and paralleling it was a railroad spur that ran from Rastenburg to Wolf's Lair. Beyond it signs warned that the pine forest was mined.

Stauffenberg knew he could not use the excuse of Heydi's call to leave. There was no way he could get word to Heydi to phone earlier.

He would have to bluff his way out.

At least he would have Sepp behind the wheel, not a motor pool driver. He had talked Streve into letting Sepp drive; it had not been difficult. Stauffenberg had almost died driving through a minefield in Africa. That he felt comfortable with no one but his own driver behind the wheel was understandable.

Sepp pulled up at the Security Zone A checkpoint. Security was stricter there at the inner gate and Stauffenberg had a chance to look around. The low ugly buildings were prefab single-storey fibreboard. The tall pines had not been cut down inside the barbed wire and except for them Security Zone A looked more like a concentration camp than a G.H.Q.

Sepp put the Volkswagen in gear and they rattled north seventy-five yards to the small parking area between the kitchen and Bormann's quarters.

'Everybody out,' said Streve cheerfully. He told Sepp: 'The mechanics usually keep a game of skat going at the garage, sergeant. In back of the theatre there.'

Sepp pulled a folded copy of *Das Reich* from his back pocket. 'I think I'll catch upon the news, Herr Oberstleutnant.'

Streve patted his shoulder. 'Good man,' he said.

Stauffenberg tossed General Stieff a salute. The hunch-backed general's assignment was in the Signals Office in the next compound. First, to phone the Bendlerstrasse in Berlin after the bomb had exploded. Then to back up Colonel General Fellgiebel, Chief of Communications, O.K.W., in blocking the signal circuits from Wolf's Lair to Berlin, ostensibly to break contact until the extent of the conspiracy could be determined.

Streve and Stauffenberg walked the forty yards from the small parking area to Marshal Keitel's quarters.

'You'll breakfast with him,' said Streve. 'He'll expect a re-hearsal of your report. Nobody wastes the Führer's time if Keitel can help it.'

'I won't waste the Führer's time,' Stauffenberg said.

Three miles away, at Rastenburg airport, the Heinkel pilot was thinking of a game of skat too. He invited Heydi to play.

'Better see that she's refuelled first,' Heydi said.

'What's the hurry?'

Heydi adjusted his monocle. 'My chief is the hurry. A holy terror if you deviate ten seconds from his schedule and he's got a conference in Berlin at 5.00 this afternoon. Believe me, don't cross him.'

'So I'll refuel the fucking plane first. I really love those Prussian shits.'

'He's Franconian.'

'Even worse,' said the pilot.

Heydi nodded. 'Don't I just know it.'

Even under ordinary circumstances breakfast with Field Marshal Keitel would have been a trying experience. Like so many military deskmen, the O.K.W. Chief-of-Staff disliked field officers. Possibly, Stauffenberg thought, because he felt inferior to them. It was common knowledge that Keitel had got where he was by assiduous toadying to Hitler. No wonder he was called Lakeitel – lackey – behind his back.

Stauffenberg's pedigree also built a barrier between them. His father had been Prime Minister to the royal houses of Württemberg and Bavaria, his mother was the granddaughter of General Count von Gneisenau who had, a hundred years ago, organised the Prussian General Staff. In peacetime a parvenu like Wilhelm Keitel would be dismissed summarily by Graf von Stauffenberg.

Stauffenberg finished his third cup of coffee at 12.20. He had already run through the report verbally twice. They were in the small sitting-room of Keitel's quarters, the briefcase on the floor at Stauffenberg's feet.

'Then that's it,' Keitel said. He was looking at his watch. 'I count on you not to be verbose.'

'I won't be, Herr Generalfeldmarschall.'

'The Führer may surprise you with his questions. His well-known intuition is quite justified, I assure you.'

'I understand,' said Stauffenberg. He cleared his throat. 'About the transportation for the new divisions,' he said.

'Yes, you weren't clear on that point, were you?'

'They're working on it at the Bendlerstrasse right now. I'm expecting a call.'

If only he could reach Heydi, he thought.

'You mean while you're with the Führer?'

'I'm sorry, sir, but the conference being advanced – I'm afraid it's likely.'

'It's irregular.'

'But necessary if I'm to give the Führer the entire picture.'

'Keep the call short, then.'

There was still a little time; Keitel allowed himself some small talk. 'The Countess is well?'

'Yes, sir.'

'Expecting your sixth, isn't she?'

Stauffenberg didn't want to think about Nina and the children. About what might happen to them if he failed. He nodded.

'Excellent. The Führer has always favoured large families of good Aryan stock.'

Keitel stood. Stauffenberg reached down for the briefcase and got to his feet. He held the briefcase awkwardly with the three fingers of his left hand.

'Here, let me take that for you,' Keitel said.

'Have I time for a visit to the W.C.?' Stauffenberg asked quickly.

Keitel chuckled. 'A conference with the Führer does that to a man, doesn't it?' His tone of voice was condescending. 'It's through there, first door on the left.'

Stauffenberg limped into the bathroom. He set the briefcase on the edge of the sink and stood for a moment looking at himself in the mirror. The eyepatch, the right sleeve pinned, the maimed left hand gloved in black leather. Suddenly it welled up in him. He had been a skilled horseman, a first-rate pianist. Horses and music had been his life. He almost wanted to remain in the conference room after he placed the bomb.

He shook off the feeling, swiftly unfastened the briefcase straps. Groped for the pliers, gripped them. It took little time. He had practised often enough. He stripped the shirt away, plunged the pliers through the wrapping paper. Snipped. Heard the faint tinkle of breaking glass.

Ten minutes.

He remembered to flush the toilet, then rejoined Field Marshal Keitel for the short walk to the guest barracks. A smell of pine heavy in the still air. The barracks building, the reassuring sight of its thick concrete shell. Inside. The noon heat stifling. Fibreboard walls, cloakroom, small communications centre with its battery of phones. Sergeant-major in charge, red porcine face.

'I'm expecting an important call. Colonel Stauffenberg. Information for the Führer. You'll call me out?'

'Jawohl, Herr Oberst.'

The conference room, forty feet by fifteen. Maps spread out on the long table, brass standing all around. General Heusinger, Deputy Chief, O.K.H., talking. Typist seated at a small round table near the right wall, transcribing. Three large windows on the far wall, thrown open to catch what little breeze there was. Pines visible through them.

Adolf Hitler standing at the centre of the near side of the table, both hands on the wood, peering at a map.

12.34. Six minutes to go.

He was standing with Keitel directly behind Hitler. Keitel whispered: 'Graf Stauffenberg, Home Army. *Ersatzheer* replacements for Army Group Centre.'

A barely perceptible nod from the Führer. 'After Heusinger.'

12.36. Heusinger still talking, the words without meaning to Stauffenberg.

He eased himself forward, felt the edge of the table; stood between Luftwaffe General Korten and Heusinger's deputy, Colonel Brandt. He placed the briefcase on the floor on the inner side of the oak upright supporting the table.

Would the windows dissipate the blast?

12.37. Only three minutes. If he left, it might arouse suspicion. Stay and die? But they would need him at the Bendlerstrasse. He backed away from the table.

Keitel jerked his head around.

'The call,' Stauffenberg whispered.

He went along the short corridor outside the conference room to the communications centre. The sergeant-major, earphones on, was taking a call.

'That call I was expecting.'

Earphones off. A shrug. 'Nothing for you yet, Herr Oberst.'

'It has to have come through by now.'

'Sorry, Herr Oberst. I could check the Signals Office.'

'Never mind. I'll do it myself.'

Stauffenberg hurried from the guest barracks and past Bormann's quarters to the parking area.

Two minutes to go.

In the conference room, something had fallen against Colonel Brandt's right foot. He looked down irritably, saw a briefcase. With his foot he nudged it to the other side of the table support, the heavy oak now between it and Adolf Hitler.

Brandt's chief, General Heusinger, was winding down, which was just as well. It had not been an optimistic report. The Führer looked savagely displeased, as only the Führer could.

Heusinger was saying: ' . . . Russians driving with strong forces west of the Duna towards the north. Their spearheads are already south of Dunaberg. If our army group around Lake Peipus is not withdrawn immediately, a catastrophe . . . '

Colonel Brandt had a microsecond left in which he saw a blinding flash and heard a roaring sound, and then he died.

Excerpts from *Reich Central Security Office Bureau IV Special Commission Report for 20 July 1944.*

Reichsführer-S.S. noted during detailing of circumstances that perpetrator of attempt was presumably Graf von Stauffenberg, Colonel, Chief-of-Staff at office of Commander, Home Army. He had been present at briefing session, then withdrew without notice before the explosion. Immediately afterwards he went to Berlin by plane.

Conference room and all furnishings heavily damaged. To right of entrance, 22-inch hole in floor. For wider radius, floor pressed in and charred. Wood splinters and leather fragments impacted into fibreboard walls.

Bomb crater shows explosion occurred above surface of floor. Direction of pressure wave indicated in photographs and sketches, enclosed.

Pressure wave largely destroyed conference room but found exit through windows. Minute sifting of mass of rubble led to discovery of small leather fragments, obviously from a briefcase; of two pieces of sheet metal and two compression springs from English chemical-mechanical time-fuse firing pins; also, part of flat iron pliers. Leather fragments that have been discovered have been identified by witnesses as belonging to Stauffenberg's briefcase. Small parts of igniter found at locale of explosion.

Stauffenberg breakfasted with Commander. When ready to go to briefing session from Keitel's quarters at 12.30 p.m., Stauffenberg went to W.C. next door with his briefcase. Presumably while there he released the time-fuse with the help of pair of flat pliers.

A short time after entering, Stauffenberg left the conference room and also left Security Zone A. The telephone operator, Sgt. Adam, testified to his hurried departure. A very nervous demeanour on the part of Stauffenberg was noted.

Stauffenberg drove to Guardpost I where, having witnessed the explosion, the lieutenant on duty had already ordered the barriers closed. Stauffenberg was halted and told the guard commander he must get to the airport urgently. As his pass was in order and additionally as he was known to the guard commander, the latter let him pass; particularly as the general alarm had not yet been sounded, but came only one and a half minutes later.

At the outer southern guardpost, Stauffenberg was halted again. The guard commander, Sgt. Kolbe, at first refused to let him pass, pointing out that the general alarm had been sounded. Kolbe telephoned headquarters, on Stauffenberg's request, reaching Hauptman von Möllendorf, the adjutant, his commanding officer then being at the locale of the explosion. Stauffenberg convinced von Möllendorf that he had received the commander's permission to leave the security area, and that he had to fly by 1.15 in any event. The adjutant, not knowing why the general alarm had been sounded, agreed, and confirmed his agreement on the telephone to Sgt. Kolbe.

In this situation it is to be taken into consideration that:

1. The alarm is sounded rather frequently.
2. Stauffenberg's papers were in order.
3. Since Stauffenberg was known as a seriously disabled fighting man and an officer in excellent standing, von Möllendorf had no reason at that time to be suspicious.

Stauffenberg passed the outermost southern gate, and took off with his adjutant, Oberleutnant von Heydebrand, at 13.15 hours from Rastenburg airport to Berlin-Rangsdorf.

Twenty-Four

General Friedrich Olbricht, Deputy Commander, Home Army, stood at the window of his office at 13–14 Bendlerstrasse, a harassed look on his round face. He had no delusions about himself. Olbricht was a superb staff officer but no leader of men; like Field Marshal Keitel, he was a desk soldier.

The day was flawless, if hot, the pall of smoke that had hung over Berlin all week gone, the sky a cloudless blue. Even the sewer smell of the Landwehr Canal did not reach Olbricht's second-floor window.

It was 1.20. Stieff's call had come through from Wolf's Lair not quite half an hour ago, his message as brief as it was baffling.

'General Olbricht? Stieff here. Listen, they'll be cutting communications soon. Things are confused here. A bomb exploded in the guest barracks during the Führer conference. There's talk of a plot, a conspiracy. There were deaths. I saw them carry the Füh . . .'

The phone had gone dead. Olbricht had tried, unsuccessfully, to return the blitz call. His secretary was still trying.

On receipt of Stieff's call, Olbricht was supposed to put the machinery of Valkyrie in motion. For twenty-seven minutes Olbricht had done nothing. He remembered the premature start last Saturday, the abortive marching of the Guard Battalion, the warning from General Fromm.

Was Hitler dead?

Olbricht removed his steel-rimmed glasses and polished them.

Without them his eyes looked vague, befuddled.

To act prematurely might cost him his life. To delay acting might mean the coup's failure.

Stauffenberg would know what to do. Stauffenberg, in a slow Heinkel III, somewhere over the old Polish Corridor now. *If* Stauffenberg had left Wolf's Lair.

If only Stauffenberg was here!

Olbricht opened the partition to the colonel's office. The secretary he shared with Stauffenberg was putting down the phone.

'Any luck with Stieff?' he asked.

'I'm sorry, sir. The circuits are still busy.'

'Keep trying.' Olbricht ran a hand nervously through his thinning hair. 'No, wait, Delia. Get me Oberleutnant von Heydebrand's home number.'

At that moment the outer door opened and he saw General Fromm standing in the doorway, Fromm looking as pugnacious as ever, his cleft slab of a jaw jutting.

'Just what the goddamn hell is going on at Rastenburg?' he demanded.

Olbricht felt a pulse pounding in his throat. 'Going on? What do you mean, sir?'

'The lines are out. I can't get through.'

Before Olbricht could answer, Delia Ziegler said: 'Begging the Herr General's pardon, but we're having the same trouble. I've been unable to reach General Stieff.'

'What do you want with Stieff?' Fromm asked Olbricht.

'Transportation arrangements for the replacements for Army Group Centre,' Olbricht said.

'Stieff? Not Stauffenberg?'

'He's attending the Führer conference,' Olbricht said. 'Stieff was to relay . . . '

'The conference is over by now. It was put forward half an hour.'

'I didn't know that.'

'This office was notified.'

'Oh dear,' said Frau Ziegler. 'I'm terribly sorry, sir. I forgot to . . . '

Fromm's voice overrode hers. 'Listen to me, Olbricht. Something's going on out there. I can't even raise them by radio.'

'Well, I don't exactly . . . '

'Inside,' Fromm snapped. He led the way into Olbricht's inner office, slid the partition.

'One way to get yourself shot,' he said, his voice low and

without inflection, 'is to treat me like a fool. You've all been doing it – you, Stauffenberg, Stieff – hinting about countering an S.S. putsch. But we both know this has nothing to do with the S.S. Don't we?'

Olbricht said nothing.

Fromm said: 'Let me remind you of something you signed – we all signed – in 1934.' He recited: ' "I swear by God this sacred oath, that I will render unconditional obedience to Adolf Hitler, the Führer of the German Reich and people, Supreme Commander of the Armed Forces, and will be ready as a brave soldier to risk my life at any time for this oath." You do remember?'

Olbricht said that he remembered.

'It is on that oath that I stand, General Olbricht. Whatever happens. And whatever happens, I don't want to see a repeat of last Saturday. That is a direct order.'

In a subdued voice Olbricht acknowledged the order. After Fromm left he told Frau Ziegler to cancel the call to Heydebrand's home number.

Ludwig Beck sat up in bed, his back propped by pillows. The morphia had made the pain recede but he felt weak and listless.

'Nothing yet?' he asked as Elisabeth came in.

She shook her head.

Beck debated calling the Bendlerstrasse himself, decided to wait.

Elisabeth hung his dark suit on the outside of the wardrobe door. She sat on the edge of the bed.

'How is Carl?' he asked.

Elisabeth had returned last night to the safe house where she had taken Goerdeler on Tuesday. A Jewish family named Gruenberg were already there, parents and two children. The girl, eight-year-old Hannah, had a sore throat and a chest cold, and was running a fever. Her cough worried the Gruenbergs. It might give them away.

'You know Mayor Goerdeler,' Elisabeth said. 'He's like a caged lion. He fully expects to be Chancellor of Germany before the day is over.'

'I wish I shared his faith,' Beck said softly.

Elisabeth looked at the bottle of morphia tablets on the bedside table. 'Could I have some of those?'

'What in the world for?' Beck asked.

Elisabeth explained about the little Gruenberg girl.

'You're going back there?'

Elisabeth knew that her uncle did not want to be alone until he left for the Bendlerstrasse. 'After you leave,' she said. 'I promised them.'

'There will be troops in the streets,' Beck told her. 'Martial law.'

'I'll be all right. It's not far. Just over on Dorotheenstrasse.'

Stauffenberg pushed open the door of the control shack at Rangsdorf airport. He was breathing hard. So was Heydi, who followed him inside. The Heinkel had encountered headwinds on the flight back from East Prussia. It was now well after four o'clock.

'Where's your phone?'

The dispatcher wore Luftwaffe overalls with sergeant's stripes. He did not look up from his clipboard.

'Where's your phone, goddamn it!'

The sergeant looked up and stiffened. 'Forgive me, Herr Oberst. In there.'

The phone was on the wall of a short hall that led to a storeroom. There was no door. It was less than a dozen feet from where the dispatcher sat. Stauffenberg fumbled the receiver off the hook with his gloved left hand.

Heydi smiled at the dispatcher and began to talk volubly. 'One of these days they're going to put those Heinkels in a museum where they belong.'

'I know what you mean, Herr Oberleutnant.'

'I almost had the feeling we could have done better with a pair of oars. Been busy here?'

'Three flights out all day. Rangsdorf's not exactly Tempelhof, Herr Oberleutnant.'

'Too far from town, that's the problem.'

Heydi kept talking. Stauffenberg's voice could be heard from the corridor. Just his voice, not what he was saying. Heydi saw a photograph of a buck-toothed woman on the desk. 'The wife?' he said. 'Do you live in Berlin?'

'Better yet. Right here in Rangsdorf.'

'You're lucky.'

Behind them, Stauffenberg had got through to Frau Ziegler. She was saying, 'I think he's in with Colonel Mertz.'

'Get him. Hurry.'

A minute passed, then: 'Olbricht speaking.'

'Has it started?'

'Klaus! Where are you?' Stauffenberg heard the relief in his voice.

'Rangsdorf. We just landed. Has it started?'

'The situation is confused here. Stieff didn't . . .'

'Has it started or hasn't it?'

'Not yet. Stieff said . . . '

'Send Valkyrie Order One.'

'It went . . . all right out there?'

'Like a direct hit from a 150mm shell. Get moving. I'll be with you inside of half an hour.'

Stauffenberg hung up and raced outside with Heydi to where Sepp was waiting in the Tatra staff car.

Most of the fifty machines in the Bendlerstrasse teletype room were chattering, non-coms sending and receiving. Olbricht found the captain in charge.

'Stop all traffic. Top priority. Issue Valkyrie One to all points.'

'Jawohl, Herr General.'

Olbricht ran upstairs to his office, got his gunbelt, buckled on the holstered Walther PPK. Then he went into General Fromm's office.

Fromm was dictating to his secretary.

'Get her out of here,' Olbricht said.

Fromm saw the gunbelt, the expression on Olbricht's usually bland face. 'If you please, Frau Binding,' he said, and she left. 'Well?'

'The Führer is dead.'

The two generals looked at each other. Fromm's face went pale. 'How do you know that?'

'Believe me, I know. We have prepared directives for you to issue. They're ready for your signature.'

Fromm rubbed a hand over his jutting jaw. 'Give me proof.'

'You're wasting time,' Olbricht said. 'This is your last chance. If you refuse, those directives can be signed in your name by your Chief-of-Staff.'

'I need proof.'

'Call Rastenburg,' Olbricht said.

'You know perfectly well we haven't been able to get through.'

'Try. Try it now.'

Fromm picked up the phone. 'Frau Binding, blitz call to Wolf's Lair. Marshal Keitel.'

They waited. Fromm's hands were shaking as he lit a cigarette. He had not finished smoking it when the phone buzzed.

'Hello? Yes, Fromm here, Herr Generalfeldmarschall.'

Olbricht's knees felt suddenly weak. He gripped the edge of the desk, watching Fromm's face.

'There are rumours that . . . the Führer has been killed. No, sir. No more than that. I . . . yes. Yes, I see.' Fromm kept rubbing his jaw; he was blinking rapidly. He said nothing for a full minute. Then: 'No, Graf Stauffenberg hasn't returned yet. Jawohl, Herr Generalfeldmarschall. Yes, I absolutely guarantee it.'

He hung up and told Olbricht: 'A bomb exploded in the guest barracks. There were casualties. The Führer was only slightly injured.'

'Keitel's lying,' Olbricht said desperately. 'It wouldn't be the first time.'

Fromm stood. 'I must ask you to place yourself under arrest, Olbricht. You are not to leave the building under any circumstances.'

Olbricht groped at his side, brought up the Walther PPK. The knowledge that Stauffenberg was on his way gave him the strength to say, 'I'm sorry, Herr General. It is you who are under arrest.'

At *Grossdeutschland* Guard Battalion headquarters in Moabit, Oberleutnant Bleiner, the National Socialist Guidance Officer, was delivering his weekly lecture to the battalion officers and non-coms in the mess-hall.

Bleiner had been droning on for half an hour about the advantages of the shortened line of defence in the East. The phlegmatic Austrian gave little attention to the mimeographed text he was reading. He considered himself over-educated for the simplistic lecture prepared by the army desk at the Promi. Bleiner had served at that desk himself before being assigned to the battalion. The experience had left him cynical.

'Should the Wehrmacht fall back on German soil temporarily,' he was saying, 'all the better. Once the Red Army supply lines become overextended, our forces will be in a position to contain, surround, and isolate the enemy's forward salients. To yield the centre preparatory to an envelopment on the flanks . . . '

The door burst open and Major Jaeger hurried into the room.

'Attention!' Bleiner shouted. Benches scraped back as officers and non-coms sprang to their feet.

'At ease, gentlemen,' Jaeger said. 'You will march your platoons, starting with Platoon A, One Company, to supply. Full battle-dress, riot-control equipment.' He nodded to Bleiner and hurried out.

'Dismissed!' Bleiner shouted, and watched the mess-hall empty in two quick orderly files. He met Hauptmann Haller at the door.

'Last Saturday all over again?' Bleiner asked; as imperturbable as ever.

'I wasn't with the battalion last Saturday.'

'No, that's true. One thing I learned in this war – never assume the Bendlerstrasse will do anything right. The major is something else again. Give him six months and he'll make full colonel,' Bleiner assured the Exec. 'Did he ever tell you how he escaped from a Russian P.O.W. camp? Ask him some time. That's quite a man. It's a privilege to serve under him, don't you agree?'

What light entered the cellar room in the bombed-out building on Dorotheenstrasse came from a high window facing the enclosed courtyard. The two windows on the opposite wall had been boarded over.

Six-year-old Maximillian Gruenberg was staring up at the rectangle of blue sky visible through the courtyard window. He brought his attention back to Elisabeth who stood at the high carpentry table in one corner of the room crushing white tablets between two spoons. He tugged at Elisabeth's skirt.

'Will it make her all better?'

'It will make her more comfortable. She won't cough so much.'

'I hate medicine.'

Elisabeth carefully distributed the white powder on to four small squares of paper. Three tablets, twelve doses of morphia – enough for three days. She folded each square of paper into a small packet.

'I'm hungry,' the boy said. He had red hair and his face was sallow under a sprinkling of freckles.

'My friend went to get us something to eat,' Elisabeth told him.

A passage connected the cellar of the bombed-out building with the adjacent apartment house. A family named Franz who lived there was part of the Emil network. For the few days that the Gruenbergs stayed on Dorotheenstrasse the Franzes were responsible for supplying food. It meant they themselves would not have enough to eat.

Carl Goerdeler had gone for the evening meal.

'Is he a Jew like us?' the boy asked.

'Max, leave the lady alone,' Frau Gruenberg said. She was a small, extremely thin woman, red-haired and freckled like her son. She might have been pretty once. Her skin was like parchment drawn tight over prominent cheekbones.

'I just wanted to know,' Maximillian said.

'Give her one every few hours,' Elisabeth told Frau Gruenberg. 'It will make her drowsy.'

Herr Gruenberg poured water carefully from a jerry-can into a chipped cup. He took one of the packets Elisabeth had prepared and stirred the white powder into the water. Elisabeth watched his graceful, long-fingered hands. Herr Gruenberg had been a 'cellist with the Kroll Opera House orchestra. He went to the cot where Hannah lay shivering under a coarse wool blanket despite the heat.

'A little medicine for you, liebchen,' he said, placing one hand behind the girl's back and raising her. Her face was flushed and her eyes, glassy with fever, widened at the sound of trucks rumbling along Dorotheenstrasse.

'They're coming to get us!' the little girl whimpered.

The sound of the trucks receded along the street.

'It has nothing to do with us, liebchen. See? They're gone.'

Hannah held the cup in both hands and began to cough rackingly. Herr Gruenberg took the cup from her and patted her back, pulling her close against him.

For one terrible moment Frau Gruenberg looked at her daughter with hate-filled eyes. The coughing could betray them all. Then the red-haired woman shook her head and her eyes misted over. She went to the cot and took her daughter's hand.

Hannah's coughing subsided and she drank from the cup.

Elisabeth felt a savage hatred for her own people, for all that eleven years of Nazism had done to them, the brutalisation and the indifference that were responsible for the so forgivable look she had seen in Frau Gruenberg's eyes.

She could even, she thought, forgive Richard Haller for

what he had come here to do. He was no more to blame than Frau Gruenberg was for her terrible moment of hatred. And he had, finally, been unable to do it.

Forgive him? What was she thinking of? He was blameless and brave, and no one, not Heydi, not herself, not even her uncle had the right to judge him. Elisabeth knew she had to tell him that, knew she must not give forgiveness but beg it for her lack of trust.

Something thudded against the door twice, three times. The wood splintered, shattered. Frau Gruenberg screamed.

Carl Goerdeler came along the passage with a basket of potatoes and beets and three small salted herrings wrapped in newspaper. A feast. The Gruenbergs would be amazed when he showed them the herrings.

He heard a man's voice, its tone savagely mocking.

'Move your kosher ass, Israel, hurry it up. You won't need all that Jewish shit where you're going.'

Goerdeler halted for an instant, then turned and hurried back along the passage.

He returned to the Franz apartment, but there was no need to tell them. They stood at the window watching the two Gestapo cars driving off.

'Stay with us,' Kurt Franz urged. 'Twenty tenants in the building. It will be safe, at least for today.'

Goerdeler shook his head. He had to let Ludwig Beck know his niece had been taken. In the confusion following the success of Operation Valkyrie anything might happen.

It did not occur to Goerdeler that the coup might fail. Failure was unthinkable.

Five minutes later he was walking along Dorotheenstrasse to the military checkpoint that had been set up at the corner of Neue Wilhelmstrasse. A big Mercedes truck was blocking the intersection and two soldiers in full battle-dress with potato-masher grenades hanging from their belts and sub-machine guns from their shoulders stopped him.

'Your papers.'

With total calm Carl Goerdeler produced his internal passport. The soldiers waved him through.

Unter den Linden was deserted except for a single motorcycle racing east towards the Brandenburg Gate. More trucks blocked the roadways through the great triumphal arch. The Pariserplatz checkpoint had been set up outside the Adlon

Hotel. He had to show his papers again there.
'All civilians off the streets of the government quarter,' he was told.
He thought it wise to show some curiosity. 'What's going on, anyway?'
'Routine military exercise,' the corporal told him. It was clear he didn't know any more than that.
Goerdeler went around to the back of Heydi's place and opened the gate in the garden wall. He used a rock to break a panel of glass in the french doors and let himself in.
He almost decided to wait out the day there. But with uncharacteristic pessimism he allowed himself to consider the possibility of failure for the first time. He tried to call Olbricht at the Bendlerstrasse. The circuits were busy.
He scrawled a note and left it on the dining-room table. Once more he tried the phone without success.
Ten minutes later he was waiting in the Brandenburg Gate station of the Nord-Sud Bahn. The underground platform was crowded with people leaving the restricted area.
He could not go back to his own apartment, he knew. He would find a quiet café and wait until the radio told him the *coup d'état* had succeeded.
He let the crowd shove him into the U-bahn car. Soon it was clattering through the tunnel south under Hermann Goeringstrasse.
Elisabeth, he thought. My God, they've got Elisabeth.

Twenty-Five

Within ten minutes after Stauffenberg's arrival at the Bendlerstrasse at 4.45, Valkyrie moved into high gear. The fifty teletypes and eight hundred phones of Armed Forces High Command Headquarters worked to capacity, contacting District headquarters and command posts throughout Germany and Occupied Europe.
Valkyrie General Order Number One, by 5.00, had reached the far corners of the Greater German Reich.
FROM OKW BERLIN TO COMMANDERS IN CHIEF ALL MILITARY DISTRICTS.
THE FÜHRER IS DEAD.

MARTIAL LAW IS DECLARED. EXECUTIVE POWER, EFFECTIVE AT ONCE, IS PLACED IN THE HANDS OF THE WEHRMACHT.

FOR THE ZONE OF THE INTERIOR, COMMANDER, HOME ARMY. FOR THE OCCUPIED AREAS OF THE WEST, COMMANDER IN CHIEF, ARMY GROUP D. FOR NORTHERN ITALY, COMMANDER IN CHIEF, ARMY GROUP C. FOR THE EASTERN FRONT, RESPECTIVE COMMANDERS ARMY GROUP SOUTH UKRAINE, ARMY GROUP NORTH UKRAINE, ARMY GROUP CENTRE, ARMY GROUP NORTH.

NON-COMBATANT NSDAP LEADERS AND SS OFFICERS ARE ATTEMPTING TO EXPLOIT THE SITUATION RESULTING FROM THE FÜHRER'S DEATH.

THE FOLLOWING ARE TO BE REMOVED IMMEDIATELY FROM THEIR POSTS AND HELD IN INDIVIDUAL ARREST: ALL NSDAP GAULEITERS, REICH GOVERNORS, SENIOR SS AND POLICE LEADERS, GESTAPO LEADERS AND CHIEFS OF SS AND PROPAGANDA OFFICES.

ALL CONCENTRATION CAMPS ARE TO BE OCCUPIED SPEEDILY, THE CAMP COMMANDERS ARRESTED, THE GUARDS CONFINED TO BARRACKS, THE PRISONERS TO BE INFORMED THAT THEY MUST ABSTAIN FROM ALL RALLIES AND INDIVIDUAL MEASURES UNTIL THEIR DISCHARGE. ALL AVAILABLE MEDICAL UNITS ARE ORDERED TO ASSIST IN THE OCCUPATION OF THE CONCENTRATION CAMPS.

THE EXECUTIVE AUTHORITIES-DESIGNATE ARE RESPONSIBLE FOR THE MAINTENANCE OF TRAFFIC AND SUPPLY ORGANISATIONS, FOR THE MAINTENANCE OF PUBLIC ORDER AND SAFETY, FOR THE SECURITY OF ALL SIGNALS INSTALLATIONS.

THE EXECUTIVE AUTHORITIES-DESIGNATE ARE RESPONSIBLE TO THE COMMANDER IN CHIEF ARMED FORCES HIGH COMMAND AND REGENT OF THE PROVISIONAL GOVERNMENT COLONEL GENERAL LUDWIG BECK.

—GRAF STAUFFENBERG, CHIEF OF STAFF, HOME ARMY, FOR THE COMMANDER IN CHIEF OKW.

Stauffenberg raced back to Olbricht's office from the communications centre.

'Where's Fromm?'

'In his office. Under guard. Never mind Fromm. Is Hitler dead? Because if he's not, we are.' Olbricht's face was bathed in sweat.

'I saw the explosion. Like a direct artillery hit. There were no survivors.'

'Are you sure?'

For a moment Stauffenberg lost his icy control. 'Never mind Hitler, God damn it. We delayed four hours, that's what could get us killed. What about the Guard Battalion?'

'They've set up their C.P. at the Armoury. Some units are already in position elsewhere.'

The phone rang. Stauffenberg answered. Helldorf was on the line.

'I've withdrawn my men from traffic control. I can give you four thousand people.'

'Not yet,' Stauffenberg said. A smile touched his drawn face. 'Have you sealed off those whorehouses?'

'Yes.'

'I'll get back to you.'

Just as Stauffenberg hung up, Beck came into the office. 'I've heard from Paris.'

'Affirmative?'

'They're moving faster than we are.' Beck looked weary. 'They're worried about Army Group D. Von Klüge hasn't made up his mind.'

Stauffenberg pointed to the phone. 'You're old friends, aren't you? Call him.'

Beck placed a blitz call to La Roche-Guyon, Headquarters, Army Group D. Klüge was noncommittal. He would not go over to the conspirators until he heard from Rastenburg that Hitler was dead. He promised to call back in half an hour.

'He won't call back,' Olbricht said. 'Not Klüge.'

'If we succeed in Berlin,' Stauffenberg told him, 'it doesn't matter what Klüge does.'

Olbricht picked up the phone. 'Try Rastenburg again, Delia.'

Stauffenberg went to the window. A dozen Austro-Daimler personnel trucks were pulling up along the quay. Soldiers in combat dress leaped out, took up positions around the entrance and along the canal. Stauffenberg watched them piling sandbags for machine-gun emplacements.

Heydi hurried in. 'Two Company, Guard Battalion,' he said.

Again a smile touched Stauffenberg's drawn face. 'Right on schedule. That's one thing we have going for us. With a dedicated Nazi like Jaeger, orders are orders.'

Two miles to the north-east, Jaeger stood outside the Armoury at Unter den Linden 1. He looked west along the boulevard past the gutted shell of the State Opera House. He held a teletype of Valkyrie General Order Number One in his hand and watched the trucks bringing Four Company from Moabit. Four Company would soon be deployed here at the Armoury and on the streets leading to the Alexanderplatz station.

Bleiner came out of the building. 'Three Company in position, sir.'

Jaeger nodded absently. He had a troubled look on his face. 'Read this.' He handed the teletype to Bleiner.

'I read it when it came in.'

'I've been wondering,' Jaeger said.

'Sir?'

'These orders call for us, among other things, to cordon off the Prinz Albrechtstrasse.'

'B Platoon of Three Company are already in the area, Herr Major. On Anhalterstrasse.'

'That isn't what I meant. Why would we have to do it? You don't seriously believe the S.S. would move against the Wehrmacht, do you?'

'General Order Number One says . . .'

'I know what it says. It also says – here, this part: "The following are to be removed from their posts and held in individual arrest: all N.S.D.A.P. Gauleiters, Reich Governors, etc., etc. . . . and chiefs of propaganda offices."'

He waited for Bleiner to pick up his cue. The phlegmatic Austrian said nothing.

'If we follow these orders,' Jaeger said with a puzzled frown, 'we'd have to place Dr Goebbels under arrest.'

'Goebbels?'

'As Gauleiter of Berlin *and* Propaganda Minister.' Jaeger laughed harshly. 'How would you like an assignment like that, Bleiner?'

'Himmel Herrgott,' said the Austrian.

'So I've been wondering,' Jaeger went on, and then he shook his head. 'No, it's too damn far-fetched.'

Bleiner waited.

'Look,' Jaeger said with apparent reluctance, 'somebody brings a washed-up general like Beck into Berlin and puts him in supreme command. Somebody tells us to seal off the Prinz Albrechtstrasse. Somebody tells us to arrest Dr Goebbels of all people.'

'We have no specific orders to do that, Herr Major.'

'It's specific enough. Somebody, Bleiner. The question is, who?'

Now Bleiner looked puzzled. 'I'm sorry, sir, I don't follow.'

'Every word of this General Order Number One,' Jaeger said slowly, 'could be construed as an attempt to counter an anticipated S.S. putsch.'

'Well, of course, sir. That much is clear anyway.'

'Is it? Every word could also be construed as a cover for a putsch by the Bendlerstrasse.'

Bleiner gaped.

'By the Bendlerstrasse against the Führer,' Jaeger said. 'The more I think of it – look, how do we even know the Führer's dead? The only way we know is . . . ' Jaeger paused and this time Bleiner picked up the cue.

'Is this piece of paper from the Bendlerstrasse.'

'Exactly. Tell me, when you worked at the Promi did you ever meet Dr Goebbels?'

'On several occasions. The Minister took a great interest in the Wehrmacht guidance programme.'

'Could you get in to see him now?'

Haller, the battalion Exec., came down the steps behind them. 'Four Company in position across the river,' he said. 'They just reported in. They've got a problem – several thousand police converging on the Alexanderplatz.'

'Keep the line open,' Jaeger said. 'See what develops.'

Haller looked surprised. He had taken over communications only temporarily from Bleiner.

Bleiner said: 'You mean you want me to speak to Dr Goebbels, Herr Major?'

'You're going to have some crossed wires,' Haller said, 'if I hold down that switchboard much longer.'

'It won't be much longer,' Jaeger assured him.

Bleiner said: 'Or do you want an appointment with him yourself, sir?'

'With Minister Goebbels?' Haller asked. 'What's going on?'

'Get back on to Four Company,' Jaeger said. 'At once, Herr Hauptmann.'

Haller stood looking from Jaeger to Bleiner and back.

'That's an order.'

Haller saluted and returned inside the building.

'I want to see Dr Goebbels as soon as possible,' Jaeger told Bleiner.

The Austrian hurried towards the line of motor cycles parked just west of the Armoury.

At 6.00 Kaltenbrunner called the R.S.H.A. bureau chiefs into his office. A few minutes earlier his S.S. military liaison officer had finally managed to get his hands on a copy of Valkyrie General Order Number One.

Kaltenbrunner read it aloud, his face impassive. He was standing; so were the others. The R.S.H.A. director towered over Gestapo Mueller, Kripo Chief Artur Nebe, and the S.D.s Schellenberg and Ohlendorf.

'Well, gentlemen?'

Schellenberg was furious, his beefy face mottled. 'If we'd moved against those Prussian shits when I wanted to, this wouldn't have happened.'

Everybody began to talk at once.

Kaltenbrunner shouted: 'Shut up, all of you! Does anyone know when Himmler's due back?'

Artur Nebe laughed. 'Der treue Heinrich,' he said, 'is conveniently in Leipzig for the afternoon.'

'I know where he is. I asked . . . '

'The operative word,' said Nebe, is "conveniently".'

'He knew?'

'We all knew. What we didn't know was when. Himmler left as soon as it was clear Rastenburg was cut off.'

'That's a filthy slander,' Schellenberg said. The chief of S.S. Security Exterior also served as Himmler's personal deputy and was the only man in the room who considered the Reichsführer-S.S. his friend. He stared levelly at Kaltenbrunner. 'Will you give me the go-ahead to order the Waffen-S.S. into the city?'

Kaltenbrunner thought that over.

Gestapo Mueller said: 'It would be a mistake.'

'What the hell do you mean, a mistake?' Schellenberg demanded. 'Will you get it through your thick Bavarian skull that we're facing a military putsch?'

Mueller ignored the insult. 'Has it occurred to you the Führer really could be dead? Or that no matter what we do the Bendlerstrasse could overthrow the government?'

Kaltenbrunner asked him: 'What do you suggest?'

'That we wait. Himmler knew what he was doing when he

went to Leipzig. Give me that,' he told Kaltenbrunner, and the R.S.H.A. director handed him the teletype sheet. Mueller read aloud the section dealing with the concentration camps. 'Just one of the things we'll all be held to account for if the putsch succeeds,' he said calmly.

Authority in the room had passed from Kaltenbrunner to Mueller along with the teletype sheet. Kaltenbrunner looked relieved.

'We will all have documents to . . . dispose of,' Gestapo Mueller said. 'We should spend our time preparing for that eventuality.'

'The Reichsführer-S.S. would never . . . ' Schellenberg began.

'Just how short is your memory?' Mueller cut him off. 'Who did he send to Stockholm last spring?'

The mission had been Schellenberg's, its purpose to feel out the Swedish Count Folke Bernadotte on the possibility of surrendering to the Western Allies. Schellenberg had got nowhere.

'Himmler was thinking of survival even then, personal survival,' Mueller went on. 'It's what we all should be thinking of now.'

Schellenberg could not dispute that, nor could Ohlendorf. Kaltenbrunner lacked the strength of will to dispute anything. It was irrelevant to Artur Nebe.

'We'll meet again in, shall we say, an hour?' Mueller suggested. 'Perhaps the situation will be clearer by then. Meanwhile, we all have things to do.'

Five minutes later Mueller returned to his own office. His secretary, Barbara Hellmuth, was covering her typewriter.

'If you don't need me for anything, Herr Gruppenführer?'

He shook his head. 'You've had a long day. Better stay off the streets, Barbara. Take the U-bahn.'

'What's happening out there, anyway?' she asked.

'A minor disturbance, nothing more. But there's no harm in being careful.'

After she was gone Mueller opened his safe. He took out the Walther PPK and buckled it on over his tunic. He removed an armload of file folders and brought them to the desk. Then he returned to the safe. It was empty except for an envelope containing fifty thousand Reichsmarks.

And the Ritter list.

He slammed the steel door shut and twirled the dials.

An hour and a half later at Unter den Linden 1, Haller was

alone in the communications room. The small room contained a telephone switchboard and a short-wave radio, its frequency set to that of the battalion's four Krupp communications trucks.

Jaeger had left the Armoury a moment ago and Haller had immediately sent the Signals sergeant for coffee. He figured he had no more than three minutes.

Quickly he put on the switchboard earphones, inserted a plug, and dialled Stauffenberg's office at the Bendlerstrasse.

The radio beeped and he heard: 'Fox Four to C.P., do you read me? Fox Four to C.P.'

Haller flipped the radio toggle to sending. 'C.P. to Fox Four. We have a blitz here. Back to you in a minute. C.P. out.'

The phone again, a buzzing sound. Then Heydi's voice.

'Oberleutnant Heydebrand speaking.'

'This is Haller. Jaeger's suspicious. He's on his way to Goebbels. NSU motor cycle, no sidecar. Figure he'll go west on Unter den Linden and south on Mauerstrasse. Can you intercept? He'll have to go through his own checkpoints. You may have enough time.'

Heydi began to speak. Haller heard footsteps outside. He broke the connection.

The signals sergeant came in with a steaming mug of coffee. 'Hot for once,' he said.

Bleiner came in, sub-machine gun slung over his shoulder. He looked at the mug of coffee. 'Take ten, sergeant. And bring me some coffee when you come back.'

The sergeant left. Haller was just able to smile as he removed the headset and got up. 'All yours, lieutenant. I wasn't cut out for this. Better get back to Fox Four. They just radioed.'

Bleiner took two steps towards the radio table, unslinging the sub-machine gun. Turning with the tubular metal stock under his arm, he pointed the gun at Haller.

Jaeger turned the NSU south on Friedrichstrasse. He had decided to cut west on Leipziger and then north on Hermann Goering. Goebbels wasn't at the Promi but at his home at 20 Hermann Goeringstrasse.

It was the long way round but Jaeger knew he would save time by avoiding most of the checkpoints he had set up.

He wondered if Bleiner was man enough for the job he had given him. The Guidance Officer had been shocked by the extent of the conspiracy Jaeger had outlined to him. The Bendlerstrasse had even planted an informer in the Guard Battalion itself. That the man was Hauptmann Haller had dismayed Bleiner; he liked the new Exec. But he knew that Major Jaeger was not one to make mistakes.

Haller threw the mug and went in low after it. The mug struck Bleiner's cheek, hot coffee splashing. Bleiner shouted. Outside, a truck engine started with a roar. Haller grabbed the sub-machine gun barrel with his left hand, slammed two body punches low with his right, doubling Bleiner over. Haller clubbed the back of his neck and as Bleiner went down he got the sub-machine gun.

Bleiner was writhing on the floor, clutching his belly. The switchboard buzzed. Haller went to the door, locked it.

'Fox Four to C.P., Fox Four to C.P.,' the radio squawked.

Haller knelt near Bleiner and slapped his face twice. Bleiner moaned, tried to sit up. Haller thrust him back, the sub-machine gun's tubular metal stock across his throat. Bleiner's eyes were unfocused. His face had already begun to blister.

'Jaeger's idea?' Haller said. He increased the pressure on the Austrian's throat. Bleiner nodded.

'Why?'

More pressure. Bleiner's eyes widened and focused on Haller's face.

'Arrest you,' he gasped.

'I said why.'

'Bendlerstrasse. Plant.'

'And the sergeant?' Haller said. 'Why'd you send him out?'

Bleiner remained mute. Haller leaned on the stock of the gun. Again Bleiner's eyes widened frantically.

Haller eased the pressure.

'Shoot you. Resisting arrest.'

'Why not just arrest me?'

'I don't know!'

More pressure.

'Fox Four to C.P. Come in, C.P. Urgent.'

'I swear to God I don't know!'

Haller waited three seconds. Why? Why not just arrest him? Why have him killed?

No time. And Bleiner probably didn't know anyway.

He crashed the sub-machine gun barrel against the side of Bleiner's head, got up, went to the door, unlocked it. Locked it from the outside. Went fast but not too fast along the corridor, slinging the sub-machine gun. Met the sergeant coming in with two mugs of coffee.

Seconds now. Downstairs past the pedestals and smashed statues outside the Armoury. Along the street to the rank of motorcycles. Salute given by and returned to the Transport corporal.

'What do you have that's fast?'

'Take the BMW, Herr Hauptman.'

He climbed astride, kicked the starter. The engine caught, stuttered and died. He kicked the starter again. The engine raced. He throttled down and lurched away from the kerb.

Where? Guard Battalion Two Company was at the Bendlerstrasse. He couldn't go there.

The Alexanderplatz. Helldorf.

He took back streets north-east as far as Klosterstrasse, then turned south. He had the same advantage Jaeger had. He knew the location of the battalion checkpoints.

Twenty-Six

He wore white, as he often did at home. It set off his black hair and swarthy skin, his dark piercing eyes. A white linen suit, rumpled now as he sat in the small downstairs office chain-smoking.

Speer was with him, the Armaments Minister droning on about production figures. More planes, more tanks, more guns this July 1944 than in any previous month, despite the terror raids. Speer's voice was background sound, like static, like a distant wind. Through the open window he heard jackboots thudding, an occasional shouted order. It reminded him of the old days when Radio Section covered every parade, the man with the microphone holding it inches from the pavement as the military units goose-stepped by, the sound of boots crashing like thunder in every home, on every street-corner loudspeaker in the Reich.

He had eaten an early dinner of herring and boiled potatoes with Speer. He liked Speer; Speer had a quick intelligence and Speer was not tall, not broad-shouldered, not blond.

He lit another cigarette. Speer said Messerschmitts, Speer said Panzers, Speer said ball bearings. The herring and potatoes were like ball bearings in his stomach.

He had sent Magda and the children upstairs. They had been prisoners here in the house on Hermann Goeringstrasse, all of them, for more than an hour now. A single battalion, eight hundred men with the future of the Reich in their hands.

Where was Jaeger? How would the man respond?

He looked at the green telephone on the desk, green like the Ministerial pencil. A green jotting in the margin of a report was almost the same as a Führer directive. Germans understood the symbolism of power.

The green telephone was a direct line to the Führer. He hadn't used it. He was afraid to.

The mythic Führer, from whom all flowed, to whom all looked. Not a leader – The Leader. Lonely and omnipotent. Irreplaceable.

His creation in a way. And he believed in it.

He lit another cigarette. He had used the other phone, tried to call Himmler. Himmler was out of town. Called Helldorf. Equivocation. With the Guard Battalion in the streets, Helldorf had withdrawn his police from traffic control. Helldorf was waiting. I can't fight the Bendlerstrasse with traffic cops, Helldorf had said. Reasonable enough, and yet . . .

Had Helldorf gone over to the enemy? Had he always been with them?

The green telephone terrified him. If he got through and learned that Hitler was dead?

He was bound to the myth. The myth was placenta and umbilicus; the myth kept him alive.

The German people had failed the myth, needed punishment. Only he and the myth he had created understood that. The blond and blue-eyed Aryan, hateful now, like the Jew, as if the Aryan and the Jew had merged, become one. To be destroyed.

He lit another cigarette, heard a knock at the door. Prince Friedrich of Schaumburg-Lippe, his adjutant, in red-white-black Promi uniform. That had always awed Magda and the children. Fetch and carry, Prince. Thank you, Prince, you may go.

Long nose, drawling voice. 'There is a Major Jaeger to see you, Herr Reichsminister.'

'Yes, very well.'

Schaumburg-Lippe sniffed. 'Hardly suitably attired,' he said.

The other one, Bleiner, had hardly been suitably attired either.

He had a feeling then, an intuition, that everything would be all right. The certainty that he would die when Hitler died receded to the back of his mind.

'Show the gentleman in,' Joseph Goebbels said in his deep, sonorous voice.

Haller rounded the corner on to Königstrasse and braked the BMW momentarily. Ahead, Alexanderplatz swarmed with uniforms, the green of Helldorf's police and the field-grey of Four Company, *Grossdeutschland* Guard Battalion.

He hesitated, then gunned the motorcycle, swung left again and skidded to a halt beside the U-bahn station. He would duck down the stairs, cross under the square through the subway tunnel, and come up directly in front of police headquarters. With luck he could get inside and to Helldorf without anyone in Four Company seeing him. He had to assume Bleiner by now had radioed the scattered units of the battalion to be on the lookout for him. Probably to shoot him on sight.

He should have killed Bleiner.

He shook his head and pushed through the station doors. It was too late for that now. Anyway, killing Bleiner would have done no good. He had already broken every rule in the book.

First rule: Never become vulnerable. Get in, do the job, and get out fast.

But he could not get out. That much was not his fault. It was just bad luck.

Or was it? If he had done the job Baker Street had sent him to do, and done it fast, he could have got out. Instead he had delayed, debated, indulged his conscience. Until the Swede was dead in an air raid. He had made his own bad luck.

Second rule: Never let the enemy know you have become vulnerable.

He should have killed Monika Jaeger.

She could identify him as an Allied agent. Killing her would have been the routine professional thing to do, the one essential requirement for his own survival. A brand new graduate of Beaulieu would have done it without batting an eye. But he was sick of killing, sick of being a professional.

At the time it had only seemed another harmless personal indulgence. After he left Monika Jaeger on Sunday, he thought he would disappear, an ordinary-looking German officer in a city of four million. Heydi would get him new papers. Heydi's office, after all, dealt in replacement troops. It would not be long until Valkyrie day, not much longer until the end of the war. Heydi would find a place for him.

How could he have known Helldorf would suggest assigning him to Major Jaeger?

Never become vulnerable.

Why had he taken the assignment, said nothing to Heydi? There was every chance Jaeger knew his real identity. Monika would have told her husband, if not from patriotism then from pure malice. Taking the assignment was suicidal.

Never become vulnerable.

He had deliberately placed himself in jeopardy. And in the process had jeopardised Operation Valkyrie as well.

Haller stopped suddenly in the deserted U-bahn tunnel.

Was it possible after all that some part of him, deep inside, was still working for Baker Street?

He leaned his head against the cool tile of the tunnel wall. He would not let himself think about it.

After a long moment he straightened and walked up the stairs to police headquarters.

The best way to play it, Jaeger knew as he entered, was awed, earnest, confused, and loyal. The ultimate question being, of course, where his loyalty lay. Let Goebbels convince him.

He drew his heels together. 'Heil Hitler!'

Goebbels was not alone. But the other man, Armaments Minister Speer, at once withdrew to a corner of the room, seating himself in a white leather chair, crossing his legs, removing himself from the interview as effectively as if he'd left the room.

'Those are your men out there?' said Joseph Goebbels.

'Yes, Herr Reichsminister.'

'Their orders?'

Jaeger shuffled his feet, looked down at the swastika-decorated carpet. 'You might say, Herr Reichsminister, you might say . . .'

'Say it,' said Joseph Goebbels.

'House arrest, Herr Reichsminister.'

'On what authority?'

'Orders from the Bendlerstrasse.'

'Why?'

'Begging the Herr Reichsminister's pardon, it is not for me to ask why.'

'But you had the sense to see me first?'

Jaeger looked up. 'I've risked a court martial coming here,' he said.

'You were told the Führer is dead?'

Jaeger nodded sullenly.

'And that an unscrupulous group of noncombatant Party officials, not to mention the S.S., were trying to exploit the situation?'

'Executive power has passed into the hands of the Wehrmacht,' Jaeger said. 'But I couldn't help wondering . . . '

'Never mind that. You remember your Soldier's Oath, don't you, Herr Major? Or have you conveniently forgotten it tonight?'

'Jawohl,' said Jaeger. He sounded confused.

'Jawohl what?'

'That oath is my life. But they said the Führer is dead. Still, I can't help wondering . . . ' Jaeger began again, and let his voice trail off.

'If perhaps it is a filthy trick? The filthiest trick in history, Herr Major? You would agree with me that the Führer could countermand your orders?'

'They told me he was dead,' Jaeger said stubbornly.

Joseph Goebbels reached for the green phone.

His demeanour then amazed Albert Speer. His self-assurance was magnificent. He needed a foil; he had always needed one.

It took less than sixty seconds for him to get through. He spoke briefly in that rich, deep voice. Jaeger heard the voice, not the words. The voice was mesmerising.

Joseph Goebbels handed the green telephone receiver to Jaeger.

'The Führer,' he said.

At 8.40 Stauffenberg was in the Bendlerstrasse Communications Centre. The first Panzer unit to reach Berlin from Krampnitz had made radio contact.

'Where are you?' Stauffenberg asked.

'Tiergarten. Near the Victory Column. Herr Oberst, I have . . . '

'How many?'

'Twelve Panthers, but . . . '

'Deploy three at the Brandenburg Gate. Seal off the Prinz Albrechtstrasse with the rest.'

'Herr Oberst, I must tell you I have just received a signal from Krampnitz.' The Panzer leader sounded not contrite but resigned. 'Voice relay of a teletype from Führer Headquarters, Rastenburg. I've been ordered back to Krampnitz.'

'From Rastenburg? The circuits are open?'

'Marshal Keitel himself.'

Stauffenberg realised he wasn't breathing.

'I'm sorry, Herr Oberst.'

'You are under the command of General Beck, Commander-in-Chief of the Wehrmacht and Regent of the Provisional Government,' Stauffenberg said. He knew it was no use.

'That's all finished now.' Again the Panzer leader said, 'I'm sorry, Herr Oberst.'

Stauffenberg swayed back from the table. Most of the teletype machines in the Communications Centre were silent now, their operators huddled in small groups, talking.

A radio in one corner of the room was playing martial music softly. The music cut out and when someone turned the volume up Stauffenberg heard the announcer's voice:

'Citizens of the Greater German Reich! Radio Germany brings you an urgent message . . . '

Then the second best known voice in Germany, the sonorous tones at once recognisable.

'It is my duty to inform you that earlier today an attempt was made on the life of the Führer by a small clique of unscrupulous army officers who hoped to betray the cause for which we have struggled so hard and long. The Führer is alive. You are to remain calm and confident. Later tonight the Führer will personally address the nation.'

Stauffenberg leaned his one hand on the table. He was shaking.

'Herr Oberst, Vienna calling.'

'Herr Oberst, Paris on the line.'

'Herr Oberst, Army Group North.'

'Herr Oberst . . . '

Stauffenberg slowly walked from the room.

Jaeger sat astride his idling motorcycle on the roadway of the Friedrichstrasse bridge across the River Spree. Tiger I heavy tanks from the second unit to reach Berlin blocked the northern end of the roadway, their powerful Maybach V-12 engines thundering, their 88mm guns low, levelled straight across the bridge. A Panzer grenadier in black uniform was trotting towards Jaeger, unfastened helmet straps slapping against his cheeks.

'Who is in command here?' Jaeger demanded.
'Oberstleutnant Glaesemer, Herr Major.'

Jaeger rode the NSU to the northern end of the bridge. Panzer grenadiers had left their machines, were milling about. A lieutenant colonel alighted nimbly from the turret of the first Tiger.

'Oberstleutnant Glaesemer, Third Panzer Battalion, Krampnitz,' he said, returning Jaeger's salute.

'I have direct orders from the Führer,' Jaeger said, 'to turn all Panzer units back to their bases.'

Jaeger waited. He knew he was finished if Glaesemer refused the order.

The lieutenant colonel smiled. 'That's lucky for you,' he told Jaeger. 'If you'd said anything else I'd have shot you.'

Jaeger watched as the tanks wheeled ponderously and headed north.

Then he rode the motorcycle south towards 20 Hermann Goeringstrasse, the new battalion C.P.

Sweat drenched Helldorf's green twill shirt. His brooding eyes stared at Haller as he put down the phone. It was past 10.30, the long summer twilight fading outside the Alexanderplatz.

'Stauffenberg wants my men,' he said bleakly. 'It's too late for that now. The Waffen-S.S. are marching on the city. I've withdrawn the roadblocks. I won't have my people slaughtered.'

Haller said nothing. More than Helldorf's police would be slaughtered.

'What else could I do?' the police chief said. 'Once Goebbels decided to move, it was as good as over.'

Not Goebbels, Haller thought. Jaeger.

Why had Jaeger wanted him shot? Taken into custody, yes. But why killed? Because Monika Jaeger had told him who Haller really was? Even that didn't explain it. If Jaeger could deliver an Allied agent to the Prinz Albrechtstrasse alive, wouldn't he have done it?

Jaeger, in the right place at the right time, just as Haller himself was.

Jaeger, the professional officer, the Nazi who could be expected to follow orders. Of course Goebbels would send for him, he was the one man in a position to . . .

It was the other way around. Goebbels hadn't sent for him. Jaeger had sent Bleiner to arrange the meeting.

If Haller had been carrying out Baker Street's orders, and

if he had been in Jaeger's position, wouldn't he have made the same audacious move?

Each of them in the right place at the right time, which was no coincidence if Jaeger . . .

If Moscow. If Moscow knew what Baker Street knew.

Bleiner, admiration in his voice: *Ask him to tell you how he escaped from a Russian P.O.W. camp.*

It all made sense, a crazy kind of sense.

Jaeger, his opposite number. One from the West, one from the East. Both sent in for the same reason. Their meeting no coincidence. Their meeting inevitable.

But still, why wouldn't Jaeger hand him over to the Prinz Albrechtstrasse? The final coup, the ultimate triumph, to deliver up the Doppelgänger.

Why?

Because Jaeger feared Haller would eventually reach the conclusion he had reached now? Because silencing Haller was protecting himself? Was that it?

It hardly mattered. Jaeger had won, he had lost. And Jaeger, doing Moscow's work, had also done Baker Street's. The final irony.

Twenty-Seven

The quiet that had settled with darkness on the quay along the Landwehr Canal was broken suddenly by the sound of approaching trucks.

Heydi put down the phone. He had tried to call his own apartment for the third time. Still no answer. Where was Elisabeth?

He went to the window of Stauffenberg's office and stood beside the secretary, Delia Ziegler. Through the fibreboard partition he could hear General Beck's voice, the tone more whining than bitter. Beck sounded like a querulous old man.

'Not even the radio station,' he was saying. 'We never got that far. Not even our own headquarters. You don't think those men are out there to protect us, do you? Do you?' Querulous and accusatory now, the accusation levelled at Stauffenberg. 'You said he was dead. You said the bomb killed him. Not that either, Klaus. Nothing.'

Olbricht chimed in. 'Why didn't you stay long enough to see that he was dead? What made you come rushing back here?'
'All right,' Stauffenberg said. 'All right.'
At the window Frau Ziegler turned to Heydi. The truck engines were idling noisily in the heat of the night. Here and there along the quay a light winked briefly, went out.
'Why doesn't he tell them?' she said. 'They were nothing without him, nothing. He had to hurry back. They were too afraid to do anything until he got here. It was their fault it failed. And now they're crucifying him.'
Abruptly the quay blazed with light – A.A. searchlights mounted on flatbed trucks. Machine gun emplacements and patrolling sentries seemed to leap out of the darkness.
'Still no answer?' Frau Ziegler asked.
'She's not there.'
'She'll be all right. You'll see.' She touched his arm in a gesture of reassurance.
Through the partition Heydi heard Stauffenberg speaking. 'And if we have failed?' he said, the arrogance gone from his voice, the impatience of the perfectionist replaced by a serenity, as if he had been touched by a state of grace the others could not comprehend. 'Still the attempt had to be made. Even if Hitler survived the bomb.'
'If?' Olbricht shouted. 'He's alive, you fool!'
'That changes nothing,' Stauffenberg said. 'The seizure of power still had to be attempted here in Berlin.'
'With Hitler alive we never had a chance.'
'You miss the point,' Stauffenberg said. 'No matter what the outcome, it had to be tried. To show the world that Germans – Germans, can't you understand? – dared to take this step.'
Heydi saw a dozen men in combat dress, steel-helmeted, carrying sub-machine guns, running up the broad stone staircase to disappear under the portico.
'They're on their way in.' Olbricht's voice, softly now from the other side of the partition, his anger spent.
And General Beck finally, like all of them in hope or despair, bowing to the strength of Stauffenberg's will: 'I regret nothing. Nothing, gentlemen.'

Lieutenant Schlee, Commanding Officer, Two Company, *Grossdeutschland* Guard Battalion, was the first to enter the room. Crowding in behind him came Sergeant Pflaum followed by four enlisted men with sub-machine guns. Schlee looked out of his depth, the pink-cheeked beardless Hitler Youth graduate masquerading as a combat officer.

Schlee *was* out of his depth, Pflaum knew. Pflaum was enjoying himself. It wasn't every day you got to shove it into the brass and break it off. He watched Schlee come to quivering attention and salute the round-faced, bespectacled general. Schlee was not going to do this right, that was obvious.

'Generaloberst Beck?' he said. 'It is my duty to inform you . . . '

'I am General Beck,' said the old man in the dark civilian suit.

Schlee was sweating. 'It is my duty . . . I must tell you . . . '

Pflaum stepped forward. Schlee would take all night. 'We have orders to place under arrest the following men.' Pflaum did not say officers. 'Beck, Olbricht, Stauffenberg, Heydebrand.'

Just then another enlisted man came into the room. With him was General Fromm.

'We found this one locked in his office, Herr Oberleutnant.'

Schlee gave a vague, confused look to Fromm.

Fromm strode into the room, stood before Stauffenberg. 'Contemptible crippled swine,' he said, and rocked the colonel with a hard open-palmed blow to the face.

On the other side of the partition Heydi heard the words, the sound of the blow. He tensed, reached for his holstered Walther.

Frau Ziegler grasped his arm. Her lips formed the word no.

Heydi stood frozen. He heard the sound of a scuffle, and then a single shot. Frau Ziegler's eyes pleaded with him. No, stay here, you can do nothing.

It was Olbricht who had yanked the Walther from his holster, Pflaum who had immediately lunged at him, grappled with him, the pistol firing once before Pflaum gained possession of it.

Stauffenberg slumped against the wall, blood seeping through the left sleeve of his tunic.

Fromm began to talk, and even Pflaum listened. They had no orders to arrest Generaloberst Friedrich Fromm, C.O., Home Army. Far from it. Their orders were to find Fromm if Fromm was still alive. Fromm could restore order in the

Bendlerstrasse. Fromm might make a full-scale assault on the building unnecessary.

'You are to be congratulated, Herr Oberleutnant,' Fromm told Schlee. 'You have three of the ringleaders here. On what authority are you acting, by the way?'

'Major Jaeger, Commanding Officer, *Grossdeutschland* Guard Battalion, Herr General.'

'Get him.'

'He's not here. He's at the Battalion C.P., Herr General. 20 Hermann Goeringstrasse.'

Fromm thought swiftly. Goebbels. He didn't like that. Goebbels would sanction no drumhead court martial. He would want to learn the full extent of the conspiracy. Fromm had very little time and he knew it. His own life was hanging by a thread. The fact that he had vacillated too long was bound to come out if Beck, Olbricht, and Stauffenberg were allowed to survive the night.

'You have three of them,' he told Schlee. 'A fourth is missing.' He looked at Stauffenberg. 'Where is your adjutant?'

Stauffenberg's right arm moved, the pinned sleeve touching his left shoulder, as if with the missing hand he hoped to stanch the flow of blood.

'Lieutenant von Heydebrand,' he said contemptuously, 'learned that he lacked the stomach for this.'

'Where is he?'

'If I knew that, he would be dead by now. He left the building hours ago.'

Fromm said after a moment: 'Who's in there?'

He walked across the room towards the partition. It began to slide as he reached it.

Heydi watched Frau Ziegler walk out, casually leaving the partition open six inches. If Fromm entered the room, he would shoot him.

He heard Frau Ziegler cry out. 'He's hurt, the colonel's hurt! What's the matter, all of you? Get bandages, hurry, there's a first-aid kit in the ante-room.'

Fromm ignored her. 'We will need field-grade officers and at least one general for a court martial,' he told Schlee. He rattled off names. 'My office in five minutes, no later.'

Heydi heard footsteps, heard metal scrape against a wall, heard the door slam.

He waited a minute, another. Not a sound from beyond the

partition, and then he heard Frau Ziegler crying softly. He slid the partition. She was alone in the office.

'Go, please go. There's nothing you can do here, Heydi.' She had never used his familiar name before.

She opened the door to the ante-room. 'Now. Hurry.'

The corridor was empty. He got as far as the Stairway C landing. No one. He went down, reached the deserted lobby. The wide entrance was brilliantly lit from outside by an A.A. searchlight. Two sentries stood there, facing inwards.

Heydi screwed his monocle into place. 'Where is Major Jaeger?' he demanded. Full Prussian voice.

'Sir?'

'Where is your commanding officer? Don't you understand German?'

'He's not here, Herr Oberleutnant.'

Full Prussian voice, now laden with sarcasm. 'Now that we know where he isn't, could you perhaps bring yourself to tell me where I can find him?'

He had learned how to do that from a master, from Haller.

Where was Haller now?

Where was Elisabeth?

'At the Battalion C.P., sir. It has been moved to . . .'

'Yes, yes, I know all that.'

'If the Herr Oberleutnant requires communications facilities or transportation . . .'

'I can arrange my own transportation.' Heydi looked at them scathingly through his monocle and waited for them to salute.

He returned their salutes and went down the stairs. He could see nothing but the light. The light was blinding. He kept walking.

Artur Nebe came into Helldorf's office shortly after 12.30. For once he was wearing S.S. black.

'Don't look at me like that,' he told the police chief. 'It's easier getting around in this uniform right now.'

Nebe placed an attaché case on the desk. He glanced at Haller.

'Don't worry, he's with us,' Helldorf said.

Nebe rubbed his long nose. 'You mean someone still is?'

Helldorf waved a hand. 'No. No, it's over. I tried the Bendlerstrasse ten minutes ago. *Grossdeutschland*'s manning the phones.'

Nebe opened the attaché case. In it were banded stacks of

Reichsmarks. 'Thirty thousand,' he told Helldorf. 'Could it help you get away?'

Nebe did not mention getting away himself.

Helldorf said: 'Where would you suggest?'

'Of course. Where. But they're yours if you want them.'

Helldorf shrugged. 'You know,' he said, 'if it had gone the other way they'd be doing this right now at the Prinz Albrechtstrasse.'

'They were pissing in their pants for a while,' Nebe said with a tired smile. 'Now Himmler's on his way back and they're drinking champagne. Kaltenbrunner, Schellenberg, Ohlendorf.'

'Not Mueller?'

'He's the one who kept the fear of God in them this long. I was there.'

'What happened?'

Nebe told him about the meeting earlier that evening.

'Anyway,' Nebe said caustically, 'the hero of the day came in just before I left. You can bet your acorns he got the royal treatment from the R.S.H.A. He's with Mueller, or was a few minutes ago.'

'Goebbels?' said Helldorf.

'No, the son of a bitch who gave the city to him. Major Jaeger.'

Haller said: 'What?'

'The C.O. of the Guard Battalion. As I said, they were giving him the royal treatment. Can you blame them?'

Haller let out his breath.

The Ritter list.

Jaeger all along had the access to it that Haller could never hope to have. His wife worked for Gestapo Mueller.

'Could you take me there?'

'If you mean the Prinz Albrechtstrasse, I could,' Nebe said testily. 'Why should I? Precisely who are you, anyway?'

Haller looked at Helldorf. Helldorf nodded.

Haller answered Nebe's question.

When the pistol shot cracked flatly, muffled by the closed door, Lieutenant Schlee winced as if the bullet had struck him. Schlee's face looked green. A regular basket case already, Sergeant Pflaum thought. He hadn't expected anything else.

General Fromm, who had given the old general in the dark civilian suit the chance to die with dignity, alone in Fromm's office with Fromm's own service pistol, now opened the door and looked in.

'Better help the old gentleman,' he said, turning. While Schlee was still fumbling awkwardly with the holster at his side, Pflaum himself entered the room.

Ludwig Beck sat slumped in a large brown leather chair near the window, his head to one side, blood dripping from the shallow furrow the bullet had made along his temple. At the last instant he had been unable to do it, had moved his hand. The Walther was on the floor, black like the polished military shoes he wore. His eyes were open. He watched Pflaum approach, Pflaum drawing his sidearm, a Luger.

The old man said something. Pflaum thought he heard, '. . . remember in the First War when . . .' and then Pflaum pulled the trigger. Old like that and reminiscing, and a single shot at the base of the skull from a distance of less than a foot, it wasn't bad, it was almost like dying in bed. Who ever thought he'd get to kill a fucking general?

Pflaum went out and General Fromm led the way along the corridor and down Stairway B at the far end and outside to the courtyard between the two wings of the building where an A.A. searchlight pinned a brilliant white circle against what was left of a brick wall. A squad of B Platoon riflemen had already lined up on either side of the flatbed truck where the searchlight was mounted. Schlee stumbled against Pflaum. What the hell could you expect from the Hitler Youth graduate?

General Fromm stood back, somewhere to one side of the truck, out of view behind the firing squad, and so did Schlee. A captain and a major Pflaum had never seen before marched the condemned men out. Their arms were bound behind their backs. Their uniforms were stripped of insignia and badges. The one who had been a general, Pflaum did not recall his name now, the one with glasses, walked falteringly, and it was a simple matter for the other one, the one-eyed colonel, to slip his arm loose because he had no right hand. He brought his right arm up and touched the round-faced general's shoulder, and there was more strength in that gesture and the touch of that handless arm than Pflaum had ever seen. It made the general whose name Pflaum had forgotten throw back his shoulders and march erect at his companion's side. It was like a benediction, and Pflaum knew then that he would not do what he had planned to do, he would not drag it out but would get it over quickly.

General Fromm appeared in the cone of light just as the condemned men reached the wall and turned to face the firing squad. With Fromm was Schlee, the lieutenant holding with a hand that shook less than Pflaum would have expected two handkerchiefs that would serve as blindfolds. Pflaum could hear the one-eyed colonel decline, and then the round-faced general, who could not talk but only shake his head, apparently declined too, because General Fromm and Schlee stepped back quickly out of view.

Pflaum himself stepped forward and waited for no orders. He gave the commands rapidly, his voice loud, and from a distance of ten yards the one-eyed colonel seemed to stare at Pflaum, who, of course, he was unable to see with the light dazzling him, but Pflaum had the eerie feeling that the one-eyed colonel was forgiving him.

Pflaum shouted, 'Fire!' and the twelve Mausers made almost one sound. What about that now – the squad was pretty good after all.

The cone of light was immediately an opaque swirl of gunsmoke.

When it cleared, the two figures were down at the base of the wall, General Fromm approaching with a sidearm to administer the coup de grace, which he did as quickly and expertly as Pflaum and the B Platoon squad had done the rest of it.

Pflaum fought back a crazy wild impulse that could do nothing but get him killed. He wanted to shoot General Fromm.

Fucking war was really getting to him.

Twenty-Eight

Mueller stood at the open door of the safe.

'I'll tell you something, Jaeger,' he said. 'Your bosses in the Kremlin are not the mystics you think they are. They don't believe they are answerable to history as a religious man is answerable to God. They believe in power. The dictatorship of the proletariat is just that – a dictatorship like any other. That's why Stalin and Hitler understand each other. And

Comrade Cell is no different. He wants Germany. He wants power. He will have both.'

The nondescript little man in the black uniform opened the round door wider, revealing stacks of file folders. 'What I want is in there. As you said, if it comes to that, a bureau of my own at Kropotkin Square. That, and my own life. I am a gambler, you see. We have won tonight. But the victory is temporary. Like all true gamblers I quit when I am ahead. I believe this is what you came for?'

He held out the Ritter notebook. Jaeger took it.

'How do I know you haven't a copy?'

Mueller shrugged. 'Would it matter?'

Jaeger adjusted the strap of the Erma sub-machine gun more comfortably on his shoulder. 'It would matter,' he said, 'if the Ritter list fell into the wrong hands before the Red Army takes Berlin. Almost half the names in this notebook are Communist.'

'There is no copy.'

Jaeger looked at him and Mueller laughed. 'Of course, I could be lying. And if I were, there is nothing you could do about it.'

Mueller slammed the door of the safe, his back to Jaeger. He waited five seconds and when he turned Jaeger had gone.

There were no copies of the files, and no copy of the Ritter list. Where could he have hidden them? He trusted no one. That was another reason he had survived.

He hated being dominated, and Jaeger had done that to him. At least he had kept the final satisfaction from Jaeger.

He left the office, making sure to lock the door. It was time to drink a glass of champagne with Kaltenbrunner and the others. To toast the life of the Führer and the good fortune of the German Reich.

The Skoda 1100 made a right turn from Friedrichstrasse onto Prinz Albrecht, Artur Nebe at the wheel, Haller beside him with Bleiner's sub-machine gun across his lap. A few hundred yards ahead, lights blazed in front of the Reich Air Ministry and R.S.H.A. headquarters.

'Like Christmas trees,' Artur Nebe said, shaking his head. 'It makes a man think.'

Haller looked at him.

'The R.A.F. picked a hell of a night to keep its planes on the ground.'

When the Skoda entered the zone of light Haller heard the

shriek of sirens. Six motorcycles came racing along Prinz Albrechtstrasse from the opposite direction, escorting a black Mercedes touring car. The sirens wound down and the limousine pulled in front of the R.S.H.A. headquarters.

Nebe applied the brakes. 'Himmler,' he said, 'has decided Berlin is once again safe.'

Waffen-S.S. guards came quickly from the building to form two ranks through which the Reichsführer-S.S. marched stiffly across the street. He went up the steps and past the black marble columns and inside.

Nebe brought the Skoda to a stop at the kerb a hundred feet short of the building. Haller watched the ranks of the Waffen-S.S. break. Some went inside, some stood on the pavement lighting cigarettes. Two came along the street towards the Skoda and approached the window on Haller's side of the car, one of them smoking.

Artur Nebe's voice was like a whiplash. 'Put that cigarette out. Get back inside the building.'

The man looked past Haller. He stiffened. 'Jawohl, Herr Gruppenführer!'

Haller watched the two Waffen-S.S. men turn and quick-march back along the street.

Then he saw Jaeger coming down the steps.

Jaeger felt the weight of the notebook bulging the gusseted pocket of his tunic. A pair of Waffen-S.S. saluted him with out-thrust arms. He returned a crisp military salute and kept walking. He'd left the motorcycle in the darkness of Mauerstrasse; another hundred yards of those damn A.A. lights to go.

One powerful searchlight blinked out, then another. A third. Himmler, in the building now, decreeing the emergency over. A fourth light went out. Another half dozen of them between here and Mauerstrasse. He hurried his steps.

Then stopped as if he'd hit an invisible wall. Heard an enormous voice amplified by the street corner loudspeakers.

MY COMRADES, MEN AND WOMEN OF THE GERMAN REICH! I SPEAK TO YOU TONIGHT SO THAT YOU CAN HEAR MY VOICE AND KNOW I AM UNHURT AND WELL . . .

Hitler.

A Skoda convertible, canvas top up, was parked at the kerb. Not empty. Two men inside.

. . . THE DETAILS OF A CRIME THAT IS WITHOUT EQUAL IN GERMAN HISTORY . . .

Jaeger slipped the strap of the sub-machine gun from his shoulder.

The voice froze Haller for an instant.

. . . SMALL CLIQUE OF DISHONOURABLE AND CRIMINALLY STUPID OFFICERS HAVE CONSPIRED TO REMOVE ME AND OVERTHROW THE LEADERSHIP OF THE GERMAN ARMY . . .

Haller opened the door just as Jaeger came abreast of the hood of the car. He brought the Erma up. There was no time to do anything but kill Jaeger and get away fast with the Ritter list. If Jaeger had it.

Only two searchlights remained.

. . . BOMB PLANTED BY COLONEL GRAF VON STAUFFENBERG EXPLODED . . .

Haller heard the chattering roar an instant before he fired. Jaeger had been a split-second quicker.

Jaeger felt the Erma bucking in his hands, up and to the right as the damn things always did. Bullets ripped into metal, shattered glass. He had recognised Haller just before the last light went.

A sledge-hammer blow hit his right side, spun him backwards and down.

. . . I MYSELF AM ABSOLUTELY UNHURT EXCEPT FOR MINOR BRUISES AND BURNS. THIS IS A CONFIRMATION OF THE ORDER OF PROVIDENCE THAT I CONTINUE TO PURSUE THE GOAL OF MY LIFE . . .

Jaeger rolled over, sat on the pavement, firing blindly.

He got to his feet, backed away, still firing. Then he ran stumbling through darkness.

Artur Nebe was dead behind the wheel of the car, his face a mask of blood, blood soaking the upholstery. Jaeger had been hit, how badly Haller didn't know.

. . . ONLY A FEW TODAY CAN IMAGINE WHAT FATE WOULD HAVE BEFALLEN GERMANY IF THE PLOT HAD SUCCEEDED . . .

Jackboots pounding down the street.

Haller began to run. He knew where the wounded Jaeger would go if he had the Ritter list. Anywhere else, a hospital, a first-aid station, even his own battalion, and he might lose possession of the notebook.

. . . WE ARE GOING TO SETTLE ACCOUNTS AS WE NATIONAL SOCIALISTS SO WELL KNOW HOW . . .

'A drink. Anything. Hurry.'

Monika looked at him. Face like putty, tunic and breeches drenched with blood.

He staggered to the sofa, threw himself down, the sub-machine gun at his side on the cushions.

'I said a drink.'

Monika in an old robe, not the silk kimono. Both her eyes puffed and purple, the left one swollen shut. Her nose swollen under a wide adhesive strip.

He got up, steadied himself against the wall, made it to the Empire desk, sat heavily, head down on folded arms for a moment.

Monika got a bottle, the first one her hand touched. The odd shaped pinched bottle, Scotch whisky. She poured a tumblerful.

He brought it to his mouth, spilling half. He drank and shuddered and drank the rest. The glass dropped from his hand, rolled on the Persian carpet, not breaking. He slumped across the desk again.

Monika picked up the glass, poured more whisky and put it on the desk. She sat on the sofa watching him. Two minutes, three. Her hand went up, touched her swollen face, the adhesive on her nose. Her hand dropped to her side.

Touched the tubular steel stock of the sub-machine gun.

His head came up slowly. He drank again and fumbled at his side pocket. Took out Gottfried Ritter's black notebook.

Monika kept watching him. Her fingers were gripping the tubular steel.

Haller walked the last hundred yards to let his breathing return to normal. That proved to be unnecessary. The lobby was deserted. He hurried up the stairs.

Jaeger opened the notebook. The letter code would not be

difficult. It was a question of sorting the Communist entries out, destroying them and making two copies of the remainder – one for himself and one for the S.D.

Not Gestapo Mueller but the failed intellectuals of the S.S. Security Department were the true fanatic Nazis. And whoever they didn't liquidate could be disposed of later.

The pain began in his side then, stabbing through the numbness. Above the hip. Hadn't hit bone. Finish the job now, then have Monika get a doctor.

The pain was nothing. He had won.

Something moved behind him. He turned and saw her, just beyond the reach of his arms, face ugly and swollen, one eye puffed shut, the other a slit, the sub-machine gun held awkwardly away from her body.

If you ever mark my face I'll kill you.

Not Mueller, not even Haller. Monika.

The gun kicked and hammered as she squeezed the trigger, forcing her arms up and to the right so that she had to use all her strength to hold on.

Jaeger jerked out of the chair and slammed across the desk, field-grey dissolving into red, one hand clutching the notebook.

When he tumbled to the floor she stood over him and kept firing, not seeing anything any longer through the smoke, until the magazine was empty.

Haller found them like that.

An hour later he was with Heydi in the Pariserplatz apartment. They could hear heavy traffic rolling through the roadways of the Brandenburg Gate.

'Waffen-S.S.,' Heydi said. He didn't sound as if he cared.

He had already shown Goerdeler's note to Haller.

'I was going to run,' Heydi said. 'Take some clothing, a little money.' He shook his head. 'Where the hell could I go?'

Haller recalled almost the same words spoken by Helldorf at the Alexanderplatz.

Both of them were right, of course. There was nowhere to go, nowhere to hide, no possibility of escape.

'A drumhead court martial for Klaus. For Olbricht,' Heydi said. 'And they've got Elisabeth. Let the fucking bastards come

Haller's orders regarding Special Project Bennett had been for me.'

specific enough. Take the Ritter list out with you.

Very goddamn funny.

He opened the notebook, its pages sticky with Jaeger's blood. He looked at a few names, the letter codes following them, the brief biographies.

None of them older than Heydi, most of them younger. All of them anti-Nazis, their lives first in Gottfried Ritter's hands, then in Mueller's, then for a few moments in Jaeger's, now in his.

Germany's future, if Germany was to have a future.

He was making too much of it, he told himself. Two hundred students were not the future, not in Germany or anywhere. Even Baker Street hadn't attached much importance to the list. What was important to Baker Street was Adolf Hitler.

Alive, not dead.

They had what they wanted now, no thanks to Haller.

Heydi brought a bottle, glasses. Haller poured the harsh schnapps down his throat and felt nothing.

'You know what he said? What Klaus said, when he knew he was going to die?'

Heydi couldn't stand still. He paced to the french doors and back, his lethargy gone. He reminded Haller of someone and at first Haller didn't know who, and then he did.

'He said no matter what, it had to be tried. No matter what the outcome.' Heydi at the french doors, and back. 'To show the world that Germans – that's what they didn't understand, not even General Beck – that *Germans* could dare to take such a step.'

Craggy face, sabre scar, monocle and all, how old was he? Twenty-five? Two hundred more like him, like Elisabeth, like Sieglinde Meier, their lives in Haller's hands for a few minutes longer.

The briefing at Baker Street – four days for the life, not the death, of Adolf Hitler; twenty minutes for the Ritter list. *Some of them will be Red; some our kind. We gather there's a code. Don't worry about that. Just bring it out and we'll do the sorting.* And something else, he remembered then, an army colonel with a flat midwestern accent. *There's always the chance your escape route will be cut.*

Yes, Haller told himself now, there always is that chance.

In which case, try to break the code. Destroy our part of the list. Let them have the other half.

The obverse of what Jaeger would have done, he was sure

of that. Only he didn't have the time and if he did, he wasn't Jaeger.

He began to rip the pages from the notebook.

'What kind of stove do you have in there?'

'What kind of what?'

'I said what kind of stove?'

'What do you expect in Berlin in 1944? It burns wood. So what?' A touch of arrogance along with the impatience in Heydi's voice.

'Light it,' Haller said.

Ten minutes later the Ritter list was gone.

The Waffen-S.S. came just before dawn, two of them kicking in the front door and four more coming through the french doors in the back. The captain in charge wore the monogram LAH on his shoulder straps, emblematic of the First S.S. Panzer Division, Leibstandarte Adolf Hitler. He had the faintly oriental cast of features sometimes found in East Prussia.

'Oberleutnant von Heydebrand?'

Heydi admitted to his identity.

'I have a warrant for your arrest, Herr Oberleutnant.' The faintly oriental face remained impassive. The voice sounded as if the man was less than happy with his assignment. 'And who is this officer?'

From somewhere Heydi dredged up a slow grin and his face, so austere in repose, then looked boyish, almost mischievous. 'In a manner of speaking,' he began, staring not at the Leibstandarte Adolf Hitler captain but at Haller, 'in a manner of speaking, he's a tourist.'

Epilogue

The shooting stopped not quite ten months later, at midnight, 8 May 1945. The war had lasted five years, eight months, and seven days. In it, more than forty million people died in fulfilment of Adolf Hitler's cosmic death wish, almost nine million of them between July 1944 and the end.

Of the fate of those who figured prominently in the events of 20 July, a few words should be said. Adolf Hitler, of course, shot himself in the Führerbunker under the New Reich Chancellory on the afternoon of 30 April 1945. Joseph Goebbels put a bullet through his head a few hours later. Himmler was captured by British troops at Bremervörde near Bremen and on 23 May swallowed a capsule of cyanide of potassium, so-called 'marching powder', dying instantly.

Three of his underlings in the Reich Central Security Office were brought before the International Military Tribunal at Nuremberg. Ernst Kaltenbrunner was executed by hanging at Nuremberg on 16 October 1946. Otto Ohlendorf met the same fate on 8 June 1951. Walter Schellenberg, sentenced to six years' imprisonment, was released in 1950. He died of cancer in Italy two years later.

Gestapo Mueller was last seen in Germany on 28 April 1945 at the Führerbunker, forty-eight hours before Hitler's death. He was next seen in Moscow three years later. He died there of natural causes in 1952.

Walter Ulbricht, alias Comrade Cell, returned to Berlin in 1945 in the uniform of a Red Army colonel. He became Secretary General of the Communist Party of the German Democratic Republic in 1949 and the most feared and hated political leader in Eastern Europe. He died in East Berlin on 1 February 1973. The London *Times* obituary read in part: 'It is difficult to mourn Herr Ulbricht as a politician because he added little or nothing to the sum of human happiness. It is difficult to mourn him as a human being because he showed so few signs of being one.'

Among the German military, Field Marshal Wilhelm Keitel, tried before the International Tribunal, was executed at Nuremberg on 16 October 1946. General Friedrich Fromm, C.-in-C., Home Army, who had tried to save himself by the summary executions of Beck, Stauffenberg, and Olbricht, was arrested by the Nazis, convicted of cowardice, and executed by firing squad in March 1945. General Helmut Stieff, for his part in the Valkyrie conspiracy, was tortured in the Prinz Albrechtstrasse cellars and tried before Roland Freisler's dread People's Court on 8 August 1944. The next day he was hanged with piano wire from a meat hook in Plötzensee Prison, Moabit, one of almost five thousand Germans with direct or tenuous connections to the July Plot who were the victims of Hitler's vengeance. Berlin Police Chief Helldorf met a similar fate one week later; Julius Esser on 3 January 1945. Motion pictures of their trials and death agonies were prepared – thirty-one miles of such film were shot before editing – and became Hitler's favourite viewing in his final months.

Carl Goerdeler, who would have become Chancellor of the Provisional Government had the plot succeeded, remained at large for three weeks. Then the most wanted fugitive in the Reich, he was identified and denounced by a member of the Luftwaffe Women's Corps at a gasthaus in Konradswalde, East Prussia. He was executed at Plötzensee on 2 February 1945.

Freiherr von Heydebrand, held and interrogated until early 1945, went before Freisler's People's Court on the morning of 3 February. The U.S.A.A.F. came over Berlin that day, a high explosive bomb from a Flying Fortress demolishing the court, killing Freisler, and destroying the dossier on Heydebrand. Monika Jaeger, awaiting trial in nearby Plötzensee for the murder of her husband, died in the same air raid. The injured Heydebrand was remanded to Flossenburg concentration camp near the Czech border while the R.S.H.A., with Teutonic attention to detail, tried to reconstruct his case.

Richard Haller, in accordance with the rules of war, should have been executed without trial for being captured in a German army uniform. Instead, he was shuttled back and forth for a period of months from Lehrterstrasse Prison to the Prinz Albrechtstrasse cellars, where Gestapo Mueller personally took charge of his interrogation, hoping to prove by Haller's presence in Berlin that the Anglo-Americans had masterminded the plot to kill Hitler. When this failed, Haller too was remanded early in 1945 to the small Flossenburg concentration camp, one of the few not yet liberated by the armies advancing from east and west. There, Haller was imprisoned with an odd assortment of twenty German and foreign internees who became known as 'Hitler's Hostages'. The idea was probably Himmler's, not Hitler's, the far-fetched hope being that the lives of these prisoners could be traded off for easier peace terms with the West. 'Hitler's Hostages' included, aside from Haller, the German economist Hjalmar Horace Greeley Schacht; Kurt von Schuschnigg, the last pre-war Chancellor of Austria; Léon Blum, the Jewish former Premier of the French Third Republic; and two British Intelligence officers who had been kidnapped across the Dutch border by Schellenberg in September 1939.

When units of the U.S. Seventh Army approached Flossenburg, its inmates were marched by the S.S. south-west to a holding camp at Niederndorf in the Austrian Tyrol, not fifty miles from Hitler's Alpine retreat at Berchtesgaden. Many of the general inmates died along the way. 'Hitler's Hostages' fared better. They went by truck.

At dawn on 4 May 1945 Haller awoke in his cell at Niederndorf. Like all of 'Hitler's Hostages' he had been placed, on arrival, in solitary confinement. Like all of them, paradoxically, he received better food than the general inmates.

Haller was waiting to die.

Each of the past three mornings he had heard the jackboots thudding along the corridor, a single cell door creaking open on rusty hinges, rifle fire a few minutes later. The S.S. had decided it was time to execute the hostages, capriciously, one at a time.

The day had dawned bright and clear, and through the small high barred window Haller could see a carpet of wild flowers on a sloping hillside that climbed to pine woods and snow-covered peaks.

The camp was quiet. It always was at this hour, until the roll call of general inmates faintly heard a quarter of a mile away in the barracks square, until the jackboots came thudding along the corridor.

Haller heard no roll call, no jackboots. Nor did the warder come to shove his bowl of ersatz coffee and chunk of black bread through the grate.

An hour after dawn Haller heard the distant stuttering hammer of machine-gun fire. It went on for fifteen minutes. Then the silence settled again on Niederndorf.

Haller judged it was almost noon when he heard the thud of boots, the jangle of keys, the creak of rusty hinges. Not just one door – they were opening door after door along the corridor. All of 'Hitler's Hostages' would buy it today. Haller was ready. He was amazed he had survived so long.

He heard voices, and the boots approaching; heard the key inserted in the lock of his own door. Haller stood. Far off from the direction of the barracks he heard shouting.

The door swung out and two soldiers in green fatigues stood in the doorway flanking the S.S. warder. Haller looked at them. Both carried rifles, both needed shaves, both had grenades and canteens dangling from their belts. The steel helmets were wrong. They weren't the familiar coal scuttles.

The two soldiers were grinning and Haller realised one of them shouting at him in a strange sort of German. At first he didn't understand the words and then he did.

'Alles ge-finished! S.S. kaput! Frei! Nicht killen. Amerikanisch Army, best in ganz Welt, nein?'

The soldier grinned at Haller.

Haller grinned at the soldier. 'Where the hell did you learn how to speak German?' he said.

Heydi had lost almost fifty pounds during his months of captivity and whether or not he would ever walk normally on the right leg that had been broken during a session of 'sharpened interrogation' in the Gestapo cellars was, the American doctor had told him, questionable. The leg was now reset. The white plaster cast contrasted with the yellow of his skin. Among other things Heydi was suffering from jaundice.

His debilitation was almost complete, but at least he had not been put in the ward for moribund patients. He lay on his back in the makeshift hospital and he did not think he could so much as screw his monocle in place, if he had one.

The medics came and went, the day wore on, Heydi drifted off to sleep and awoke later that afternoon to see a U.S. Army captain in crisp khakis and stiff garrison cap with the gold American eagle staring down at him. The captain said nothing and neither did Heydi.

Then Heydi sat up. It took some effort, but he did it. He said: 'You know what I think?'

'No,' said Haller. 'What?'

'That uniform sure suits you better than field-grey.'

They brought Heydi to the dayroom for the first time a few days later in a wheelchair. By then Haller had made contact with the C.I.C. unit attached to Headquarters, United States Third Army.

'I've done some preliminary digging,' Haller said. He shook his head.

'Nothing?'

'They've got maybe two million D.P.s in American-occupied territory already, and almost as many in the north where the British are moving in. And a lot of the concentration camp records have been destroyed.' Haller didn't want to say the other part of it. Heydi said it for him.

'And then of course there are the Russians.'

Haller nodded. 'I've got permission to go up to Third Army Headquarters tomorrow. They're trying to sort things out. It could take months.'

'We'll find her,' Heydi said.

Glossary

ABWEHR. German military counter-intelligence, discredited prior to 1944 and absorbed into R.S.H.A.
the ALEXANDERPLATZ. Berlin police headquarters.
ALTE KÄMPFER. Old Fighters. Veteran Nazi Party members.
ANTIFA. Anti-fascist. Applied to Red Underground cells in pre-war Germany.
BAHNHOF. Railway station.
BAKER STREET. London headquarters, Special Operations Executive.
the BENDLERSTRASSE. Berlin headquarters, Armed Forces High Command.
BERGHOF. Hitler's mountain retreat on the Obersalzberg above Berchtesgaden.
BREAKERS. O.S.S. code name for German anti-Nazi conspirators.
BROWN SHIRTS. The S.A.
EINSATZGRUPPEN. Special task forces for liquidation in occupied territories, primarily Russia.
FELDGENDARMERIE. German military police.
FREIHERR. Baron.
FÜHRERLEXIKON. Who's Who of Nazi leadership.
FÜHRERPRINZIP. Principle of authoritarian rule in Nazi Germany.
GASTHAUS. Inn.
GAULEITER. District Leader.
GENERALFELDMARSCHALL. Field Marshal.

GENERALMAJOR. Major General.

GENERALOBERST. Colonel General. Army rank immediately below Field Marshal.

GESTAPO. *Geheime Staatspolizei.* Secret State Police, R.S.H.A. Bureau IV.

GÖTTERDÄMMERUNG. Twilight of the Gods. Cataclysm expected at the end of war.

GRAF. Count.

GRÄFIN. Countess.

GRENADIER. German infantryman.

GRÖFAZ. *Grösster Feldherr aller Zeiten.* Greatest Commander-in-Chief of All Time. Epithet of cynical Berliners for Hitler.

GROSSDEUTSCHLAND GUARD BATTALION. Military unit responsible for security in Berlin.

GRUPPENFÜHRER. S.S. rank equivalent to lieutenant general.

HAUPTMANN. Captain, rank in German army.

HAUPTWACHTMEISTER. Sergeant-major, rank in German police.

KÖNIGSBAU. Munich headquarters, Gestapo.

KRIPO. *Kriminalpolizei.* Criminal Police, R.S.H.A. Bureau V.

KROPOTKIN SQUARE. Moscow headquarters, Central Intelligence Directorate.

LEIBSTANDARTE-S.S. ADOLF HITLER. Hitler's S.S. Bodyguard Regiment. Later expanded into First S.S. Panzer Division.

LOKAL. Neighbourhood bar.

MARK. *See* REICHSMARK.

MEISTER. Sergeant-major, rank in German police.

NACHTMARSCHGERÄT. Night march apparatus. Blackout tail-lights for military vehicles.

N.K.V.D. Red Army Intelligence and Counter-espionage.

NORD–SUD BAHN. Main north–south subway line in Berlin.

N.S.D.A.P. *Nationalsozialistische Deutsche Arbeiterpartei.* National Socialist German Workers' Party. The Nazi Party.

OBERFELDWEBEL. Master-sergeant, rank in German army.

OBERLEUTNANT. First Lieutenant, rank in Germany army.

OBERSALZBERG. Mountain above Berchtesgaden, location of Hitler's Alpine retreat.

OBERST. Colonel, rank in German army.

OBERSTLEUTNANT. Lieutenant-colonel, rank in German army.

OBERWACHTMEISTER. Staff-sergeant, rank in German police.
O.K.H. *Oberkommando des Heeres.* Army High Command.
O.K.W. *Oberkommando der Wehrmacht.* Armed Forces High Command.
ORGANIZATION TODT (O.T.) Paramilitary heavy construction and repair unit.
O.S.S. Office of Strategic Services.
the PRINZ ALBRECHTSTRASSE. Berlin headquarters, R.S.H.A. Colloquially, the Gestapo.
PROMI. Propaganda Ministry.
RAZVEDUPR. *Glavnoe Razvedyvatelnoe Upravlenie.* Central Intelligence Directorate, Moscow.
REICHSMARK. Unit of German currency. Equivalent in 1944 to approximately 25 cents.
REICHSFÜHRER-S.S. Himmler's title as chief of S.S.
R.S.H.A. *Reichssicherheitshauptamt.* Reich Central Security Office.
S.A. *Sturmabteilung.* Storm Troops. Private army of early Nazi Party; after 1934, largely ceremonial.
SCHÜTZE. Private, rank in German army.
SCHWABING. Student district of Munich.
S.D. *Sicherheitsdienst.* Security Department. Intelligence branch of S.S.
SIPO *Sicherheitspolizei.* Security Police, comprising Gestapo and Kripo.
S.O.E. Special Operations Executive. British wartime organisation for clandestine operations in enemy territory.
S.S. *Schutzstaffel.* Defence Detachment. Originally, Hitler's élite guard. Ultimately the vehicle for enforcing Nazi domination in Germany and occupied Europe.
STORM TROOPS. *see* S.A.
STANDARTENFÜHRER. S.S. rank equivalent to colonel.
STURMBANNFÜHRER. S.S. rank equivalent to major.
STURMMANN. S.S. rank equivalent to private first-class.
U-BAHN. Berlin underground.
U-BOATS. Term for Jews in hiding in Germany and occupied Europe.
UMGEBUNGSKARTE. Map of city and environs.
UNCLE EMIL. Berlin network for hiding Jews.
VALKYRIE. Code name for Hilter-approved plan for military takeover of German cities in event of slave labour uprising. Subsequently adopted by anti-Hitler officers for conspiracy to assassinate Führer and overthrow Nazi government.

V-MAN. *Vertrauensmann.* Confidant. Gestapo informant and *agent provocateur.*

WAFFEN-S.S. Combat branch of S.S.

WHITE ROSE. Anti-Nazi student organisation, University of Munich.

WOLF'S LAIR. Hitler's field headquarters near Rastenburg, East Prussia.